TRAP 'N' TRACE

FEDERAL K-9 SERIES

TRAP 'N' TRACE

FEDERAL K-9 SERIES

TEE O'FALLON

This book is a work of fiction. Names, characters, places, and incidents are the product of the author's imagination or are used fictitiously. Any resemblance to actual events, locales, or persons, living or dead, is coincidental.

Copyright © 2020 by Tee O'Fallon. All rights reserved, including the right to reproduce, distribute, or transmit in any form or by any means. For information regarding subsidiary rights, please contact the Publisher.

Entangled Publishing, LLC
10940 S Parker Rd
Suite 327
Parker, CO 80134
rights@entangledpublishing.com

Amara is an imprint of Entangled Publishing, LLC.

Edited by Candace Havens
Cover design by EDH Graphics
Cover photography by romancephotos/DepositPhotos
Andrew F. Kazmierski and shutswis/123.RF
Eric Isselee/Shutterstock

Manufactured in the United States of America

First Edition June 2020

AMARA

To my family, human and *canine. To my readers, for your unfailing support and heartfelt appreciation of my books. And to first responders and frontline workers everywhere. Thank you for keeping us safe during this crazy time.*

Chapter One

"Angus, stop squirming!"

Kat kicked the Escalade's door shut, barely able to hold on to the wriggling puppy in her arms. Angus was adorable, but he had enough energy in his furry little body to fuel a jet engine.

She headed up the brick path to the small ranch house office, noting a blue SUV parked in the driveway. "That's a good sign, Angus. Somebody's home."

The puppy got in a slobbery kiss on Kat's chin, making her smile. Angus sure liked to lick. He'd only been staying with her at the Canine Haven since last night, but she missed him already. His bubbly puppy personality had been just the ticket to get her mind off other things. Like getting dumped. That had definitely sucked.

A large wood sign in the front yard confirmed she was in the right place. *Garman Investigations*. The phone number on the sign was the same as the one on Angus's dog tag.

Kat had called the number twice last night and once this morning. No one had returned her voicemail messages regarding the puppy being found wandering in the neighborhood.

A plaque on the front door said, *Come on in.* She hefted Angus against her shoulder, holding him tighter. The door opened into a small reception area with several chairs against a wall and a table littered with magazines.

"Hello?" She closed the door behind her then waited. No one answered. "Hello? Is anyone here? I have Angus." The place was deathly quiet.

She continued through the reception area to a short hallway. An overturned dog bowl and several dog toys lay on the floor by the back door. Kat grimaced at the metallic and sickly, rancid odor. "Ooh." She held her hand over her nose, as if that could actually filter out the smell. It didn't.

The puppy went utterly still, like someone had unplugged his little generator. His tiny black nostrils flared. Whatever the smell was, Angus didn't like it, either.

Hair on her nape tingled. Another door off the hallway was open. Cautiously, she moved closer until the edge of a desk came into view. The metallic scent grew more pungent and she began breathing through her mouth, which helped. Some, anyway. A bad feeling edged its way into her mind. At the open doorway, she raised her hand to knock, then gasped.

Bile rose in her throat. She blinked then blinked again. *Oh. God.* Not even the worst slasher movie could have prepared her for this.

A woman's body lay on the floor. Her eyes open and sightless. The entire torso was covered in various shades of red. *Blood.*

Kat stumbled backward. Her shoulder slammed against the doorframe. She sucked in quick, shallow breaths, swallowing repeatedly to keep from throwing up, then darted her eyes to the hallway.

This can't be real. But it was.

What if whoever did this was still here?

Angus's high-pitched whimper broke through the haze of shock, and she ran through the reception area, hugging the puppy tightly to her chest. She flung open the door then bolted down the steps and across the front lawn to her car, glancing over her shoulder twice before she made it to the street.

Breathing heavily, she jerked open the door and hoisted herself and Angus inside. After setting the puppy on the passenger seat, she slammed the door shut and punched the lock button.

With shaking hands, she fumbled to release her cell phone from the hands-free contraption on the dash. Finally, she clicked open the release. Her fingers were so unsteady she nearly dropped the phone, snagging it in the nick of time.

Then she did something she'd never done before in her life—dialed 911.

The operator answered.

"Blood!" was the only word she managed before having to swallow again or vomit. "So much of it. Please, hurry."

But there *was* no hurry. Not really. The woman was not only dead, she was...

Desecrated.

Chapter Two

Dayne stared at the lifeless, bloody body, pressing his lips together and willing the tightness in his chest to ease. He'd seen his share of homicide victims, but this was different.

He fisted his hands so tightly, his nails dug into his palms. *I'll find whoever did this, Becca. I swear it.*

FBI Special Agent Rebecca Garman had been Dayne's mentor when he'd graduated from Quantico and been assigned to the Newark Field Office. Becca retired several years ago and started her own private investigation firm in Tappan, New York. She'd been one hell of an agent, a tenacious PI, and a friend. Now she was dead. He still couldn't believe it.

From a corner of the reception area, he watched the CSU guys methodically set out evidence tags around the body, the blood-soaked carpet, and then begin photographing every square inch of the office. As he looked into Becca's lifeless eyes, the backs of his own eyes stung, and for a moment, his vision blurred. He blinked rapidly. No one deserved to die like this, especially not Becca. He'd find the sick fuck that did this to her.

He took a deep breath and slowly let it out, forcing himself to view the crime scene as a trained agent would, not as a friend of the victim.

Unfortunately, there were no surveillance cameras anywhere. People who hired PIs generally wanted their affairs to remain private. Peep cams would have cut Becca's clientele in half.

Stacked on the desk were a few manila file folders. No laptop that he could see, but he didn't doubt she had one. Several desk drawers were partially open, as if someone had searched them and hadn't found what they were looking for. Other than that, nothing appeared out of place. *Except for Becca.*

She'd been stabbed multiple times in the chest, neck, and abdomen. That level of violence usually indicated either a crime of passion, or one of intense hatred. Becca's relationship with her husband was solid, so he'd go with intense hatred.

He didn't know Ted Garman well but was relieved Becca's husband was in Seattle on a business trip. They had no reason to believe Ted killed his wife, but when a victim's body was cut up by so many stab wounds the husband or boyfriend was always at the top of the suspect list. Thankfully, Ted had a rock-solid alibi by virtue of being three thousand miles away. The man was catching a flight home that evening, as were Becca's adult children.

The CSU tech's camera clicked and flashed. Behind him, the detective assigned to the case, Mike Paulson, took down information from the uniformed cop who'd been first on scene. Paulson was about to interview the witness who'd discovered the body.

According to this witness, the front door had been closed but unlocked. The entire office had already been dusted for prints. If they were lucky, they'd get a hit, but it was never that easy. They'd have to pore through Becca's files, her laptop, and her cell phone, searching for clues. Then they'd interview all the neighbors in case they saw anything suspicious.

"I understand you knew the victim." Paulson waved his pen in the direction of Becca's body. "I'm sorry for your loss."

He cleared the lump from his throat. "Yeah, thanks." He felt guilty for not staying in touch with Becca more after she retired. She'd seen things in him no one else had. *She made me a better agent.* "Mind if I listen in when you talk to the witness?"

Paulson hesitated, twisting his lips slightly and giving Dayne the clear impression that he *did* mind. "Sure thing." The detective executed a stiff about-face and headed for the back door.

Early in his career Dayne figured out that a lot of PDs resented it when the feds crashed their party. The FBI didn't normally get involved in straight-up homicides, but because the victim was a former FBI agent, they couldn't be certain if her murder was connected to a case she worked as a PI, or something she did while employed by the FBI. Dayne had been directed to keep tabs on the case until a determination could be made.

He followed Paulson down the hall, sidestepping some dog toys and an overturned dog bowl by the back door, although he hadn't seen a dog anywhere.

Patrol cars and dark sedans lined the road, their red-and-blue strobes flashing. Several reporters and videographers crowded the sidewalk outside the police tape.

It was a beautiful early-spring day, warm enough that he'd shed his jacket and lowered the windows of his Interceptor so Remy could get some fresh air. His K-9's brown and black head stuck out the window, bobbing up and down as she took in all the scents in the air.

Flowerbeds with bright yellow daffodils and red tulips swaying in the breeze surrounded the house. Becca loved her garden. She'd once told him April flowers were a sign of rebirth.

Dayne nearly choked on the irony. Today, they were a sign of death and the funeral yet to come.

A white Escalade sat at the curb, its passenger door open. The woman on the seat held a squirming golden retriever puppy.

Dayne frowned. *Whoa.* "Is that Katrina Vandenburg?"

"The one and only," the detective said over his shoulder as they took the last few steps down the sloped yard to the sidewalk. "Once it leaked out that she found the body, the press swarmed in like sharks at a feeding frenzy."

Great.

Dayne had only met Katrina Vandenburg once, a month ago when his best friend's fiancée was picking out a dog at the Canine Haven. He and Katrina hadn't exactly hit it off.

He couldn't think of a single reason why the woman would be meeting with a private investigator. She had enough millions in the bank to buy her way out of anything. *Actually, she's got billions.*

As they approached, Katrina Vandenburg looked up. If he'd had any doubt as to her identity before, there was absolutely none now. Nobody else had eyes like hers. *Amethyst.* Other than that, she looked nothing like the image he hadn't realized until now had been seared into his memory.

She'd been wearing a glittery, silver evening gown and sporting enough diamonds to fill a display case at Tiffany's. She'd whipped on a long silk wrap, practically smacking him in the face with it, then slid gracefully into a white limo.

Today, her attire surprised him. Jeans, sneakers, and a light blue sweatshirt. Deep chestnut hair pulled back into a tight ponytail. The only jewelry were the small diamond studs twinkling from her delicate earlobes.

"Miss Vandenburg, I'm Detective Paulson with the

Orangetown Police Department, and this is FBI Special Agent Andrews." Paulson indicated Dayne with a quick nod. "I'd like to ask you some questions. I understand you discovered the body."

He raised a brow at Paulson's repeated use of the word *I*, instead of *we*, a not too subtle dig that this was Paulson's interview, not Dayne's.

"Yes, I did." She tucked a wayward strand of hair behind her ear, calling attention to the fact that she wore no makeup and was still pretty as hell.

"What time did you get here?" Paulson asked.

"About ten this morning."

The puppy, which Dayne guessed was about nine weeks old, wriggled like a worm on a hook. With long, graceful fingers she stroked the dog's belly, calming him. Short nails, no polish, and no rings.

"Did you have an appointment with Rebecca Garman?" Paulson's pen poised over his pad.

"No, I—" She stared at Dayne. "I know you. Don't I?" The melodic timbre of her voice lowered. No doubt she was recalling their one and only meeting, which had been about as pleasant as a bee sting.

"We've met," Dayne admitted. "At the Canine Haven about a month ago."

"Oh." Her eyes widened, giving him an even clearer glimpse of the dark black rings surrounding the light purple irises. "*Oh*. I remember now. You're friends with Jesse, Eric, and Tess." Pink lips compressed, and her eyes narrowed a fraction. "You told me not to get my diamonds dirty."

Yep, I did. The snarky comment had flown from his lips before he could stop them, but he'd felt like a dick about it afterward. "That was me."

"Well, Mister *Just Dayne*," she said, recalling the way she'd addressed him that day, "how…*nice* to see you again."

No missing the sarcasm there. Not that he didn't deserve it. "Nice seeing you again, too." He gave her a stiff, subtle bow. He was, after all, a civil servant. Granted, one armed with a big-ass Glock and a partner with teeth sharp enough to bite through sheet metal.

"Miss Vandenburg," Paulson continued, "if you didn't have an appointment with Rebecca Garman, why were you here?"

"To return Angus."

Paulson's brows met. "Who's Angus?"

"The puppy." She nodded to the squirming ball of fluff on her lap. "One of the women who volunteers at the Canine Haven, Julia Hernandez, lives at the end of this street. Last night, Julia found Angus wandering through the neighborhood. She tried calling the number on the tag, but no one answered. She had to catch a flight to Florida with her family, so I agreed to care for Angus at the Haven until I could reach his owner."

Paulson pointed his pen in the general direction of Piermont. "Are you talking about that dog pound on Tweed Boulevard?"

"It's a *rescue* shelter," she corrected. "We take in dogs and find good homes for them or train them to be service animals for the community."

"I see." Paulson scribbled on his pad. "I take it the number on the dog tag came back to Garman Investigations at this address?"

Katrina nodded. "I did a search and the number popped right up. I tried calling last night and then again, this morning. No one answered, and I had errands to run in the area, so I swung by."

Errands? Wouldn't someone else do those for her?

"The front door was unlocked, and I went in," she continued. "That's when I"—she swallowed, drawing attention to the graceful column of her throat—"found the body."

Not many people discovered a dead body, let alone one that had been so heinously ravaged. He expected the waterworks to turn on any second, but she surprised him by keeping her shit together. She hugged Angus, as if the puppy could magically erase the ugliness of what she'd seen.

Katrina reached down by her feet and grabbed a chewed up rubber toy that looked like a tiny orange dumbbell covered with dark nubby bumps. "You're teething, aren't you?" She held the toy in front of Angus's muzzle. "Here you go, sweetie."

Angus bit down and the toy made soft whistling sounds.

"Was anyone else inside the house when you got here?" Paulson asked.

Katrina shook her head, and another wisp of thick, chestnut-brown hair escaped her ponytail, cradling her almond-shaped face. "No."

"Did you touch anything or move anything?"

"No."

"What did you do after you found the body?"

"I ran outside to my car and called 911."

Paulson made a few more notes then reached into his suit jacket pocket and handed her a business card. "I think that's it for now. I'll call if I have any more questions."

"Actually," Dayne interjected as Katrina accepted the card, "I have a few more questions."

Beside him, Paulson exhaled an impatient groan that Dayne ignored. It was obvious the man wanted to get the hell out of there, and Dayne couldn't figure out why.

"After you came out of the house to call 911, did anyone else go inside?" he asked.

"No, I'm sure of it. I sat here the whole time and could see the door." Again, she shook her head. "I suppose that was stupid. I should have driven away in case whoever did this was still nearby."

Maybe so, but he gave her credit for having the backbone to stick around until the PD showed up.

"Let's dial this back to when you first got here." Twenty feet away, the press hounds eyed them like vultures scoping out their next meal. Only the uniforms prevented the reporters and their video guys from charging over. "Sometimes, a witness doesn't realize they've seen things that are critical to an investigation. Try closing your eyes. Visualize everything from the moment you turned onto the street. Say anything that pops into your head, even if you think it's not important."

She took a deep breath and shut her eyes. Perfectly arched brows furrowed. "As soon as I turned onto Kings Highway, I saw the commercial sign on the front lawn then pulled in front of the house and parked."

"Was there a vehicle in the driveway?" He glanced at Becca's Toyota Highlander.

"Yes." She nodded, smoothing her hand over the puppy's head while he chewed on his toy. "A blue SUV. I didn't notice what kind."

"Were there any other vehicles parked in front of you or behind you?"

Again, her brows furrowed. "There was a gray car parked halfway down the street. When I came back out of the house and got into my car, it drove away."

"Was the driver a man or a woman?"

"I think it was a man. Or a woman with short hair."

"Could you tell what the make of the car was?"

"No." She rolled her lips inward. "But there was something about the back of the car."

"A bumper sticker?" he suggested. "Or a parking sticker?"

"No, nothing like that. I got it!" Her eyes flew open. "The

bumper was dented pretty badly on one side."

"Right side or left?"

"Left."

"Could you read the license plate?"

Again, she closed her eyes. Angus dropped the toy onto his little belly and licked Katrina's chin. "No. I'm sorry."

"What state license plate was it?"

"New Jersey," she said firmly. "Black on a beige background."

"Good." Might be nothing, but some murderers liked to stick around for that moment when the body was discovered or when the press showed up. "That's all I have."

"Detective," one of the uniforms called out, holding up a cell phone. "The chief wants you."

"Miss Vandenburg, thank you for your time." Paulson beat feet to take his boss's call.

"If you don't mind, *Mister* Dayne," Katrina said, standing and cradling the puppy in her arms like a baby, "I'd like to leave before Angus pees on my lap." The dog toy fell to the sidewalk beside the Escalade.

Dayne scooped up the toy then held it out to Angus, who promptly clamped his jaws around it. The huddle of reporters closed in tighter, some photographers snapping shots.

"Oh no." A tortured expression clouded her features. "I hate reporters."

Dayne held back a snort. That might be the one and only thing they had in common.

Katrina twisted her neck in all directions, searching for an escape route. Patrol cars blocked in her Escalade. Dayne's Interceptor, however, was in the clear.

She bit her lower lip, looking more panicked by the second. He could never leave a woman in distress. It wasn't his way. Besides, if he did, his mother would smack him upside the head. When it came to courtesy, his mom was a drill sergeant.

"Hop in with me. I'll give you a ride home and you can pick up the Caddy later when the horde of vultures flies away."

She glanced again at the reporters then flashed him a wary but considering look, as if taking him up on his offer was the lesser of two evils. "Thank you," she said then hastily followed him across the street.

At their approach, Remy stuck her head farther out of the open window. He opened the passenger door and swiveled the mobile computer aside to make room for her and Angus. Using his body as a shield, he stepped in front of the encroaching reporters while Katrina slid onto the seat, clutching the puppy to her chest.

"Oh, come on," a female reporter with platinum blond hair and fire engine-red lipstick whined. "We only want to ask a few questions."

"Not gonna happen." Reporters and photographers surrounded the vehicle. As soon as he got in, he blasted the air horn, sending the press bolting to avoid being run down. A snide snicker erupted from his throat.

Katrina laughed. "You enjoyed that, didn't you?"

"Yep." He gunned the SUV down the road to the traffic light, which, thankfully, was green, then shot through the intersection.

She tucked Angus's head beneath her chin. "They really are vultures."

"I'd think you'd be used to it by now." It wasn't that he kept track of her in the newspapers or on TV, but he'd caught a few clips here and there of her being photographed and interviewed at charity events around the city.

"Well, I'm *not* used to it, so that's the second incorrect preconceived notion you have about me."

"The second?" He slanted her a sideways look, inhaling her subtle perfume. *Roses.* "What's the first?"

"That I would *ever* allow my diamonds to get dirty." There was no hiding the snark in her comeback.

He'd stepped right into that minefield like a rookie fresh out of Quantico. "Okay, I deserved that."

"Yes, you did." This time, she was the one to snicker. "Do you remember how to get to the Haven?" she asked then gave a startled gasp when Remy shoved her muzzle through the kennel window.

"Sorry." He reached over his shoulder and tugged the cage window closed, although that didn't stop Remy from pressing her snout through the bars as she investigated Angus. "I usually leave it open."

"Female?" Katrina eyed his K-9, as did the pup.

The puppy craned his neck to touch noses with Remy's. "Yeah. Most people assume she's a *he* because of her size."

"I spend a lot of time with dogs at the Haven." She surprised him by touching her fingers to Remy's snout. "I can usually tell what sex they are by their facial bone structure. She's beautiful."

"That she is," Dayne agreed, stepping on the gas when the light turned.

"What's her name?"

"Remy."

"That's a fun name. Did you name her after *Remy Martin*, the French cognac?"

"No. Remington, the gun."

Her laugh was more of a full-blown snort. "I should have guessed. And for the record, *Mister* Dayne, call me Kat."

Not likely. To him, she would always be *Miss* Katrina Vandenburg.

Turning onto Tweed Boulevard, he gunned the SUV up the steep road that led to Clausland Mountain and the Canine Haven. Clausland Mountain was a mix of state park land and private property located on the Palisades cliff overlooking the Hudson River some five hundred feet below. Hell, even the dogs at this shelter had a better view than he did.

At the sign for the Canine Haven, he turned right into the heavily wooded property. Tall evergreens and deciduous trees lined both sides of the road. No fencing. Anyone could waltz right onto the property unannounced and armed to the teeth. At the main entrance, he slowed.

"Keep going." She waved a finger. "The house is up ahead."

Dayne stepped on the gas. "You're not dropping Angus off here?"

"He's so little I think he'll be more comfortable at the house with me. Besides, I like his company."

A large iron gate blocked the road. About ten feet before the gate stood a coded lock box attached to a pole. At least the woman had *some* kind of security system, although it was laughable at best. Even if the fence surrounded every square inch of the property, any lowlife could scale it and walk right in. He stopped and lowered the window.

"The code is four-two-six-five."

After punching in the code, the gates slowly swung open with an eerie creak and he drove through. Trees gave way to low shrubs and Kat's house came into view. Not that anyone in their right mind would ever refer to this place as a *house*.

A hundred feet ahead, perched near the edge of the cliff, sat a gothic castle, complete with pointed turrets and ivy-covered stone walls. The only things missing were a moat, drawbridge, and the Knights of the freaking Round Table.

Dayne drove onto a circular white gravel driveway, stopping in front of a wide stone staircase. "If you don't mind, I've got a few more questions."

"Okay, sure." Briefly, she pressed a hand to her forehead, as if she had a headache. She got out and set Angus on the ground. "Remy can come in. She probably needs water."

Well, there was an invitation Remy didn't get too often. At all, really. Most people were afraid to go anywhere near his dog, let alone invite her in. "Thanks." As Kat headed for the door, her face looked a little pale.

Angus peed then bounded around the front of the SUV, charging right up to his K-9. He wasn't worried about Remy hurting the little guy. Remy might be a cop, but she was also one of the most maternal dogs he'd ever known. She never met a puppy she didn't like, and Angus was no exception.

Dayne supervised while Angus yipped and nipped at Remy's legs. Sure enough, his K-9 took it all in stride and stood there unmoving, content to let the puppy vent its energy. Kat waited on the top step, again pressing a hand to her forehead. Then she wavered unsteadily, staggering sideways like a drunken sailor.

"Kat?" He'd already started toward her when her eyes rolled back in her head. *Shit.* He bolted to the stairs.

Chapter Three

Kat's world went dark, misting over with thick gray fog. Then she was floating. *No, flying.* Something big and warm wrapped around her like a soothing, protective cocoon.

She snuggled closer to the warmth and found it firm against her cheek. Firm. Hard. And smelling oh-so-good. Like spring showers and fabric softener mingled with an unfamiliar scent. Subtle, masculine, woodsy cologne. *Not* Chad's. *Good thing, the rat bastard.*

"It's all right. I've got you," a deep voice rumbled. A sound she liked.

Pounding shattered the peacefulness surrounding her, followed by shouting. *Urgent* shouting. "Police, open the door!"

I didn't call the police again. Did I?

"Oh my god! What happened? Is she all right?" *Emily.* "Come in, come in! Should I call an ambulance?"

Yipping filtered through the murky haze.

"Get me a blanket," the deep voice ordered. *No, commanded.* Like a soldier barking orders at his troops.

Soft cushions beneath her back and head. More yipping.

"Angus." She struggled to sit up. Strong hands gently pushed her down. "Where's the puppy?" Her voice was slightly slurred, but she hadn't been drinking.

"He's right here," the deep voice assured.

A wet nose nuzzled her hand, and her tension eased. Then the events of the day hit her like a freight train.

The deep, rumbling voice had come from the FBI agent. Mister Just Dayne aka Special Agent Andrews. The last thing she remembered was walking up the steps then...*lights out.*

Slowly, the fog melted away. Clear, emerald-green eyes fringed by the thickest, darkest lashes she'd ever seen on a man stared back at her, so stunning in their intensity they were almost pretty. That's where the pretty ended.

A face as ruggedly masculine as his—all granite-jawed and sculpted cheekbones—could never be considered *pretty* by any stretch. She'd had that exact thought during their two-minute encounter over a month ago. Although it was more than his appearance that had intrigued her then. The man was striking but not in the same manicured way all the men in her world were. Where the men she knew were polished and refined, Special Agent Dayne Andrews was fierce and totally sexy. *That's* what she remembered most about him.

"Here's that blanket." Emily, her personal assistant, handed a blanket to Agent Andrews, who knelt on the floor beside her.

Remy, his enormous German shepherd, sat next to him. Little Angus stood with his paws on the sofa cushion by her right elbow, chomping down on the squeaky toy.

"Did you eat anything today?" Agent Andrews draped the blanket over her body.

She started to shake her head then thought better of it when the room began spinning. "No. I didn't get around to it."

"Is she going to be okay?" Emily wrung her hands. "Should I call an ambulance?"

"No," she mumbled. "No ambulance." This was embarrassing enough.

Agent Andrews nodded to Emily. "Do you have something sweet to drink, like orange juice?"

"I'll get some." Emily rushed to the kitchen, returning quickly with a glass of juice.

Kat struggled to sit up.

"Wait." Agent Andrews slid his arm beneath her back, lifting her upper body then wedging himself between her and the sofa. His very hard, very muscular chest pressed against her back. He held out his hand, and Emily handed him the glass. "Think you can drink some of this?" He held the glass to her lips. Her hands automatically came around his. "I've got this. Just drink."

She did as ordered, and the tangy-sweet juice hit her taste buds then trickled down her throat, gradually reawakening her senses.

"What happened?" She looked at Emily's concerned hazel eyes. The woman was not only Kat's assistant but one of her few trusted friends.

"You fainted," Agent Andrews said matter-of-factly.

"Fainted?" When she twisted her neck to look at him, her cheek grazed his chin. A very chiseled chin with a fine bristle of dark hair. "I *never* faint."

"You did today." He chuckled against the side of her face.

The sensation wasn't entirely unpleasant. Despite the blanket and the warmth provided by his broad chest pressing so intimately against her body, she shivered.

Emily sat in the Chippendale armchair facing the sofa. Worry lines creased her forehead. "Can I get you anything else?"

She shook her head, feeling better already. "No. Thank

you. But I don't think we'll be doing any kickboxing today."

"Probably a wise decision," Emily agreed.

"*You* kickbox?" Agent Andrews asked.

She turned to find his dark brows raised. "What? Only men are allowed to work out and get sweaty?" Yet again, he'd made a snap judgment about her. Most people did, and she hated being a foregone conclusion. "I've got a great gym in the basement. Emily and I work out together almost every day. Keeps us in shape, and it's a great way to vent frustration." *Why am I telling him this?* The man could care less about her physical fitness, let alone her personal issues.

Angus whimpered and tried hopping up beside her, but his front paws barely made it to the top cushion. Remy dipped her head and gave the puppy a shove with her snout, launching him onto Kat's lap where he promptly curled up with his toy. "Remy seems to know just what Angus needs."

In an unexpectedly tender gesture, Agent Andrews stroked the top of his dog's head. "There are three things she loves most in the world. Me, catching bad guys, and puppies."

She rubbed the shepherd's soft ears and was rewarded with a contented groan. "I don't understand why I fainted."

"Part of your problem is low blood sugar. Think you can hold this by yourself?" She nodded, and he eased his hands from beneath hers on the glass.

"What's the other part?" she asked between sips.

"Shock and stress." Warm breath feathered her ear, sending tingles down her neck and back. "Finding a dead body is enough to yank the rug out from under anyone."

"*What* dead body?" Emily straightened, glaring at Kat. "You didn't say anything about a dead body."

"I was taking Angus back to his owner," Kat began, only now realizing Emily still had no idea what was going on. "Unfortunately, she was…dead."

Emily's eyes went wide. "Holy shit."

"There was so much blood. All those cuts on her body... What kind of animal would do such a thing?"

"That's what I'm here to find out." His jaw tightened, reemphasizing the rugged masculinity of his face.

"Does the FBI investigate *all* murders?" Most of what she knew about the FBI from the news concerned things like terrorism and bank robberies.

"No." A long moment of dead silence followed before he added, "The Orangetown PD has primary jurisdiction, but Rebecca Garman was an FBI agent before she became a private investigator. I'm assisting in case it turns out she was killed because of something she did for the FBI."

"How will you figure that out?" She found herself suddenly intrigued by the investigative process.

"By sticking close to Detective Paulson and by reviewing every stitch of evidence."

Feeling awkward about his proximity, she tugged the blanket closer around her shoulders. "Did you know Rebecca Garman personally?"

"Yeah." A shadow darkened his eyes, something more than just anger. *Grief.* She easily recognized it. "When I graduated from the academy, she was my training agent."

"I'm sorry." It couldn't be easy losing a mentor. She suspected Rebecca Garman had also been his friend.

"Thanks." There was deep emotion in that one word. After their first encounter, perhaps she, too, was guilty of prejudgment. Maybe he was human after all.

Remy lowered her head to his thigh, watching him with big, expressive eyes.

"Did she have family?"

He rested his big hand on the dog's head, gently sifting long fingers through the golden-brown fur. "Her husband is flying back from a business trip, and her children will be here tomorrow."

To plan Rebecca's funeral.

The organ-like doorbell echoed throughout the foyer and living room.

Agent Andrews tensed. "What *is* that?"

Remy snorted. Angus lifted his head and stared at the door.

"*That* would be the doorbell. I'll get it." Emily stood. "It's probably the press. Once in a while they climb the fence."

Kat groaned. "I'm not in the mood for this." Actually, she was never in the mood to be interviewed but tolerated it because it was good publicity for the Haven and the other charities she supported. Another downside to being a Vandenburg. Most days, it seemed like there were more downsides than up.

"In that case, I've got this." Agent Andrews slipped out from behind her then went to the door before Emily could open it. Remy trotted after him, picking up on some unspoken command.

That one simple act left her wondering if she'd ever be so in sync with anyone. Doubtful. Not after Chad, and certainly not after being so duped by him.

The doorbell chimed again, but she wasn't worried. As big and intimidating as the agent and his dog were, she didn't doubt he could kick any trespassers into the next county.

. . .

Dayne opened the door, preparing to tell the vultures to take a hike or get arrested.

A man wearing a suit that probably cost more than two of his biweekly paychecks stared at him from ice-cold gray eyes. Behind him, a silver Jaguar glinted in the sunlight. When he tried pushing past, Dayne planted a hand in the guy's chest, sending him stumbling back.

Remy lowered her head, uttering a low growl.

"What the hell?" the guy sputtered. "Let me in."

"No." Dayne hooked his thumbs on his belt, intentionally drawing attention to the gold badge and holstered Glock.

"Step. Aside."

"Not happening." Dayne crossed his arms, meeting the other man's glare and taking an instant dislike to the guy. He couldn't be certain, but he thought he heard Emily biting back a snicker.

"It's all right," Kat called out. "Emily, tell him Colin can come in."

For an instant longer, their gazes remained locked, Dayne's with a warning that whoever he was, he'd better play nice.

"Katrina," the guy—Colin—called out as Dayne allowed him in.

Not that Dayne cared, but she'd told *him* to call her *Kat*.

He shut the door then turned to see Colin lean down to kiss Kat on the lips, but she presented him with her cheek, instead. Again, not that he cared, but whatever their relationship was, it wasn't romantic. Whoever Colin was, he must have had the code to the gate or his pricy Jag wouldn't be parked outside the front door.

"Katrina?" Colin sat beside her, arching a derisive brow at the now-wriggling puppy. He rested an arm possessively around her shoulders and threaded the fingers of his other hand through one of hers. "It's all over the news. Did you really find a dead body?"

"Unfortunately, yes." She patted his hand then pulled both of hers away to calm Angus, who was doing his best to greet Colin aka Mr. Stick-Up-His-Ass with a sound licking. "Speaking of which… Emily, would you please let the Haven staff, Francine, and Walter know what's happened? I don't want them to hear about it first on TV."

"Of course." Emily nodded then went into the kitchen.

Dayne was itching to get out of there, but he still needed to ask Kat a few more questions and make sure she had his business card in case she remembered anything else.

"What's that puppy doing here?" Colin's face wrinkled like he'd just sucked a lemon. "Why isn't it at the shelter?"

"He's too little, and I like the company. Angus is only here temporarily," she reassured him.

The guy was a dog hater if ever Dayne saw one.

Colin leaned back against an enormous sofa with intricate carvings on the wood-framed top. *Expensive. Like the rest of the place.*

A crystal chandelier hung over Dayne's head, and the column he leaned against—one of many in the place—rose to high ceilings painted with colorful scenery. Everywhere he looked there were layers and layers of floor and ceiling molding.

Kat's voice drew his attention back to the open-space living room, which was as big as a football field. Another giant chandelier hung from the ceiling, and the room's black granite fireplace was large enough to park a Sherman tank in.

"Are you all right?" Colin asked Kat. The man's eyes narrowed as he glared across the foyer at Dayne. "And what's that cop doing here?"

"I'm fine, and he's not a cop." Kat continued stroking Angus's belly. "He's an FBI agent."

Colin threw him a derogatory look. "Then what's an FBI agent doing in the house?"

"He drove me home," Kat said.

"Colin, can I get you anything?" Emily asked, returning from the kitchen.

"No." He didn't even offer Kat's assistant the courtesy of looking at her, telling Dayne precisely what the guy thought of hired help. Why would someone like Kat—who was turning out to be nicer than he expected—have anything to do with such a douche bag?

Dayne went back into the living room and sat on the edge of the sofa. Remy sat beside him, keeping a wary eye on Colin. "You okay, now?"

"Yes." She mustered a smile. "Thank you for, um, carrying me here."

Colin's brows lowered. "What does that mean? What aren't you telling me?"

"It's nothing. I didn't eat anything today and apparently, I passed out. Lack of food, shock, stress… Agent Andrews caught me before I took a swan dive off the stairs."

His lips compressed. "You should have called me."

"I didn't see the need." Kat didn't notice because she'd begun stroking Angus's ears, but Colin's face began turning an embarrassed shade of douche bag-red.

Dayne tugged a business card from his thigh pocket and handed it to her. "I'll stop by another time to talk to you."

"Okay." She nodded. "And Angus can stay with me until the Garmans are ready to have him back."

Colin cleared his throat. "Thank you for taking care of her, Agent Andrews. I can handle things from here."

Did somebody say dis-missed? "Remy." His dog stood, eager to get back to work. "Nice to meet you, Emily."

"Same. Come back anytime." The genuine smile Kat's assistant gave him said she was appreciative of being noticed.

Seconds later, he was out the door. He waited for Remy to hop in the kennel then took one last look at the castle. Something about all that wealth brought back shitty memories he'd stashed deep inside a locked part of his brain.

Just before he'd pulled that velvet box from his pocket, he'd given Britt the exciting news that he was abandoning his plans for med school and joining the FBI. He thought she'd be proud. Instead her eyes had bulged, and she'd gaped at him like a largemouth bass. Then she'd dumped his ass. Said she needed to be married to a rich surgeon who could buy her an expensive home, fancy cars, jewelry, and take her on trips to Europe twice a year.

As he drove away from the castle, he gunned the SUV toward the looming iron gates. He couldn't get out of there fast enough.

Chapter Four

"Katrina, we need to talk." Colin set his mug on the coffee table.

Emily had stayed late to make sure she was okay, and Francine—her cook and housekeeper—had left roasted tomato bisque and a warm, gooey Gruyere Panini. Colin had joined her for dinner, and she'd polished off her food.

"Isn't that what we've *been* doing?" Well into the night, to be precise.

After driving her to pick up her car, they'd talked for hours. Now, Angus's little snores were making her envious. The puppy was fast asleep on the dog bed she'd set in a corner of the living room. What she really wanted was to take a hot bath then fall into bed. Unfortunately, Colin had insisted on hearing every last detail.

"Not about that." He clasped her hand, something he'd been doing a lot lately. Ever since her breakup with Chad. "About our future."

Our future? The mug in her other hand froze halfway to her lips.

"We're not kids anymore," he continued. "You're thirty-three, and I'm thirty-six. Your birthday is right around the corner."

"I know that." They'd grown up together and, despite his occasional snobbishness, had been friends for over twenty years. The food she'd just eaten soured in her stomach.

He squeezed her hand. "It's time for us to settle down and have a family."

She blinked. Surely, she'd misheard him. "What exactly do you mean?"

"I mean, you and me. We're a good match. A good fit."

"A good *fit*?" She couldn't believe what she was hearing. "You make it sound like a business merger."

"You know what I mean." The look on his face became more determined, and the souring food in her belly turned into pure vinegar. "We come from the same backgrounds. We understand each other, and I would never hurt you."

"What you mean is, you would never hurt me like Chad did." She tugged her hand from his and set down her mug. The constant reminder of her latest failed relationship and very public breakup was a thorn in her side that she couldn't pull out.

He nodded. "Yes, that's exactly what I mean. You know I don't need your money."

The tightness in her chest was her heart shriveling. Was this really what her personal life had boiled down to, a business transaction? *That can't be all there is.* She shook her head. "I want to marry for love." The words sounded naive, even to her. Especially considering how she'd all but given up on that ever happening, and he knew it because she'd vented to him about it. "But you don't love me. Not like that, anyway."

"I love you as a friend, and I respect you. I know you feel the same about me." When he cupped her face, she willed her body to offer up some kind of physical response. It didn't. Ironically, being in Agent Andrews's arms *had*. "We're different from other people, and we understand each other. We *can* make this work. We're not getting any younger."

That much was true, and until that moment she hadn't realized that even men had biological clocks, and Colin had decided his was ticking away.

She dragged a hand down her face. Hers was, too. That didn't mean she was ready to compromise all her hopes and dreams.

He let his hand drop. "Tell me what you're thinking."

"I'm thinking that a marriage of convenience isn't right for me, especially not for money reasons. I refuse to believe that I'm only destined to be with someone whose bank account rivals my own. That would pretty much eliminate all but one percent of the world's male population. Maybe more." It might also eliminate the possibility of ever finding someone who truly loved her. Her parents had married for love, and she always assumed she would, too.

"You should consider it, anyway. In time, I think you'll change your mind. I'll call you." He leaned over and before she could turn away, he kissed her on the lips.

Again, not a flicker of sexual awareness. A moment later, he was gone. That was it. Business meeting over. Not that she would actually consider it, but was this what a marriage to Colin would be like? All business and no passion?

Yes, the nausea in her belly warned.

She stood and went to the window. It was too dark outside to see much except the soft glow of lights on the Tappan Zee Bridge. Despite rejecting Colin's offer, she was tired of being alone without someone to share her life with. She'd even considered online dating under a made-up name. That would have been the only way to meet men without constantly wondering if they were secretly calculating her net worth.

But she didn't like the idea of being dishonest. Too bad she couldn't pick the perfect guy from a catalogue.

It was tough, especially with all the world watching her every move.

Taking a deep breath, she straightened her slumped posture. She had to stay strong. Whatever happened, she was *not* marrying Colin.

Wind buffeted the windows and heavy rain obscured most of the view. She couldn't make them out in the darkness, but knew the Hudson was alive and dancing with whitecaps. It never ceased to amaze her how the river could be as shiny and reflective as a mirror one minute, rough and violent the next. Beautiful but at times, deadly.

Images of Rebecca Garman's body flashed before Kat's eyes, and a shiver ran through her. There was no possible way to imagine the pain that woman must have suffered at the hands of her killer.

Angus padded over and dropped his rubber toy on the floor for her to toss. One look at his angelic, furry face was enough to cleanse her mind of the terrible images. Temporarily, anyway.

She picked up the toy, shaking it like a rattle. When she threw it into the foyer, he barked with glee and scampered after it.

Kat shook her head, still trying to make sense of Colin's baffling and emotionless proposal. Had she said or done something to make him believe she'd actually take him up on his offer? For some inexplicable reason, Dayne Andrews's face flitted before her eyes.

He was around her age, maybe a few years older. In addition to his raw masculinity and tough good looks, he had a power and strength she was unaccustomed to. Men in her social circles had power, but that came from their checkbooks. Dayne's came from an inherent confidence and self-assuredness. That kind of man wouldn't pull any punches. He'd say what he meant and mean what he said. Her father always told her that was a good quality.

Angus returned with his toy, so she tossed it once more, watching his little legs scrabble on the marble tile floor. When the puppy didn't come back, she went in search of him and found him sniffing around his empty food bowl. She went to get the bag then realized she'd forgotten to get more at the shelter.

"I'm not going to let you go hungry tonight." She grabbed her keys from the table in the foyer then gave Angus a quick pat. "I'll be back in a few minutes. Be a good boy and don't chew anything you shouldn't while I'm gone." Trusting the little guy to follow her order was probably foolish, but she'd only be gone a few minutes. Luckily, he'd already peed his little heart out on the driveway before the rain started pounding. The puppy gave a high-pitched bark. "I'll take you out again before bedtime."

Seconds later, she drove through the gate. The deluge impeded visibility, but as she neared the Haven's main entrance, she could make out a car parked in one of the designated employee parking spaces. The vehicle belonged to Amy, her manager. But the Haven closed its doors to the public at six sharp. Amy should have gone home hours ago.

The Haven was completely dark inside. Odd, since Amy was still here. She could have forgotten to turn the night-lights on. Then again, in the two years since the woman had been hired, she'd never once forgotten. There was a first time for everything. Like fainting.

Talk about embarrassment. Being physically and mentally strong was important to her. Fainting definitely did not fall into that category. *Nor does falling into an FBI agent's arms.*

She shut off the engine and stepped out, splashing through puddles as she ran. Water soaked her hair and dripped into her eyes. She unlocked the door and went inside. "Amy?"

A hint of light that hadn't been there before now glowed from the corridor behind the reception desk. She flipped on the light switch, illuminating the reception space. "Amy?"

She went down the hallway. A few feet from the kibble room, the lights went out. Goose bumps prickled her back and neck. Slowly, she reached inside and flipped on the wall switch.

"Amy?" She walked farther into the room, between two rows of shelves. At the end of the shelving unit, she turned and nearly tripped.

Kat gasped. Amy lay on the floor.

A dark blur moved from the shadows. She screamed. A man wearing a black ski mask over his face slammed into her, shoving her backward against a shelf. Something toppled down and hit her attacker in the head.

Move your ass! She raced into the corridor. A hand grabbed her arm, wrenching it back so hard, she screamed again.

He spun her then gripped her arms and shook her. "Where is it?" Furious dark brown eyes bored into her. "Where the fuck is it?"

Dogs in the adjacent kennel barked. Her pulse raced, and she sucked in ragged breaths. Part of her brain still didn't believe this was really happening. She shook her head, barely comprehending the words. "We don't keep any cash here."

"*Not* cash. I want the—"

She drove her knee up as hard as she could, aiming for his groin, but he sidestepped, and she missed.

Strong hands gripped her throat. *Can't. Breathe.* She clawed uselessly at his fingers. Her pulse pounded in her ears, and she could hear her own pathetic attempts to take in a breath. *Oh. Hell. No!* She rammed the palm of her hand straight up into his nose. His head rocked back, and he loosened his hold around her neck.

She sucked in a breath, filling her lungs with much-needed air. "Asshole." Fisting her hand, she punched the side of his head. He released her and staggered back. She cocked her arm again for a right cross when he grabbed her wrist and squeezed. Pain blasted up her arm and she uttered a sharp cry.

Fury gleamed through the eye slits of the mask as his lips curled into a sadistic grin. He liked inflicting pain.

Kat struggled in his grip then began clawing at his face. Her fingers caught on the mask and she yanked it up to his forehead. Blood trickled from his nose onto his mustache.

"Bitch." He yanked the mask back into place then pulled something from his belt.

Light glinted off the pointed weapon in his hand. *A knife.* Her heart began racing so fast her chest hurt. She sucked in quick breaths and began backing away. Time seemed to slow. Bloody images of that sharp blade cutting into her soft flesh flashed through her mind.

Kickboxing classes in her private gym were one thing, but it didn't prepare her for a knife-wielding lunatic. Long before she could get away, he'd ram it in her back.

I'm going to die.

• • •

Dayne parked next to Kat's car. It was after nine p.m. He'd figured on driving up to the castle to deliver the puppy kibble and more toys Becca's husband had given him for Angus. Remy pinned him with intense chocolate-brown eyes. "Suits me fine," he muttered, not relishing going back to Kat's "house" again.

"Back in a minute, girl." Outside, rain pelted him, quickly soaking his shirt and dripping down his face like tears. Like

Ted Garman's tears.

When he'd stopped by Becca's house, he'd felt helpless seeing the man's grief and unable to do anything except pay his respects.

He hefted the sack of food over his shoulder, grabbed the bag of toys, then kicked the door shut. As he started toward the Haven, wind howled through the trees, sounding exactly like—

A woman's scream.

Kat.

He dropped the bags and bolted toward the door, punching the door popper on his belt to release Remy. Before he'd gotten halfway up the sidewalk, she darted past him.

Dayne drew his Glock and yanked open the glass door. As a team, he and Remy entered the vestibule. The overhead light was off, but a glow from the corridor behind the reception desk lit the space enough to see. With his gun extended, he "sliced the pie," scanning in incremental wedges.

"Kat!" he shouted. A thump came from somewhere down the corridor.

Remy pranced, her nails clicking on the floor as she waited for his command. *"Revier!"* His K-9 took off, her feet scrambling as she rounded the desk and disappeared.

Dayne raced after his dog. Warning prickles lit up his nerve endings.

As he edged around the desk, a door slammed. Remy barked. Leading with his gun, he peered down the hallway. His dog stood on her hind legs, clawing at the door. Kat lay slumped against the wall, breathing raggedly and clutching her hand to her neck.

His breath froze in his throat like a solid ball of ice.

Light came from the room opposite where she lay. He took a quick scan through the open door. No one visible. He trusted his partner. If anyone inside that room posed a threat,

Remy would have alerted him. Instead, his K-9 continued barking at the exit door.

"*Bleiben.*" Remy lowered and stilled. As much as he wanted to let her out to run the asshole down, he couldn't leave Kat alone, and he wouldn't risk sending his partner out there in the dark without knowing what she'd be up against. This fucker could have a gun or a knife, or a four-foot-long samurai sword.

He holstered his gun then tugged out his cell phone, dialing 911 as he knelt in front of Kat. Her eyes were closed, but her breathing had evened out. While he waited for the operator, he scanned her body for injuries. None that he could see. No visible blood, anyway.

When the 911 operator answered, he ID'd himself then quickly described the situation, requesting police backup and an ambulance. Then he issued a warning to all responding units to be on the lookout for anyone in the vicinity who didn't look like they belonged there.

Kat moaned then leaned her head back against the wall, dropping her hand from her throat. Pale red marks in the shape of fingers encircled her neck.

Dayne clamped his jaw together. *Jesus.* He cued up another number. "Paulson," he said when the detective answered. "Get over to the Canine Haven. Someone just attacked Katrina Vandenburg. I already called 911."

Swearing came through loud and clear. "On my way."

Remy remained by the door as ordered, her body vibrating with tension.

Kat reached up again to touch her throat, but he caught her wrist, gently pulling it away. "Try not to touch your neck. We might be able to pull some DNA off skin cells left by whoever did this." It was a stretch, but it might be possible. When she didn't respond, a shaft of worry crept up his spine. "Talk to me. You okay?" Other than the obvious.

"Yes," she whispered, and he let out a huge breath. Judging by the fact that her eyes weren't bloodshot and her voice wasn't raspy, he'd guess the asshole hadn't had his hands wrapped around her neck for very long. "But"—she coughed several times—"he wore gloves. And a ski mask."

Damn. So much for DNA or prints.

Kat shifted, trying to get up, when she winced.

With one hand on her shoulder, he urged her to stay put. "Are you hurt?"

"No." She shook her head, wincing again.

"Be straight with me. Did he hurt you?"

She let out a resigned breath. "He threw me against the wall. My shoulder hit the fire extinguisher box."

He glanced up at the metal and glass case housing a large red extinguisher and was doubly glad he'd called for an ambulance. "You said 'he.' Was there just the one guy?" She nodded. "Can you describe him? Height, weight, eyes, hair?"

"He was taller than I am, and strong. *Really* strong." She took a deep breath, drawing Dayne's gaze back to the ligature marks on her throat. "I'm five-five, so I'd guess he was about five-ten."

"Was he skinny? Fat?"

"He was…average. Not skinny, not fat."

"What do you remember about the clothes he wore and what color they were?" He wanted to get a more detailed description out over the radio ASAP.

"The mask was black. His eyes were brown. He had a beard and mustache. I don't remember what else he was wearing."

"Wait. If he was wearing a mask, how do you know he had a beard and mustache?"

"Because when we were struggling, my fingers caught on the mask and it pulled partially up. Then I—" Her eyes went wide. "Oh god. *Amy.* Help her, please!" She tried pushing off the floor.

He admired her game but held her down. "Where is she?" Kat pointed to the open door on the other side of the corridor. "Stay here." With his hand on his gun, he got to his feet.

"Remy, *such.*" His dog bolted inside the storage room. Rows and rows of tall metal shelving loaded with supplies crammed every bit of space.

Remy barked once. He followed the sound and rounded the end of the last row. A woman lay face up on the floor. Red ligature marks ringed her throat. The woman's eyes were open and sightless.

He dropped to her side, touching his fingers to her carotid. *Nada.* Her skin was still warm. Training kicked in and he positioned her head and neck to start mouth-to-mouth resuscitation and CPR. He whipped out a tiny red packet from his thigh pocket—a breathing barrier—then placed it over her mouth. After pinching her nostrils closed, he administered two rescue breaths. He hadn't gotten in two rounds of chest compressions when sirens screamed outside. A soft sob came from the doorway.

"Please, no," Kat whispered. "Is she dead?"

"Not if I can help it," he managed between compressions.

"Police, call out!" someone shouted.

"In here!" He gave two more rescue breaths, switching back to compressions. "Go get the EMTs."

She ran from the room. Seconds later, two EMTs hustled in, followed by several cops.

"We'll take over," one of the EMTs said.

Dayne backed off to give them room to work. "See anyone on the way up here?" he asked.

"Negative." The first cop shook his head. "We've got units patrolling the area. We could use a little more description."

Kat's brow wrinkled, and her eyes shimmered with tears

as she watched the EMTs tend to her friend.

"Let's talk somewhere else." He placed his hand at the small of her back and urged her to the vestibule. Along the way, he tipped his head to his K-9. "Remy." She trotted behind them with her head down, disappointed at not being green-lighted to give chase.

At the reception desk, he pulled out a chair. "You'd better sit down." He eyed Kat closely for other aftereffects of the attack. The woman had had one hell of a day. It was a miracle she was still upright.

Paulson came through the front door, frowning as he took in the pink marks on her neck. "Are you all right, Miss Vandenburg?"

"I'm fine, Detective." She peered around Paulson's shoulder in the direction of where the other woman was being worked on.

Dayne didn't say so, but his gut told him the EMTs' efforts would be futile. Kat's eyes met his, then her chin dropped, and she let out a heavy sigh. She knew it, too.

Remy nudged her muzzle beneath Kat's hand, forcing her to pet the top of his dog's head. Remy's maternal instinct didn't surprise him, but *his* next move did. He cupped Kat's face. "As soon as they know something, they'll tell us. I promise." Her glistening eyes reminded him of purple gemstones. "Okay?" She nodded, blinking rapidly and stemming the tears with admirable guts and determination. "Walk us through everything from the moment you got here."

"I came here to get food for Angus," she said in a steady voice. "I noticed Amy's—the Haven's manager, Amy Thorpe—car was still parked outside."

"What time was that?" Paulson tugged a pad and pen from his jacket's breast pocket.

"About nine. The lights were off. I came in, then called out for Amy. When she didn't answer, I went to the storage room. The lights were on. Then they went out. I turned them back on and found Amy on the floor. That's when he attacked me. He threw me against the shelves and I ran. Then he grabbed me and started choking me. When he heard you coming, he shoved me against the fire extinguisher box and ran out the back door."

"Did he say anything?" Dayne asked.

Her smooth brow wrinkled. "He asked me where *it* was."

"It?" Paulson looked up. "It *what*?"

"I don't know. I told him we don't keep cash here, but he said he didn't want cash."

"Is there anything else here of value?" Dayne asked. "A safe?"

"No, nothing. We don't even require a fee to adopt any of the dogs here, so there's no need for one. The only things we keep here are dog food, bowls, leashes, collars, toys, and other supplies."

"What about drugs?" Paulson asked. "Do you keep any painkillers on site? Injectable or pills?"

"Yes, but not in this building." She pointed to the other side of the vestibule. "We have an infirmary attached to the main kennel. Everything stronger than over-the-counter meds is kept in a locked cabinet. I can show it to you."

Paulson nodded, making a few more notes. "Could be the guy was looking to score some prescription meds."

"Could be." But Dayne didn't think so. Two women murdered on the same day and less than five miles apart... This area wasn't exactly the homicide capital of the county.

"I'll need the names of everyone who works here," Paulson said, and Kat gave him six names, two that worked full time, the others part time.

"Where are the recordings for your security cameras maintained?" Dayne tipped his head to a camera on the ceiling.

"In a closet next to the storage room." She pointed to the corridor then turned her hand over, looking oddly at it.

Dayne watched her, curious. "What?"

"I forgot. I hit him in the nose with a palm strike. I may have broken his nose. He was bleeding. Not much, just a little trickle from one of his nostrils. I was looking to see if there was any blood on my hand that you could get DNA from."

"You *hit* him?"

"I told you Emily and I did kickboxing together."

He *had* forgotten about that.

"I'll make sure the CSU guys check her hands and under her fingernails for blood." Paulson made another notation. "Meantime, don't touch anything."

"While you're at it," Dayne said, "I don't see any blood on Remy's muzzle, but I can swab her in case she got a piece of the guy."

A team of CSU officers came through the door, each carrying a large duffel and a black hard-sided plastic case.

Paulson motioned them over to Kat. "Swab her hands and take nail scrapings. Then swab that K-9's mouth."

"You got it." The older of the two CSU techs perched his duffel on the desk and took out gloves, Q-Tips, and plastic evidence bags, handing one set to his partner for Remy while he got to work on Kat's fingers. The younger technician didn't get the swab within two feet of Remy when she lowered her head and growled. The tech jumped back.

"Better let me do that." Dayne dug out another pair of gloves from the tech's bag and slipped them on. He held out his hand for the swab, which the other man gratefully turned over.

Dayne knelt in front of Remy. "Smile."

Remy pulled back her lips, exposing her teeth and looking exactly like she was grinning.

The tech shook his head. "That's some trick."

"Makes this a lot easier." He made quick work of swabbing Remy's teeth and gums. After depositing the swab in the evidence baggie, he tugged off the gloves and tossed them in a nearby garbage can.

The other tech still worked on Kat's fingers and nails. They *looked* clean, but maybe she scraped some DNA off the guy's face after all. "How much of a look did you get of him?"

"A few seconds, maybe."

He and Paulson exchanged knowing looks. They might not get any DNA, but maybe Kat could ID the guy.

One of the EMT's emerged from the corridor. The man's expression was grim. He gave a subtle shake of his head.

"No," Kat whispered. "Nooo." She stood and took a step toward the corridor.

He caught her gently, being careful not to squeeze her injured shoulder. "Kat, don't. I know you want to go to her, but there's nothing you can do. The crime scene unit needs to catalogue everything. We'll only make it harder for them to do their job."

When her body shook with sobs, something inside him broke and he took her in his arms, holding her while she cried. Over her shoulder, he and Paulson again exchanged looks. He and the detective weren't necessarily in sync on everything, but on this, they agreed. Both murders had one common denominator.

Katrina Vandenburg.

Not only had she been the one to discover both bodies, but now someone had tried to kill her.

And she'd seen the guy's face.

Chapter Five

Dayne pushed a button on his wristwatch, backlighting the dial in a fluorescent green hue. It was nearly midnight. He and Remy had been searching the woods surrounding the Haven and the castle for nearly two hours.

Remy shook, sending water droplets flying. Rain dripped from Dayne's hair and he wiped it from his forehead before it ran into his eyes. His K-9 was one of the best trackers in the Tri-state area, but with the constant deluge, finding a lasting scent was impossible. She'd picked up a trail outside the exit door, lost it, only to find it again an hour later and track it to the road where it disappeared. Chances were Kat's attacker had a car parked somewhere and was long gone by now. The uniforms patrolling the nearby streets had also come up empty.

He cursed under his breath. "Let's go, girl. We're done for the night."

They headed back to the Haven, stomping through puddle after puddle. A few police cars still sat out front, including Paulson's Charger. Inside the Haven, the tech guys were packing up their cases. Paulson sat on a corner of the reception desk, reviewing his notes.

"Anything?" Dayne hitched his head to the tech guys.

Paulson flipped a page on his pad. "No obvious traces of blood on the floor or on Miss Vandenburg's clothing. We took photos of her neck and swabbed her skin for DNA. The camera outside the rear exit door was covered with a cloth. No drugs are missing from the infirmary, but maybe he just hadn't found them yet. That could have been what he meant when he asked her where 'it' was."

"Maybe." He still didn't buy that theory. His gut told him the two homicides were connected, and drugs weren't the connection. "Or maybe we're just not seeing it yet."

"Seeing what?"

He wasn't sure. "The killer came here for something, and I don't think it was to kill the manager. Kat is the connection between Becca Garman and the Haven, not Amy Thorpe."

"But all she did was find the body," Paulson countered. "She said she didn't see anyone else."

"We're still missing something." Speaking of which... "Who's with Kat at the hospital?"

Paulson arched a brow. "*Miss* Vandenburg refused to go to the hospital."

The detective's intentional dig at Dayne's familiar use of Kat's nickname was as subtle as a nuclear bomb.

"Also," Paulson continued, "she got on the phone with my chief and made him swear not to do a press conference about the attack. Said she was afraid they'd put some kind of crazy spin on it that would have a negative impact on the charities she supports."

That it might. The media would put whatever spin on things they wanted. That was how they made their living. He took a quick scan of the vestibule, then the corridor. "Where is she?"

"Home."

"Great," he muttered, not liking the idea that a doctor hadn't checked out her throat and shoulder. "Who's with her?"

"I assigned a couple of uniforms for the overnight, but she wasn't happy about it. Said she'd hire a security company with armed guards first thing tomorrow."

Just what they *didn't* need. A bunch of yahoo cop-wannabes with Rambo delusions roaming the property.

"Can you have your sketch artist at the station tomorrow?" Dayne wanted to get a picture of the guy before Kat started forgetting details.

Paulson grunted. "Unlike the great and powerful FBI, most humble police departments such as ours don't have sufficient funding to retain a sketch artist at their beck and call."

"I'll take care of it." The local FBI office *did* have a sketch artist. "I'll also make sure Kat gets to the station tomorrow."

"*You'll* make sure?" Paulson took a step closer, trying to get in Dayne's face. *Good luck with that.* The man was at least five inches shorter than Dayne's six-four. "Don't forget, Feeb, she's *my* witness."

Remy inserted herself between them, growling low in her throat as she glared up at the detective. When Paulson leaped back, Dayne couldn't prevent the not-so-tiny smirk quirking his lips.

"Easy, girl." He leaned down to rest his hand on Remy's head. To Paulson, he said, "She's also an FBI witness."

Paulson gave Remy a cautionary glance. "How do you figure that?"

"Retired or not, Becca Garman will always be FBI, so like it or not, you just got yourself a new partner for the duration of this investigation. Remy, let's go." He didn't miss the look of resentment on Paulson's face.

Tough shit, dude.

Two minutes later, he parked behind two police cruisers in the castle's driveway. Rain still fell but had finally begun to ease.

He gave Remy a quick chin rub, then grabbed the bag of Angus's toys he'd retrieved from where he'd dropped them outside the Haven. The kibble, unfortunately, was a soggy mess that he'd disposed of in a dumpster. He left the SUV running with its heat vents directed toward the kennel so his K-9's thick coat would start to dry. He didn't like leaving Remy in the vehicle, but her coat was a mess and she smelled exactly like what she was. A wet dog.

The window on one of the cruisers rolled down, and he badged himself to the young cop. "FBI Special Agent Andrews. Is your partner inside?"

"Yeah." The cop, who looked no more than fifteen but had to be at least twenty-one, jerked his thumb to the house. "But I'm not sure for how long. His wife just went into labor. It's their first kid. We're trying to get a replacement so he can leave."

Dayne grinned. Two of his best friends, Matt Connors and Nick Houston, had recently become fathers and they were happier than pigs in shit. "I'm going in. Notify your partner, will ya?"

"Ten-four."

Dayne understood the other cop needing to hightail it to the hospital. If he and Britt had married, they might have had several kids by now. He'd have walked through fire and brimstone to be at her side for every birth. But Britt had taken off and never looked back.

At the top step, a red light lodged in a corner of the roof caught his eye. A security camera. Tomorrow, he'd do a thorough inspection of the entire system. Maybe he'd even call Kade for an assist.

Before hiring on with Homeland Security, Kade Sampson had been a security system specialist. Kade was a master at installing systems while Dayne was an expert at getting past them, a trade he'd learned as a kid on the streets of Newark. If they hadn't gone the law enforcement route, they could have started their own company and made a mint.

He assumed Kat had long since gone to bed. Not wanting to wake her by using the church organ doorbell, he knocked softly. Another cop, this one in his early thirties and wearing a pin that said T. Morales, answered the door with a cell phone pressed to his ear.

"Honey, I'll be there as soon as my relief shows up." Morales closed the door after Dayne stepped inside.

Angus bounded into the foyer, his ears flapping against the sides of his head. In his mouth was the same gnarly chew toy. Dayne knelt and scratched the puppy's ears. He emptied the bag of toys on the floor, expecting Angus to dive right in. Instead he maintained a firm grip on the ratty one in his mouth, ignoring all the other options, which included a black puppy *Kong*, a rope with a ball on one end, and a blue stuffed animal with bulging yellow eyes, the species of which was unidentifiable.

"Congratulations." He stood when the cop pocketed his phone. "Your first?"

"Yeah." Morales grinned, but the smile quickly morphed into a frown as he glanced at his watch. "My wife will have my balls on a platter if I don't get my ass to the hospital ASAP."

Angus scampered off.

"When's your replacement due?" Gurgling sounds floated into the foyer, the kind made by a coffeepot.

"They won't say." Morales dragged a hand down his face, looking desperate.

Dayne's only experience with kids was with his niece and nephew, but that didn't make him immune to the cop's predicament. "How is Ka—Miss Vandenburg—doing?"

"She's okay, I guess. She's upstairs, but still awake." Something buzzed, and Morales pulled out his phone and began reading a text.

Angus bumped his toy against Dayne's knee. He tugged it from the puppy's mouth and tossed it for him to chase after.

He followed Angus into an enormous library paneled in dark wood. Three more crystal chandeliers, each the size of a small Chevy, dangled over his head. He didn't know much about rugs, but the floor was littered with them. Thick red and blue ones. The rugs alone probably cost thousands.

The place really was over the top. There had to be at least thirty rooms but no big screen or beat-up leather chair for watching baseball and football.

His boots clumped as he walked into another room that made his heart sing. A full-size pool table took up most of the room. No dart board on the wall, though. Instead every inch of wall was covered with paintings of men and women glaring down at him. *Kat's ancestors?*

Dayne arched a brow. He didn't know who his own father was, let alone any of his ancestors. Hell, he'd barely known his own mother.

Hushed cursing drew him back to the foyer where Morales held his cell to his ear again. "Yes, sir. I understand." The cop ended the call, looking about as sad sack as a guy could get.

Clearly, getting a replacement was still a no-go. Dayne exhaled a long breath. As much as it killed him, the brotherhood demanded he do it. "I'll stay here in your place."

Morales jerked his head up, one corner of his mouth lifting. "Seriously?" Dayne nodded and the cop's grin broadened. "Just let me run it by my CO."

A minute later, Morales got the green light to beat feet and Dayne was pouring himself a cup of coffee in the kitchen. The other cop was still outside in his patrol car.

A vase on the end of the island held a bunch of slightly wilted pink roses. Already bored, he counted the flowers. Eleven, not a dozen as he'd expected.

A creak came from the staircase and Angus scampered off with his rubber chew toy. Dayne set the mug on the counter, resting his hand on his Glock. He stepped quietly into the living room to find Kat kneeling, stroking Angus's ears. She'd changed out of her jeans and sweatshirt and now wore a long purple robe.

The puppy dropped the chew toy and stood on his hind legs, begging to be picked up. She cooed to him, dropping gentle little kisses on the top of his head, the same way a mother would kiss a child. Apparently, like his K-9, Kat had a maternal streak a mile wide. And this puppy wasn't even hers.

"You are *so* cute. I wish I could keep you." When Angus landed a puppy lick to her face, she smiled.

He'd seen her smile before, but not like this. This one was genuine. The other times, they'd been perfunctory and then only because protocol dictated it.

Angus yipped, and Kat reached down to scoop him into her arms. When she rose, she sucked in a tight breath. Her eyes squeezed shut and her lips compressed, but she didn't let go of the puppy.

"Are you all right?" Any idiot could see she wasn't.

She spun to face him, wide-eyed. Neither of them uttered a word. He couldn't say why *she* was speechless, but he knew why *he* was. Whatever material that robe was made of clung to a set of long, shapely legs, defining every sleek muscle.

"Agent Andrews, what are you doing here?"

"Call me Dayne." It seemed silly not to when he'd been using *her* first name all this time. "Morales—the cop who was here—had to leave. His wife just went into labor."

"That's wonderful news." Again, she smiled, but pain

rimmed the tight lines of her mouth, and only then did he notice how red her eyes were. "And you took his place? How noble."

Was there a touch of sarcasm behind her words? *Maybe.* Then again, she was one of the most polite people he'd ever met.

One of Angus's tiny paws rested on her collarbone. He sobered at the pale pink marks on her neck. "Why didn't you go to the hospital?"

"I don't like hospitals." She went past him into the kitchen.

"Nobody does."

"My parents died there."

"I'm sorry." Man, he couldn't seem to say anything right around her. "What happened?"

"Plane crash. I was sixteen, but I remember everything. The awful hospital smell. The sadness. The terrible loneliness. The—" She stopped, as if she hadn't meant to confess something so personal. "It's just something I never forgot. Since then, the only times I go to a hospital are for charity events."

"Understandable." As favorite places to visit went, hospitals were at the rock bottom of his list, too. "Why aren't you asleep?" He thought he knew the answer but needed to hear her say it.

She leaned against one end of the counter. "Like you said, finding a dead body, let alone two in one day, would mess with anyone's head."

He gave her an assessing look. "Are you sure you're telling me everything?"

"Are you suggesting that finding two women—one of whom was my *friend*—dead doesn't bother me in the slightest?" Her voice trembled at the reference to Amy Thorpe. When Angus wriggled in her arms, she hissed in a breath.

"No. What I'm suggesting is that you're in pain. Emotional *and* physical." He lifted Angus from her arms, and as he did, one of his hands brushed against her breast. Her eyes widened. His did, too, but not because he'd accidentally touched her inappropriately. The puppy's paw had caught on the collar of the robe, tugging it from her shoulder and revealing an ugly bruise the size of a grapefruit.

He ground his jaw, angry as hell at the fucker who'd done this. Angrier still that he and Remy hadn't gotten to the Haven a few seconds sooner.

Dayne set the puppy on the floor then crossed his arms, watching her draw the robe back in place. "You've got two choices. Either you let me take you to the hospital right now to get that shoulder looked at, or you let me examine you."

"*You*?" She tightened the robe around her torso.

Yeah, he didn't think she'd like that idea.

"Does your expertise include medical training?"

"Actually, it does. In another life, I was a paramedic and pre-med."

Her brows rose. He hadn't noticed before that they were slightly darker than her hair. She sighed. "Fine."

"Fine *what*?" She *had* to have meant the hospital. *Right*?

She swallowed. "I'll let you examine me."

Fuck. He'd only given her the ultimatum to force her into seeing a doctor to make sure she hadn't broken anything. She *really* must hate hospitals.

Kat had more guts than he'd given her credit for. She'd called his bluff, leaving him no choice.

Time to play doctor.

Chapter Six

Kat swallowed again as she untied the belt. They were alone in the house and once she removed her robe, the only thing she'd have on was the matching silk and lace nightie that barely covered her thighs. But going to a hospital was scarier than having a man she barely knew—and who *wasn't* a doctor—examine her.

Her vision blurred, and she blinked. Amy was probably in a hospital morgue by now, lying on a cold metal table and draped with a white sheet. Alone. Cold. And dead. *Try not to think about it.* But it was *all* she thought about.

"Kat?" Dayne's voice cut through her morbid thoughts.

If she didn't let him do his doctor thing, she didn't doubt for one second that he'd make good on his threat to take her to the hospital.

She let the robe slip from her shoulders. Before she could catch it, the garment slithered down her legs to the floor. He tracked the movement, although she couldn't be certain if he was looking at the robe or taking in her nearly naked body, and *oh shit.* Her nipples tingled, and she crossed her arms over her breasts to cover the hard little buds. Her body had a mind of its own that clearly wasn't connected to her brain.

Dayne stepped closer. "I'll try not to hurt you," he said gruffly. "Tell me if I do, and I'll stop."

She nodded, giving him a nervous smile. "I'm in your hands, Doctor Dayne."

He clasped her wrist with one hand, resting his other on her shoulder, readying to gently manipulate her arm when she gasped.

He jerked his hand away. "Did I hurt you?"

"No." She uttered a tight laugh. "Your hands are cold."

His big body relaxed, and relief seemed to wash over him. He rubbed his hands together several times before placing them back on her shoulder and wrist. His now warm fingers were rough and calloused, yet his touch unexpectedly gentle, as if he were caressing a fragile piece of glass. "Better?" he asked.

"Um, yes." Her shoulder had been aching and throbbing to the point where she couldn't sleep. Now all she felt was the army of goose bumps racing across every inch of her skin. Funny how she'd never gotten those goose bumps from Chad's touch.

He manipulated her arm and shoulder in different directions then abruptly dropped his hands and took an awkward step back. "I don't think anything's broken, but the only way to confirm that is with X-rays. Did you take anything for the pain?"

"Yes. It didn't help."

"I can see why." He dipped his head to the ugly bruise that had pretty much doubled in size in the last hour. "Do you have an ice pack?"

"In the freezer." She nodded to the stainless steel Thermidor against the far wall. "Emily and I keep several in there in case we pull something during kickboxing."

He practically bolted to the freezer then jerked open the door with what seemed like more force than necessary. The ice packs were staring him in the face on one of the shelves, but he didn't grab one right away. He stood there with his broad back to her, his entire body frozen like a block of ice.

A long moment passed before he grabbed one of the packs then shut the freezer door. He held the pack out to her, maintaining so much distance between them it was obviously intentional. "Hold this to your shoulder for twenty minutes, three times a day for the next forty-eight hours."

"Thank you." She took the ice pack, taking extra care not to touch his hand. *What was* that *about?* One minute they'd been getting along fine—not that she cared, not really, anyway—the next, he acted as if she had the cooties.

She pressed the ice pack against the bruise, flinching as it made contact. "I told Detective Paulson I'll be hiring a security guard company first thing in the morning. That way, neither the police department *nor* the FBI will have to shoulder the burden of my safety."

His brows met. "Your safety is *not* a burden."

"Then why do you look physically ill?"

"Do I?" He shoved one hand in his pocket, making his biceps bunch.

"You do." A little, anyway.

"I'm not." A muscle in his cheek ticked. "And, I'm not going anywhere. I don't believe in coincidence, and you shouldn't, either. In case it's escaped your attention, there's a connection between the two victims."

"Okay, I'll bite." She crossed her arms, inadvertently plumping her breasts against the lacy cups of her nightie then quickly uncrossing them. "What's the connection?"

"You," he said softly. "*You* were at both locations. So, like it or not, you now have round-the-clock protection, and I'm not talking about some rent-a-cop agency."

She advanced on him until she was a foot away. "Then what *are* you talking about?"

"*Me*." He pushed from the counter, closing the gap to a few inches. "Until this investigation is over, you don't go anywhere without me glued to your six."

She snorted. "Is that alpha male jargon for *glued to my ass*?"

"It means you're stuck with me, twenty-four seven."

It took another few seconds for the full meaning of his intentions to take root. "No." She shook her head. "That's not happening." Not with him, anyway. One night was fine, but having him around all the time would drive her—and her body—crazy.

"Security guard companies hire inexperienced cheap labor. They can't protect you from this kind of violence. If this guy attacks again, by the time your security team dials 911… You'll. Be. Dead." His voice had turned hard.

Chills snaked over her body, and it had nothing to do with the ice pack.

"We can't be certain, but whoever tried to kill you may try again. We don't know if this was a crime of opportunity or something else. But you've seen his face. The fact that he came here after killing Becca tells me he's persistent and won't stop until he has whatever he's after."

Dayne didn't want to be there but was willing to stay just to keep her safe. Two people were dead. An FBI agent and her own friend. An uncontrollable shudder swept through her. *Poor Amy.* How would her husband and children get through this? Because dead was dead, and there was no bringing Amy back.

As if someone had flipped a switch in her brain, the truth of Dayne's words kicked in with brilliant clarity. *I really could be next.*

Making a decision she prayed wouldn't be a colossal

mistake, she set down the ice pack then retrieved her robe and slipped it on. "I want to see Amy's family tomorrow." She'd left messages for her husband, but he hadn't returned her calls.

"Okay," he said quietly.

"And I'll be going to the wake." She blinked to hold back the tears that had suddenly reappeared.

He regarded her closely, but with compassion in his eyes. "Okay. If you'd prefer someone else—a female agent—I can make that happen."

That was something she hadn't considered. Then again, while they had their differences, he could—and would— protect her. He was strong and intelligent. He made her feel… *Safe*. That hadn't happened in a long time–maybe ever.

"You can stay."

Something in his expression changed. She had to be mistaken because it looked like relief.

Weariness took over, and she pressed her fingers to her forehead. "Do you really think the same person who killed Rebecca Garman killed Amy?"

"I can't prove it, but yes. I do."

She lowered her hand. "Amy was such a kind person. She wouldn't hurt a fly. Why did he do this?" Why did anyone kill another human being?

"I don't know." He gave a slight shake of his head. "Yet. We've got a lot of leads we're looking into."

"I still don't understand why he went to the Haven in the first place."

"I don't know that, either." His brows lowered. "We'll figure it out. I promise."

Their gazes met and held. "I believe you."

Something wet and rough licked her bare toes. Angus's tongue.

"Where's Remy?" She peered into the living room. If

Dayne's giant German shepherd were there, she'd know it. That K-9 had the same undeniable presence that her handler did. Neither would ever be overlooked.

He tipped his head to the front door. "Out in the truck."

"She can't stay there all night. Bring her in." She headed for the door, intending to open it, but Dayne got there first, blocking her path.

"No going outside tonight. Especially in"—his eyes dipped to her silk robe—"that."

She pinched her lips, holding back the death stare she wanted to give him. Instead, she flung her hands in the air, resigned to the fact that she now had round-the-clock protection. "Fine."

"She's muddy," he warned.

"There's a hose on the side of the house." She pointed in the general direction where one was attached to the exterior wall.

Dayne arched a dark brow. "Then she'll be wet."

"I have towels. Bring her in. My house, my rules." Angus let loose with a sharp yip. "See? It's unanimous."

"Yes, ma'am." She opened her mouth, readying to also insist that he never call her "ma'am," when a corner of his mouth lifted, revealing a very nice set of white teeth. "We'll be back."

Leaving the puppy staring at the door, she went to one of the guest bedrooms on the main floor—the butler's accommodations—and plucked two fluffy white towels from the bathroom shelf. She turned to inspect the bedroom. Dayne could stay here. He'd like it. With its dark wood paneling and black comforter on the four-poster bed, it was 100 percent alpha male. *Just like him.*

Back in the foyer, Angus had parked his furry little butt two inches from the door. She cracked it open, using her foot to keep Angus from darting outside.

"Shake," Dayne commanded, and Remy shook. A few droplets hit Kat in the face, but she didn't care. "Shake," he ordered again, and again, Remy shook. "Good girl."

"She shakes on command?"

He narrowed his eyes and his lips compressed into a tight line. "I told you to stay inside."

She rolled her eyes. "I *am* inside."

"You shouldn't be standing on the threshold, exposed like that." He and Remy pushed past her then he closed and locked the door behind them.

Well, maybe he had a point. As far as safety went, guess she'd be taking orders from him from now on.

Angus yipped, standing on his hind legs, trying to nip at Remy's face. The big shepherd stood calmly, allowing Angus to burn off his excitement. "She has the patience of a saint," Kat said.

"*She* does. *I* don't." Dayne nodded to the security keypad on the wall. "What's your alarm code?"

"Four-two-six-five." She set one of the towels on the foyer table, then using her good arm, began toweling off the K-9's damp coat.

"The same code as the driveway gate?" His lips twisted into a disapproving frown. "They should be different codes."

"It's easier to remember only one code." Ignoring the annoyance on his face, she continued drying Remy. "Remy, *du bist wunderschon.*"

The dog's head bobbed, as if acknowledging Kat's compliment at how beautiful she was.

"You speak German?" Dayne asked.

"Yes." She ran the towel over Remy's back and tail.

"Exactly how many languages *do* you speak?"

"Besides English, four. German, French, Italian, and Spanish. It helps me get through meetings I have every so often with our shareholders."

Dayne grunted. "Other than English, I only know enough German for Remy and me to communicate. Right girl?" He petted his dog's head then gently caressed the back of her ear. Remy leaned into his big hand, watching him with absolute adoration in her eyes before landing a lick on his chin. His laugh was deep, rumbly, and totally uninhibited. Seemed like uninhibited laughter was reserved solely for his dog.

He caught sight of her watching them and frowned. "What?"

"Uh, nothing." She shook her head, focusing on sifting her fingers through Remy's thick golden brown and black coat. Just that for a tough, hard-as-nails federal agent, the love he and his K-9 had for each other was so…unexpected. "Teaching her to shake is a handy trick."

"It was either that, or my mother would never let her into my parents' house again. Once, I let her in when it was raining and she shook all over Mom's antique white lace tablecloth. You should have heard the scream. Mom chased Remy *and* me out of the house with a broom." He tugged the towel from her hand and began rubbing his dog's coat. "I've got this."

Maybe chivalry isn't dead after all. Genuine chivalry, that was. Everyone in her circle was usually overly solicitous and always for the wrong reasons. Because they wanted something in return. Like money or the prestige her name could give them by association.

Remy twisted her neck to watch Dayne from adoring eyes then turned back to Angus and gave him a playful nudge with her snout, sending him sprawling. Not to be deterred, the puppy reengaged and clamped his jaw around one of Remy's legs.

The shepherd strode through the foyer and into the living room, dragging the clinging puppy along the floor as she went.

"That should do it." Dayne stood then offered his hand to help her rise to her feet.

For a long moment, she stared at his hand, hesitating to take it and not completely understanding why. A second later, she did.

While his motives had been strictly for medical, analytical reasons, she'd already felt his touch…and liked it. *Gulp.*

Did I actually just gulp? She prayed he didn't hear it.

When she placed her hand in his, long, strong fingers closed around hers, pulling her gently to her feet. Warmth from his hand shot up her arm to her neck, heating her face. He didn't let go. Neither did she.

As if realizing he still held her hand, he abruptly released it. "You must be tired, and we have a busy day tomorrow. I'll take you to Amy's house then the police station to work with a sketch artist."

"Of course. I'll do anything I can to help. And again, I'm sorry. I know you lost a friend yesterday, too." Which explained why he was all business. Finding their friends' killer was the driving force behind everything he did.

"Yeah." He dragged a hand through his hair. "We'll get him. One way or the other."

"There's a guestroom on this floor where you can stay. You do sleep, don't you?"

He nodded. "I'll try and catch some shut-eye."

"This way." As Dayne, Remy, and Angus followed her through the kitchen to the guest quarters, she couldn't put a name to the prickling sense of awareness zinging through her body. "Here we are." She turned on the lights then stepped aside.

He slipped past her to check out the room. "You don't have any ser—" He cleared his throat. "I mean, any employees who stay here with you?"

"You were going to say 'servants,' weren't you?" He shrugged, giving her his answer. "No. I don't have servants. Employees, yes." Although she considered Emily, Francine, and Walter to be friends more than employees.

He raised his brows. "Why not?" She opened her mouth to object to his assumption that she retained servants when he held up his hand. "I only meant that this is a big place. Huge, actually. It must take a small army to maintain."

Remy circled twice then lay down. Angus snuggled up beside her, pressing his back against the K-9's belly.

"It does, but we manage." *Barely*. It wasn't that she didn't have the money to pay more people to run such a big estate. Hiring those she didn't know and trust was a risk, one she was no longer willing to take. Not after reading about her last breakup in the tabloids.

One of the maids had overheard her conversation with Chad and sold the story to make a few hundred dollars. Getting burned again by her own staff... *Never. Again.* The next day, she fired everyone except those she implicitly trusted.

"The people I employ have families." Her tone sounded overly bright, even to her. "Asking them to stay here overnight is unkind. Besides, during the day I'm usually surrounded by people, either at the Haven or at one event or another. Just so you're familiar, there's Emily, my personal assistant whom you met earlier, and Francine, my housekeeper and cook, who will be here at nine o'clock. My groundskeeper, Walter, works outside twice a week."

"I'll need their full names, dates of birth, and Social Security numbers. And the same for anyone else working at the Haven."

"I seriously doubt that's necessary." She crossed her arms, grimacing as a slight twinge shot to her shoulder. "They've all been with me for years. If they wanted to murder me, they could have done it a long time ago."

"I can't argue with that," Dayne admitted. "But everyone has friends, and everyone has relatives. People can be blackmailed, coerced, used by others without even being aware of it. I'm just doing my job, Kat."

"Fine." She held up her hands. "I'll get you the information tomorrow. I mean, later." Considering today was already here.

"Thank you."

"You're welcome." A trickle of water ran down his face, and she realized his clothes were soaked from being outside in the rain. She'd been so self-absorbed, she hadn't given a thought to *his* needs. "There's a laundry room next door to yours if you'd like to wash and dry your clothes."

"Thanks, maybe I will." Panting had them both glancing to Remy and Angus. Remy's tongue lolled from her mouth. The bigger dog appeared totally content to babysit the puppy. "He can stay down here tonight, if you like. I'll take care of him if he needs to go out."

When Dayne smiled her brain shorted out.

You need to answer him.

"I'll take you up on that kind offer. I'm wiped out. I'm not sure I'd hear him once I get to sleep. Good night," she managed.

"'Night."

If he washed his clothes, would he sleep nude?

Stop it. He has absolutely no interest in you that way. Poor guy is just doing his job.

She fell into bed and winced when her sore shoulder hit the mattress. Tears threatened, and she blinked them away.

Two women had died.

Two men and their children had lost their loved ones.

And no one knew why.

I *almost died*. Her throat tightened but she wouldn't allow herself to give in to the terror that had paralyzed her earlier.

She'd do whatever it took to help find the killer, so he could never hurt anyone again.

Chapter Seven

By eight a.m. the coffeepot was calling to Dayne.

He hosed off Remy and Angus's feet, eager for another cup of Kat's French frou-frou java. The early morning dog walk had done double duty, also giving him the opportunity to inspect the property in daylight and scrutinize the exterior of the castle for weaknesses. Of which there were a shitload.

During the walk down to the Haven for puppy kibble, he'd called Kade to give him the rundown on yesterday's events and to get his friend's take on installing a new security system. Kade had quickly grasped the need for exigency and promised to be at the castle in a couple of hours.

Before going back inside, he introduced himself to the outside replacement duty officer in the patrol car and notified the cop that Kat's assistant and housekeeper would be arriving at nine o'clock. He gave the guy his cell number, along with strict instructions to check IDs and send him a text when anyone approached the house.

He dried the dogs' feet then fed them in the kitchen. Aside from the sound of the dogs munching away, the castle was quiet. He took a hefty swig of coffee, shutting his eyes and savoring the deep, rich flavor. This shit was damn good.

Taking his mug with him, he headed for his servants' quarters. He had just enough time to toss his clothes in the wash and grab a shower. After trekking around in the muddy woods for two days straight, his cargo pants and polo shirt were covered with mud splatter. Even he had to admit he *and* his clothes smelled like a herd of buffalo.

He stripped down then grabbed a towel from the bathroom and tied it around his waist. Quietly, he padded to the small laundry room and stuffed his clothes in the washing machine. Even the washer and dryer were top of the line and with enough buttons to fill a computer keyboard. When he pushed the quick wash button an LED lit up telling him the cycle would be done in fifteen minutes. Good thing or he'd be doing protection duty wearing nothing but a towel.

Back in his quarters, he cranked on the shower and when the glass door steamed up, tugged off the towel and stepped in. Resting his palms on the tile, he bowed his head, allowing the hot water to massage his neck and back, nearly groaning from sheer bliss.

This assignment was more stressful than he anticipated. *Because it's Becca.* No, that wasn't it. Not all of it, anyway. Maintaining professionalism was the cornerstone of his career, and his was being tested. Because he liked Kat. A little *too* much.

She could have been killed, and that bothered him more than he cared to admit. Not because she was a critical witness. Because she was…her, and that woman was more down to earth and gutsier than he'd expected. On top of that, the woman was stunning, right down to her toes. He doubted even a sex-deprived monk would be immune to her beauty.

He slapped the bar of soap back onto the ledge and squeezed out a gob of shampoo, rubbing it vigorously into his hair. *Don't even think it.*

It was beyond ridiculous. He wasn't for her, and she wasn't for him. Under *any* circumstances. He wasn't in the same solar system or even the same universe as the Katrina Vandenburgs of the world. But something had been brewing between them last night. Something intense and hot and…

His dick twitched, and he groaned.

Cold or no, she'd trembled at his touch, and her pulse had sped up. He'd had to stand in front of the open freezer to cool the fuck off. When he'd reached for one of the ice packs, he'd been tempted to grab two. One for her shoulder. One for the ache at his crotch. The only thing he could think of at that moment was putting physical distance between them.

No wonder he was still single. Smoothness where women were concerned was as elusive to him as a unicorn. Protecting her was what he should focus on.

He shut off the water. He'd pulled that hairbrained idea out of his ass without knowing if his SAC would even approve it.

After drying off, he tied the towel around his waist then poked his head into the bedroom. Remy's tail thumped when she caught sight of him. Angus still snuggled against her belly, fast asleep.

He padded to the laundry room and transferred his clothes to the dryer. After pushing the quick dry button, he returned to the bedroom and lay back on the bed while he made some calls.

The first call was to his ASAC, updating her on the situation and pitching his protection idea. Miraculously, ASAC Barstow agreed, adding that agents were combing through Becca's old FBI case files for anyone with enough of a grudge to want her dead.

His next call was to Paulson, who answered on the fourth ring. "Paulson," the man said on a yawn.

"It's Dayne Andrews." He waited for a wisecrack about how early it was and was surprised when it didn't come. "Just checking in. Anything new?"

"Yes and no." Sheets rustled. "We're waiting on fingerprint analysis in AFIS. Although, if he really wore gloves, the prints we find should belong to Katrina Vandenburg and her employees, since they're the only ones allowed past the reception desk."

"What else?"

"We interviewed everyone on the same block as Rebecca Garman's office. No one saw a thing, except for one person who thinks they saw the puppy alone in the front yard Tuesday afternoon around four p.m. We took all the case files from the office, and we'll start reviewing them for anyone who stands out as a suspect. The husband confirmed that his wife had a digital camera and a laptop, and that she only did PI casework on the laptop."

"Did he know where the camera and laptop are?"

"No. Said they were with his wife. We didn't find them in the office or in her vehicle."

Dayne frowned. "So the killer stole them."

"Looks like. But we'll do a search of her emails, see if that gets us anywhere."

"And her cell phone?"

"County tech guys are doing a dump on it. We'll interview everyone she spoke with during the days preceding her death. Today, I'll serve a subpoena on the carrier for toll and text records for the last twelve months. If we have to, we'll interview everyone in her list of contacts."

"What about a mapping app on the phone?" It wouldn't tell them every location where Becca had been, but it might give them something else to go on. Right now, the only possible lead lay in Kat's ability to give them a decent sketch.

"I'll add that to the list," the detective grumbled. "But we don't have unlimited resources."

Through the cracked door, Dayne heard Kat calling for Angus. He'd expected her to sleep later.

"I know that. Which is why I'll be taking over your department's protection duties."

A pause, then, "She said she was hiring her own security company."

"She is, but they'll be supplemental. They can't protect her as well as I can."

"On that we agree," Paulson said.

"We'll be at the station by eleven to meet with the sketch artist."

"Later."

When the dryer buzzed, he grabbed his clothes and returned to the bedroom. He stepped into his pants then turned to find Kat standing in the open doorway. Her eyes widened as she took in his bare abs. A blush crept to her cheeks. *Pink looks good on her.*

"I'm sorry, I—" The blush deepened, and he quickly zipped up his pants and fastened the button. "I-I didn't mean to wake you."

Smooth recovery. For a woman in her thirties, Kat had more poise and grace than most people twice her age.

"You didn't," he reassured her with a slight smile, amused and stupidly pleased at how his semi nakedness affected her. "I've been up for a couple hours."

"Well, I, uh…" She put her hand to her throat, reminding him of a prim and proper schoolteacher and calling his attention to the marks on her neck. Even the gray sweater and slacks she wore were conservative, but he'd bet a bucket of bullets the outfit was expensive. "I was looking for Angus to take him outside before he has an accident. Nine-week-old puppies can't hold it for very long."

"He's good." Dayne opened the door wider so Kat could

see Angus happily snoring away. Remy's tail thumped again, this time for Kat's benefit. "I already took the dogs out and fed them."

Her brows rose. "Thank you. You didn't have to do that. Angus can be quite a handful."

"Remy keeps him in line." The puppy's eyes remained closed as he continued making little puppy snores. "He does whatever she tells him to do."

"She really is maternal, isn't she?" Kat tucked a wayward strand of hair behind her ear, revealing the gold stud at her lobe.

"How's your shoulder?" If he detected the barest hint that her answer was evasive, he'd drag her to the hospital whether she liked it or not.

"Better. It still aches but I took something for the pain."

Her eyes remained solidly fixed on his. No shifting up and to the right, a typical indication of deceit. "Good, but there's something else we need to discuss."

"Your attire?" Her lips twitched, then she made a point of checking out his abs again. "What there is of it."

He narrowed his eyes. "My clothes were dirty enough to stand up all by themselves. I walked the property, and we need to talk about your security system, specifically the virtual lack thereof. All you've got is a locked gate, but anyone can climb over the fence. A ten-year-old could disarm the alarm." As he'd done many times to similar systems when he'd been a kid living on the street. "The gate is bad enough. Your house is a castle—literally—but it's a break-in waiting to happen. The security system at the Haven isn't much better," he added. "In fact, it's the same rinky-dink version you've got here."

Closing her eyes, she took a deep breath, as if holding back the annoyance she wanted to unleash in his face.

"You need to upgrade the security here, especially the

cameras. There aren't enough of them, and the ones you have look old enough to take Polaroids. The wiring can be cut from the outside, and the entire system looks as if it was installed forty years ago." She fidgeted with the thin gold chain around her neck, twisting it with her finger and refusing to look him in the eye. "Exactly how old *is* the system?"

"I appreciate your concern, really, and I'm not trying to be difficult. Despite what you may think, I do understand the dangers." She rolled her shoulders back. "But if you install cameras everywhere, I'll feel like eyes are on me all the time, even more than I do already, and I don't want that. This is the only private place I have left in the world. I can't lose that. I just *can't*."

Whoa. Hot emotion flashed in her eyes. *Fear*.

Last night, when she'd been explaining why there wasn't more hired help on the premises, he'd detected she was holding something back. Now he was dead sure of it.

"Okay. No more cameras," he said softly. He didn't like seeing her this way—upset and frightened. The opposite of how security systems were supposed to make a person feel. "All I'm saying is that anyone can walk right into the Haven with a gun or scale the fence and break in here. Right now, the only things stopping that from happening are me and the cop outside."

She waved her hand in the air. "Do you think I should hire guards to frisk everyone who comes here?"

He really wasn't handling this well. "Actually," he added quickly, sorely needing to diffuse things and really, *really* wanting to erase the look of stark desperation on her face, "I was thinking of snipers with .50 caliber machine guns mounted on the turrets and electrical fencing surrounding the perimeter." Kat's eyes went as wide as saucers. "Okay, maybe that's a little overkill. At a minimum, I'd suggest a moat stocked with man-eating alligators or flesh-eating piranhas. My personal favorite."

"Ha. Ha." A smile played at her lips. Lips glossed shimmery pink. "Very funny. Who knew FBI agents have a sense of humor?"

He breathed an inward sigh of relief. "At times, I'm funnier than a stand-up comedian." A little part of his brain was happy as shit that he'd made her smile.

"A stand-up comedian?" She arched a brow. "I seriously doubt that."

"Don't. I have hidden talents."

Her eyes flared a fraction wider. *Yeah, that didn't come out the way I intended.*

The doorbell gonged at the same time his cell phone dinged with an incoming text. Remy barked then leaped over Angus and shot past them into the kitchen. Angus lifted his head, his sleepy eyes staring after Remy.

Raised voices—*female* voices—shrieked. Dayne hauled ass after his dog.

Sonofabitch. The outside duty officer was supposed to notify him *before* anyone approached the house. A lot of good it did *after*.

"Remy, *bleiben*!" His dog skidded to a stop, her body still tense and ready for action.

Dayne took in the wide-eyed expressions of five people cowering in the foyer. Behind them stood the duty officer. All wore identical looks of shock on their faces because here he was in Kat's house, wearing nothing but his pants.

Just what he needed. Their thoughts might as well have been written on the wall.

Now it was his turn to blush.

• • •

Kat rushed after Dayne and Remy, her heart pounding like

a snare drum at the Met. Behind her, Angus scampered to catch up.

Cowering in front of the open door were her personal staff and two of the Haven's full-time employees. The police officer stood behind them on the front stoop. In all, six sets of human eyes were locked on Dayne, although none said a word. They didn't have to. The implication was clear: They'd been having sex.

"Everything all right?" The cop looked at Dayne.

"We're fine," he snapped, and was he...*blushing?* "Remy, *hier.*"

The shepherd obediently sat at his side. The young officer turned, but not before she caught the smirk on his face.

Awk-ward. As much as she wanted to, courtesy dictated she *not* roll her eyes. Instead, she cleared her throat. "Kevin," she said to the Haven's assistant manager, "would you please close the door?" She waited until the door clicked shut. "I asked you all to come in early today because a lot's happened that you need to be aware of. First, I'd like to introduce you to Special Agent Andrews. He's with the FBI."

Walter grunted, narrowing his dark eyes on Dayne. The look of disapproval on the grizzled man's face was easy to read. Her groundskeeper was old school and a stickler for propriety.

"Seriously?" Kevin's blond brows shot straight to his hairline. "And what's with the cop outside? And the police tape blocking off the back rooms at the Haven?"

"Dayne, this is Kevin Acosta, the Haven's assistant manager." Dayne tipped his head in Kevin's direction. "And Fiona, the Haven's only other full-time staffer." Now that Amy was dead. Her throat constricted. She could still barely think it, let alone say it.

"Fiona," Dayne acknowledged the younger woman.

"Emily, you remember Special Agent Andrews from

yesterday?"

"I do." Her assistant grinned as she took in his bare chest. "Nice to, uh, *see* you again, Agent Andrews."

Dayne's jaw tightened.

As much as she willed herself not to, she grinned. Watching this badass federal agent feel the heat was too entertaining not to.

"This is Walter." Kat looked nervously from the older man to Dayne. "Walter is my groundskeeper. He's been with my family for over forty years." Meaning he'd known her since birth. Since the day her parents died, Walter had insisted on meeting every one of her boyfriends. To vet them on behalf of her parents, he'd proclaimed. Not that Dayne was her date, or anything.

"Son." Walter angled his head to look Dayne in the eye. "I sure do hope you have something else to wear besides those pants."

"Yes, sir. I do." She'd thought Dayne's jaw was tight before. Now, it went harder than the kitchen's granite counters.

Walter was testing Dayne's mettle. To his credit, Dayne held fast, not flinching or looking away. Even she understood that if he did, the old groundskeeper would take it as a sign of weakness. *Weak* was a word she would never use to describe Dayne.

"And this is Francine." She indicated the older woman who'd been a stand-in mother to her for the past twenty years. "My housekeeper and the best chef in the Hudson Valley."

True to form, Francine walked right up to Dayne and extended her hand. "Pleased to meet you, Special Agent." A tiny smile curved her lips as she checked out his abs.

A corner of Dayne's mouth lifted. "The feeling is mutual."

"Everyone, let's go into the kitchen and sit down for a few minutes." Kat's heart dipped at the prospect of notifying her staff that Amy had been murdered. Again, her throat choked with so much grief that she had to swallow repeatedly.

"If you'll excuse me," Dayne said, "I'll get dressed."

"Good idea." Walter's eyes narrowed to thin slits.

"Remy, *hier*." Man, and dog, then disappeared down the hallway to his bedroom.

"Would anyone like coffee?" she asked as the people she now considered her family seated themselves on the counter stools. Given the news she was about to deliver, offering refreshment seemed so…ridiculous. But she needed something to do with her hands.

As one, they declined and watched her from somber faces. They knew her well enough to understand something bad was coming.

Kat stood at one end of the counter, uncertain of where to start. Blurting out that one of their own had been murdered seemed abrupt. "Dayne—Special Agent Andrews," she corrected, not wanting to add more fuel to the fire regarding their relationship, which was strictly professional, "is staying here to protect me."

"Protect you from what?" Kevin asked. "Emily called us all yesterday about you finding a dead body but said you were okay. We all saw it on TV last night. But why do *you* need protection?"

Kat hesitated. They needed to hear it, all of it, and not just for *her* protection but for theirs. In case the killer came back. "Last night, someone broke into the Haven."

"Oh no." Francine gasped. "Are the dogs all right?" Francine was a huge dog lover, second only to herself. That was one of the reasons they'd connected in the first place.

"The dogs are fine," she reassured them.

"Did they take anything?" Fiona's blue eyes widened. "Did they break into the drug cabinet?"

"No." Kat rested her hands flat on the counter. "They didn't take anything. But—" There simply was no protocol for what she had to say. "Amy was murdered."

"*What?*" Emily and Kevin cried, their mouths falling open and their expressions one of disbelief.

"Oh my goodness." Francine's hand flew to her mouth.

"I don't believe it." Fiona began shaking her head.

Kevin opened his mouth then closed it. His face went pale.

"What in God's name happened?" Walter fisted his grizzled hand on the counter.

"We don't know. She may simply have been in the wrong place at the wrong time."

"Kat," Walter said quietly, "were you there, too?"

Unable to speak due to that lump of grief in her throat getting bigger by the second, she nodded.

Francine's eyes widened as she pointed. "Are those fingerprints on your neck?"

Again, she nodded. "I interrupted whoever killed Amy, and they tried to kill me, too."

Collective gasps went around the table.

"Are you all right?" Emily clasped one of Kat's hands. Francine grabbed the other, squeezing it.

"I'm fine." Tears burned the backs of her eyes. *Not really. Not at all.*

"Have you spoken with Amy's husband?" Kevin asked. "Is there anything we can do?"

"Not right now." She shook her head. "Emily, would you please cancel all my appointments for the week?"

Emily nodded, sniffing back a sob. "Of course."

"Thank you. I'm going to Amy's house today. I'll let everyone know when the wake is, and I'll close the Haven that day so we can all attend."

The kitchen was deathly quiet as her friends absorbed and processed the horrible news. Only the sound of Angus chewing on his squeaky toy interrupted the morbid silence.

"So now she has twenty-four seven protection," Dayne said as he joined them in the kitchen, fully dressed. Remy trailed him to the counter. "I'll be with Kat around the clock. Kat will hire security guards to supplement outside the castle and at the Haven. Two other agents will be arriving this morning to install a new alarm system."

"*What?*" She smacked her hand on the counter. "This is *my* home, *not* yours, and you agreed... No. More. Cameras." On this, she had no intention of budging.

He loomed over her, stepping into her personal space. "I agreed to no more cameras, but not to keeping a system that can be disarmed from the outside with a paper clip and a plastic straw. And I can see you care about these people. It isn't just you who needs to be protected."

A paper clip? Is it really that easy? What if it was?

Trust him, the rational side of her brain said. If nothing else, he really did have her—and her friends'— safety at heart. "Fine."

"Young man." Walter focused on Dayne. "What do you need from us? We'll do anything to help."

"What I need," Dayne said, "is for you all to be vigilant. Report anything or anyone that seems out of place. Don't take any chances. The killer was looking for something, but we don't know what."

"Honey, what happened to Amy was..." Francine squeezed her hand again. "We're just glad *you're* okay."

Dayne tugged a cell phone from his belt. "Excuse me." He started for the door, as did his K-9. "Remy, *bleib,*" he said over his shoulder, eliciting a disappointed snort from the dog who now stood motionless.

Not being fluent in German, Angus trotted into the foyer. When Dayne opened the door, her eyes went wide. Three enormous men stood on the threshold, each of them as tall and as broad as Dayne.

One of them gave Dayne a bear hug.

"Yo, bro." The next man clapped Dayne on the shoulder.

The third man's jaw went tight as he scanned the interior of the house. Kat couldn't put her finger on it, but something about his countenance screamed: *keep back*. After he and Dayne shook hands, Dayne led them all to the kitchen. She had a mental flash of four giant jungle cats, all power and grace as they stalked their prey.

"Everyone," Dayne said, "this is Kade Sampson, Jaime Pataglio, and Markus York. Kade is with Homeland Security, Jaime is with the Port Authority, and Markus is with Secret Service."

She'd already guessed they were law enforcement. Like Dayne's, not only was their physical fitness totally off the charts, but it was in their bearing and demeanor. Confident. Authoritative. Cautious.

"This is Katrina Vandenburg." Dayne caught her eye and a spurt of heat shot up the back of her neck.

Kade extended his hand and smiled, flashing a set of boyish dimples that softened the hard features of his face. The man was beyond handsome, but… *No heat.*

"Always a pleasure to meet a beautiful woman." Dark eyes twinkled as Jaime brought her hand to his lips, dropping a chaste kiss on her fingers.

"Down, boy." Dayne's eyes glittered like shards of green ice.

Jaime held up both hands then knelt to pet Remy and greet Angus. "Hello, little man."

Angus barked with unabashed joy at the attention.

"Ma'am." Markus York shook her hand, although his overall demeanor was still distinctly different from those of his friends. Brooding, even, and there was something else reflected in his obsidian eyes. *Pain*. She still hated the ma'am thing, but with Markus, she let it go. This man was hurting.

She knew it because she'd seen it in the mirror. *Too many times.* "I don't mean to insult you, but your security for this place is some of the worst I've ever seen."

"So I've heard." Too many feds couldn't all be wrong. Maybe she did need more security.

Next, Dayne introduced Kat's staff one by one and by their first names. As she watched and listened, the depths of her love and friendship with these people hit her with stark clarity. They were everything to her.

Anguish squeezed her heart like a vise. Three months ago, they'd all sat around this same kitchen counter, sipping on beer, wine, and eggnog for the annual Christmas party she threw for all of them. Amy had been there. But Amy would never be at another Christmas party. Anywhere.

Her chest tightened to the point where she couldn't breathe. *Was this my fault?* By not wanting to turn her property into more of a prison than it already was to her, had she compromised her friends' safety?

She pinned her arms over her stomach. Guilt ate at her insides like a cancer. If she'd had better security at the Haven, maybe this wouldn't have happened. Perhaps Amy would have gotten some kind of advanced warning that the killer had gotten inside. Maybe she wouldn't be dead. *Maybe, maybe, maybe…*

She wanted to scream. There was only one thing she could think of that *she* could do. For those she loved, she'd tolerate anything.

"Kat?" Dayne's brows drew together. "Are you alright?"

"Yes." *As much as I can be, anyway.* "I've changed my mind. Install as many cameras as you think are necessary to keep us safe. *All* of us. Especially at the Haven." She choked back a cry of rage. "I don't care what it costs."

Chapter Eight

Dayne shot Kat a quick glance as he turned onto the Palisades Parkway. "What made you change your mind?"

"About what?" Her voice was clipped, her hands clasped so tightly together he thought they'd crack.

"The security system. More cameras." Right before she'd authorized a blank check for any system upgrades he recommended, there'd been an about-face shift in her attitude. Up until that moment, she'd been dead set against it.

"I don't want any more of my friends murdered. I was being thoughtless and stupid." The last word came out on a decidedly bitter note.

Understanding smacked him in the face. With it came a healthy dose of compassion. For all her outward composure, she really was scared to death of losing her privacy. A simple thing most people took for granted. *Something she's willing to give up to safeguard those she cares about most.* In his world, not everyone was so selfless. "If I had cameras pointed at me every time I went out in public, the last thing I'd want was more of them all over my home. What you're doing is a good thing."

"Good thing." She uttered a sound of disgust. "I never should have questioned you in the first place."

"Don't be so hard on yourself." He squeezed her hand, releasing it just as quickly because it felt too good beneath his rough fingers. He cranked the warm air and was rewarded with a whiff of roses. She really did smell pretty.

Remy stuck her head through the opening, her nostrils flaring as she breathed in Kat's perfume.

"Hello, Remy." The tone of her voice wasn't angry anymore, just sad. He wished he could whip up something upbeat to say. Not a damn thing came to mind. His dog nuzzled Kat's cheek, and she sifted her fingers through Remy's thick ruff. "Thank you, girl."

Remy was good like that. When someone needed canine love, she was all in.

Dayne shot into the left lane, heading north on the parkway. The dashboard clock read 9:30 a.m. They had just enough time for Kat to pay her respects at the Thorpes then a quick stop at his place to grab a few things.

A few minutes later, her hands fell to her lap, again clasped tightly.

"Do me a favor." He pointed to the glove box. "Grab me a fresh roll."

"A fresh roll of *what*?" Her brow furrowed. "Toilet paper?"

A snort flew from his lips. "Now who's a comedienne? Just open it. You'll see what I mean."

Kat did as he asked. "What *are* these?" She pulled out one of the three-inch wide rolls of paper studded with brightly colored candy dots.

"Dots." He indicated the wood dispenser he'd installed on the dashboard between the driver and passenger seats. "It's old fashion candy. You can buy it by the inch, but I eat so much of it, I order it by the roll. My favorite is the red one. Rootie Tootie Raspberry. Hang it up for me, will you?"

Ironically, her crack about toilet paper was spot on. The wood hanger his dad had specially constructed was pretty much identical to a toilet paper dispenser.

She pulled out the wooden dowel, stuck it through the center of the roll, then reinserted the ends of the dowel into the bracket.

"Try one." All he wanted was to make her smile again. Even for a few minutes because things weren't about to improve any time soon. Not with a killer on the loose and two funerals on the horizon.

From the corner of his eye he caught her look of skepticism as she examined the roll of candy. Finally she peeled off a red dot, popped it into her mouth, and crunched down. "These are good."

"Knock yourself out. Tear off a few inches."

She did and began popping different colored dots into her mouth. "Is this candy standard issue for all FBI agents?" she asked between crunches.

"No." He chuckled. "There's no line item for candy in the Department of Justice's budget. My mother used to buy it for me when I was a kid." One of the few good things he remembered about his mom. "The sugar keeps me going when I'm on the road, and the crunch keeps me awake when I work nights."

"Does she still buy you candy?"

He shook his head. "She died when I was ten." From a crack overdose.

"Oh. I'm sorry."

"It was a long time ago, but I remember the dots." And finding his mother's body.

"So you were raised by your father?"

He grunted. "I never knew my father. I'm not even certain

my *mother* knew who he was." He'd never told that to *anyone* before. Not even his closest friends.

After exiting the parkway, he stopped at a red light and caught Kat staring at him, her features soft as she gave him a weak smile.

"What?" He frowned. *Ah, shit*. "Don't feel sorry for me."

"It's not that." She stared out the windshield, crumpling the now-empty strip of paper in her fist. "I just feel…empathy."

He exhaled an angry breath because, *fuck*. Last night, she'd told him her parents died when she was sixteen, so after that, she'd grown up with no parents at all. At least *he'd* had his adopted parents. Compared to her, he'd been lucky.

The light turned green and he jerked the wheel left, harder than intended. Being around her reignited not only his old insecurities about growing up without a cent to his name, but about Britt. Still, that was in the past and it wasn't fair to judge Kat by the actions of others. She really was turning out to be a decent person. "Sorry. If anyone can empathize, it's you."

"No." She shook her head. "I shouldn't have pried into your personal life. It's none of my business." Her cell phone dinged, and she dug it from her leather purse. "Emily found several security companies to choose from. She's emailing the details."

"Give her my email and have her copy me on it. Don't hire anyone until I review everything."

"Bossy, aren't you?" An impish grin tugged at her lips.

"It's an FBI thing. We like to take charge."

"Apparently." Her grin broadened, making him feel slightly less shitty.

He gave her his agency email address and cell phone number, so she'd have it plugged into her phone. "And send me a text so I have your number."

"Again with the orders."

"Hey." He braked at a stop sign and twisted in his seat to face her. "I'm doing this to protect you."

Her smile faded, and she gave him a subtle nod of acceptance. "I know."

"Good." He nodded back. It was important to him that she understood how seriously he took his job, and that he wouldn't let anything happen to her.

Two minutes later, they pulled alongside a 1970s tract house that looked the same as every other one on the street. Several cars were parked in front of the place, including a marked patrol unit.

There'd been no such support for him when he'd found his mother—his only living relative—unmoving on that ratty sofa. She'd been twenty-six when she died and left him alone.

"Ready?" He shrugged into a black fleece vest to cover his weapon.

"Yes." After taking a deep breath, she opened the door and got out.

Remy watched him, waiting for a sign that she was coming with them.

"Not this time, girl." He lowered one of the windows so his dog could get some fresh air, then gave her a quick scruff on the head and got out of the vehicle. Remy was accustomed to remaining behind, but that didn't stop her from uttering a sad little whine.

Kat was already at the top step in front of the house. She pressed the bell, and a few moments later the door opened. A forty-ish man stood in the doorway, his eyes red-rimmed.

"Kat, thank you for coming." He opened his arms and embraced her tightly.

They stood that way for several seconds, wordlessly expressing their grief.

Kat pulled away, clasping the man's hands in hers. "Michael, I'm so sorry," she said in a shaky voice. "I feel responsible, and I—"

"It's not your fault," Michael said.

She swallowed repeatedly, valiantly trying to hold her emotions in check, and that's when it hit him. No way was this an act. She really cared about everyone who worked for her. All this time he'd assumed this visit to Amy's family was a required aspect of the courtesy and protocol she took to an art form. *I really am a judgmental dick.*

"I'm sorry for your loss," Dayne said. "May we come in?" He urged Kat into the house. The last thing he wanted was her standing in an open doorway.

"Forgive me," she said as they moved inside. "This is Special Agent Andrews with the FBI. He's investigating Amy's...murder." Kat momentarily squeezed her eyes shut.

Several people standing in the kitchen, along with an older couple in the living room, watched them.

Michael closed the door, narrowing his eyes on Dayne. "Why is the FBI involved?"

Over Michael's shoulder, two teenage boys with features similar to their father's eyed him solemnly from the living room.

"There may be a connection between your wife's murder and the murder of a retired FBI agent."

"What possible connection could there be?" Michael's brows furrowed.

Dayne glanced at Kat, not wanting to publicly voice his opinion that *she* was the connection. Outing that information wouldn't bring the man's wife back, and it would do nothing to ease his family's pain.

"We're not sure yet, but we're working with the Orangetown PD to investigate every possible lead. We'll find out who did this. I promise."

The man stared at him a moment longer, before blinking rapidly and pinching the bridge of his nose.

Kat rested her hand on Michael's shoulder, rubbing it gently. "How are the boys holding up?"

"Not much better than I am. We're all in shock." Michael looked at his boys. "I'm sure they'd like to talk with you."

"I'd be happy to." She squeezed his shoulder once more before joining the boys.

Michael nodded to Kat as she hugged first one boy then the other, each clinging to her as if she were close family. "The first time Amy brought Luke and Tommy to the Haven, Kat took them on a personal tour. When they got home, they couldn't stop talking about the dogs *or* her. I think they're secretly in love with her."

Dayne grunted. *What teenage boy wouldn't be?*

While he couldn't hear what Kat was saying, Luke and Tommy listened with rapt attention.

"Can we speak privately?" Dayne indicated a corner of the kitchen that was currently unoccupied, and where he could still keep Kat in sight.

"Of course." Michael led the way to a table loaded with aluminum trays of food. Someone had gone all-out making sure the family wouldn't have to cook for the next month.

"Has Detective Paulson been by to ask you any questions?"

"Yes." Michael nodded. "Late last night, but I don't think I was able to help much. I was in shock—hell, I still am."

"Would you mind if I asked a few questions?" He glanced at Kat where she now sat on the sofa, with Luke and Tommy on either side of her.

The other man took a deep breath. "I'll do anything I can to help."

"Thank you." As an FBI K-9 agent, he didn't normally take point on homicide investigations—except to locate a body. But this was an exception. Timing was everything, and he had a bad feeling time was not on their side. "Did you or your wife know Rebecca Garman?"

"No." Michael shook his head. "The only reason I know the name is because it was all over the news yesterday that she was murdered, and that Kat discovered the body."

"Did you or Amy ever retain the services of a private investigator?"

Again, he shook his head. "No."

"Is it possible Amy ran into Rebecca Garman and you weren't aware of it?"

"I don't think so. We had no secrets from each other. We talked about everything, including our friends. Amy was always excited when she met someone new, especially someone who had an interesting job, like a private investigator. I'm sure she would have told me if she'd ever met Rebecca Garman." He paused to swipe at his watery eyes. "Were they after drugs or money?"

"Possibly." But he still doubted it.

Kat managed to wring wan smiles from the boys. Whatever they'd been discussing, she'd found a way to make them feel just a little better. She always seemed to know just what to say. A skill he didn't have and wished he did.

"Did anyone hold a grudge against your wife, or was she threatened lately?" Given the fact that the killer had demanded to know where *it* was, he didn't really think Amy was killed because of something in her past, but he had to ask.

"No, everyone loved her." Michael pressed a hand to his forehead then dragged it down his face. "She was a sweetheart who wouldn't hurt or offend a soul."

Not wanting to upset the man more, Dayne abandoned his line of questioning. Truth was, he believed it was a waste of time. "If you think of anything else, please give me or Detective Paulson a call right away." He tugged a business card from his pocket.

"I will." Michael accepted the card then clutched it tightly in his fist. "Agent Andrews, please find who did this and-and"—his voice shook—"make them pay."

As if sensing their father's distress, Luke and Tommy came to his side.

Dayne wanted nothing more at that moment than to plow his fist into the face of the homicidal motherfucker that had torn Amy's family apart. A renewed shot of determination ripped through him, and he clasped the other man's shoulder. "I will. You have my word."

Kat joined them, casting a sympathetic look at Michael and his sons. "We should give you some privacy." She hooked her arm around Dayne's. The look in her eyes was soft and gentle, her brows slightly raised in question.

Shit. He hadn't realized he'd been wearing his emotions on his sleeve.

Michael hugged Kat one last time. "Thank you for coming," he whispered.

"If there's anything you need, or anything you think of that I can do to help, please don't hesitate to ask."

Michael sniffled. "I won't. Thank you for all the food and the beautiful flowers. Amy would have loved them. How did you know orchids were her favorite?"

Kat smiled sadly. "While we cleaned out the kennels, we talked about all kinds of things. Gardening, flowers, and dogs, of course."

The piles of food and flowers had all been from Kat. *And she cleans kennels?*

"Will we see you at the wake on Saturday?" Michael asked.

"Of course." She gave Luke and Tommy quick hugs. "You guys take care of each other."

They said their goodbyes then headed outside. Remy's head appeared at the open window. He opened the passenger side door for Kat, but instead of getting right in, she paused to give Remy a sound scratching behind her ears. She buried her face in Remy's neck and wrapped her arms around his dog. Her upper body heaved with a sigh, then she released Remy and got into the truck.

As he rounded the hood of the SUV, again he was struck by what an enigma this woman was. Filthy rich, yet generous, caring, and sensitive to the needs of others. She wasn't hung up on status, and he liked that about her.

He reached for the door handle then froze. Two blocks away, a blue vehicle sat at a stop sign, unmoving. No oncoming traffic in either direction. There could be twenty reasons why the car didn't take off, but Dayne's heart thumped faster, and adrenaline shot through his system just the same. The vehicle was too far away to see the driver's face, and the angle wasn't right to read the tag.

Every muscle in his body tightened. Seconds later, the car drove straight through the intersection. Curiosity—and a healthy dose of suspicion—had him wanting to give chase, but it was probably nothing.

After getting into the SUV, he took in Kat's somber expression and swore inwardly. He needed to keep his shit together and not get sidetracked. If he allowed that to happen, he wouldn't be able to do his job, and there could be another family minus a loved one.

The Vandenburg family.

Chapter Nine

Kat stole occasional glances at Dayne as they drove back down the Palisades Parkway to the Orangetown Police Department. Since leaving Amy's house, he hadn't said a single word, not even to give her another bossy FBI directive.

"Is anything wrong?" she asked.

He frowned. "You mean, aside from the fact that Tommy and Luke's mother was murdered by some motherfu— homicidal maniac? No." His thick forearms bunched and rippled as he gripped the wheel tighter.

Contrary to his words, he wasn't great. That much was clear, even if he wouldn't admit it. As if sensing his mood, Remy rested her muzzle on the ledge.

There'd been a moment back at the house, albeit a fleeting one, when the emotions on his face and in his body language had given him away. He was grieving, but he was so strong and confident it was easy to forget that, like her, he'd also lost a close friend. "Don't you want to say something bossy and controlling?" She smiled, hoping to crack through that thick armor shell he wore like a second skin.

Dayne snorted. "Maybe later." He rewarded her with the slight upturn of his mouth.

She hated seeing anyone in pain. Cops and federal agents were always portrayed on TV and in movies as a tough breed that never confessed their inner feelings. Not to a virtual stranger, anyway. She didn't want them to be strangers. Quite the opposite.

"I know I said I wouldn't pry into your personal life again, but—"

"Go for it." He slowed the vehicle as he took the exit for Orangeburg.

That was easier than she'd expected. "You said you didn't know your father, and your mother died when you were just a boy. Who took care of you?"

"When I was twelve, a great family adopted me. I was the luckiest kid on the planet." He guided the SUV into the police station, a large two-story brick building with an American flag whipping back and forth on a pole.

"Wait, you said your mother died when you were ten. Where were you for the two years before you were adopted?"

He parked in the lot reserved for police personnel. "Some of that time I spent in the system. Mostly, I lived on the street."

She widened her eyes. "You lived on the *street*? As a ten-year-old?" How was that possible in this day and age? Her heart went out to the little boy Dayne used to be. She couldn't imagine being so young and so alone in a big city. "How did you survive?"

He shoved the gearshift into park and stared straight ahead. "I wasn't alone. I—" He shook his head, as if to clear it. "We need to get inside."

She pressed her lips together, wishing he wouldn't shut her out and wondering why she cared so much that he had.

After cranking on the AC, he shoved open the driver side

door then came around to her side. Remy uttered a mournful whimper as Dayne clicked the locks shut.

"Will she be okay in there?" Kat glanced over her shoulder to see Remy's nose pressed to the window, leaving a wet rosette on the glass.

"As long as the AC's on." He hustled her to the station steps, looking in all directions and casting one last glance behind them before they went inside.

The reception desk, if one could call it that, was encased by tinted glass on all sides and was higher than the lobby floor, enabling the officer behind the glass to look down on anyone entering the station. She'd bet the glass was bulletproof.

Dayne tugged a black wallet from his back pocket, flipped it open, and held it up for the officer. "Special Agent Andrews and Katrina Vandenburg to see Detective Paulson. He's expecting us."

"Yes, sir. He's been waiting for you. Stand by." The officer, whom she could barely see through the tinted glass, picked up the desk phone and said something she couldn't hear. "He's coming right out."

Less than half a minute later, a door on the far wall opened.

"C'mon in," Detective Paulson said. "Your sketch artist got here a few minutes ago. He's setting up his laptop."

They hadn't taken two steps when the lobby door opened, and several people entered the building. Dayne inserted himself between her and the new arrivals, eyeing them cautiously.

Would the killer really come for her inside a police station? The thought seemed ludicrous, but she appreciated Dayne's protectiveness. Around him, her sense of safety was a solid ten out of ten.

The heavy door clunked shut behind them and they followed Paulson down a long, gray-walled corridor. They passed several uniformed officers and another man wearing a suit and tie. They all stared at her as if she were a leper. To Dayne, they offered curt greetings with quick nods.

Paulson led them into the last room on the right. Two other men in dark suits, detectives, she assumed, sat behind desks. Another man dressed more casually, in khakis and a blue polo shirt, sat at another.

"Guys," Paulson said, "this is FBI agent Dayne Andrews and Katrina Vandenburg, the witness. She'll be working with the sketch artist this morning." The other detectives rose from their chairs. Both were tall and fit and could have been poster boys for police recruitment ads, but neither was as tall as Dayne or, by her estimation, as fit. "Detectives Toby Jacobs and Ron Ganelli. They're assisting on this case."

"Ma'am." Detective Jacobs nodded to her then held out his hand for Dayne to shake.

Ma'am. She still hated that. Was it something they taught at police academies? It might be worth calling in a favor in Albany to change that.

Detective Ganelli gave her a polite nod, staring a bit longer than necessary and ramping up her discomfort even more. Neither man had made a move to shake *her* hand. Was it because she was a witness? Either way, she hadn't been this nervous since her first cotillion.

"Jim, good to see you." Dayne went to the third man at the desk in the corner, who stood.

"You, too, Dayne." The two men shook hands. "Sorry to hear about Becca."

"Thanks." His gave a tight nod. "Kat, this is Jim Snow, the best composite sketch artist in the agency."

Jim laughed. "Well, I don't know about that, but hopefully I can earn that distinction today. Nice to meet you." Mercifully, he held out his hand, giving her a genuine smile and putting her instantly at ease. "Have a seat and we'll get started." He pulled out the chair he'd been sitting in, waiting for her to sit before rolling over another chair next to hers.

"I'll fill you in on what we've learned since yesterday," Paulson said, walking off and indicating Dayne should follow.

"Where are you going?" Her voice was unintentionally high-pitched. She sounded like a scared rabbit.

"I'll be right over there." He canted his head to the fourth desk in the room where Paulson was seating himself. "I'll check in on you."

She nodded. It wasn't that she didn't think these other men who also wore guns the size of small cannons wouldn't protect her if the killer appeared out of thin air. Around Dayne she felt safer. Maybe it was because she knew him. But she didn't, not really. *So what is it about him?* She honestly couldn't say.

"Dayne already filled me in on the generalities." Jim's fingers flew over the keyboard, and the screen filled with individual boxes containing blank head shapes with varying hairlines. "This app has hundreds of variables to choose from. Face shape, hair, nose, lips, scars, facial hair. This little baby has it all." He gave the top of the laptop an affectionate pat.

Across the room, Dayne sat in a chair opposite Paulson's desk and accepted a handful of documents the detective handed him. The skin between his brows and just over his nose crinkled.

She turned to see Jim's lips quirk. "Dayne's a good guy and an outstanding agent. He and Remy are the best K-9 team in the business. So don't worry. They've got your back." Jim refocused his attention on the screen. "Let's get started. Take a look at these face shapes. When you see one that resembles the guy from last night, touch your finger to the screen over the same box. You can also scroll down to find more shapes."

"There are so many. I don't know if I can remember all that detail." After all, she'd only seen his face for a few seconds, and the mask still covered the top of his head.

"That's okay." His tone was gentle and patient. "Pick the best one you can to start, and then keep going with the other features. We can always come back and change it. Usually, what happens is, you select all the features, look at the image, then things start coming back to you. Like his nose is too long. Or his eyes aren't set deep enough. Take your time. We'll get there."

Overwhelmed. That was the word that came to mind as she scrolled through the options. Finally, she stopped at a face that was neither oval nor angular. It was just plain average. When she touched her finger to one of the options, the face shape filled the screen. The left margin populated with different-shaped ears.

"Now choose the ears. Did they stick out or lie flat against the sides of his head?"

"A little of both. Somewhere in between." Again, average. She dragged her fingers on the screen then tapped one of the images. Ears appeared on the sides of the face.

"Did you see his hair?"

"Only for a moment. He was wearing a mask that I pulled up for a few seconds. It was short, but not crew cut."

"Color?"

"Brown."

"Eyebrows. Were they thick or thin? Arched or straight?"

"Brown. No, maybe black. I'm not sure." She tapped her finger on the desk as the image began drifting away.

Jim took over and quickly added some features. "Eye color?"

Squeezing her eyes shut, she struggled to recall his face. A shudder ran through her as she remembered his hands wrapped around her throat, cutting off her airway.

"Easy." Gentle hands rested on her shoulders, and she flinched. "You're safe here." She released a tight breath. For such a big man, Dayne moved with the stealth and silence of a cougar. "Keep your eyes closed and try to remember."

She might be having difficulty remembering the man who tried to end her life, but she distinctly recalled Dayne's familiar touch from last night while he'd been inspecting her injuries.

Warm breath skimmed across her ear as he leaned down to view the screen. She trembled again, not from fear this time. All Dayne had to do was stand behind her, and her nerve endings went haywire. "Think back to last night and tell me what you saw."

With his big hands keeping her grounded, she let herself drift back to that awful moment. Her attacker's eyes were indeed brown but with a glint of deadly intent she would never forget. "Brown eyes. Dark brown hair. Straight brows."

"That's it." His low, soothing voice kept her in the moment. "What else do you see?"

"A beard and a mustache. Not thick and bushy. Trimmed neat and close to his face." Still keeping her eyes closed, she heard Jim's movements as he adjusted the image on his laptop. "His nose was a bit rounded on the bottom, but not too much. His lips were pressed together, so it's hard to know if they were really that thin. His chin was slightly pointed, but not too much and definitely not a cleft chin."

"Open your eyes," Dayne said. "Does that look like him?"

She twisted her lips. "Almost. There was more space between his eyebrows and eyes."

Using his thumb and forefinger on the screen, Jim adjusted the space.

"His nose was a little longer." She waited for Jim to make more adjustments. When he finished, a chill crept up her spine. The likeness was so startling she could barely breathe.

Because she was staring at the face of the man who'd tried to kill her.

Chapter Ten

"Is that him?" Dayne asked. Kat didn't look at him, didn't utter a word. Her body was as unmoving as a marble statue. "Kat?"

Slowly, she nodded, the movement almost imperceptible. "Yes," she whispered. "I think so."

The image depicted a man so generic there was nothing about him that would ever stand out in a crowd. On a scale of one to ten the chances of getting a definitive hit off facial recognition were about zilch because he'd look like half the men in every database. They'd get way too many hits to follow up on.

"Good job." He gave her shoulder a gentle squeeze. To Jim he said, "Can you send the image to me and Detective Paulson?"

Paulson rattled off his department email.

"You got it." Jim clicked the mouse to save the image.

"Make sure you copy ASAC Barstow and SAC Peters," Dayne added. "I'll call them in a minute to have someone run it through NGI." The FBI's Next Generation Identification

System and many states' DMVs now used state-of-the-art facial recognition technology. It was a long shot, but still worth a try.

"I'll print out some color copies and distribute them to everyone in the department. I can also put out a county-wide alert." Paulson headed back to his desk. A minute later, the printer on a nearby credenza began spewing out copies. The detective retrieved the sheets, handing one to Dayne and one to Kat.

"What is it?" he asked, when she frowned at the image.

"Something about the eyes still isn't right. They were cloudy."

"In what way?"

"I once wore green contact lenses to a Halloween charity event. I dressed up as a witch. The contacts made my eyes look green, but also cloudy."

"So he could be wearing contacts. If that's the case, his eyes could be *any* color."

"Which means," Paulson interjected, "it will be that much harder to get a positive ID on the guy."

"We good here?" Jim caught his eye. "I've got another appointment downtown."

"We're good, man. Thanks for coming."

A minute later, Jim had packed up his equipment and was out the door. Kat continued staring at the image, gripping the edges of the paper tighter until her knuckles whitened.

"What's wrong?" Her face had paled considerably.

"I just can't believe I'm sitting here in a police station, looking at a sketch of the man who murdered two people and tried to kill me, too. It's surreal." He glimpsed her pain, and something he hadn't felt in a very long time pierced his gut.

Like many cops, he'd witnessed so many victims of violent crimes he'd been forced to build walls to protect his sanity. Watching her suffer pounded at those self-imposed boundaries. Not penetrating, just leaving little indentations in his emotional armor. Even more shocking was that he wanted to comfort her. *Bad idea.* His brain never got the message, and he reached out to rest his hand on her shoulder when both their cell phones dinged.

He cued up the email Emily had sent regarding security company options, quickly scrolling down the screen. Beside him, Kat did the same on her phone.

"I can't tell one company from the other." Her brows scrunched as she read the email. "Emily says your friends have completely taken over the castle."

He chuckled. "Kade's the best." He continued scrolling through the list of companies. "Hire All Time Security and make sure they can have people on duty by this afternoon." He started typing in the manpower and scheduling he wanted. "You'll need three guards twenty-four seven. One outside the Haven, two outside the castle."

"You really do like giving orders, don't you?" Amusement glimmered in her eyes.

"Like I said, it's an FBI thing." He couldn't stop the grin forming on his lips, or the idiotic way his heart thumped a little faster.

She gave an utterly feminine snort. "And where will *you* be stationed during all of this?"

"With you, at all times. Wherever you are, that's where I'll be." The realization of what he'd just committed to had him gripping the phone tighter. Having personal feelings for a witness could turn into a shitstorm.

"Oh." Her eyes widened. "I hadn't realized that—"

"That I'd be with you every second of the day? Yep, that's the plan." Along with not letting her out of his sight. Except while she slept, of course.

"I see." She began typing out a reply to Emily.

He gave a mental sigh of relief that she gave in so easily.

Protective services weren't his forte, but he didn't trust her safety to anyone else. That, and it would have trashed his ego if she'd told him to pound sand.

When she'd finished typing, she dropped her phone back into her purse. Again, she swallowed, only this time it was accompanied by a deep breath and the tip of her tongue darting over her lips. She was worried, and she should be. Hell, he was worried, too.

"Between the security guards, the new alarm system, and me and Remy with you, you'll be safe. I promise." This time when he reached out and rested his hand on her shoulder, the tension in her body seemed to lessen. "Okay?"

Their gazes locked. "Okay."

Unspoken understanding passed between them, along with something else he wouldn't—no, *shouldn't*—put a label on, let alone give voice to. It was in the way his heart skittered faster and how parts of his body had just gone on red alert. No matter how much he fought it, that *something else* zinging between them could only be one thing. *Desire.*

Paulson returned to the office and Dayne yanked his hand away, feeling like a teenage kid caught by his girlfriend's father. From the smirk plastering the detective's face, he hadn't missed a thing.

"If you can spare a few minutes," Paulson said, "I'll give you an update."

"Be right there." He gave Paulson a dismissive nod, waiting for him to return to his desk before continuing. "Tell Emily I want those guards on duty no later than four p.m."

The corners of her mouth twitched, and she raised her free hand to her forehead, giving him a sharp salute. "Yes, sir, officer, sir."

He lowered his brows, feigning annoyance. "The term you're looking for is *special agent. Not* officer."

"Then, yes, sir, special agent, sir." Her eyes twinkled with mirth, and he was glad to see her expression lighten, even if temporarily. Because she'd been right about one thing. Her freedom *and* her privacy were headed straight for the nonexistent zone.

He winked. "You're learning."

Paulson picked up a document. "We're running every print the tech guys pulled from the Garman and Thorpe homicides."

"The DNA results will take a while," Dayne said absently, noting the stiffness in Kat's back as she spoke on her cell phone. "What lab has Becca's cell?"

"The Rockland County Sheriff's Office." Paulson glanced at a chain of custody form. "Their computer crime unit does forensic analysis for just about every department in the county."

Dayne hoped they were as capable as the FBI lab. He didn't dare voice the thought and risk falling to the rock-bottom position on Paulson's shit list. Still… "Make sure they download all the addresses in her GPS app. It might help us trace her movements right before she died."

He took a deep breath to steady himself. Getting wrapped up in the world of Katrina Vandenburg had kept him so busy, he hadn't had time to fully process that Becca was really gone.

"Will do." Paulson made a note on a pad, and Dayne was gratified to see the words "To Do" at the top. The guy might not like him, but he seemed motivated, and that was all that mattered.

He focused on the chains of custody and the list of evidence the department had collected at both crime scenes, including more than a dozen boxes of case files. "Did you get the subpoena for Becca's phone?"

The detective pursed his lips, arching a brow as he held up a piece of paper with the words *Grand Jury Subpoena* in large bold letters.

"Yeah." Dayne took the subpoena, giving it a quick once-over. "Sorry." He really needed to stop second-guessing the guy. He handed the document back then reread the chains of custody. "You took a lot of case files. Need help looking through them?"

"Actually, yeah." Paulson nodded.

Dayne cued up his ASAC's number on his own cell phone. Seconds later, his boss answered.

"So, Dayne...what's it like guarding the richest woman in the state?" Lydia Barstow, the Assistant Special Agent-in-Charge of the FBI's Newark office, asked.

One of the detectives had given Kat a bottle of water and was now sporting a grin so broad the guy reminded Dayne of a kid talking to the prettiest girl in school. The other detective joined in and perched on the edge of the desk. Kat held out her hand and Dayne thought the guy was going to kiss it. She said something he couldn't hear. Whatever it was, the guy blushed. It was like watching a queen hold court, and her minions were eating up every word.

Teenage boy or grown man, if they had blood flowing through their veins, they'd be drawn to her like iron to a magnet.

Goddammit. He could lie to himself until he was blue in the face. That flare of irritation in his gut was none other than good old-fashioned jealousy.

"Dayne, you still there?" came Lydia's voice.

"Yeah. The Orangetown PD took all of Becca's case files from her office. Can you assign some agents to review them at the PD?"

"I'll send two agents right over."

Dayne rattled off the address. "Anything on Becca's arrestees?" Statistically, ex-cons seeking revenge did it within days of being released, and it was usually violent, fitting the

MO of a stabbing.

Becca had been a hard-hitting agent, racking up a fuck ton of arrests on the west coast before transferring to the Newark office. She'd put some violent people behind bars. There was always the possibility that one of them had been sitting in a jail cell, seething until the day he—or she, for that matter—could exact revenge.

"One name popped up on the list. Kelso Donnelly. You know him?"

"Yeah." He frowned, remembering the case he'd worked on with Becca. Kelso Donnelly had thrown a conniption when he'd been sentenced to ten years in federal lockup.

Donnelly was a beast of a man. At six-two and weighing in at about three-fifty, he was intimidating as hell. Added to that was the twisted mind of a pedophile. If they hadn't caught up with him before he'd left the country with eight-year-old Melinda White… Dayne's stomach roiled at the thought of what would have been that little girl's fate.

"Where is he?" Dayne asked.

"That's the problem," Lydia continued. "He was released two weeks ago, but no one's seen him. Not his family, his ex-wife, or anyone who knew him. He's from Pennsylvania, and I have two teams out there now trying to find him."

Donnelly definitely fit the profile, and now he was on the loose. But the guy looked nothing like the digital sketch Kat and Jim had come up with. Then again, a decade in prison could change a man. Inside *and* out.

"Can you email me his rap sheet and a recent photo? I want to share them with the PD."

"Already did."

On cue, his cell phone pinged. "Thanks, Lydia." He ended the call and forwarded Donnelly's criminal history and color photo to Paulson's email. "Two agents are on their way to read through Becca's case files. I just sent you a rap sheet. Becca and I arrested this guy ten years ago. She was the case agent, and he swore he'd come after her the second he got released."

"Maybe he did." Paulson pulled up the email on his desktop and opened the attachment. As expected, Donnelly's arrest photo looked nothing like Kat's sketch. But Lydia had included another photo, one dated less than a year ago and taken in prison. Compared to the way the guy had looked the day he and Becca had arrested him, the face staring back at him was gaunt. Donnelly must have lost two hundred pounds. Now that his chin and cheekbones were visible, his face looked average.

Like the man in Kat's sketch.

"Kat." The conversation she'd been having with the young detectives immediately ceased. "Can you come over here?"

Kat rose regally, smoothing her hands down her slacks before gliding over to Paulson's desk.

"Take a look at this photo." He indicated Paulson's monitor. "Is this the man who attacked you?"

Slowly, she shook her head. "I can't be sure. It all happened so fast." She leaned in closer. "Are his eyes blue?"

Paulson scrolled back to the rap sheet, but Dayne already knew the answer because he'd never forget the bastard's eyes or the disgusting way he'd watched as they'd carried Melinda out of the tiny bedroom he'd kept her in. "Yes. They're blue," he answered before Paulson had even gotten to the man's physical description.

"Whatever color they are, this asshole's now a suspect." Paulson printed out several copies of Donnelly's photo. "I'll put out a BOLO and make sure every department in the area sees it."

While the detective logged into NYSPIN, Dayne urged Kat to the nearest chair then retrieved the photos from the printer and grabbed a black pen from the desk. He set the photo on the desk then scribbled on Donnelly's chin, doing his best to draw a beard and mustache similar to the one in Kat's sketch. He put the photo and Kat's sketch side by side.

The images were similar in terms of overall features, but the features in both were so average, even he could see it would be difficult for anyone to say with a reasonable degree of certainty that these were the same men.

After staring alternately from one image to the other, she looked up at him, her eyes filled with regret. "I'm sorry. I just can't tell."

"That's okay." Although he was disappointed. Not with her. She was doing far better than he could have expected.

"No." She grabbed his hand, and when her fingers tightened around his, he felt the contact clear down to his toes. "It's not okay. I *saw* him, but I can't identify him. How is that possible? Why can't I be sure? It's as if the image is becoming more and more fuzzy over time."

He clasped her hands in his. "What you're experiencing is normal. Lots of witnesses go through the same thing, thinking that because they got a quick look at someone, they should instantly be able to pick them out of a lineup. It's never that simple. There are emotions involved and stress. The more time that goes by, the harder it is to recall detail."

Her head lowered. He expected her to release his hand. She didn't. When she looked up, shadows flickered in her eyes. *Dark* shadows, as if she were suddenly bone-tired.

"Please," she whispered. "Get me out of here."

So he did. He would have done anything to ease her pain.

Chapter Eleven

By the time Dayne pulled up to the wrought iron gate on Kat's property, it was nearly five o'clock.

They'd detoured to his house to pick up some clothes for him and more food for Remy. After that, they'd stopped at the Canine Haven where he'd introduced himself to one of the newly hired security guards, John Benton. They'd exchanged cell phone numbers so each could be reached in an emergency, and he'd given John several of his business cards to share with whoever took over the next shift. He'd do the same with the two guards on duty outside the castle. Last, he instructed Benton to notify him and the other guards anytime someone approached the gate.

When he lowered the window to punch in the new code Kade had texted him earlier, a cool breeze hit him in the face. Remy stuck her head through the kennel opening to sniff the fresh air.

"I'll need to give the new gate code to my staff," Kat said.

"Fine, but don't give it to anyone else."

During the drive from his house, Kat had busied herself

reading emails and talking on the phone with Emily about some big charity fund-raiser she'd be attending in the city. From the number of times he'd caught her grimacing during that conversation, he'd gotten the distinct impression that she was more than willing to donate money to a cause she believed in but didn't particularly want to be there in person, hogging the spotlight.

Interesting. And unexpected.

No more so than him talking about his birth mother.

The guys all knew he and his sister Lily were adopted, but his birth mother was a topic he'd always tucked away in a private box. Only Lily knew the details of what he'd gone through as a kid.

He drove through the gate, checking his rearview mirror to assure himself it was closing behind them. Who knew how many nights he'd be spending in her house? *Hopefully, not many.* Because there was no denying the spark of attraction between them. He needed to focus on protecting her, not getting into her pants.

As they approached the castle, he was gratified to see the other two guards on duty heading around to the rear of the property. Kade, Jaime, and Markus came around the other side of the castle, carrying toolboxes.

When he parked the SUV, Kat reached for the door handle but stopped before opening the door.

"Can I get out?"

He expected to find an expression of sarcasm on her face. What he saw was genuine question. He trusted that his friends or the guards would have notified him of any threats. "Yeah. I'll meet you inside. I want to talk to the guys about the new system." And give his cell number to the security guards. Communication was everything.

She stopped briefly to exchange greetings with Kade, Jaime, and Markus, who all grinned like idiots. Seeing

Markus grin was a sight to behold. These days, the man rarely smiled. At anything.

"You gonna let her out?" Kade's lips quirked as he and the others walked over.

Dayne narrowed his eyes. "Let *who* out?"

"Remy." Jaime indicated the SUV, inside of which his dog whined. "The *other* female in your life."

"Very funny." He glared at his friends a moment before opening Remy's door. She leaped out, wagging her tail.

"She's quite a woman." Kade canted his head to the castle as he leaned down to scratch Remy's ears.

In response to his ministrations, Remy leaned her head against the side of Kade's leg, demanding he not stop.

"Beautiful, too," Jaime added.

"Yeah, so?" Dayne had a feeling he wouldn't like where this was going. His friends didn't disappoint.

"Is she married?" Kade asked. "Boyfriend? With a bank account like hers, I wouldn't be surprised if there were dozens of men prowling around after her."

Dayne's scowl deepened. It was none of his business how many men drooled after Katrina Vandenburg. "There's more to her than just her bankroll."

"I stand corrected." Kade gave a little bow.

"Cut the crap," Dayne said, although this time there was intended humor in his voice. "Tell me about the upgrades."

"Thought you'd never ask." Kade grinned so broadly it brought out both his dimples, features Dayne had seen dozens of women swoon over. "We installed plenty of new cameras at the Haven and outside the castle. They can all be accessed via cell phone and computer. In addition to the new keypad at the gate, we installed a keypad outside the main entrance to the Haven and here, inside." He jerked his thumb to the castle. "She'll have to set a new code because this one uses five digits, not the four she's used to. If someone drives up to the gate, you can buzz them in if you want to. We also installed glass-break sensors on all the first-story windows, along with window and door sensors. No one's getting in without you knowing it."

"What about the rest of the property?" He indicated with his arm. "There must be over twenty acres."

"And a pool, a vintage carriage house, and a concrete storage bunker in the middle of the woods," Markus added. "Did you know about that?"

Dayne shook his head. "What's in it?"

"Not much." Markus shook his head. "A desk and some old filing cabinets. Looked like there'd been a fire in there a while back."

"Wiring up the whole place is impossible," Kade continued. "The property's like a small-scale nature preserve. There's so much wildlife in all these woods there's no way to install motion sensors without some animal setting it off every minute."

"We installed cameras at every door," Markus said. "We set a monitor up in your, uh"—Markus coughed—"bedroom. There's a remote control that allows you to shift from one camera's view to the others."

The front door to the castle opened. Kat held Angus in her arms. When the puppy caught sight of Remy, he wriggled furiously and let loose with a series of high-pitched yips.

Unable to hold the struggling puppy, she set him on the stoop. Before Angus got halfway down the stairs, Remy bolted to the puppy's side, nipping him playfully on his flanks then dancing away with the easy grace of an athletic shepherd.

Kat shrugged, calling out, "He was making such a fuss I had to let him out."

"She's a lot more down to earth than I expected." Kade smiled.

"That's the truth," Dayne muttered.

"What did you expect?" Markus asked.

"Dunno." *Liar.* He'd assumed she'd be stuck up and condescending. Especially to cops.

"I like her," Jaime added. "If I were you, I'd be all over that like a dog on a two-inch thick ribeye."

"Yeah, well you're not me, so forget it." Dayne glared at his friend, not liking the insinuation. "I'm only here to keep her safe."

"Okay, man." Jaime threw up his hands in defeat.

"Why don't we go inside and help the lady key in her new code?" Markus suggested.

"Good idea." Dayne followed Markus to the castle then veered off to meet one of the guards. "Be there in a minute."

Remy and Angus followed his friends inside while Dayne exchanged cell numbers with the guards. His phone buzzed with a text. A delivery van—Hudson Valley Floral—was approaching the gate.

Less than a minute later, a white van ambled up the road and pulled into the driveway. Dayne set down the bags as a man in his late thirties or early forties, with brown hair, a mustache, and beard, got out carrying a long box. Ignoring Dayne, he rounded the van and made for the stairs. The embroidered tag on the guy's jacket said Manny. And he had a passing resemblance to Kat's police sketch.

Dayne stepped into Manny's path. "I'll take those." The fewer people who went inside, the better.

Ignoring his order, Manny tried brushing past, and again, Dayne blocked him. "I said, I'll take those."

Manny's eyes rounded, and his jaw clamped shut as he stared at Dayne. "But I *always* take them in," he insisted.

When Manny started past Dayne again, he planted a firm hand on the guy's chest and gave a not-too-subtle shake of his head. "Not today, you don't." Not ever, if Dayne had his way. There was something off about him, and it wasn't just because he looked somewhat like the sketch. Dayne widened his stance, preparing to flatten the guy if he didn't back off.

Manny's face flushed angry red and his lower lip trembled. "Who the fuck are you?" The guy's words might be tough, but his delivery lacked punch.

"I'm the fucker that says you're not going inside." Manny's eyes glossed over, and Dayne thought the guy was about to cry. *Ah, hell.* He pulled his wallet from his back pocket and tugged out a $5 bill. "Take it and go."

Manny's eyes flicked briefly to the front door, as if assessing his chances.

Don't be stupid, pal.

Manny's nostrils flared like a bull ready to charge headfirst at a matador. Then he hung his head and let out a dejected breath, his brief moment of bravado deflating like a popped balloon. He thrust the box at Dayne's chest and snatched the bill, shoving it in his pants pocket as he spun and got back in the van. White stone spit from beneath the van's rear tires as it sped down the drive.

"What the heck was that about?" Dayne took his eyes off the van only long enough to text John Benton to confirm when the vehicle had left the property. After the text came in, he balanced the flower box under one arm, grabbing his and Remy's bags. He fully intended to have a serious sit-down with Kat about letting outsiders into her house because Manny just pinged a solid ten on his creepy-as-shit-delivery-guy radar.

He was greeted with the now-familiar sight of Remy stalking around with Angus's jaws clamped around one of her legs, dragging the puppy along the floor.

Laughter came from the kitchen where Kat, Emily, and his friends watched.

"I'll take those." Emily hopped off a stool and slipped the box from under his arm. "I take it you met Manny. Kat orders a dozen roses every week, and every week, Manny delivers them like clockwork."

"Yeah. About Manny—" His phone buzzed with another incoming text and he set down the bags. *Silver Jag approaching.* Seconds later, the new keypad by the door dinged.

"C'mon," Kade said to Kat. "I'll show you how the new system works." He stopped with her by the keypad. "Press this button and you can talk to whoever's at the gate."

She pressed the button and spoke into the intercom. "Who is it?"

"Colin," an impatient voice snapped. "The code isn't working."

"I know." She grimaced. "I'll buzz you in."

Emily cleared her throat. "I'd better get these in water then pack up and go home. Kat, I'll talk with you tomorrow about your schedule for next week." Hastily, she took the box of roses into the kitchen.

Outside, a car door slammed. Then the door handle jiggled. The guy actually thought he could walk right in as if he owned the place. *Or has a special place in Kat's life.* Maybe he did. Dayne hoped not. Not for personal reasons. She deserved better than a pompous prick like Colin.

Kat opened the door to a scowling Colin.

"Why didn't you give me the new code?" He set his shiny briefcase on the floor then leaned down to kiss her. In a perfunctory fashion, she turned her head, offering him her cheek.

"Who *are* these people?" Dayne didn't miss the condescending emphasis. "And what's wrong with your neck?"

Ignoring his last question, she indicated Dayne. "This is Dayne, whom, of course, you've already met, and these are his friends." When she introduced Kade, Jaime, and Markus, he acknowledged them with a grunt. Dayne, he completely ignored. "They just installed a new security system. Don't feel bad about not knowing the new code. Even *I* don't know it yet."

"Let's talk over here." He led her into the living room out of earshot.

"Who's the dick?" Jaime hooked his thumb in the direction of the living room.

"Boyfriend?" Markus raised his brows.

Dayne crossed his arms. "Not sure." Kat and Colin's relationship was still a mystery to him. Not that he cared what the guy was to her, as long as he didn't get in the way. But he had to admit, he was curious about the mixed signals bouncing back and forth between them, so who knew?

Kade began packing up the last of their tools. "As much as we'd love to stay and watch this episode of Keeping Up with The Vandenburgs play out, me and the boys got a date with a case of beer and a stack of poker chips. Sorry you can't join us."

"Something tells me," Jaime said as he tossed a screwdriver into another toolbox, "he's got his hands full."

Markus shot him a look of sympathy. "True that."

"Let's get the new code set." He went into the living room, making no pretense of pretending he wasn't barging in on Colin's private conversation. "Kade's leaving and needs to show you how to set the new code."

When Kat rose from the sofa, so did Colin. "Good. I'll need it. I still can't believe you didn't call me after getting attacked last night."

"I told you, I'm fine. I didn't want to worry you."

The moment she walked past Dayne, he blocked the other man's path. "Give her privacy to set the code."

Colin's face went red with indignation. "*Nothing* about her life is private. Not from me."

"Do you live here?" Dayne asked with a sharp edge to his voice.

"No," he spat out. "But I should know the code. I'm here all the time, and I'm her lawyer."

Well, that's news. "Then make yourself useful. Go write a legal brief or something, because you're not getting the code." He maintained his position, blocking both Colin's view and his path to the door.

"Kat!" he shouted around Dayne's shoulder. "This is ridiculous. I've always known the code to the gate."

"Colin, please." She sent him a pleading look. "I'm trying to concentrate here."

"Oh, for Christ's sake." Colin crossed his arms, wisely taking a step back.

"Only those with a need-to-know are getting that code." Dayne locked eyes with the man again, not fully understanding his adolescent dislike for the guy but still content to go with his gut on this one. His gut had never steered him wrong before. "And you're definitely not on that list. As her attorney, you should be more concerned with her well-being than having access to her property." Whether that property included her body was anyone's guess.

"She's all set," Kade called out, picking up his toolbox. "We're outta here, boys."

"Later, man." Jaime clapped Dayne on the shoulder.

Markus shook Dayne's hand, sending an undisguised warning look at Colin. "Call if you need us."

"Will do. Thanks, guys." Dayne walked his friends to the door.

Emily appeared with her jacket draped over her arm and her purse in her hand. Over her shoulder, Dayne noticed the vase of wilted pink roses on the kitchen island had been replaced by a fresh bunch of yellow ones. Courtesy of creepy Manny. "I'll see you tomorrow," Emily said, smiling at him and Kat. "Colin," she added, although when she looked at the other man her smile was frosty, confirming his earlier suspicion.

The door shut and the three of them were alone. Remy sniffed Colin's expensive-looking briefcase.

Colin rushed over, inserting his foot none too gently between Remy's snout and the briefcase. Remy's lips drew back in a snarl, revealing sharp incisors that had taken a chunk out of more criminals than Dayne could remember.

"Remy, *nein*!" As entertaining as it would be if his K-9 clamped her teeth around Colin's ankle, that wouldn't go over too big with his SAC or the FBI director. Being a lawyer, and, as Jaime so succinctly put it—a dick—he didn't doubt for one second Colin would sue the agency *and* him, personally.

Obediently and reluctantly, Remy backed off, still keeping a watchful eye on the other man.

"Colin!" Kat inserted herself between him and Remy. "She was just curious."

Ignoring her ire, Colin pointed to the two large duffels. "What are those?"

"Overnight bags," Dayne answered bluntly, knowing it would piss Colin off.

His eyes widened. "Why does he need overnight bags?"

Kat led Colin back into the living room, sitting a good three feet from him on the sofa.

Dayne leaned against a fluted column between the foyer and the living room, allowing him to see and hear everything. Giving this douche bag any privacy wasn't at the top of his list.

Kat patted Colin's hands. "Dayne is my official bodyguard until the person who killed Amy and the private investigator is caught. He's staying in the guest room."

Colin's jaw went hard. "The hell he is." Over Kat's shoulder, he glared at Dayne. "You've got a security team outside and a brand-new system inside. You don't need him. *I'll* stay with you. I can protect you just as well as he can."

"No. You can't." Dayne ground his teeth as he pushed away from the column. "You aren't armed, and you aren't trained in physical combat. Do you even know what to do if someone breaks in?"

"I'll call 911." He rose and gave Dayne what he assumed was intended to be an intimidating glare that wouldn't have scared a field mouse.

He snorted. "By the time the police arrive, she could be dead." Something he'd never allow to happen.

Kat dragged a hand down her face, weariness evident in her eyes and the slump of her shoulders. "I'm in good hands and it's already settled, so just let it go."

"Fine." The man's face softened. "But call me if you need anything."

"I will." She took him by the elbow and led him to the door. "Thank you."

He began to reach for his briefcase then froze in mid-reach. The briefcase was gone.

"Where the hell is my—"

Chewing sounds came from the kitchen. Remy lay in the middle of the floor, chomping away on one corner of Colin's briefcase, while Angus licked noisily at another. Both corners of the leather were mangled and glistening with saliva. A big hunk of leather hung off Remy's end. His dog took that moment to lift her head, panting in a way that made her look like she was smiling.

She is. Dayne fought the urge to give his K-9 a high five. He should have known she'd seek retribution against the dude because he'd nearly kicked her in the face. Remy was extremely well mannered, but when someone was mean to her, *watch the fuck out*.

Colin's eyes rounded, and he charged over, grabbing the

handle and trying unsuccessfully to wrench the case from Remy's jaws. "Let go, dammit."

His dog growled under her breath, maintaining a solid grip on the briefcase as she and Colin battled in a tug-of-war.

"I've got this." Dayne swung into action, clamping onto Colin's arm and jerking him away. "Remy, *aus*."

His dog released the briefcase, which promptly fell on Colin's foot.

"Ouch." He jerked his foot away.

Wimp. "Sorry about that." Dayne handed Colin back his property, teeth marks and all. A gooey chunk of leather hit the floor with a sloppy, wet *splat*. "Bad dog," he admonished. *Good girl.* "She's always had a taste for fine imported Italian leather, which I assume this is made of. If you like, I can forward you an FBI property damage claim form." One that would take at least six months to be processed.

"No need." Colin's eyes burned with rage and indignation. "I have ten others just like it."

Dayne arched a brow. "Of course you do."

Colin turned with a huff. "I'll call you tomorrow," he said to Kat, and, as before, she offered her cheek, not her lips, for him to kiss.

The door slammed shut behind Colin. A few seconds later, his car started with a throaty rumble and roared as he gunned it down the driveway. For a moment, neither of them said a word. Then he shared something with Kat he rarely shared with anyone.

They both burst into laughter.

Chapter Twelve

Saturday morning, Kat looked at herself in the antique English Regency Cheval mirror—her mother's mirror, and one of Kat's favorite pieces. It had been several days since she and Dayne had laughed together over Remy destroying Colin's briefcase. She couldn't have come up with a more fitting punishment for his rude behavior. Although he probably did have ten others just like it.

His family's law firm was enormous and one of the most prestigious in the city. Colin's father, and his father and grandfather before him, had been her family's legal representatives over the decades.

"Maybe it's finally time for some changes," she muttered.

Angus lifted his head to watch her from the foot of her bed. He cocked his head, first one way then the other, looking totally adorable. Aside from that one bout of laughter with Dayne, Angus and Remy were the only ones who elicited any smiles from her lately. Not even Colin made her smile anymore. It hurt to acknowledge it, but he was no longer the boy she'd once known.

As a child, he'd been fun to play with. As a teenager, he'd been her constant companion. After he graduated from law school, she began noticing changes. At first, they were subtle. Once he started working for his family's law firm, his disrespect and rudeness toward those outside his social and financial stratosphere became more obvious. Lately, it had been snowballing.

"Angus, what do *you* think of Colin?" The puppy gave a quick shake of his head.

"I know what you mean." Added to his growing list of negatives, she'd never felt that special tug for him in her heart. That was probably why she could never consider marrying him and why it never occurred to her to call him after being attacked.

She fingered the thin strand of pearls around her neck, examining the black jacket and skirt suit she'd dug from the back of her closet. Black clothing was something she hated. This was an outfit she only wore for one type of occasion. Funerals.

Her heart felt as heavy as a ten-pound brick. Today, hers and Dayne's schedules held nothing but grief.

Rebecca Garman's wake was in the morning, followed by Amy's in the afternoon. Even if Dayne hadn't insisted she accompany him to Rebecca Garman's wake, she would have gone anyway. To support Dayne and because of an oddly morbid connection she felt to the woman.

She took Angus's soft little face in her hands, staring into his dark eyes. "Were you there when it happened?" she whispered. "Did you see who killed her?"

Angus's eyes were sad, as if he, too, understood the solemnity of what was happening today. She was also quite certain he missed Remy. Dayne and his K-9 had left an hour ago so he could drop by the police station then his house to pick up a suit. Kade was downstairs covering for him while he was gone.

She slipped into a pair of shiny black Dolce & Gabbana pumps. Over the last couple of days, Dayne was always there, watching over her, but he'd done it coldly, efficiently. It was almost as if he were distancing himself, doing his duty to protect her but with as little human or personal interaction as possible.

They'd shared meals Francine left for them on the stove, but no sooner did he clear his plate than he'd go outside to walk the property with Remy and one of the guards, or busy himself on his laptop reading emails or whatever reports Detective Paulson sent him. He always stayed up until she went to bed. They'd been coexisting, nothing more.

Once, she'd tiptoed down the stairs, stopping just short of the one stair she knew creaked and would give her away, to find him in the kitchen, watching a Yankees game on the tiny countertop TV. Aside from their mutual distaste for nosy reporters, that might very well be the only thing they had in common. Baseball.

Her parents had been huge Yankees fans, sharing their love of the sport with their only child. To this day, she made a point of watching as many games as possible to keep track of the team's standing throughout the season.

A bell chimed on the new white intercom by her bedroom door, indicating the front door had opened. *Dayne was home. Her* home, anyway.

Angus jumped off the bed and scampered out the door, barking the entire way down the stairs. The puppy's excitement over Remy returning was infectious. She liked seeing the two dogs so happy together.

Taking one last look in the mirror, she smoothed down the lapels of her jacket and grabbed her cell phone from the nightstand. Halfway down the stairs, low voices drifted to her. Dayne and Kade's. When they caught sight of her, the conversation immediately ceased.

Her throat went dry. Words didn't come because Dayne was no longer wearing the black polo shirt and cargo pants she was accustomed to seeing. The black suit he wore made him look taller and more powerful, accentuating what she already knew was a sculpted chest and abs, and thickly muscled arms. A crisp white dress shirt with a blue silk tie gleamed beneath his suit jacket. And he was freshly shaven. The man looked good. *Really* good. *No, make that amazingly handsome.* In a way that would have women staring at him while he walked toward them and watching his perfect backside as he walked away.

She heard pounding, *felt* pounding. Was someone at the door? *Nope.* It was her own stupid, completely irrational heart thumping faster in her chest.

His green gaze dipped briefly down her body like a gentle caress. She cleared her throat. "Good morning, gentlemen."

"Morning." Kade's dimples deepened as he glanced from her to Dayne. Vaguely, she noted Kade also wore a suit, a dark gray one. "Well, then, I guess I'll be going. We'll meet you at the wake."

"Thanks, man." Dayne clapped him on the back then watched his friend leave.

Something vibrated, and Dayne tugged out his phone. "Andrews," he said. "Yeah."

While Dayne took his call, she checked her own cell phone, knowing there were several messages she'd been ignoring for days. Several were from Colin. One was from Penny, announcing that if she didn't hear back from her by this evening, she and "the girls" were coming over. "Shit." That was the absolute last thing she needed after what was sure to be a sad, depressing day.

She shook her head in disbelief. Never in her entire life had she thought—let alone spoken—so many curse words, and for once in her life she didn't care. Didn't give a shit, more like it.

Life had just thrown her so many curve balls she couldn't keep up. Changes were happening whether she wanted them or not.

"We should go," Dayne said. "Will anyone else be here today? Francine or Emily?"

"No." She went to the closet and slipped on a light, three-quarter length black coat over her suit. Remy joined her by the door, waiting for Dayne. "I give everyone the weekends off."

"What do you want to do with Angus?" The puppy dropped his rubber squeaky toy at Dayne's feet and began sniffing his dress shoes. "The fringe on all those living room pillows looks mighty tasty."

"Good point. That, and there'd be yellow puddles everywhere." She picked up the puppy, cradling him in her arms and wincing slightly when he squirmed and whacked his head against her injured shoulder. "We can drop him off at the Haven for the day. Would you mind grabbing that?" She pointed to the toy.

"Sure." He picked it up then held it to Angus's mouth for him to grab hold. "You need to give your shoulder a rest. Let me take him." Without waiting for an answer, he took the puppy from her.

A tiny bit of warmth bloomed in her chest, and it wasn't from the brief contact as they'd transferred the puppy to his arms. "Thank you." *A law enforcement officer* and *a gentleman*. Not that she should be surprised, by now. He'd been nothing *but* gentlemanly since the day he'd blown into her life. *I wonder what he's like when he cuts loose?*

Angus promptly licked Dayne's cheek then began squirming again. "Easy does it, little guy." He nuzzled his chin against the puppy's head, instantly calming him.

The man certainly had a way with dogs. And infinite patience.

After setting the new security code, they went outside. She followed Remy and Dayne down the steps and nearly slammed into Dayne's broad back.

"Don't move," he said in a gravelly voice laced with warning. "Stay behind me."

"What's wrong?" She peered around his body, which was as rigid as a piece of sheet metal.

One of the guards on the north corner of the house lifted a hand in greeting. The other, standing a few feet away, did the same.

Dayne's eyes narrowed and his jaw set as he searched the property. Kat didn't see a thing out of place. The tension in Dayne's body said otherwise.

Beneath her coat, the hair on her forearms prickled. Remy watched Dayne, her body as tense as her handler's, although she didn't alert. The wind blew away from them, whispering through the distant trees.

"Dayne? What is it?" When he didn't answer, her pulse kicked up. "Do you see something?"

"No, I just..." He tipped his head to his SUV. "Let's get out of here."

As they drove to the Haven, Kat couldn't stop from glancing repeatedly in the sideview mirror. She licked her lips, her tongue having gone as dry as a piece of cardboard. She couldn't shake the unsettling feeling that time was running out. On what, she didn't know, but there it was.

Along with the firm belief that things would only get worse before they got better.

• • •

Two blocks from the funeral home, the streets were lined

with marked police cars and dark sedans and SUVs.

Dayne drove directly to the entrance of the large white building. Only one spot at the curb in front was empty, blocked off with orange cones. A man waved them in and moved the cones out of the way.

"Is that Detective Paulson?" she asked.

"Yeah." Dayne quickly parallel parked. "I had him reserve us a space near the front. Quick in, quick out."

"I see." He didn't want her outside and exposed any longer than necessary. The man's protective nature knew no bounds. "Thank you."

"Wait a minute before getting out." He lowered the rear windows before shutting off the engine and coming around to her side. As usual, he searched the street in both directions, then the sidewalks, which were filling with uniformed policemen and women, and others in dark suits, many wearing tiny badge-shaped lapel pins.

The door opened, and he held out his hand. She tried to ignore how good his fingers felt around hers and the stab of disappointment when he released it.

He accompanied her to the walkway where Detective Paulson waited. The funeral home was packed, yet a hushed silence hung over the long line of people waiting to pay their respects.

"We should have most of the lab reports later today." Detective Paulson indicated they should follow him to a corner of the waiting area.

Several people nodded to Dayne then stared at her. Considering she was often interviewed on live TV, not to mention the fact that she'd recently been identified in the news as the person who'd found Rebecca's body, she shouldn't have been surprised. Lately, however, being gaped at as if she were a new species was beginning to grate like sandpaper on her already frayed nerves.

Dayne looked around the crowded room, which must have been easy for him, since he was at least several inches taller than everyone else. "We have agents stationed inside and out," he said to Paulson. "In case Kelso Donnelly shows his face."

Donnelly. Her stomach dropped at the mention of the ex-con. He was still out there, somewhere, and he may have murdered Rebecca.

"We do, too," the detective said. "We'll also have people staked out at Amy Thorpe's wake."

"Why would Kelso Donnelly show up here if he murdered Rebecca?" she asked. "Wouldn't he be worried someone would spot him?"

"It's not unheard of for a killer to return to the scene of the crime," Dayne answered. "Or to attend the victim's funeral."

Kat made a face. "That's twisted."

"It *is* twisted." Dayne acknowledged Kade, Markus, and Jaime coming in the front door. "They enjoy the pageantry of watching law enforcement at the crime scene. Makes them feel important. Seeing the distress of their victim's family at the funeral turns them on, gives them a sick rush of excitement."

"Speaking of which," Paulson added, "I've had a patrol unit watching the Garman Investigations building. So far, no one's come by except the press."

"And no one's been skulking around the Canine Haven," Dayne added. "There's a three-man guard unit stationed on the property at all times."

She touched her fingers to her throat, grateful that the pink marks had all but disappeared.

Marks left by the man who tried to kill me. Donnelly? Or someone else? Someone they had yet to identify? Either way, it was impossible not to keep reliving the moment when she'd nearly died.

The first two nights after the attack, she'd had listless nights with little sleep, waking up and feeling as if she were choking to death. Last night had been her first dreamless night since it had happened.

"Let's go." Dayne directed her back into the crowd.

He stopped briefly to introduce her to his supervisors, Special Agent-in-Charge Mark Peters and Assistant Special Agent-in-Charge Lydia Barstow. They were about to enter the reception room when someone called his name.

A woman whose face she couldn't see hugged Dayne, intimately rubbing his back. When the woman pulled away, Kat's pulse raced. Was this Dayne's wife? Until that moment, she hadn't considered that he might be married.

Feeling as if she were spying, she turned away and took a fortifying breath. It shouldn't come as a surprise that his wife was there, and it shouldn't bother her so much that she was. Any loving wife would support her husband when his friend or colleague had passed away.

"Kat, there's someone I'd like you to meet."

She turned back just as he wrapped an arm around the woman, tugging her to his side.

Her heart thumped harder. The idea of meeting Dayne's wife made her anxious. Sucking up the awkwardness, she pasted on her best protocol face.

"Kat, this is Lily." He gave Lily an affectionate squeeze. "My sister."

"Your—" *Sister?*

"Hello." Lily held out her hand. Numbly, Kat shook it.

Dayne's sister was beautiful, with dark brown, almond-shaped eyes set against the most perfect ebony skin she'd ever seen. Her African heritage was obvious, but it was her genuine smile that had Kat forming an instant liking for her.

"I'm—"

"Katrina Vandenburg," Lily cut her off. "I've seen you on TV and in the social pages. It's a pleasure to meet you."

"You, too." She smiled back—a genuine one, this time.

"I can't stay," Lily said. "I have to get back to the shop, but I wanted to be here for you." She looped her long, graceful arms around Dayne's neck then pressed her lips to his cheek.

"Thanks for coming, Lil," he said.

Lily cast a quick glance at Kat. "Can you make it to Mom and Dad's tomorrow night?"

"I'll do my best," he promised.

"Try." She pointed an admonishing finger at him then left.

"She seems very nice," Kat said.

"She's the best." His voice held a warmth she'd never heard before. "C'mon. We're not waiting in this line."

He led her to the front of the receiving line, politely excusing himself along the way for cutting in front of everyone. Near the casket, which was closed, stood a man with graying hair, his face haggard and his eyes red-rimmed. Rebecca's husband, she assumed. Beside him stood two younger couples in their twenties. One of the women held the hand of a little girl of about six, with the prettiest head of blond curls Kat had ever seen.

Dayne swung the child into his arms, twirling her around before kissing her on the cheek. "Hiya, Suzie."

"Unca Dayne." She giggled, kissing him back.

For such a tough guy, he had a natural way with children. Despite the somber mood, people in line smiled, including her. His big, strong hands held the little girl as if she were a delicate piece of crystal and had her wondering if she'd ever have the pleasure of watching her own husband coo at their daughter with the same adoration beaming from his face.

The image of Dayne as that man flickered in the back of her mind. Ridiculous, considering she'd known the man for five days.

Still holding the child in one arm, he held out his other hand to her. "Come meet Becca's family." He led her to the older man first. "This is Ted Garman, Becca's husband. Ted, this is Katrina Vandenburg."

It was painstakingly obvious from the man's tortured expression that he'd just lost his entire world. "I'm so sorry for your loss," was the only thing she could think to say.

"Thank you." He clasped her outstretched hand. To Dayne, he said, "We're glad you're here."

"Unfortunately, we can't stay long." He set Suzie on the floor by her mother.

"Let me know when you catch the bastard." Ted blinked rapidly.

"Count on it." Dayne pulled the man into a tight embrace. The bond he shared with Kade, Markus, and Jaime obviously extended to the Garman family, as well. Friendship was important to him, and she respected that.

After quick introductions to the rest of the Garmans, Dayne led her outside to the Interceptor. At their approach, Remy stuck her head out the window. The dog's lips curled back, baring her teeth. Hair on the K-9's spine stood straight up.

Dayne stopped walking and held out one arm in front of her. His lips tightened as he scanned the sidewalk in both directions. *Again?* No one lingered in the area, but something had spooked his K-9. The question was what.

He clasped her hand, urging her to follow him.

"What is it?" she asked, taking in the worry lines creasing his forehead and the deadly glint in his eyes. In her high heels, she struggled to keep up with his brisk pace.

"I don't know." He slowed then put his arm around her shoulder, tugging her to his side and protecting her with his body. "But I'm getting you out of here."

As they neared the vehicle, her breath quickened, and her pulse began racing. Dayne clicked open the passenger door and opened it, again scanning in all directions as she slid onto the seat. He shut the door and started rounding the hood but stopped. Tucked beneath the wiper was a single red rose.

Dayne grabbed the rose and threw it to the sidewalk. He got in and slammed the door shut. A second later, he gunned the SUV down the road.

Remy's pants sounded more like growls as she paced back and forth behind them. Both man and dog were agitated, which only made Kat's heart thump faster.

A muscle in Dayne's jaw ticked as he maneuvered the residential streets.

She took a steadying breath and let it out, still trying to slow her racing heart. "What happened back there?"

"Not sure." He didn't look at her, just stared straight ahead. "Remy reacted to something or some*one*. That rose…" His jaw tightened. "I don't like it."

"Don't like what?" She grabbed his arm, feeling the stiffness in his muscles. "It probably just fell out of a funeral bouquet and someone stuck it on the windshield."

"Maybe. Maybe not." He eased his grip on the wheel, and the tension that had been radiating from his big body seemed to recede like the Hudson's ebbing tide. "I think you may have a stalker. Manny."

Her jaw dropped. "The guy who delivers my roses? I don't believe it. He's been delivering me flowers every week for the past two years. He's harmless."

"*Nobody* is harmless." His phone vibrated, and she released his arm, settling back into the seat. "Andrews," he answered. "When?" The tension that had made his body as rigid as a board only moments ago was back, worse now. "Keep me posted."

What now? As if there wasn't enough craziness happening all around her already.

He gunned the SUV back onto the highway. Judging by his reaction to the phone call, whatever news he'd just received couldn't be good. She waited for him to clue her in. He didn't.

"Well?" she prodded. This was her life on the line, and she didn't want to be kept in the dark.

"State Police just pulled Kelso Donnelly over on the New Jersey Turnpike."

Chapter Thirteen

Dayne shoved his hands into his pockets, waiting impatiently for Paulson to pull up the video of Kelso Donnelly's interview. As much as he'd wanted to be the one to grill Donnelly's ass, he couldn't be in two places at the same time. Besides, he had enough to deal with as it was.

When they'd left the castle earlier, he could swear someone was out there. Remy hadn't alerted, and he didn't see a thing. It was just a feeling, one that hadn't gone away then and didn't now. Then, outside the funeral home, he'd been hit with the same sensation.

They were being watched.

And that damned rose. No matter how much Kat didn't want to believe him, his gut told him it *was* Manny. Still, he needed more than just a gut feeling to justify filing a formal complaint, let alone slapping an order of protection on the guy.

He stole a glance at the adjacent office where she sat behind a spare desk, talking on her cell phone. He'd seen women in black suits before, but black had never looked so good. The way that slim skirt and snug little jacket hugged her curves… Hell, the woman could make a burlap sack look like high fashion.

Paulson's monitor flickered as the video finished loading. State troopers had reacted swiftly to the nationwide BOLO on Donnelly and pulled the man in for questioning. The Newark FBI SAC office sent their two best interviewers, Diaz and Caldwell, to assist with the interrogation. That had been two hours ago.

While the interview was in progress, he and Kat had grabbed some chow at a nearby deli. While they ate, he ran a cursory check on Manny, whose name turned out to be Emanuel Gomes. No criminal record. By the end of the meal, Kat had taken no fewer than five phone calls, including making one to Emily, during which they'd reviewed several charity grant proposals. Until that moment, he'd assumed Emily did all the heavy lifting. Man, was he wrong. Being the caretaker of so much money was, apparently, a full-time job.

Paulson's monitor filled with the interior of a holding cell. A significantly slimmer Kelso Donnelly sat in a chair, with Agents Diaz and Caldwell sitting opposite him.

"For the record," Agent Diaz said, "the time is one p.m. Present are FBI Special Agents Thomas Diaz and Daniel Caldwell, interviewing Kelso Donnelly at the New Jersey State Police Barracks in Moorestown, New Jersey." Tommy Diaz paused then looked at Donnelly. "Where were you this past Tuesday?"

The day Becca was killed, according to the county medical examiner's preliminary report.

Donnelly yawned, as if he didn't have a freaking care in the world. "Driving cross country from the west coast."

"What was your destination?"

"New York."

Dayne sat on the edge of Paulson's desk.

"Where in New York?"

"Tappan."

"Specifically, where in Tappan?"

"FBI Special Agent Rebecca Garman's office." The grin Donnelly made was more of a sneer, his lip curling back and revealing teeth yellowed from years of chewing tobacco.

"Why did you want to see Special Agent Garman?"

Dayne knew the answer before Donnelly said a word.

"To kill her." He spat on the floor at Diaz's feet.

No way. This is too easy.

"Did you? Kill her?"

"Fuck, no." Donnelly's eyes narrowed to angry slits, and the sneer on his face now was one of pure rage. "Some asshole beat me to it."

"So you didn't kill Rebecca Garman?"

Donnelly held out his arms. "Haven't you idiots heard a goddamn word I've been saying? No! I didn't kill her. But I wish to fuck I had. The bitch deserved to die."

"Can you prove where you were all day this past Tuesday?"

"How did she die? Was it painful?" Donnelly's sneering grin returned. "I hope so."

Dayne fisted his hands. It was probably a good thing, after all, that he hadn't been in that cell interrogating the guy.

"Again," Diaz said, "can you prove where you were on Tuesday?"

Dayne had already heard from the troopers that Donnelly didn't have an EZPass transmitter on his vehicle, so they couldn't track him that way.

"I don't know. Somewhere between California and New York."

"Did you stop anywhere? A motel, gas station, or a convenience store?" Caldwell asked. "Got any receipts?"

"I'm not under arrest, so why should I tell you anything?"

"Because," Caldwell countered, "if you don't talk to us, and you can't provide an alibi, we can hold you for twenty-four hours. Who knows what other reasons we can drum up to keep you longer? I'm sure you haven't been a saint since you were released last week."

A flicker of fear flashed in Donnelly's eyes. The man had something to hide, but Dayne didn't think he killed Becca.

Donnelly shifted in the chair then tugged a wallet from his rear pants pocket and pulled out a folded piece of paper that he tossed to Caldwell. The agent unfolded the paper, reading out loud for the video recording. "This is a receipt for the Red Pump Inn in Missouri. It says you arrived last Tuesday night and checked out Wednesday morning."

Donnelly nodded. "That sounds about right."

Which meant there was no way he could have been in Tappan Tuesday afternoon. *Stabbing Becca to death.*

"We'll check it out."

The agents left the room, but the video remained on. Dayne and Paulson watched Donnelly picking dirt from under his nails. Ten minutes more into the video, and Donnelly stared directly at the camera then flipped the bird, mouthing the words *"Fuck you."*

"He's some piece of work," Paulson said in a disgusted tone.

"Yeah." More like, piece of shit.

When his phone vibrated, Dayne set down his coffee cup to take the call.

"Dayne, it's Tommy Diaz." He quickly recognized the other agent's voice. "We sent two agents to the Red Pump Inn in Missouri. Not only did they confirm the receipt, but they also sent us the photocopy of Donnelly's expired driver license. He used that as ID when he checked in. They also pulled the hotel's video. Donnelly checked in Tuesday night around seven p.m. and left Wednesday morning about eight thirty. Looks like his alibi checks out."

He exhaled a frustrated breath. "You sure it's him in the video?"

"Yeah. The video system at the inn was brand spanking new. The images couldn't be any clearer."

"Any chance he could have snuck out a side or back door, then caught a plane to New York?"

"I don't see how," Tommy said. "Our guys reviewed footage from cameras at all the exits and they didn't see him leaving until Wednesday morning."

"Thanks, Tommy." He ended the call then gave Paulson the bad news. "Donnelly was in Missouri Tuesday night through Wednesday morning. It's not him." He pressed two fingers to the bridge of his nose.

Donnelly made no bones about wanting revenge against Becca. They had a history. But assuming Becca and Amy's murders were committed by the same person, he couldn't come up with a single reason why Donnelly would have needed to go to the Canine Haven or kill the Haven's manager.

So far, they were ass-deep in nowhere-land. Except for his witness. *Kat.*

While he wouldn't put her protection in anyone else's hands, part of him itched for a more proactive role in the investigation. He texted one of the agents from his office who'd been reviewing Becca's case files. A minute later, Special Agent Bart Danchuk came into the detectives' squad room, holding a yellow pad.

Danchuk was still as skinny as Dayne remembered from their Quantico days, and his hair was still as orange as a pumpkin. The only thing new was the cheaters perched on top of his head.

After making quick introductions to Paulson, Dayne glanced at the pad in Bart's hand. "What've you got?"

"For a PI in business just over a year, Becca had a lot of case files, and I do mean a *lot*." He slid the cheaters onto his nose and focused on his notes. "We've still got five full boxes to go through. Philandering spouses, adopted people searching for their birth mothers, phony insurance claims. Nothing jumps out."

"Which of those cases was she actively working?" Now that they'd eliminated Donnelly and his long sought-after revenge, maybe one of her current cases was connected to her death.

"Actually, she was only working one case, but there were multiple targets. An insurance fraud investigation. About three months ago, she scored a big contract with an insurance company. According to the contract, Becca was hired to investigate drivers intentionally causing accidents then faking injuries and threatening to file lawsuits. One of the company auditors figured out the number of these cases far exceeded what was normal for the industry."

"So," Dayne concluded, "in an effort to avoid drawn-out court battles and exorbitant legal fees, the company had been settling out of court and finally got sick and tired of having their bank account sucked dry."

"Yep," Bart confirmed.

"Was Becca successful in finding anyone committing insurance fraud?"

"She was." Bart tapped the pad with his pen. "Last month two individuals were arrested, along with a doctor who was signing off on phony diagnoses. Turns out the driver of the offending vehicle and the injured driver he slammed into from behind were actually cousins who were going to split the settlement. They had different last names, and it was Becca's surveillance photos that pounded the nail into their coffins. She actually caught them in a bar, celebrating."

Dayne swallowed another sip of muddy coffee. "How

much would that settlement have been?"

"Half a million."

Paulson whistled. "I can think of a lot of people who'd do a lot of bad things for half a mil."

"Where are the two people who got arrested?" Dayne asked. "Chances are they wouldn't have gotten jail time, so they're probably out on probation." And could have paid Becca a visit.

"Already on it," Bart said. "I sent the names to ASAC Barstow, and she's sending another team to interview them."

"Good." Dayne appreciated that Bart was on the ball. "How many other cases like this was she actively working?"

Bart flipped a page. "Seven with the same MO, but there could be eight."

Something about the way Bart tapped the pad faster with his pen caught his attention. "*Could* be?"

"Becca's file-keeping system was impeccable. Since she got her license, she worked a total of fifty-seven cases. She numbered every file folder sequentially and kept an inventory sheet with case numbers, along with the open and closure dates of each case."

Dayne beat Bart to the punch. "One of the case files is missing."

"Yep."

"Does the inventory list any subject names for each case number?"

"Negative." Bart shook his head.

He took another drag of coffee. "Becca's husband said she never took work files home. So, in addition to the laptop and camera, now there's a missing file." He tucked that tidbit of information away in the back of his mind. They had no way of knowing if the missing file was relevant, but sometimes key evidence could materialize from otherwise seemingly inconsequential bits of information. "Okay. Thanks, Bart.

Let me know if you find anything else."

"Will do."

When Bart had left the squad room, Paulson pulled up his email. "The ME's final report is in. So are most of the lab reports for both crime scenes." He printed out two copies of everything, handing one set to Dayne.

"Time of death," Paulson read aloud, "estimated to be between four p.m. and midnight, Tuesday, March twenty-eighth. Cause of death…"

Before Paulson finished the sentence, the contents of Dayne's stomach gave a vicious roll. Not that there'd been any doubt as to the COD, but still.

"…severe lacerative trauma to all major internal organs. Specifically, forty-seven stab wounds. Probable weapon was a smooth-edged blade, approximately five inches in length and two inches in diameter."

They both read on in silence.

Many of the wounds on Becca's back contained carpet fibers, indicating they'd been inflicted when she was lying on her back on the office floor. Meaning, the fucker kept stabbing her when she was already down.

Many of the wounds were nonlethal, but there were so many to her heart and lungs the organs were all but hacked to pieces. Her neck had been stabbed so many times and with such brutal force, her head had practically been severed from her body.

He'd seen a lot of bodies in his career, but reading such a gory report on someone he knew was enough to make his lunch launch right out of his throat. To prevent that from happening, he dragged in several deep breaths.

The rest of the ME's findings on Becca and Amy were as expected. Blood toxicology for both was negative for alcohol, methamphetamines, marijuana, and traces of any other illegal substance. Amy's COD was strangulation. Bruises in the shape of fingers confirmed the killer had used his hands. The lab reports were easier to stomach. Unfortunately, they provided very few, if any, leads.

The only blood in Becca's office was her own. As expected, the place was covered with fingerprints, including Becca's and a few of her clients who had minor criminal records. Nothing that spiked high on his would-be-homicide list, but it was worth following up on. All the other prints came back "not on file" and could belong to anyone. The postal carrier, the cleaning service Becca used, her husband, just to name a few. Process of elimination would take a while, but they'd be thorough just the same. Not having prints on file didn't mean a person wasn't capable of committing murder. They were better off using their time following up on a possible motive.

One that was, for the moment, elusive.

"DNA results were negative." Paulson took a slug of coffee. "No one else's DNA was present on Katrina Vandenburg or Amy Thorpe's neck, or on the swabs from your dog's mouth. And before you ask, CCU called me this morning. They only just got into the cell phone. It was encrypted and took a while. They'll keep me posted on what they find."

"What about this footprint in the mud outside the Canine Haven?" Dayne asked, flipping to the next page. Unless the killer wore shoes with unique tread or had an abnormally large or small shoe size, that wouldn't give them much to go on.

Paulson set his mug down. "One decent imprint, approximately size ten, nothing unique about the tread."

"Any hits on facial recognition?" Dayne folded the report and stuck it in his suit jacket pocket.

Paulson scrolled through his emails. "Here it is."

Dayne began pacing in front of the detective's desk. They couldn't be so lucky as to actually get a hit from Kat's sketch.

Paulson grunted. "No positive hits. Over a thousand people in New York and New Jersey DMV made the 'possible' list."

"Great. Another dead end." As expected, the killer's features were too generic.

"Someone *else* is dead?" Kat stood in the doorway, her lips parted and her eyes brimming with shock and disbelief.

"No," he reassured her. The need to put her fears to rest was a fierce instinct burning inside him. "A dead *end*. We didn't get any database hits on your sketch."

"Oh." Her shoulders sagged with relief. "So the sketch was worthless?"

"I wouldn't say that, exactly, but we were hoping to get a lucky break." So they could put this nameless fucker behind bars where he belonged.

"We'd better go." Paulson stood and slipped on his jacket but then sat again, staring at his screen. He clicked the mouse and frowned.

"What is it?" The serious expression on Paulson's face put Dayne's instincts on high alert.

"CCU sent over the call log from Rebecca's phone."

"Print it." Dayne was already heading to the credenza. When the sheets printed, he grabbed them and went down the list of incoming and outgoing calls. He stared at the last line item on the third and final page. Date: Tuesday. The day she was killed. Duration of incoming call: three minutes. Time: 3:50 p.m. According to the ME's report, that was shortly before the time frame in which Becca was murdered.

Mobile number… "No Caller ID." *Dammit*.

"More dead ends," Paulson said, voicing Dayne's thoughts.

Or is it? His pulse ratcheted up. A symbol next to the blocked call data caught his attention—a green check mark with an eyeball. *An app symbol.*

He'd seen that symbol before. Not that he could recall the name of the app, but he was familiar with how it functioned. "Did CCU send over the list of apps on the phone?"

Paulson shook his head. "We didn't ask for that."

"Get it." Dayne's mind raced. "Tell them to dump all data—especially call lists—from any apps on the phone."

When Kat touched his arm, tingles pricked his skin. "Did you find something?"

"Maybe." No sense getting overly optimistic. "Becca has an app installed on her phone that behaves similarly to a pen register or a trap 'n' trace device."

"What's a trap 'n' trace?" Kat frowned.

"A court-ordered device that captures all incoming electrical pulses. In this case, a phone number. Even if the caller blocks their number, the app captures it in a separate log. Someone blocking their number called Becca just before four p.m. on the day she was murdered. We need to find that person. Whoever that caller was, he or she could have been the last person Becca ever spoke with."

And, possibly, her killer.

Chapter Fourteen

The funeral home was packed to the point where Dayne could barely move. Apparently, the Haven's manager was extremely well liked, and half the county had turned out to say their goodbyes.

He and Paulson hovered in the back of the room, searching for anyone who didn't seem to belong there. With his height, he could easily keep track of Kat's location and still periodically scan the room and all entrances and exits.

Sweat trickled down his back. Using his forefinger, he loosened his tie. The temperature inside the viewing room felt like it was rising a degree every second. Through it all, Kat looked as cool as a cucumber. But she wasn't.

She greeted people left and right, but when no one was looking, he glimpsed the toll this was beginning to take on her. An occasional swipe at the corner of one eye and her chest heaving from the effort it took not to lose it in front of everyone.

The Haven must have closed down for the rest of the day, because Kevin and Fiona were there, along with Emily,

Francine, and Walter. For such a supposedly close friend, Colin was nowhere in sight. You'd think the guy would remove the stick from his ass long enough to come and support Kat when she needed it.

Her friends tried urging her to the casket, but she shook her head, indicating they should go ahead without her. With obvious reluctance, they left her standing in the middle of the room, and that's when he saw it. The first real break in her armor.

She covered her mouth with her hand, and her body shuddered.

Ah, hell. As a federal agent, he could have stood by and watched her have a meltdown in the middle of a funeral home. But as a man, his heart cracked just a little bit.

"Keep an eye out," he said to Paulson then wended his way through the crowd. Kat's eyes were glossy, but her face was dry. Somehow she'd managed to hold back the floodgates.

He leaned in close. "Want me to go up there with you?"

She looked up at him with wounded, soulful eyes. "Would you?" Her tone held notes of disbelief *and* hope.

He clasped her hand, squeezing it gently. "I would." Her look of gratitude turned his already mushy heart into a pile of goo.

"Thank you."

The crowd parted for them as he held her hand all the way to the viewing area. Emily's brows rose; Kevin and Fiona gave Kat quizzical looks; Francine's eyes dipped to their joined hands, and he couldn't be certain but thought he detected a slight nod of approval. Walter looked at him with something a step above outright disapproval.

Francine whispered to Kat, whose eyes widened. He couldn't make out her response. Whatever it was, Francine gave a little smile and patted Kat's hand.

For the next ten minutes, he remained dutifully at Kat's

side, speaking briefly with Amy's family then walking her to the casket. Amy Thorpe appeared to be sleeping, nestled in her final resting place—a bed of soft green velvet. When Kat knelt on the small bench, he held her hand tighter. "Oh, Amy," Kat whispered. "None of this was supposed to happen. I'm so, so sorry." She bowed her head for a moment, and when she lifted it, Dayne expected to see tears on her face but there weren't any. Yet. It was only a matter of time.

When they were out the door, he led her to the SUV where Remy watched them through the window. He searched the street, making sure no one lingered nearby. *And no more roses.*

After getting in, Kat gave Remy a quick scratch under the chin. Moments later, he was gunning the Interceptor down Kings Highway, taking the quickest route back to the castle.

"What did Francine say to you back there?" he asked.

"It was nothing." Kat continued staring out the window.

"Liar." He chuckled.

She shook her head. "It wasn't important. Really."

"C'mon, spill it."

"She said that we made a beautiful couple."

He nearly drove off the road into a ditch, jerking the wheel in the nick of time. "And what did you say in response?" He held his breath, curious.

"I said 'thank you.' I'm sorry, I should have told her the truth—that we're not. A couple, that is. I just didn't want to discuss it any further."

"No problem. I understand." Not that he'd been harboring thoughts of them as a couple or that he ever would. Knowing what elicited such a stunned response from Kat back at the funeral home…rankled him. Just a little.

He'd become what he wanted to be—an FBI agent—and he was totally content with that. But part of him would always be that little boy who'd grown up in the filth of the streets.

When the light turned green, he stepped on the gas pedal harder than necessary and the SUV shot up Tweed Boulevard.

They stopped briefly at the Haven to collect Angus and for Dayne to confer with the guard outside. Everything had been quiet in their absence.

After rolling through the big gates and pulling up in front of the castle, he hit the door popper, allowing Remy and Angus to leap out. While the dogs played, he spoke with the guards on duty at the castle and received the same "all quiet" report.

"I have work to do," Kat said then went inside, leaving the door open.

He was about to follow her when Remy uttered a low growl and thrust her nose in the air, staring into the adjacent woods.

"Stay here," he told the guard coming around the corner, then scooped Angus into his arms and deposited the puppy inside the castle. No sooner did Angus's feet hit the floor than he tried darting back outside. "Not this time, little guy." Using his foot, he gently nudged the puppy out of the way as he closed the door.

His K-9 stared at the same location, her nostrils flaring. Remy had scented something, or *someone*. The wind blew in their direction, which meant his dog could be picking up on any number of things. Given his gut feeling that morning, Dayne wasn't taking any chances. He grabbed Remy's tracking leash from the SUV and clipped it onto her collar. *"Such."*

Remy took off, taking up the slack in the leash and sniffing the air as she led them into the woods. Enough light filtered through the mix of deciduous and coniferous trees for him to see a good hundred yards ahead. But Remy's nose was far better than Dayne's vision. Depending on wind direction, physical obstructions, and swirling air currents, she could pull in scents originating thousands of yards away.

As they pushed farther into the woods, Dayne's heart rate skyrocketed. They were so close to putting the habeas grabus on this guy, he could taste it.

They continued in a straight line through the trees, passing a vine-covered concrete bunker—the one Kade mentioned. Remy didn't track to the building so they continued on, crossing the boundary into Blauvelt State Park. In the last few days, the ground had dried, and their feet made swishing, crunching noises on the dry leaves and low scrub. If someone had been on the property, they wouldn't have left any deep footprints.

Occasionally, Remy sniffed the ground, circling several times before taking off again in the same direction they'd been heading. Which meant she was on a hot track. Which meant…

Someone *had* been there. *Not* a deer. Remy's body language was entirely different when she tracked people. Adrenaline cranked in Dayne's bloodstream. If the killer was here, they'd get him.

Five minutes later they stood in a parking lot at the edge of Bradley Hill Road, the western boundary of the park. Remy circled frantically, her nostrils flaring as she scented the asphalt again and again, but it was no use.

The scent ended there.

Dayne scanned the road. Whoever Remy had been tracking must have had a vehicle parked in the lot and driven off. He looked around for pole cameras, but there were none. The killer was too smart to make such a simple mistake. If it really was the killer. Dayne didn't have a psych degree, but he was convinced Manny Gomes was an intimacy-seeking stalker.

As the adrenaline drained from his system, he turned in

a slow three-sixty. There was no innocent reason for someone to leave a vehicle this far away and trek all the way through the park and onto the Vandenburg property. Given that Kat was a famous person, it could have been the paparazzi or a gawker looking to snap a photo.

Dayne stroked his chin. With a killer *and* a potential stalker on the loose, he couldn't assume anything that tweaked his or Remy's radar was a harmless coincidence.

He slipped his phone out and dialed one of the guards outside the castle. The guy picked up on the first ring. Dayne couldn't contain the note of anger. "Notify your partner, and report this to your head office. There was an intruder on the property." Not that it was the guards' fault. Dayne hadn't picked up on it, either. Remy had, but she was the best K-9 tracker he'd ever seen.

"Yes, sir," the guard replied, and Dayne ended the call. No sense getting into it. The guard would be extra vigilant now, and that had been Dayne's intent.

"Good girl." He patted Remy's side then tapped his chest.

His dog rose on her hind legs, resting her front paws on his chest. All K-9s viewed work as fun, and this was one of many rewards he gave her for a job well done. As another reward, he unclipped her leash and draped it around his neck, allowing her to run free during the trek back to the castle. She took full advantage and darted happily after a few chipmunks, always returning to his side.

Eventually the castle came into view. The property really was too large to put under constant surveillance or completely fence in. That joke he'd made about a piranha-filled moat and .50 caliber guns on the turrets…not so funny, now.

The safest course of action was to keep Kat inside at all times. She'd hate the idea. He could already hear the argument they'd have if he tried broaching the subject.

As he and Remy climbed the steps, he noted the guard

rounding the north corner to commence his hourly rounds. He opened the door, expecting Angus to bound out. He didn't. Dayne closed the door, straining for sounds of the puppy.

The house was quiet. *Too* quiet.

"Kat?" he called out. When she didn't answer, his heart rate began to soar. "Angus?" Again, nothing.

Common sense told him no one could have gotten inside with guards on duty, and one of them would have notified him if Kat had gone out. That didn't stop the hairs on the back of his neck from standing at full attention.

He pushed his suit jacket aside and rested his hand on his gun. The living room and kitchen were empty. Next, he went to Kat's office. Her desk was piled high with stacks of documents, some labeled "urgent." The bud vase on her desk held a solitary rose. Now he knew why the bouquet in the kitchen only had eleven roses, not a perfect dozen.

He checked every other room on the main level, including his quarters and the giant library with floor-to-ceiling bookcases. Kat wasn't in any of them.

His heart rate picked up more.

At the bottom of the stairs, he heard something. Remy's ears twitched, and she cocked her head. The same sound drifted down the stairs.

Someone moaning—*Kat*.

Shit. Drawing his weapon, he raced up the stairs. Remy charged after him. How the hell had someone gotten inside?

At the top of the stairs, he paused, straining to hear over his own heartbeat, which pounded like a goddamn freight train chugging up a hill.

The same sound came again from his left, softer this time. Glock extended, he ran to a door that was half open. In between the slams of his heart against his ribs and the pounding of his blood in his ears, he heard sniffling.

Kat lay curled up on a king-size bed with her back to him. No one else was visible, but he scanned every corner of the room and the bathroom just the same. He hung his head and let out the mother of all silent, relief-filled breaths.

Slowly, he lowered his weapon and holstered. *She's fine,* his brain screamed. Physically, at least. The sounds he'd heard were her crying. Everything she'd been holding in all week had finally erupted. He'd known the time would come. It had only been a question of when.

As his heart rate slowed, he dragged a hand down his stubbled jaw. Kat's body trembled from the occasional muffled sob. Angus sat on the foot of the bed, his puppy expression one of uncertainty. The puppy's confusion was totally understandable. Dayne didn't know what he should do, either.

What he ought to do was a quick one-eighty and hightail it back down the stairs. That message never made it from his brain to his feet. The next thing he knew, he stood at the edge of the bed. When he sat, the mattress dipped, and her eyes snapped open. A flash of fear flickered in her eyes, dissipating when she realized it was him.

"You okay?" he asked, taking in her red-rimmed eyes and the fresh stream of tears.

Ah, fuck.

Those big, sad tears were his undoing.

He cupped her face with one hand, stroking her thick, silky hair with the other. She covered his hand with one of her own, clutching his tightly. The trembling increased to the point where Remy padded to the edge of the bed, resting her head on the mattress and watching Kat from sympathetic canine eyes.

"I just c-can't believe she's gone," Kat sobbed. "This sh-shouldn't have happened. It shouldn't have."

"Shh," he whispered, continuing to stroke her hair and

trying not to think about how soft it was beneath his rough fingers. The trembling worsened, and her sobs became louder.

He didn't know what it was—instinct or fear—that if he didn't do something and do it post-haste, she'd drown in her own tears. Or maybe it was the immense tug on his heart that made him do it.

Dayne gathered her in his arms, rocking her gently while she cried, rubbing her back in slow, easy circles. With every breath, he inhaled her pretty, flowery scent into his lungs. Slim arms wrapped around his back, clinging to him like he was a human lifeline. They stayed that way for several minutes, until her sobs quieted.

He eased her back to the mattress, intending to disengage, but she held fast, forcing him to the mattress alongside her.

Their mouths were only inches apart, and Dayne's resistance deserted him in less than a second. Warm breath fanned his face. He lifted his hand and rubbed her cheekbone with the pad of his thumb, savoring the softness of her skin. With a groan, she rested her forehead against his. The movement pressed her breasts to his chest, sending streaks of lightning straight to his groin. *I'm in deep shit.* And getting deeper.

When she tilted her head, their lips grazed. He was sure the contact was unintentional, but he didn't move one single, freaking muscle. Every part of his body froze like a block of ice. *Yep, even that part.*

Like the idiot he was, he found himself wondering how soft her lips would be if he kissed her. For real and not by accident. The need to find out pounded in his brain.

He tilted his head a fraction of an inch. When their mouths made contact again, he had his answer.

They were softer and sweeter than he could have imagined.

Chapter Fifteen

Kat's pulse thumped wildly as their tongues tangled and tasted. Every ounce of grief and fear and desperation that had been building since the morning she'd found Rebecca Garman's body roared through her like an unstoppable force.

She wrapped her arms around Dayne's back, digging her nails into the thick muscles beneath his suit jacket. Vaguely, she registered Angus hopping off the bed.

Doing this was a mistake, but she didn't care. A demon had taken possession of her body. For one brief moment in her all-too-structured life, she wanted—no, *needed*—to do as she pleased. She just wanted to *feel*. To eradicate the grief and most of all, to forget—just for a few minutes—that she'd lost a good friend whom she loved dearly.

She slipped her hands beneath Dayne's jacket, sliding them up his ripped abdominals to his pecs. His big body shuddered beneath her seeking fingers.

Too many clothes.

She wanted to feel bare, naked skin.

His kiss grew hotter, or maybe that was her body

temperature soaring out of control. As she dragged the jacket off his shoulders, he broke the kiss and stripped it off the rest of the way. His hands stroked over her breasts, cupping and caressing, making her nipples ache and tighten until all she wanted was his mouth sucking hotly on the sensitive peaks.

He clenched his jaw, sucking in deep, unsteady breaths. "Kat, I don't think this is a good idea."

"Don't. Think." She drew his head back down to hers, kissing him with every pent-up emotion screaming to be cut loose. "*Please*," she whispered, "make me forget." Hot tears leaked from the corners of her eyes and he began kissing them away.

She angled her head, allowing him easier access as he kissed his way down her neck to her throat, then to her breasts. He unbuttoned her blouse and tugged it from the waistband of her skirt. With a flick of his thumb, her lacy white bra opened, baring her breasts.

"Jesus," he breathed. A second later, his lips were on one of her nipples, sucking it into his mouth, licking and nipping gently until sparks shot down her belly, zooming to her core.

She gasped and arched deeper into his mouth. No one had ever made her body feel so good, so alive, and she wanted more. No strings attached. No regrets, and no tomorrows.

Her core pulsed with wild need. "Hurry, Dayne. Just hurry." Before she changed her mind. Before she regretted doing something—the *only* thing—in her entire life that wasn't in perfect line with the exemplary life everyone expected her to lead.

Dayne hiked up her skirt and hooked his fingers at the waistband of her silk nylons and panties. Cool air hit her thighs and calves as he slid the garments down her legs. Her skin might be cold, but her internal body temperature was hot enough to melt chocolate.

His broad chest expanded as he took in her bare lower

body. His hands—large, strong, and hot—stroked her inner thighs until his thumbs touched her wet folds. Pleasure streaked to her core, and she arched off the bed, uttering a mewling little cry.

Kat grabbed one of his wrists, urging him to push his fingers into her. When he did, she nearly orgasmed on the spot. *Still not enough.* She wanted *him* inside her.

The gun on his waistband was barely an impediment as she undid his belt and pulled down the zipper. When she cupped him, he was long, thick, and hard.

"Kat," he grit out. "Stop."

"No," she cried. "I need you inside me. *Now.*"

"Dammit." He pulled away then sat on the edge of the mattress, sucking in deep breaths.

"What are you doing?" She levered onto her elbows. "Don't you *dare* stop."

Taking another deep breath, he glanced over his shoulder. Clear green eyes filled with regret lasered into her. "We can't do this."

"Why the hell n—" She stiffened. *Oh no. Oh god, no. What have I done?* Shame washed over her in roaring waves and her cheeks flamed. Throwing herself at him was ten shades beyond inappropriate. He was there to protect her, nothing more, and she'd taken advantage of the situation to satisfy her own selfish needs. "I'm so sorry." She took an unsteady breath to slow her pounding heart. "You're right, this *was* a mistake. I shouldn't have—"

"Attacked me and torn my clothes off?" His lips curved into a faint smile.

"You-you actually think this is funny?" She grabbed the sides of her blouse, dragging them together to cover her breasts.

"Yeah." He chuckled. When she glared at him, he sobered instantly. "I mean, no. We need to talk about what just happened."

"No." She shook her head. It would be far too embarrassing. "Just let it go. Please."

His lips flattened then his cell phone vibrated against her hip. He looked at the screen and swore. "We've got company. A limousine is approaching the gate." He pushed off the bed, tucking his shirt into his pants as he strode from the room. Remy and Angus hurried after him.

Sitting up, she stared at the door. Bile rose in her throat. *I'm a slut.* There was no other word for it. She touched her fingers to her lips. Lips that still throbbed, still wanted what she couldn't have.

My life is a living, breathing soap opera.

Slowly, she stood on wobbly legs and walked into the bathroom. She flipped on the lights and stared into the mirror. While it didn't hurt as much as yesterday, the ugly purple bruise had spread to her collarbone. That wasn't what shocked her most.

Her hair sprung in five different directions. The skin around her mouth was pink, abraded by Dayne's five-o-clock shadow, and her bra hung unhooked beside her breasts. She covered them with her hands, imagining they were Dayne's hands cupping and kneading, flicking at her tender nipples.

No! She dragged the lacy cups together, quickly refastening the bra. He was right. They shouldn't do this. Theirs was a business relationship. One of the black-and-white rules she'd learned from her father sprang to mind: Never mix business with pleasure. Because it always—*always*—complicated things beyond repair and killed the relationship.

The gate tone blared from the security box on the wall.

"Kat!" Dayne shouted up the stairs.

She clapped a hand to her forehead. *Oh shit.* Her friends had arrived. She'd completely forgotten they were coming over.

"I'll be right down," she called out. Working quickly, she buttoned her blouse then brushed her hair. Next, she went in search of her jacket and shrugged into it. Dayne's suit jacket lay on the floor. She picked it up and held it to her nose, torturing herself all over again at how good he'd smelled as he'd been on top of her.

The gate bell chimed again.

"Kat!" Dayne bellowed.

"I'm coming," she shouted back, stepping into her shoes and draping Dayne's jacket over her arm.

Coming? Hadn't she just nearly done that?

Angus and Remy waited for her at the bottom of the stairs, their tails wagging. Dayne stood in the foyer, his arms crossed and lips pursed. Light from the chandelier glinted off the gold badge clipped to his belt directly in front of his holstered gun. "You should have told me you were expecting company."

She threw his jacket on the table, not caring when it slid onto the floor.

They'd practically just made love, and all he could do was stand there and act pissed because she'd forgotten her friends were coming over? *What an a— Correction, jerk.*

The gate bell chimed again, but she ignored it, advancing on him and pointing a finger at his chest, stopping just short of actually touching him. Her heart beat harder as her temper flared. "You have no reason to be pissed at me."

"You're right I don't, and I'm not." He uncrossed his arms and took a step closer. "But you *do* need to let me know when you have people coming over. That's for your safety. And we still need to talk about what just happened."

"No. We don't." She took a step back, desperately needing space from him and the regret in his eyes. "Please, let's forget it ever did."

"Forget?" His eyes narrowed then quickly shuttered as

his expression became one of bland indifference. "Fine."

Despite her own adamancy, hurt knifed through her at how easily and emphatically he'd agreed. "Excuse me." Doing her best to ignore him—and failing miserably—she went to the intercom and pressed the button. "Penny?"

"It's about time," came Penny's voice. "Are you going to let us in, or what?"

She pressed the gate button then faced Dayne again. His eyes were frosty and there was a discernible chill in the air. She hated the awkwardness between them. If only she hadn't thrown herself at him. *Literally.*

He stalked to the door, opening it as a black limousine came to an abrupt stop at the bottom of the stairs.

Outside, the sun had set. Cool, spring evening air blew inside. The driver came around and opened the rear door. A set of four-inch heels followed by long legs barely covered by a body-hugging red sheath alighted first from the limo.

"Katrina!" Penelope Lowell aka Penny held up two bottles of champagne as she walked up the steps. Penny leaned in to land air kisses on either of Kat's cheeks, her straight-as-spaghetti dark brown hair brushing Kat's face.

Behind them, Remy snorted, and she glanced over her shoulder to see Angus backing away as if he'd just seen the Wicked Witch of the West.

Natasha Cabot came next, wearing sparkly silver stilettos and a matching strapless cocktail dress. Nat flung her arms around Kat, enveloping her in an invisible cloud of Chanel No. 5, with which her friend habitually drenched her short red bob.

Elaina Griswold's sharp hazel eyes glinted with amusement as she planted a kiss on Kat's cheek. As was typical, the woman's black silk Dior gown's neckline plunged nearly to her belly button. If it weren't for her butt-length blond hair covering her breasts, most of her bosom would be exposed for the world to see.

"Who is *that*?" Penny peered around Kat's shoulder.

Dayne leaned against the doorjamb, his arms still crossed, tightening the shirt over his muscled chest and biceps. Remy's head lowered, her eyes fastening on the other women. From the dog's rigid posture, Kat understood Remy sensed something she didn't like.

"Remy." Dayne pointed inside the house. "*Platz.*"

The shepherd looked up at Dayne then actually seemed to shake her head, as if telling him he was crazy. With obvious reluctance, she turned and padded into the house. Angus followed, his squeaky toy now firmly gripped in his jaws.

Nat let loose with a catcall.

"Mmm, yummy." Elaina licked her lips in a none-too-subtle gesture. "That's quite a big dog," she murmured huskily, making it clear she was referring to Dayne, not Remy.

Penny arched a dark brow. "You've been holding out on us, Katrina. No wonder we haven't seen you around."

Seen me around? Didn't they know Amy had been murdered?

"If I had a man like that in *my* house," Nat chimed in, "I'd never leave home, and I'd never let him out of my bed."

Kat's cheeks heated at the reminder of exactly what *had* happened in her bed. And what hadn't. Her friends followed her to the door, their heels clicking on the bluestone. "This is FBI Special Agent Dayne Andrews."

"Ladies." He made brief eye contact with each of them.

"Ooh," Elaina crooned. "Special *Agent.* Fascinating." If a person's eyes could slither, hers did unabashedly down Dayne's body.

He arched a brow then scanned the property behind where they all stood.

Ever alert. Not even three beautiful, flirtatious women could derail him from his duty.

"Will you be joining us for a little bubbly?" Penny held up the two bottles of Dom Perignon.

"Thank you, but no." He stepped aside for them to enter. "I'm on duty."

"Oh, right." Penny slipped past him, intentionally brushing her upper arm against his chest. "I forgot, Kat, that you have a *body*guard."

Kat rolled her eyes, something that was happening with increasing frequency lately. Her mother had always told her the gesture was unseemly and rude. Worse, a spurt of jealousy made her want to slap that lascivious expression right off Penny's painted face.

Lord, what is happening to me? Cursing, eye rolling, and now this—smacking her friends for being such...tramps. *Who am I to call anyone a tramp?*

"Maybe we can change your mind." Natasha started past Dayne, batting her eyelashes.

"I bet *I* can." Elaina dragged one long, blood-red polished fingernail over his bicep.

Kat nearly rolled her eyes again. For the first time in her life, she was embarrassed by her friends. They treated Dayne as if he were their new toy. *Boy toy.* It was disgusting, and it was sexual harassment, for god's sake. He was handling it surprisingly well, though. With courtesy they didn't deserve.

At about six foot four, well over two hundred pounds, and loaded with hard muscle, there was no doubting he could take care of himself physically. That didn't mean he had to suffer being pawed at like he was their next meal.

Champagne corks popped as Dayne closed the door behind them.

"Where are your glasses?" Penny began opening and closing cupboard doors.

"I'll get them." She opened the one cupboard Penny hadn't tried and took down four slender Baccarat champagne flutes. While Penny poured, Kat held her hand over her mouth and yawned. Alcohol was the last thing she wanted or needed. All she wanted was to fall into bed and sleep for a week.

A squeak came from the living room where Remy and Angus fought over the puppy's toy.

Nat accepted a flute from Penny. "Why do you let dogs in your house? They're so dirty."

"Dogs are a lot cleaner than you'd think." Reluctantly, Kat accepted a glass then glanced at her watch. *How fast can I get them out of here?*

"Can't you see she likes animals?" Elaina nodded to where Dayne reached for his jacket, the movement tightening his slacks over his extremely tight, muscular backside. "The man moves like a jungle cat. A very *hot* jungle cat."

"Knock it off." Kat gripped the stemware tighter. He was out of earshot, but she hated her friends talking about him that way. Plus, the thought of him with another woman… Well, let's just say that veil of irritation was jealous pea green.

"Where does he sleep?" Penny whispered.

Dayne joined them in the kitchen, heading straight to the coffeepot and scooping fresh coffee into a filter. He had to have heard Penny's insinuating question. From the tight set of his jaw, he didn't like it.

"Please, ignore her," Nat said. "It's that time of the month and she's in heat."

"In that case"—Elaina winked—"it's *always* that time of the month for her."

The women snickered.

Kat tapped her finger on the rim of the glass, finding their sexual banter and innuendos increasingly obnoxious, to the point where she was on the verge of kicking them out. *Twenty minutes. Thirty, tops.* Just to be polite.

Penny draped an arm over Kat's shoulder. "So tell us,

what was it like finding a dead body?"

She stared at the tiny bubbles floating to the surface of her glass. *Try* two *bodies*. Reliving those moments was the last thing she wanted.

"Leave her alone," Elaina said. "Let's talk about something else. Did Nat tell you she's seeing Chad?"

Kat jerked her head up, staring first at Elaina then Nat. *Chad?* My *Chad?* Well, not hers, not anymore. *Reality check. He was never mine.*

Dayne caught sight of what must have been a horrified look on her face and stopped filling the coffeemaker with water. What did it say about her friends when he was the only one to pick up on her feelings? He didn't even know who Chad was to her.

Losing Chad didn't matter. Not anymore. That last thought surprised her, and she loosened the death grip she'd had on the champagne flute. The anger she'd expected to feel at Nat for moving in so quickly on her ex wasn't there. Betrayal, however, was.

Nat should have been the one to tell her first. Hearing it from someone else, the same way Penny had so bluntly delivered the news that Chad was dumping her because he heard he'd have to sign a prenup, was totally insensitive.

"Well, not *seeing* him exactly," Elaina added, "but definitely sleeping with him."

"Elaina, that's enough!" Nat slapped Elaina's shoulder. Champagne slopped over the edge of Elaina's glass.

Kat stared at the wet floor. She didn't care that they were sleeping together, either. Drawing on years of ingrained courtesy, she mustered a smile.

"Ladies, have a good evening." Dayne grabbed a mug and the entire carafe, taking it with him into the library.

All three women repositioned themselves to eye Dayne's backside.

Elaina's lips curved in a decidedly feline smile. "That man is *fine*."

Yuck. Her friends' behavior had always been this way, and in that regard, they were consistent to a fault. The problem wasn't that *they* hadn't changed. *She* had.

Tolerating them wasn't as easy as it once had been. Or maybe she was finally seeing them for what they really were: a trio of rude, snobby bitches.

What's happening to me?

The only thing certain was the driving need to get them out of her home.

• • •

Dayne held the first edition Sherlock Holmes novel in one hand, his mug of coffee in the other. His *fourth* mug. It was eight o'clock, and he'd been sucking down java for the last three hours. At this point, he was more wired than the inside of a computer. He was caffeinated as fuck.

Blood pumped through his veins at light speed, but he actually found Kat's library peaceful. Peace that was interrupted by sounds he hadn't known a human being could make.

He'd left the library door partially open. Not enough to protect his eardrums from the occasional high-pitched squeals and giggles. Not once did he hear Kat's voice. He imagined her sitting calmly in one of those big overstuffed chairs, listening politely while her friends rambled on. Those women knew no boundaries. Definitely the kiss-and-tell type.

Yeah, and speaking of kissing…

Blood shot straight to his dick, and he shut his eyes, reliving every hot, wild moment in Kat's bed. His body had been on fire, and hers had been soft and pliant beneath him. When she'd dragged her short nails down his back and dug her fingers into his muscles, his entire body hummed with the need to sink deep inside her. Maintaining distance from her had gone totally to hell. Things were all good until she'd reached for him. That's all it had taken. One touch and he'd gone ballistic in her arms.

He snapped the book shut. *Weak.* That's what he was around her. He'd been drawn to her from the start and knew it was wrong. Screwing his witness would be supremely unprofessional and *way* past irresponsible. He was sworn to protect her. Not make love to her like his next breath depended on getting inside her.

Didn't matter that she'd been a willing participant *or* that she'd instigated it. He'd been right there with her. He'd wanted her and still did. When he agreed to sex amnesia, he'd been lying his ass off. He'd seen the hurt in her eyes. It was brief, but it had been there, and it was like a justifiable kick in the balls. But it was his best armor against her because it couldn't happen again.

Shortly after he'd made his escape to the library, the dogs had slunk in to take refuge and now slept in the center of the ornate Persian rug. The library truly was amazing. With its fourteen-foot high ceiling, and every square inch of wall space jam-packed with books, it was like a museum, just for books.

Laughter from the living room had Remy's ears twitching. Angus's hind legs kicked as if he were running in his sleep. The women's voices grew louder as they entered the foyer. *Thank you, Jesus. They're leaving.*

He pulled his phone from his belt and texted the guards. If the guys were smart, they'd hide inside their vehicles until Kat's friends were off the property.

Friends my ass.

He'd wanted to say something but held back. Who was he to criticize the people she surrounded herself with? His role in her life was temporary. Whom she hung out with was none of his business. Just like it was none of his business who Chad was. Sounded like the guy was a total prick. But Nat was worse for going after him without telling Kat.

Let it go.

Why couldn't he?

Because he cared. The admission had him mentally kicking himself. Involving his emotions in a homicide investigation was a bad idea. Emotions got people killed.

Another minute went by before the front door opened and closed, followed by the limousine pulling away. He exhaled a long, caffeine-laden breath. The plan was to walk off all his pent-up energy outside with the dogs then try to get some shut-eye.

Kat's heels sounded as she came into the library. "I need to apologize." Dark circles shadowed her eyes, and her shoulders sagged. "I won't have them over again as long as you're here. In fact, I may never have them over again at all."

"It's your home." He set the book on the table and stood. "You can have anyone over that you like. I'm a big boy. I can take care of myself."

She shook her head. "You shouldn't have to."

He shoved his hands in his pockets. The white elephant in the room was gaining weight by the second, and they both knew it. If he could go back in time, would he change anything?

I never should have touched her.

She bit her lower lip, looking adorable but upset. "The only thing I want to say about what happened upstairs, is that I'm sorry."

"Never be sorry for that. You were hurting. You still are." *We both are.* "For the record, I wanted to, but I can't. You're a witness. My job is to protect you, not..." Yeah, he didn't have to say it.

"I know." Still not looking at him directly, she went to a corner of the library and pulled a book from the shelf. As she flipped through it, several worn pages slipped out and drifted to the floor. Dropping to her knees, she began gathering the sheets. Dayne joined her and picked up one of the pages, handing it to her.

"Thank you." Taking excessive care not to touch him, she tucked the pages back into the book then ran her hand reverently over the cover's worn, faded edges. There was no picture on the cover, only the title: *Dogs of Character*, by Cecil Aldin. "As a child, this was my favorite book. My father gave it to me. I must have read it fifty times. I even read it again last year. It's so fragile now the pages practically disintegrate in my hands."

"What's it about?" He tried imagining her as a little girl sitting on one of the giant leather sofas, snuggled up with the book in her hands.

"The author wrote it for children to help them decide what breed of dog would suit them best and how to train it. There are so many beautiful illustrations inside. The last promise my father ever made to me was that he would find a first edition signed by the author, one that *wasn't* falling apart." She smiled tiredly.

"I take it he never did."

"No." Her smile faded as she returned the book to the shelf. "Not for lack of trying. The book is rare, written in 1927. There are a few available on the internet. The problem is finding one in good condition, and the author only signed two hundred fifty first editions. Growing up, this book—and, dogs, of course—were my best friends." She sighed. "I thought I was lucky to have found real friends, but sometimes I never know why people want to be around me. Not for sure."

"Do you consider those women your friends?" He hoped not. With backstabbing friends like that, he'd be looking over his shoulder twenty-four seven.

She hesitated. "I've known them since I was a child."

"The amount of time you've known someone doesn't automatically make them a friend. In case you didn't notice, not once in the last three hours did they ask how you were or say anything about you losing a close friend. None of them—including Colin—was there for you at the funeral home, but they show up here with champagne to celebrate?"

Her lips compressed. "Don't you think that's being a little harsh?"

"It's the truth."

She lifted her chin high, pressing her lips together. "Maybe I just didn't see it until now."

"See what?"

Her shoulders sagged more, as if she carried the weight of the world on them. "That most people are only my friends because they want something from me."

"Money?"

"Yes, but not always. Sometimes, all they want is association. Wealth, fame, and the power that comes with it has to be wielded wisely and with compassion."

"That's a heavy burden." One he couldn't imagine. He was also beginning to understand her need to isolate herself in this castle. These walls were her protection. She had everything yet just might be the loneliest person he'd ever met.

"I'll survive." The phony smile she pasted on didn't convince him. "Not to worry. I've lived with it all my life."

"I'm not worrying, I—" *Liar.* He'd crossed way over the line and stepped ass-deep into her personal life. A mistake he kept repeating. He shoved a hand through his hair. The best thing he could do was to make a tactical retreat before he opened his big mouth again. "I'm sorry. I shouldn't have said anything. It's not my place. It's just that—" *Don't say it.*

"You deserve better."

Turning abruptly, he snapped his fingers. "Remy. Angus." The dogs leaped to their feet and followed him. He went outside, nodding to the guard who'd stepped from his vehicle.

Dayne started down the driveway as the dogs scampered onto the grass, sniffing and doing their stuff. The night air was cool and felt good on his face. If there was any chance at all that he could get some sleep, he needed to walk off all the caffeine shooting through his system faster than a speeding bullet.

Caffeine wasn't why he was so twisted up inside. It was because she *did* deserve better. Better than those sycophantic women masquerading as her friends. Better than Colin or that faceless asshole, Chad.

Better than me.

He stopped in his tracks. *That* was the realization eating him alive.

He'd never be good enough for her, either.

Chapter Sixteen

Kat woke to the French mantel clock ticking away on her nightstand. Green onyx surrounded the gilded metal face that told her she needed to get her lazy ass out of bed.

Turning her face into the pillow, she swore she could smell Dayne's aftershave. She drew him into her lungs, reliving every lust-filled moment.

She snapped her eyes open. *What am I doing?* Daydreaming about what happened was self-destructive and would only get them both into trouble again. Damn him for comforting her and holding her while she cried her eyes out. *Damn me for reaching for him.*

"I'm an idiot," she whispered.

Last night, when she'd gone downstairs, she'd lit into him. Now she felt horrible. The blame was more hers than it was his. She'd wanted something and taken it. Tried to, anyway. Acting recklessly was *so* outside the box for her. Everything about Dayne was outside her neat, always-tidy box. He'd done something to her that could never be undone.

He'd made her want him.

Despite their extreme differences, she'd genuinely begun to like him, and that only made it worse. Not only was she ridiculously attracted to him, now she had feelings for him. *Strong* feelings.

Last night, he'd been a perfect gentleman to people who didn't deserve it. He'd done it for her. Because they were her friends. In the span of five days, he'd done more for her and exhibited more kindness to her than most people had. Then again, maybe it was only out of a sense of duty.

She flung back the covers and threw on a pair of black nylon sweatpants and racerback bra. After tying her hair in a high, tight ponytail, she tiptoed down the stairs, hoping to miss Dayne. Despite their nice little chat in the library last night, the awkwardness between them was still thick enough to cut with a knife.

Neither of the dogs or Dayne was in sight as she slunk through the kitchen and down the basement stairs. A quick stretch later and she was kicking and punching the living daylights out of the heavy bag hanging by a chain from the ceiling.

Jab-squat. Squat-kick. Of all the equipment in her gym, this was by far the most used piece. The bag's leather cover was worn down in places from all the workouts she and Emily had given it over the years. Not having worked out for the past week made a difference. Sweat trickled down her temples. Her muscles ached, and her breaths came hard and fast.

Jab-cross-jab. Again, again, again. Her hair was soaked. Her bra stuck to her body. *Keep moving. Don't stop.*

Forty minutes later, her chest heaved and she leaned over, resting her forearms on her thighs. Even her knuckle guards dripped with sweat.

"No wonder you broke his nose."

Kat jerked her head up. If she hadn't already been sucking in air, she would have gasped at the shock of finding Dayne watching her. With all her heavy breathing, she hadn't heard him come down the stairs. Knowing he could have been there for several minutes made her self-conscious. The man was in such amazing shape.

His jeans weren't tight, but they showcased every muscle in his butt, thighs, and calves. The black Henley tucked into his belt molded itself to his pecs, shoulders, and biceps. *Shirts like that should be outlawed.*

"How long have you been standing there?" she managed when her heart rate slowed.

"Long enough."

She could swear his lips twitched. "Long enough for what?"

"Long enough to admire your incredible...equipment." For a moment he stared at her, and she couldn't be sure if he was referring to the gym equipment or *her.* He turned to look first at the free weights, then the barbells, dumbbells, treadmill, cross-trainer, and bevy of other workout machinery. "Would you mind if I used your gym while I'm staying here?"

"Of course not." She ripped off her knuckle guards and grabbed a bottle of water from the mini-fridge, twisting the cap off and sucking down a long draught.

"Thanks."

When he didn't go back upstairs, she narrowed her eyes. He'd come down here for a reason, and it hadn't been to check out her *equipment.*

"I need to go somewhere this afternoon." Something in his tone set off alarm bells in her head.

"Okay." She wiped her brow. "I'll be fine here without you."

"You're coming with me."

Today was Sunday so... "Are you going to church?"

He scratched his freshly shaven and extremely sculpted jaw. "It's my parents' fortieth wedding anniversary. I have to go and I'm not leaving you here."

"Oh no." She shook her head gently at first then with more emphasis. "I'm *not* going." After last night, what she needed was *more* personal space from him. Not less. Attending his parents' party was straying way too far into the personal zone.

"Yes. You are." That sculpted jaw hardened, and he crossed his arms in a way that tightened the black Henley snugger across those incredible biceps. "It's not open to negotiation."

"Fine," she flung back, realizing he had more control over her life at the moment than she did. She could practically read his mind: *suck it up, princess.* "What time?"

"Three o'clock." He turned to leave when his cell phone rang, and he unclipped it from his belt. "Andrews." He straightened from where he'd been leaning casually against the wall. "What's the address?" He ended the call. "We need to leave an hour earlier."

"Why? What's happened?" His stiff body posture told her something was up.

"The tech guys just pulled something critical from Becca's phone."

. . .

Dayne alternated between the rear and sideview mirrors, keeping tabs on the gray sedan that had stuck with them for the last few minutes. He tested his theory by pressing his foot down on the accelerator and...*shit*. When he sped up, so did the sedan. Sure enough, when he eased off the gas, the other driver slowed. Could be nothing. Then again, maybe they really were being followed.

He kept watching the vehicle, trying not to let Kat see. He'd finally gotten around to telling her he thought someone had been on the property yesterday. She was edgy enough as it was. The last thing she needed was his paranoia making it worse.

"Where are we going?" Kat plucked another raspberry candy dot from the roll of paper. She'd been popping them like a drug addict craving a fix, cleaning off more than four inches of paper.

"Englewood. The Sylvus Corporate Center. It was the last location Becca entered into her GPS phone app the day she was killed." He shot another look in the rearview mirror and tightened his grip on the wheel. *Still there.*

Delicately, she put the candy in her mouth and crunched. Remy stuck her head through the opening, her nostrils flaring as the scent of raspberry filled the SUV's interior. Yep, his dog had a sweet tooth. Angus whimpered, and his little paws hooked over the ledge as he tried unsuccessfully to peer into the passenger compartment.

Kat twisted to pet Remy and give Angus's little paws a quick squeeze. She wore gray slacks and a lavender sweater. The only jewelry she had on was a pair of amethyst studs that matched the color of her eyes. She really did have the prettiest eyes and—

Don't think about how pretty the rest of her is, either.

"Who exactly will be at this party?" She plucked off another dot.

"Just my parents." He made a left turn and checked the mirror. The sedan hung back, creating more distance. "And Lily."

Kat tore off two more inches from the roll and plucked off several dots at once, shoving them into her mouth. "Why do you keep looking in the rearview mirror?"

"Because," he said, flicking on the wipers as raindrops dotted the windshield, "somebody might be following us."

"*What?* Who?"

"Don't know." He could easily flip on the lights, hang

a *uey*, then pull over the sedan to find out, but that went against every rule of protection in the book. If the killer were actually following them, pulling the asshole over would only put less distance between the guy and Kat, which would be monumentally stupid.

Plus, he still couldn't be certain about the sedan. And Lily would macerate his balls if they were late for the party. He cued up the universal police department frequency then grabbed the mic to make an official request for a marked unit to pull over the sedan.

"Is he still back there?" Kat twisted in her seat to look behind them.

"Don't." He shot out a hand to clasp her upper arm and, in the process, unintentionally copped a feel of her warm, perfect breast. "The rear window is pretty well tinted, but I don't want the driver to know we're checking him out."

Kat settled into the seat but he glimpsed the pink stain creeping up her neck. She was as much affected by his clumsy *faux pas* as he was.

Her nipple puckered against the lavender sweater, jutting out like a plump little berry. If only his peripheral wasn't so good, because he really, *really* didn't need to see that. All the more reason to keep things from getting physical between them again.

Refocusing, he glanced in the mirror again. "Shit."

"*Now* what?" Kat made an exaggerated gesture with her hand.

"He's gone." The road behind them was empty.

"Isn't that a good thing?"

"Yeah." Except that he'd been totally, inexcusably distracted and missed which road the vehicle turned onto. His feelings for her were affecting his job. He could still ask for reassignment, at least for inside-duty at the castle, but he didn't want that, either. Didn't trust anyone else to keep her safe. Problem was, after last night, his awareness of her was exponentially over the top. Now she was 200 percent off-limits.

What he needed was distance. As soon as the killer was caught, he'd be outta there. Meantime, he needed to keep a lid on his libido. They *both* did.

He noted the time and their location. If a marked unit didn't catch up to the sedan which, at this point, would probably be the case, another agent could run the same route they'd taken and check for video cameras. If they were lucky, the car would be on one of them.

"We're here." He turned into the parking lot of a four-story building then rolled down his window to snap a photo. *Nothing's ever easy.* According to the sign, half a dozen companies maintained offices here. Three law firms, one marketing company, and two accounting firms. He forwarded the image to Paulson's email then drove slowly through the lot.

"What are you looking for?" Kat asked.

"A needle in a haystack."

"Why do you say that?"

"There must be hundreds of employees working in this building. During business hours, there'll be nearly as many vehicles in the lot. Even if there is a connection between the gray sedan that *may* have been following us, or the car you saw outside Becca's office the day you found her, half these cars will fit that description."

"Do you know why she came here?"

"Not yet. First thing tomorrow, we'll send an agent to every company in the building to find out if anyone working there knew Becca. We'll also cross-check her case files with this address, along with the names of all the employees. That is, if these companies cooperate. Not all of them will. Before they fork over the names of their people, it's a guarantee that, at a minimum, the legal firms will demand a subpoena."

"How long does *that* take?"

"Depends." He guided the Interceptor around the building then exited back onto Route 9W, heading south. "The official compliance date for a subpoena is usually two weeks from the date of issuance, but I've seen companies weasel out of responding for months. Especially, law firms that come up with every excuse in the book. Sometimes just to be difficult."

"Great." The resignation in Kat's voice echoed his thoughts exactly.

There'd be no wrapping up these homicides overnight.

More rain hit the windshield. Seconds later, mini-hurricane force wind and rain pounded the SUV. Just as he flipped on the wipers, his cell rang. He clamped it into a dashboard cradle and put the caller—Paulson—on speaker.

"Did you get the photo?" he asked without preamble.

"Got it. I'm drafting subpoenas as we speak. The second the DA's office opens in the morning, I'll be standing on their doorstep."

"Outstanding." This guy was turning out to be more of a kick-ass detective than he'd first thought. "The FBI can assign more agents to help you canvass the company employees."

"Thanks, but that's not why I'm calling." Dayne tensed. Either good news was coming, or something really bad. He hoped to hell it was the former. They needed a break in the case, and they needed it yesterday. "We got into the trap 'n' trace app log."

Hoo-yah. "And?"

"We pulled the last number to call Rebecca before she died. It's an unlisted cell phone."

"What's the number?" Dayne pulled a pad and pen from the console and jotted down the 201 New Jersey number. "Did you call it?"

"Yeah. No answer and no voicemail."

"What number did you use to call?" Paulson wouldn't be the first detective to make a rookie mistake by using his own police cell. Worse, a department hard line. If they gave the killer a heads-up they were on to him, he'd disappear in the wind.

"A UC line," Paulson replied. "Comes back to a fictitious online sporting goods company we set up a few years back. If he calls it, it should pass muster."

Paulson just jumped a couple more ratings on Dayne's CC—cop competency—scale.

"And before you ask," Paulson added, "the carrier is Verizon and we're getting a subpoena for the phone's subscriber information, along with a search warrant for Google so we can view all Rebecca's emails."

Dayne couldn't have done it better if he were the lead investigator. *Go Paulson.* "Did you look at her Facebook page? She doesn't have a personal account, but she started one for her business about six months ago."

"I'll check it out as soon as I get this affidavit and subpoenas done."

"We'll check in with you tomorrow." Dayne ended the call and took the I-95 south ramp toward Newark. The rain had eased somewhat, and he gunned the SUV onto the highway.

"What did all that mean?" Kat asked.

"It means we're covering all the bases. Case files. Email. Phone. Social media. Forensic and ME reports."

"Then why do you look so annoyed?"

Do I? He was, though. Not just with the snail's pace of the investigation. Apparently, he'd been telegraphing his thoughts and mood. Something he never did. In just under a week, Kat could read him as well—if not better—than his closest friends and family.

"Well?" she prodded. "Why *do* you look so irritated?"

"Because"—he changed lanes, doing his best to focus on the road, rather than what was really bugging him—"we're staring at the ass-end of nowhere, struggling to catch up."

That was half of it, anyway. The other half he couldn't tell her.

They were doing everything in their investigative repertoire, but going by the book was taking too long.

Time was on the killer's side, and the killer *would* strike again. He was certain of it.

Chapter Seventeen

Kat resisted inspecting her tongue in the mirror. It had to be fluorescent red by now. Meeting Lily at the wake was one thing. Meeting Dayne's parents was fixing to be awkward at best. What would they think? *That I'm his girlfriend? That we're sleeping together?*

It didn't matter that they almost had, because they definitely weren't now.

Her body began heating from the inside out, starting low in her belly before flooding her torso. The mere thought of making love with Dayne did that. *Think about something else.* Colin's face popped into her head. Her core temperature instantly dropped into the frigid zone.

When Dayne exited the Turnpike she clasped her hands to keep from stripping the entire roll of candy bare. "You never got around to telling me about your parents," she said.

His face lit up. "They're the best." He headed west on Route 280 toward the Oranges. "They own a hardware store in Newark, one of the few holdouts competing with the big warehouses. In the forty years they've had the store, they've built up a loyal customer base that keeps them in business. I used to work there after school and summers when I was in college. I loved working there."

"Were they disappointed you didn't stay with the family business?"

"Just the opposite. They were proud as hell when I became an FBI agent. Dad still laughs at the irony."

"Irony?"

"Well, yeah. Considering I was a pretty good thief when I was a kid."

"A thief?" Now *that* was hard to believe.

"Yep." He drove into a semi-rural neighborhood. "I told you I grew up on the street after my mother died. That's when I figured out I have a knack for breaking into places. I got pretty good at shoplifting. Nothing of much value and only when I couldn't get my dinner from a dumpster."

"A dumpster?" Her jaw dropped. "You ate food from a *dumpster*?"

Again, he chuckled. "You'd be surprised at how much decent food restaurants throw out every day. I've had more than my share of lobster."

Oh my god. While she was being served vichyssoise in fine china, he was dumpster diving in back alleys to survive.

Shame sliced through her. Not that it was her fault that she'd been born into wealth, but this certainly explained a lot. Like their first encounter. A man with Dayne's backstory might very well resent someone like her who'd had everything handed to her on a silver platter. *Literally.*

"You seemed shocked to hear that." There was no censure in his eyes or his voice. Only fact, and his assumption was the correct one.

"I *am* shocked," she admitted.

"Why? You must know kids like that actually exist."

"Of course I do. I donate a lot of money annually to

several children's organizations. It's just…just…" How to say it without sounding like a snob? "It's because you're so confident in who and what you are." One of many things she admired about him. The only time she had that level of confidence was in the boardroom. In her personal life, not so much.

He grunted, as if he didn't agree with her assessment.

They drove deeper into the neighborhood where the houses were older, with mature trees and well-established perennial gardens. Tulips and daffodils bloomed everywhere.

She gasped. "Flowers. We need to stop for flowers. I can't go to your parents' party without bringing a gift. Flowers at the very least."

"Don't worry about it." He turned left onto another street. "Lily and I have this covered. We booked them a week-long vacation in the Florida Keys. My folks know what's going on with you. Trust me." He winked. "They'll forgive this one breach in protocol."

"You told them about me?" He nodded. "Told them *what* exactly?"

"That you're *the* Katrina Vandenburg. They can't wait to meet you."

"What else did you tell them?" She held her breath. No way would he have told them *everything. Right*?

"Nothing. Except that you're under my protection." He parked in front of a two-story Tudor house and shut off the engine. "We're here."

Relief had her slumping in the seat. She hooked a leash to Angus's collar and waited for Dayne to come around and signal her to get out. Remy ran straight to the front door, as if she'd been here a hundred times before. Angus barked and strained at the leash. She took a deep breath. A few hours, and it would all be over.

Dayne pushed open the door and Remy bounded inside.

Kat maintained a firm hold on Angus's leash, which only made the puppy strain harder and bark louder. The second Dayne unclipped the leash, Angus bounded through the hallway after Remy.

Laughter floated their way, then, "A puppy! A puppy!"

"After you." Dayne extended his arm, indicating she should follow the laughter down the hall.

They didn't make it to the kitchen before Lily met them halfway. Kat held out her hand to the other woman but was swept into a warm hug instead.

"It's nice to see you again." Lily released her. "And under better circumstances this time."

Better circumstances. That was one way to put it.

"Hi, Lily." Dayne kissed his sister on the cheek.

"Hi, yourself." She gave him a warm hug then took Kat's hand and led her the rest of the way to the kitchen. "I need to check on dinner. C'mon in and meet everyone."

Only then did she realize Lily wore an apron and the house smelled amazing. Garlic, herbs, and something meaty permeated the air, making her stomach growl.

Four sets of eyes turned to her. Two from the couple seated at the round oak table—Dayne's parents—and two from the kitchen floor, where a boy and a girl stopped playing with Angus and Remy to stare at her.

"Kat," Dayne's deep voice resonated behind her, "this is my mother and father, Renee and Bill Andrews."

When Renee rose from the table, Kat extended her hand but Dayne's mother ignored it and enveloped her in a hug. "If you haven't figured it out by now, we're huggers in this family."

Renee released her then stepped aside for Bill, who did the same. "It's a pleasure to meet you, young lady."

Renee and Bill were in their late sixties, she guessed, with gray hair and warm brown eyes. They exuded a kindness she hadn't experienced in a long time. Since her parents died.

"Hi, Mom." Dayne hugged his mother tightly then gave his dad a giant bear hug, clapping him on the back. "Dad. Happy anniversary."

"Thank you, son." To Kat, he said, "Can I get you a glass of wine?" He pointed to the bottles of Cabernet and Chardonnay on the table.

"Yes. Thank you." *Try a whole bottle.*

"Leave me some of that Cab for the sauce," Lily said from the stove, where she stirred something in a saucepan.

"Uncle Dayne, where'd you get the puppy?" the boy—who looked to be about ten—asked.

"Guys. Get off your tiny heinies and come here." Dayne held out his arms, and when the children went to his side, he draped an arm over their shoulders. "This is Miss Vandenburg. Kat, this is my nephew, Jimmy, and my niece, Adele."

Jimmy held out his hand. On the cuteness scale, this kid was a solid ten. As she shook the boy's hand, he sucked his lower lip between his teeth. Big, beautiful brown eyes stared up at her. "Pleased to meet you, Miss Vandenburg."

"Pleased to meet you as well, Jimmy." She doubted *her* manners were as good as Jimmy's at this age.

"What's your puppy's name?" he asked.

"His name is Angus, although he's not really mine. I'm just taking care of him for a while."

"Can I play with him?" Jimmy's brows rose, his face brimming with hopefulness.

"Of course you can."

"Addie?" Dayne gave his niece a slight nudge and the girl extended her hand.

"Pleased to meet you," Addie said. "Are your eyes really purple?"

Kat smiled at the wonder in the child's eyes. "Yes, they

are."

"Wowww." When Addie stepped closer, Kat knelt to let her get a better look. The girl stared for a good five seconds. "They're so pretty. Mommy, can I have purple eyes, too?"

Lily stopped stirring and laughed. "No, baby. You have to be born with them."

Kat touched Addie's cheek. "I think your eyes are beautiful just the way they are."

"Say 'thank you,'" Dayne said.

"Thank you, Miss Vandenburg."

"Son, can I get you a beer?" Bill asked Dayne.

"No thanks, Dad."

"Come sit by me, Katrina." Renee patted the chair next to her. "We're looking at old photo albums." Dayne groaned. "Dayne doesn't like it when we walk down memory lane. Sweetheart, you were such a handsome boy." His mother lovingly stroked her fingers down a photo of Dayne in a football uniform.

"*Were*?" Dayne's face twisted with mock disappointment.

He wasn't kidding. Contrary to what she'd assumed, he really did have a sense of humor, after all.

When Renee turned another page in the album, Bill headed to the refrigerator and pulled out a beer.

"I think I'll take that beer after all, Dad." Dayne grimaced like a little boy about to be embarrassed by his mother.

"Figured that." He popped the cap off then handed the bottle to Dayne. "It's River Horse Ale. Your favorite."

"Thanks." He took a long slug.

"Did you know a hippo spends ninety percent of its life underwater?" Jimmy asked Kat.

She shook her head, smiling. "I didn't know that." Jimmy really was adorable. Both Lily's children were.

"Jimmy wants to be a veterinarian when he grows up," Lily said. "His father always took him to the zoo. That's where he fell in love with animals."

"Why don't you and Addie take the dogs into the backyard to play?" Dayne suggested.

"Okay!" Jimmy shouted, delight written all over his face. "C'mon, Angus. C'mon, Remy." He ran to the kitchen door and flung it open.

Remy and Angus charged outside, with Jimmy two steps behind.

"Wait for me!" Addie scrambled after her brother.

"Don't be too long," Lily called after them, still stirring. "Dinner's soon and you have to wash your hands before coming to the table."

"Did Dayne tell you he was an All-American running back?" Renee flipped the page to more photos of Dayne in his football uniform.

"No, he didn't." She gave him an exaggerated smile, and as she turned back to Dayne's mother, caught the narrowing of his eyes. *This could be fun*. Since he'd given her no choice about being here in the first place, she intended to make the most of it. Especially if it involved anything that made him uncomfortable. *Right back at ya, Mr. Federal Agent man.* Payback was a bitch.

"Well, he told us an awful lot about *you*." Renee winked at her son. "Like where you live, what you were like, and all about the Canine Haven."

"Mom." The word came out on a strangled growl. "I told you all that so you'd understand where she comes from."

Where I come from? What did *that* mean? *Oh, right. Wealth.* She shot him an icy glare.

He tipped the bottle back and it took all her willpower to stop staring at the strong column of his throat as he swallowed.

Bill came around the table and rested his hand affectionately on his wife's shoulder as they both looked at the photos. Dayne sat in a chair opposite Kat, his face softening as he watched his parents. He had a major soft spot for his family.

The kitchen door swung open. Remy and Angus barreled inside, followed by Addie and Jimmy. Addie ran to Dayne and held up her arms. He tugged the little girl onto his lap. First, the little girl at Becca's wake and now his niece and nephew... The man really was great with children.

"JJ, wash up before dinner." Lily poured herself a glass of wine and joined them at the table. "And you're next, young lady."

"Okay, Mommy." Addie snuggled deeper into Dayne's arms.

"JJ?" Kat asked.

"Jim Junior. Jimmy was named after his father." Lily pointed to a wedding photo of her and a tall, red-haired man in a police uniform. "He was killed in the line of duty. Four years ago."

Kat went completely still. Her heart ached for Lily's loss. "I'm so sorry." She couldn't imagine what it must be like to fall in love then lose that person so early in life.

"Me, too." Lily pressed a hand to her breastbone. "But we're doing okay now. I don't know how I would have managed without Mom and Dad helping me, and especially, my brother." Lily looked across the table at Dayne, the love and affection so obvious in her eyes. "Thank god Mom and Dad adopted both of us."

She studied him from across the table. "He's just full of surprises, isn't he?" she muttered, mostly to herself. Aside from him being an FBI agent and being adopted, she didn't know much about him. Maybe he didn't want to get too personal, either. Could that be the real reason why he'd stopped things before they'd actually made love? Or maybe he'd realized long before she had that having sex with a witness was mixing business with pleasure. *No problem. I may have been late to the meeting, but I did get the memo.*

"If they hadn't taken us in," Dayne said, ignoring her last comment, "we'd both have rap sheets as long as my arm."

"You, brother dear," Lily said, slanting her brother a sarcastic look, "would probably still be in jail."

Still? Kat caught the subtle shake of Dayne's head as he glared at his sister. How had someone who'd been arrested become an FBI agent? Clearly, there was a story there that he didn't want told.

"Okay, okay." Lily threw up her hands. "Just sayin' is all."

Bill draped an arm over Dayne's shoulders. "I think you both turned out pretty darned well if I do say so. Two extremely law-abiding citizens."

"Oh, Mom." Lily grimaced as she pointed to the album. "I thought you got rid of all the photos of her."

Renee made a disgusted sound. "I must have missed this one." She peeled back the plastic sheet and plucked out the photo of a younger Dayne with a beautiful woman. She crumpled the photo and tossed it on the table.

"Wonderful," Dayne grumbled then took another slug of beer.

Lily pointed to what was left of the photo. "That is—or, rather *was*—Britt Somers, one of Dayne's ex-girlfriends." *One of them?* She shouldn't be surprised. A man with his looks probably had a long list of exes. "Britt was a gold-digging bi—"

"Lily! Not in front of the children." Renee nodded to Addie and JJ, who'd returned from washing his hands.

"Sorry, Mom." Lily cupped the side of her face so only Kat could see her mouth the word *bitch*. "I call it as I see it. I'm glad that woman showed her true colors before you married her."

So Dayne had been engaged. No matter how much she willed it not to, that pea-green veil clouded her vision again.

"Don't you have something to do at the stove?" Dayne growled. "Like, I don't know...cook?"

There was definitely another story there. The man's list of secrets was growing by the minute. She shouldn't be curious. Shouldn't want to know everything there was to know about the man. But she did. *Dammit.*

"Fine." Again, Lily threw up her hands. "All I'm saying is you're better off without her."

"That's one thing we agree on." Dayne gently set Addie on her feet then stood. "I need to feed the dogs." He went to the pantry and began scooping kibble. As soon as it hit the bowls, Remy and Angus began Hoovering their food.

"Can I help with anything?" Kat asked Lily.

"No, you relax with Mom and Dad," Lily said over her shoulder. "If Dayne didn't mention it, I'm a caterer. I've got things well in hand."

Judging by the wonderful smells emanating from the stove, Lily did, indeed, have things well in hand. There was also a beautiful four-inch high sheet cake perched on the counter, one with dark chocolate frosting and yellow roses.

Dayne's warning about Manny came to mind, but she pushed it away. Even if it was only for a few hours, she didn't want to think about all the lurking threats in her life.

For the first time since she had arrived, Kat looked around the kitchen, admiring the warm yellow walls and the worn table that had probably hosted many a family gathering. Photos and kids' drawings dotted nearly every square inch of the refrigerator, held there by tape and magnets. This house was filled with light, warmth, and love. *I miss that.*

When her parents were alive, evening meals were a time and place for them to come together as a family and talk about everything. Dad's business deals. Mom's charity organizations and everything going on in Kat's life. Her parents always had time for her, and they showed it with their love.

"Dear, are you all right?" Renee asked. "You've been through so much this past week."

"We're sorry to hear about your friend who was killed," Bill said to her, then to Dayne, "*Both* your friends. You must miss them."

Dayne nodded but didn't say anything.

"I do." A lump formed in her throat. "Terribly." And last night, she'd almost found a way to take her mind off the grief. With their son.

Something touched her shoulder—Dayne's hand, gentle and reassuring. Though it was a simple gesture of support, she appreciated it. More than she should.

Two hours later, Kat's stomach was about to burst.

"Lily, your chicken piccata was delicious, and this chocolate mousse cake…" She had no words for how wonderfully chocolatey and rich the cake was. "It makes my heart sing."

Lily's face beamed. "I'm happy you enjoyed it."

"JJ." Dayne snagged the boy's arm. "Stop feeding Angus cake. Chocolate's not good for dogs. It can make them very sick, and I don't want him puking on the way home."

"Aww, Uncle Dayne." JJ gave his uncle a sheepish look.

"You, too." Dayne stopped Addie from slipping a frosting-laden gob of cake to Remy.

Both children giggled, and then everyone at the table was giggling. Except Dayne.

"Yeah, very funny," he said. "You're not the ones who'll have to wash out the kennel. Maybe if I made all of you clean up dog vomit you'd think twice."

"Dayne." Renee swatted his arm. "The dinner table is no place to discuss vomit."

Another round of laughter went around the table, and this time, Dayne joined in.

"Do you have a business card?" Kat asked Lily. "I periodically host charity events and I'd love to have you cater one. If you'd like to, that is."

"Are you kidding?" Lily's brows shot up. "Of course I would. I appreciate the opportunity."

Kat clasped Renee's hand, smiling warmly at Dayne's mother and father. "Thank you—*both* of you—for allowing me to intrude on your special day." It really had been more fun than she'd expected.

"It was our pleasure," Bill said.

Renee squeezed her hand. "You're welcome to join us anytime."

"Thank you." She wished she *could* join them again but doubted it would ever happen. "This was wonderful. Unfortunately, I have to get up very early tomorrow. I have meetings all day in the city."

Dayne's brows lowered. "You didn't tell me that."

"I forgot." Actually, she hadn't. Until that moment, she'd planned on canceling all her morning meetings, but she had to get out of the house. Anything to keep her busy. Because she'd enjoyed tonight far too much.

Being with Dayne and his family hadn't been awkward at all. It had been nice. *Too* nice. The only thing she could think of to keep her mind off that was meetings. *Lots* of meetings.

"I'm sorry," she added. "It must have slipped my mind."

His brows lowered more, silently voicing what he wouldn't say out loud: *bullshit*.

He's right. It *was* bullshit. *I never should have agreed to come here tonight.* Now that she had, she liked him even more. Liked his family and the way they all were together. She wanted that. *With someone.*

The very real possibility that she would wind up an old maid—single, alone, and rambling around the walls of her castle…broke her heart.

Dayne pulled out his phone. His brows drew together, and his lips compressed into a tight line.

"Not at the table." Renee rested her hand on his forearm.

"Sorry, Mom." He put the phone away. "It's work."

Meaning, it was about *her*.

"Anything wrong?" Bill asked.

"Nothing I can't handle." His eyes met hers and one thing instantly became clear.

The pleasantries of the evening had just come to a grinding halt.

...

Two hours later, Kat had rearranged her sock drawer, rehung everything in her closet according to color, and reorganized all her shoes and boots in their shoe cubbies. Still, the jittery feeling in her belly wouldn't go away. Not after what Dayne had told her on the way home.

The text during dinner had come from his boss, Lydia Barstow. One of Rebecca's cases had resulted in two men—cousins—being arrested for insurance fraud, and Lydia had sent a team of agents out to Long Island to interview both men. One had been found and had an alibi for the nights Rebecca was killed and she was attacked. The other, Jonathan Bale, was missing. And he had a history of violence.

A thump came from downstairs. Kat flinched, holding her breath. Her heart pounded like a herd of stampeding hippos in her chest.

The thump came again, sounding like...a pot in the kitchen. Probably just Dayne making coffee.

She let out her breath with a loud *whoosh*. Until six days ago, she'd felt perfectly safe in her own home. Now, she didn't.

Jonathan Bale had sworn to "kick the shit" out of Rebecca Garman. The motivation was clear. Why he would have come to the Haven and killed Amy was anyone's guess. But the man was missing and, according to city cameras, had left Long Island earlier this evening, crossed over the Triboro Bridge into Manhattan, and from there, taken the George Washington Bridge into New Jersey. The last camera Bale's car had shown up on had him heading north on the Palisades Parkway. In the same general direction as the Haven.

As Dayne had explained, suburbs didn't have the same extensive system of cameras that New York City did. After Bale had gotten on the Parkway, he'd disappeared. The man could be anywhere. Driving up Tweed Boulevard. Creeping around outside her fence...

"This is ridiculous." No way was she getting to sleep anytime soon. She grabbed her favorite pair of beaded slippers and headed downstairs.

Halfway down the stairs, she smelled it. Not coffee. *Chocolate.*

Dayne sat at the counter, scrolling through his phone, but looked up when she came into the kitchen. "Couldn't sleep?"

She shook her head, sliding onto a stool next to him.

He went to the stove and picked up a small pot, swirling it then pouring the contents into another mug already sitting on the counter. "Here. It'll help you sleep."

"Thank you." She accepted the mug, her thoughts jumbled at his unexpected thoughtfulness. But it was more than that. He'd gone out of his way and anticipated her needs. She couldn't recall a man ever doing something like that for her. So simple and genuine. With no expectation of anything in return. "How did you know I'd come downstairs?"

He shrugged. "Heard you banging around up there. Figured you'd be down sooner or later."

"I didn't realize I was *banging* so loudly." She smiled then took a sip. "This is good. But doesn't chocolate have caffeine in it?"

"Some. Not as much as coffee or tea. Mom used to make it for me when I couldn't sleep. All I know is, it worked." He grinned. "'Course, she might have spiked it with something stronger just to knock me out."

For a few minutes they sipped in silence, then she had to ask. "Anything new on Jonathan Bale?"

"He's still MIA." Dayne tapped one long finger on the side of his mug.

"There's more, isn't there?" she asked, taking another sip.

"The last camera to pick him up was at exit four on the Palisades Parkway."

She swallowed. "That's my exit." The chocolate turned bitter in her stomach.

"There's a statewide BOLO out for him. As soon as he's spotted, he'll be pulled over. He's not getting in here." Dayne rested a reassuring hand on her shoulder. "Between the guards, me, and Remy, you're safe."

Was she? Kat looked into his eyes, at the fierce expression on his handsome face. For now, yes. But he and Remy wouldn't be here forever, and they couldn't protect her indefinitely. All the more reason to keep things as impersonal as possible.

Chapter Eighteen

"You need to keep me informed about *every* aspect of your schedule." Dayne turned left on Park Avenue, holding back the curse on the tip of his tongue as a taxi cut him off.

Kat sighed. "I'll do my best."

Yeah, right. It wouldn't have surprised him one bit if there'd *been* no scheduled meetings until last night. While they hadn't talked about it back at the castle, something had happened at his parents'. One minute they'd been having a good time, and the next... She closed down and shut him out.

Now she was doing everything in her power to put emotional distance between them. Since it made *that* part of his job easier, he should be happy about it. He gripped the wheel tighter. It had the opposite effect. He was grouchy as hell and had no one else to blame but himself.

Getting involved with her—on *any* personal level—was the dumbest thing he could have done. He never should have taken her to his parents'. Seeing how she was with them, how well she fit in, only made everything worse.

She was right to keep things impersonal. *I'm a goddamn*

federal agent, for shit's sake.

"In the spirit of advance notification," she said, breaking the silence, "I'm attending a charity event this Saturday."

He slipped into an illegal spot in front of a forty-story building—Kat's building. She really did own the damn thing. "Exactly how many buildings do you own?"

"In New York? The United States? Or the world?" Her countenance was deadpan serious, *Jesus.* She *was* serious. "Assuming you'll be accompanying me, you'll need a tuxedo."

"Not a chance." His stomach lurched at the thought of wearing a monkey suit. "I don't wear tuxedos. I don't even own one."

"I'm sorry, but if you want to come with me, then you'll wear one. It's black tie."

He flipped open the center console and pulled out Remy's leash. "I don't care if it's tie-dye, I'm not wearing one."

"Then you're not going."

"Fine." Although he didn't think the FBI would foot the bill for a tux.

"Consider it my gift to you."

"What?" He threw a police placard onto the dashboard. "A tuxedo?"

"I'm forcing you to wear one, so it's only fair that I pay for it. Since you're my bodyguard, I'll consider it an investment in my physical well-being."

"I can afford to buy my own clothes," he growled.

She faced him. "That's not the point."

"Then what is?" Her mouth opened then closed. She swallowed and looked away for a moment, and he could see the gears turning in her head. "Out with it, or you'll be late for your meetings." He really was grouchy this morning. Her silence did that to him.

"Not all tuxedos are created equally. Yours has to be of the highest quality and custom tailored to your body."

"Ahh." He nodded. "You mean, it has to be *expensive*, and you don't think I have the fashion sense or good taste to purchase one that will meet your exacting, upscale standards."

Amethyst eyes blazed at him, so hot there might as well have been flames shooting at his face. "I'll arrange for a tailor to come to the house." She gathered her purse and briefcase.

"Kat, wait!" Before he could stop her, she was out the door. *For Christ's sake!* Why didn't she have this kind of kick-ass attitude toward those bitchy friends of hers the other night? Why did she have to dump all that feminine fury on *his* head?

He bolted out then leashed Remy in record time and sprinted to catch up. Not even three-inch heels or a purple skirt—one so snug he wondered how she could walk in it— slowed her pace. By the time he caught up with her she was already at the entrance where four-foot-high gold lettering announced to the world: VANDENBURG ENTERPRISES.

"Do you have a death wish? I thought we already established that you don't get out of the vehicle until I tell you it's safe." Her cavalier attitude toward her own safety was driving him up the frigging wall.

Ignoring him, she strode to the revolving door and stepped in, effectively cutting him off.

He yanked open the adjacent door and led Remy inside.

"Good morning, Miss Vandenburg," a woman said from the front desk.

"Good morning, Angela." Kat waved to the young woman and continued on to the elevators.

"I'm sorry, sir." Angela waved to a security guard in a navy-blue suit. "Only service dogs are allowed in the building."

Dayne reached into his back pocket, readying to flash his badge.

"That's all right," Kat called out over her shoulder. "He's

with me."

Of course it was all right. Considering she owned the building.

Seconds later, they were in the elevator, shooting up forty or so floors to the executive offices. Dayne stood directly in front of the doors, readying to block her path until he could verify the floor was secure. The elevator was dead silent, yet the hostile atmosphere humming between them was as loud as a machine gun.

The doors opened, and Dayne did a quick sneak and peak in either direction before stepping aside. Without so much as a passing glance, she glided past him to the reception desk.

"Good morning, Miss Vandenburg," another woman said.

"How are you, Kenya?" Kat went around the desk and gave the receptionist a warm hug.

"I'm doing well, Miss Vandenburg."

"How is your father recovering from his surgery?" Kat asked.

"He's doing physical therapy and not happy about it." The woman returned to her seat. "Thank you for asking. They're waiting for you in the boardroom."

"Thank you." Kat glided past the desk.

Dayne grunted. Seemed like she was on a first name basis with *everyone* that worked for her. In this building alone that could be hundreds. In the world…thousands.

"Uh, Miss Vandenburg?" Kenya pointed questioningly to Dayne and Remy.

"They're FBI bodyguards," she answered, again without looking at him.

Dayne followed her down a hallway, along which she stopped to greet half a dozen people as if they were her next-door neighbors. At the end of the hallway loomed two enormous wood double doors, standing by which were three stuffy-looking men who greeted Kat overly solicitously.

"It's so good to see you."

"Welcome back, Miss Vandenburg."

"Everyone is waiting inside for you."

They all eyed Remy with a mixture of fear and disdain.

Dayne snorted. *Guess not a log of dogs have graced these hallowed halls.*

Kat gave a brief nod. "My FBI bodyguards."

As if on cue, each man again had a response.

"Oh my. Yes, we read about you discovering a body last week."

"Bodyguards? The dog, too?"

"FBI? Is something amiss?"

Amiss? Dayne held back another snort. Did anyone really use that word?

He followed Kat into the boardroom, ignoring the concerned looks of the three men, along with the curious expressions on the faces of the dozen or so people seated around the table that was as long as a stretch limo. He settled into a chair in the corner of the room and pointed to the floor. Remy lay down and rested her snout between her paws.

One of the men who'd greeted her at the door held out a chair for Kat at the head of the table. Another approached Dayne cautiously, giving Remy a wide berth.

"We don't normally allow outsiders to attend board meetings," the man said. "Perhaps you'd be more comfortable waiting outside."

"Perhaps I would, but I'll be staying right here. Thank you for the kind offer."

"I don't think you understand—"

"I understand perfectly." Dayne tugged his cell from his belt, preparing to fill the time catching up on emails. "Pretend I'm not here."

"Ernst," Kat intervened from her presiding position at

the table. "I'm quite certain he won't divulge any confidential matters we discuss here today."

With an audible grumble, Ernst turned and took the seat to Kat's right. Apparently, Ernst was accustomed to getting his way.

He opened up the first of many emails from Paulson, the one concerning Becca's Facebook business account.

"The monthly meeting of the Vandenburg Enterprises charity board is called to order," Ernst announced. "There are five charities on the agenda for our review."

Kat flipped open a bound document, as did everyone else. "Are the two I specifically wanted included in this list?"

"Yes, however only one of them meets our guidelines," Ernst said. "Vets of Valor didn't make the cut."

"Why not?" Kat's brows rose. *Yeah, why not?* Even Dayne had heard that was a good charity. "I recommended that organization myself. They had excellent prospects for approval. Their program and mission were very well articulated, and their preliminary budget sheet looked good, especially their overhead ratio."

You go, girl.

Ernst set down his booklet. "They were unable to provide a well-defined method of measuring their overall success."

"Did they give us a description of their long- and short-term goals?" She turned the page. "I see they did."

This was a side of Miss Katrina Vandenburg's persona he hadn't known existed. The kick-ass side.

"Yes." Ernst tugged off his glasses. "But they failed to provide a method detailing how they plan to measure the success of their program."

"Then we'll ask them to rework their proposal for consideration next month." Kat picked up a pen and jotted something down.

"Katrina." Ernst's patently false smile and placating tone

made Dayne want to tell the man where to shove it. It was as if the guy were talking to a small child. "There are several other more worthy charities on our agenda this month. The one on page two, for example. Books for Bairns. They have an extremely articulate proposal that meets all our guidelines."

Kat took a moment to review the document, then for the next ten minutes listened patiently while Ernst sang the charity's praises. Dayne had to admit it also sounded like a worthy cause. Kat set the agenda on the table, clasping her hands on top of the document.

Sorry, Ernst. Looks like you're not getting your way today. Yeah, he knew her well enough to decipher her body language. She wasn't buying it. More to the point, she knew Ernst was trying to bully her, and in classic, composed Kat fashion, she was about to put the guy in his place. Politely, of course.

"This is an extremely comprehensive proposal. So comprehensive, in fact, it's almost as if it was written by one of our board members." She paused to look around the table. Sure enough, one of the younger board members slunk in his chair, looking guilty as hell. "While it does appear to meet our guidelines," Kat continued, "and it is certainly a worthy cause, aren't we already donating to at least two other charities with nearly identical programs and mission statements?"

"Why, yes, but—"

"And isn't this charity chaired by the mayor's wife?" All eyes turned to Ernst.

"Katrina." Ernst held out his arms. "Your parents always believed that the key to success in New York City lay in maintaining appropriate liaisons with key people in government. The city's First Lady is a critical component of—"

"Let me be clear here," Kat interrupted. "While I'd love nothing more than to see my parents seated at this table, we both know that isn't possible. And while I don't particularly feel the need to say it, I will anyway. My parents entrusted the future of this company into *my* hands."

Dayne smirked. This was getting good.

"Furthermore," she continued, "pandering to government officials, or their wives, is not our priority now, nor will it ever be. What *is* our priority—is diversification. I want Vandenburg Enterprises to donate across all lines of society.

"One area we're severely behind in is military veteran programs. Frankly, I can't believe we aren't stronger in this category. That's why I suggested Vets of Valor." Ernst opened his mouth to speak, but she held up her hand. "Mario." She turned to the man seated to her left. "Please reach out to their chairperson and courteously suggest they revise their proposal so it better meets our guidelines. Be sure to outline our area of concern. Give them a two-week deadline so it can be ready for next month's meeting."

"Yes, Miss Vandenburg."

He liked this side of her. Not only did the woman know her shit, but she put that pompous old fart in his place without missing a beat. He was torn between clapping, doing a *hooyah* fist pump, and giving her a high five.

Kat picked up the agenda and smoothly flipped to the next page. "What's next?"

For the next two hours, Dayne read emails and texted, keeping one ear on the conversation. Remy's ears occasionally flicked, but eventually she fell into a light sleep.

His first text was to Bart Danchuk, requesting he cross-check Becca's case files for the Sylvus Corporate Center address in Englewood. Minutes later, he received a response from Bart. *Negative.*

Paulson had forwarded copies of the subpoenas served on Becca's cell phone carrier and her email server. Dayne was particularly interested in the subpoena for subscriber information on the unlisted number the techies found in the trap 'n' trace app. The only other thing of note in the emails was that Jonathan Bale was still in the wind.

By the time the meeting concluded, Dayne was certain of one thing. Kat was a killer in a boardroom.

When the elevator doors opened on the ground floor, they were met by several men in dark suits. Dayne pegged them for what they were. Building security. Vandenburg Enterprises' version of Men in Black. Minus that nifty little memory-erasing gadget.

"Good morning, Tim." Kat smiled at the one wearing a nametag that said *Taggert*. "Are they here?"

"Right on schedule." Taggert nodded to the revolving doors leading to the street, behind which stood a crowd of men and women holding microphones and cameras. "We have two men outside, and we'll escort you to your car."

She started for the door but Dayne blocked her path, pressing his lips together to keep from exploding. "Do you mean to tell me you *expected* this?"

Hairs on the back of Remy's neck rose as she picked up on the tension traveling down his arm, through the leash, directly to his K-9.

"Please give us a moment, Tim." Taggert dipped his head briefly, and she waited for him and the other guards to walk out of earshot. "The press knows we hold our charity board meetings on the fourth Monday of every month."

He tried not to grind his teeth. *Un-fucking-believable.* "Don't you think you should have warned me about this? I could have made other arrangements. You wait inside while I drive around to the back entrance."

"I'll do nothing of the sort." She jutted out her chin. "I'll be going straight out the front door."

"It's not safe," he shot back. "Anyone could be in that

crowd. I'll never see it coming, and neither will your Men in Black. I can't protect you this way."

"The media is a necessary evil."

"How is allowing these vultures to harass you necessary?"

"Every charity needs publicity, but most don't have the financial means to pay for it. This is *free* publicity, and I won't do anything to jeopardize that. Plus," she added, looking guilty as hell about something, "the vultures and I have a deal."

He tightened his fingers around Remy's leash. "*What* deal?"

"When I'm in the city, which isn't often, I'll talk to them, answer their questions. But the Haven and the castle are my sanctuaries. That's why they don't show up there." He had, in fact, wondered about that, but had considered it a gift from the gods.

"So you knew this was going to happen and you intentionally kept me in the dark." Knowing he'd go ballistic, like he was trying not to do right now.

"Yes." She nodded. "I knew you'd go all Neanderthal on me and never allow it."

Neanderthal? Well, didn't that just put him in his place?

He stepped closer. "You've got five minutes. Not a second longer."

"Thank you." Her eyes softened. "I know you're only doing your job."

When she looked at him that way, all soft and sweet, most of his frustration diffused. "And you're making it very difficult." In more ways than one.

Despite their self-imposed resolutions and distancing efforts, his professionalism still teetered on the verge of self-destruction. If only he didn't know what it was like to hold her in his arms and kiss her while she— The memory was far too vivid.

"I'll go first. Stay close to me." He led the way to the doors and stepped outside. The minute the reporters caught sight of her they converged like a pack of wild animals. Cameras clicked. Microphones were shoved in her face.

Remy lowered her head and uttered a growl. Dayne wrapped her leash twice more around his hand. His dog didn't like this anymore than he did. As highly trained as Remy was, his K-9 would take the press's aggressive behavior as an attack. "Easy, girl."

"Katrina! Katrina!" Ten reporters vied for her attention.

"What was it like to find a dead body?"

"Are the rumors true that you were attacked by the same person who murdered that private investigator?"

"Why is the FBI involved?"

Maintaining unbelievable composure, she held up her hands, silencing the reporters. "Ladies and gentlemen. I'm sorry, but I can't discuss anything related to an ongoing investigation." *Good. Deflect.* "But I *would* like to mention that Vandenburg Enterprises is currently considering several new charities for our grants this month, including—"

"C'mon, Katrina. Tell us what's really going on." A burly reporter pushed past a cameraman, invading Kat's personal space and bumping into her as he shoved a digital recorder in her face.

Kat jerked back and stumbled. Her high heel caught on the edge of the step. She wobbled, about to go down hard on the concrete.

"Remy! *Gib laut!*"

He dropped Remy's leash, lunging for Kat and catching her before she fell backward on the pavement. Remy barked, snapping her jaws and forcing the reporter to back off.

"Geh voraus!" Remy swung her head left and right, still barking and growling as she cleared a path through the throng of reporters who jumped out of the way to keep from having a

set of sharp canine incisors sink deep into their flesh.

"Put me down," Kat hissed in his ear. "You're embarrassing me."

"I'm only doing my job. Remember?" He barreled his way to the curb with a struggling Kat in his arms.

Behind them, cameras clicked faster. Questions came fast and fierce.

"Is this man your bodyguard?"

"Is he FBI?"

"Are you in any danger?"

"For god's sake, put me down!" She pushed at his shoulders but he held fast, not setting her down until they'd reached the vehicle.

Once she was safely inside, he loaded Remy into the kennel. He began rounding the hood but stopped. A familiar face hovered on the edge of the crowd. Was that—? Jesus, it was. Manny—the flower delivery guy. Holding a bouquet of pink roses. If that guy wasn't stalker material, Dayne would eat his left nut.

That's all he needed. A homicidal maniac *and* a stalker to contend with. A strongly worded phone call to the flower shop was at the top of his to-do list.

With Remy no longer a threat, the media horde converged once again. As soon as Dayne closed his door, he cranked the engine, hit the strobes, and gunned the SUV into traffic.

A few blocks away, he flipped off the strobes. The second he did, Kat twisted in her seat, jabbing a finger at him.

"How *dare* you?" Her eyes flashed with enough heated anger to singe the hair off his head. "I've never been so embarrassed in my life."

He met her fury head-on. "At least you're not lying on the steps of your own building with your skull cracked open, because that's exactly what would have happened if I hadn't gotten you out of there."

"You…you…" Color crept up her neck.

"Yeah, I know. Neanderthal." The light turned green. "Buckle up."

"I hate you," she spat. "Right now, I really hate you." She huffed then clicked on her seat belt and crossed her arms.

The hostility in the SUV was hotter than a forest fire and all he could think was that if anyone tried to hurt her, he'd kill them with his bare hands. Not because she was a witness he was assigned to protect. Because he cared about her. More than he should.

"By the way," he added. "In case you didn't notice, you've definitely got a stalker."

Chapter Nineteen

Kat dug her bare toes into the plush rug. The moment they'd returned home, she'd kicked off her heels and sought out the peace and solitude of her home office. For the past two hours, she'd been reviewing business documents, with only Angus for company.

Taking a break, she threw down her pen and sighed. She still thought Manny was harmless but had to agree with Dayne. Him showing up outside her building—with roses, no less—was indeed stalker behavior she could no longer ignore. Dayne had notified the guards not to let Manny onto the property, then he'd called the flower shop to arrange for a different delivery person.

Angus pawed his chew toy, dragging it closer to her desk then flopping onto his side. The puppy would have been glued to Remy, but Dayne had taken his K-9 on patrol outside with the guards. He was probably avoiding her. Not that she could blame the man.

Since telling Dayne she hated him, they hadn't spoken. "Oh my god," she groaned. She couldn't believe she had actually said that. Right on the heels of calling him a Neanderthal. Her behavior had been inexcusable. "He just makes me so angry."

"Who does?" Emily paused in the doorway then came in and sat on a chair.

"Dayne," she admitted, pressing two fingers to her forehead.

"What did he do?" Emily set Kat's scheduler on the desk.

"Nothing. Not really." She stood and walked to the window, staring at the whitecaps dotting the river. "It wasn't his fault. He was only doing his job."

"Then what's the problem?"

When she turned back to Emily, the corners of her friend's mouth lifted. "The problem is, he makes me so angry that I say things to him I've never said to anyone. I just open my mouth and blurt out whatever I feel. Unabridged and inappropriate." And she couldn't stop thinking about him. *Or stop wanting him.*

"Sounds like he's getting to you."

"Exactly." She dropped heavily onto her chair. "When I'm around him, everything I've been taught to keep inside comes bubbling to the surface like a witch's cauldron, and that's the way I behaved today. Like a total witch." *Bitch, more like it.*

"Why do you think that is?" Angus brought Emily his toy and she tossed it to the far side of the office for him to chase.

"I don't know." She stared at her scheduler, not really seeing it.

"I don't mean to go all psycho-babble on you, but sometimes anger is just anger because someone has done you wrong. Other times, people make you angry because you care more about them and what they think of you."

Did she? Care what Dayne thought of her?

Yes. But he couldn't possibly return the sentiment. Not that she'd given him any reason to, lately.

"I know that face." Emily stood. "It's the face of a woman who just figured out the answer to her questions."

"I suppose so. Thank you, Doctor Emily."

"My pleasure. And I won't even charge you a co-payment." They both laughed, easing some of the tension. "Make sure to review your scheduler."

"I will, Em. Bye."

Kat focused on the scheduler and smiled. Today was one of her favorite days of the year. Opening Day at Yankee Stadium. First pitch was at 1:10 p.m.

All those season openers with her parents in their luxury corporate suite overlooking the stadium... Before her mother and father died, it was a family ritual. Six months after burying them, she sold the suite but still watched every season opener on TV.

She flipped the page in her scheduler and frowned. Three weeks from this Saturday's event was her birthday. Colin had planned a big bash in her honor. Celebrating was the last thing she wanted. Amy was dead. Another woman murdered. With everything going on, a party seemed like the height of bad taste, and her heart wasn't in it.

The heaviness in her chest worsened. Given the tone of her last conversation with Colin, maybe he'd cancel the event altogether. It would probably be for the best.

The front door opened then closed again. Angus perked his head up. Remy trotted in and the puppy bounded to the shepherd, licking her face and nipping her legs. Both dogs trotted out, leaving her alone again.

She picked up a gold-plated pen and began tapping it louder and louder on the scheduler. Concentrating was easier said than done. Knowing Dayne was in the house made her tense.

Somehow, she managed to review documents Emily had left for her, and before she knew it thirty minutes had gone by. It was now 1:05 p.m. Five minutes before first pitch.

She closed the scheduler and went into the living room. The TV was already on and tuned to the game. Dayne stood in front of the kitchen island. "I see you found the big screen."

A smile lit his face. "I did, and it's kick-ass."

She knew that smile wasn't directed at her but rather at the giant 80-inch flat-screen TV normally hidden away in a specially made mahogany credenza. When fully extended, the massive screen took up half the wall. Still, that smile made her belly flutter.

A wonderful scent filled the air. *Cookies?* She followed the heavenly smell into the kitchen, unable to contain the shock in her voice. "You bake?"

Dayne gave her a wry look. "I told you I have hidden talents." He pulled a tray from the oven and set it on the cooktop. "My mother—Renee—taught Lily and I how to bake. It was one of the first things she did with us after we got adopted. Helped us all to bond. Nothing fancy, mostly cookies, brownies, cakes, and pies."

"Nothing fancy? That's quite an accomplishment." She leaned over the cookie rack and inhaled. "They smell amazing. Chocolate chip?"

He nodded. "Yep. Mom said every chef needs a good chipper recipe."

"Francine tried teaching me to bake." She scrunched up her face at the memory of her very blackened, very failed attempt at making brownies. "It didn't take."

"My baking is adequate." Using a spatula, he transferred the cookies to a cooling rack. "Lily's skills are out of bounds."

"Her cake last night was decadent. I'll be having chocolate mousse dreams for weeks." He slathered one side of a cookie with frosting then sandwiched it with another. "You made frosting, too?" Her mouth watered. She dug her finger into the bowl then licked off the fluffy white icing, closing her eyes and moaning. "That's good. *Really* good."

She opened her eyes. Dayne stared at her finger then licked his lips and swallowed. "Uh. Yeah. Thanks," he muttered, and went back to slapping more cookie sandwiches together.

It was brief, but there was no missing the unspoken heat and emotion in his eyes. She'd felt it, too. That attraction, magnetic pull, or whatever it was that hung between them and refused to go away no matter how much they denied it.

He took his plate and a tall glass of milk into the living room then sat on the sofa and turned up the volume. "I hope you don't mind if I watch in here. Your 80-incher is too good to waste."

"Not at all." Considering her rude behavior earlier, it was the least she could do. "As long as you don't mind if I join you." She followed him and sat on the other side of the sofa.

His brows rose. "You're a baseball fan?"

"Not just a baseball fan. A *Yankees* fan." She paused at the look of skepticism on his face. "What, girls aren't allowed to like baseball?"

"I didn't say that." He bit off half a cookie sandwich and chewed. "I'm just surprised," he said around a mouthful of cookie.

"Well, don't be." She proceeded to tell him of her family's opening-day tradition.

"Luxury suite, huh?" He arched a brow.

"Yes, but I sold it."

His face contorted. "Why?"

"It was something we shared as a family. After my parents died, it wasn't the same without them."

He watched her for a moment, saying nothing. "That sounds like a nice tradition. I've only been in one of those suites once. I felt like I'd died and gone to baseball heaven."

She reached for a cookie, but he snatched the plate away.

"Get your own. These are mine."

She counted quickly. "All *ten* cookie sandwiches are yours?"

"I need my snacks. I'm a big boy." He shoved another cookie into his mouth, washing it down with a gulp of milk.

Yes, you are. He'd rolled his dress shirtsleeves to just below his elbows, exposing thick, flexing forearms. Instead of ogling him, she should be thankful they were talking again. Otherwise, living under the same roof until this was over would be a living, breathing hell.

"You're not serious about hoarding all those cookies," she chided. "Are you?"

He took a deep breath. "I'll let you have some on one condition."

She crossed her arms. "What's that?"

Humor twinkled in his eyes. "You fix the next batch."

"Deal. Now hand them over." She held out her hand and he presented her with the plate. After carefully selecting the two biggest cookie sandwiches, she placed her bare feet on the coffee table.

"Is that a tradition, too?" He indicated her feet.

She nodded enthusiastically as more of the tension between them eased. "You're welcome to join me."

"Don't mind if I do." He shucked his shoes and stretched out his long legs, carefully setting his feet on the table.

Kat nearly choked on the cookie she'd been chewing. The New York Yankees team emblem was printed on the sides of his socks. "Seriously?"

He shrugged. "This is *my* tradition."

"I can see that." And his feet were h-u-g-e, *huge*. "What size shoe do you wear?" The disparity between their feet was comical. His were nearly three inches longer and twice as wide.

"Lucky thirteen. You?"

"Lucky seven."

A uniformed member of the New York City Police Department belted out the national anthem, then the first pitch was thrown.

By the seventh inning stretch, they were on the edge of their seats—*literally*. The score was three-three after a controversial call that resulted in the Boston Red Sox tying the game.

"Did you *see* that?" Kat shouted, pointing to the screen. "That ump needs glasses. The runner was *so* out at first it's not funny."

Dayne nodded. "That ump makes more controversial calls than any other umpire in the league."

She fell back against the sofa and crossed her arms. "I should have him fired."

He chuckled. "You have that much pull?"

"I'd be willing to assert my influence. It's a matter of principle."

"That it is." He held up his hand, palm out for her to smack, which she did in mutual agreement.

The brief contact sent tingles of awareness shooting up her arm. Awareness she didn't want to feel. She stood, raising her arms over her head. "Time for the stretch." Dayne didn't move. His gaze was fastened on her breasts. Quickly, she lowered her arms and sat, grabbing another cookie to take her mind off thinking about him, too. It didn't help. Not when he looked at her that way.

"Tell me about Chad."

Kat froze in mid-chew. She finished chewing then swallowed. The cookie *and* the latent anger and humiliation. "There's not much to tell. He's my ex-boyfriend."

"I know that. But how long has it been?"

"About a month. We broke up a few hours before you and I first met at the Haven. At least, that's when I found out from Penny that he dumped me. Later that day, I read about it in the tabloids. One of my maids overheard the conversation and sold it for three hundred dollars."

"Ouch." He grimaced.

"Yes, ouch." Thankfully, the raw, aching pain had finally disappeared. "That's why I have such a small staff. I didn't want eyes and ears on me all the time, so that same day, I fired everyone I didn't trust."

"Understandable." He nodded. "Why did you break up?"

"He discovered that in order to marry me he'd have to sign a prenuptial agreement." *There.* She'd said it, and it felt good to unload.

Dayne's features tightened. "The man's a fool for letting you get away."

"Actually, he did me a favor. He only wanted my money. Like I said, it's kind of a recurring problem for me."

"I'll bet it is." Again, he nodded, but there was sincerity and understanding in his eyes.

She clasped her hands, staring at them. "I think what upset me most was that I would have given him anything he wanted. Anything."

"Do you still love him?"

The answer came to her with incredible clarity. "I don't think I ever did, or I wouldn't have gotten over him so quickly. I think I just wanted someone to love and marry. It's important to me. I want to have children but not with someone who doesn't love me back." She gave a self-deprecating laugh. "You probably think that's silly and naive."

"No. I don't." He took a deep inhale and let it out. "The day I got accepted into the FBI academy, I went out and bought a ring for my girlfriend. An engagement ring. I was excited to share the good news and tell her that I wanted her with me wherever I got stationed."

The young woman in the now crumpled photo. *Brit.* "I take it things didn't work out."

He grunted. "She was excited by the diamond ring, all right. Not about me becoming an FBI agent."

"Why not? I would be proud if the man I loved worked for the FBI." *Whoops.* Heat flooded her face. She hadn't meant her words to come out quite like that.

"Thanks, but she definitely wasn't proud. She expected me to go to medical school then join her father's orthopedic practice and make the big bucks of a surgeon so she could live in style. What *I* thought was happy news wound up being the very thing that split us up."

"I'm sorry." His iron-hard jaw tightened, leaving her wondering if... "Do you still love her?"

"God no." He laughed bitterly. "I just felt stupid for not seeing her for what she was."

"A gold-digging bitch?" As Lily had indicated last night.

The corners of his mouth lifted. "I guess we have more in common than we realized. The Yankees *and* people wanting to marry us for our money."

"Who knew?" Kat grabbed another cookie sandwich, touching it to his in a mock toast. *A cookie toast.* "Here's to finding the right person."

"The right fiscally *responsible* person."

They laughed and bit into their cookies. A gob of icing squirted onto her lower lip.

"Kat." Using his finger, he swiped off the frosting before it fell onto her shirt. As he licked his finger, his gaze met hers and he swallowed.

Kat's heart raced. *There it is again.* So much heat and emotion pouring off him, she could feel it straight through her blouse. *Kiss me. Kiss me, dammit.*

He leaned in closer until their mouths were inches apart.

Her heart pounded faster. If he didn't kiss her soon she'd go up in flames.

His lips grazed hers, softly at first then with more pressure. He urged her mouth open, and *oh yes. Finally.* When their tongues met, need spiked in her blood. She wanted to touch him but was afraid this was some kind of magic spell and one wrong move would shatter the moment.

Still not touching her with his hands, he deepened the kiss and it was all she could do not to groan into his mouth. He tasted of sugar, chocolate, and vanilla. The unhurried way his tongue danced with hers was more sensual than the first time they'd kissed. That kiss had been fast and furious and more about easing their grief. Then, they'd barely known each other. This time was completely different. Now they were just two people who liked and wanted each other.

With a groan, he pulled away. *No,* she wanted to scream. The look on his face mimicked what he'd said to her in the library last week: *You're a witness. My job is to protect you, not… make love to you.* He hadn't said those words then, and he didn't now. He didn't have to.

His chest expanded as he took a deep breath. "I really should take the dogs out." He shoved his feet into his shoes and headed for the door. The dogs joined him, and a moment later she was alone.

All the energy bled from her body. She sank to the sofa and grabbed one of the fluffy, frilly-fringed pillows, holding it to her chest. They were standing on either side of an emotional boundary, looking over the edge at something that could have dire consequences. He'd set that boundary. *To keep me safe.* It was a line he couldn't—or *wouldn't*—cross.

Would getting involved really undermine his ability to protect her? He seemed to think so. *Maybe it's* my *priorities that are messed up.*

Kat dug her nails deeper into the pillow. Life was a

precious gift, and someone out there wanted to end hers.

Dayne and the dogs charged back inside. "Are you sure it's him?" he said into the cell pressed to his ear. "When did he get there?"

Kat shot to her feet, tracking Dayne as he paced the foyer, looking grim. She threw the pillow to the sofa and moved closer. Whoever he was talking to, the news wasn't good. That seemed to be a recurring theme in her life.

He ended the call and slammed his phone onto the table. "Clarkstown PD found Jonathan Bale's car. Bale wasn't in it."

"Who was?" She half expected him to say they'd found another dead body.

"His girlfriend. She was on her way to visit Bale. He checked himself into rehab. A month ago, and he's still there."

Which meant Bale couldn't have killed Rebecca or Amy. Which meant…

The real killer was still out there.

Chapter Twenty

The things I do in the line of duty.

The brand-new monkey suit Dayne wore felt like a straitjacket and not because it didn't fit right. It was probably the best-fitting suit he'd ever worn. But wearing it—he was a fraud, an imposter trying to blend in someplace he didn't belong.

Remy lay in front of the fireplace then sat up to watch. Her jaws cracked and when she began panting, he could swear his dog was laughing at him.

The gate bell chimed, then his cell vibrated with two incoming texts. One from Kade, telling him they'd be here in twenty seconds, and another from the outside guard, informing him two vehicles were passing through the gates.

Kade had texted him earlier to say he needed to make a few adjustments to the security system and that he'd bring along some "company."

A moment later, someone pounded on the door. Remy barked and bolted to the foyer. When Dayne opened the door, five sets of eyes went as wide as silver dollars.

Kade, Markus, Jaime, Eric, and Eric's fiancée, Tess, gaped at him. For a full five seconds, no one said a word. Then the snarky comments flew at breakneck speed.

"Yo, double-oh-seven. You gonna let us in?"

"Heading to the prom?"

"He looks like a giant penguin."

"Bond. James Bond. Shaken, not stirred."

Tess pushed past his friends and stood on her tiptoes to drop a kiss on his cheek. "I think you look *very* handsome."

"Thank you, Tess." Dayne still felt like a complete dork. He gave Tess a quick hug then released her and stood aside to let his friends in. "One of you want to tell me what you're all doing here?"

"We were in the neighborhood." Eric shook Dayne's hand then clapped him on the shoulder. "Tess wanted to go antiquing in the area, so here we are." The groan in his friend's voice was accompanied by a sappy grin the man had been wearing since the day Tess blew back into his life.

He held back his laughter. Eric loved antiquing about as much as a dog loved fleas, but he absolutely adored Tess and would do anything for her. Since buying his fiancée a little store in Flemington, New Jersey, she'd been dragging Eric everywhere to shop for crafts, antiques, and all kinds of trinkets to stock the place with.

"The rest of us," Jaime said, crouching to ruffle Remy's ears, "are here to help Kade tweak the new system. Then we're ordering in from the Clausland Tavern for pizza."

Dayne's mouth watered. The Clausland Tavern made the best pizza around, and he wished he could join his friends. It would be a whole lot better than the snooty food he'd be getting at the gala tonight.

He held out his hand to Markus, who stood silent and grim off to the side. Something had been eating at the man since he'd shown up two years ago with one helluva deep cut on his forehead. One day, Markus would talk about it. *Bad things happen when a man keeps heavy shit bottled up inside.*

A sharp yip came from the second floor, followed by tiny puppy feet scampering down the stairs.

"Angus, my man." Jaime scooped up the puppy, letting Angus lick him a few times before holding the wriggling puppy out to Markus. "Here. You haven't been kissed in a while."

The hint of a smile curved Markus's lips as he took the pup from Jaime and let Angus clean his chin.

High heels clicked as Kat glided down the stairs into the foyer, looking so regal and so incredibly beautiful Dayne was struck utterly dumb. For the last four days, he'd tried not to think about kissing her again. Since then, they'd avoided each other as much as possible and barely spoken. Now he couldn't talk even if he wanted to.

Her rich chestnut hair was pulled back into a cluster of curls, and as she turned to greet his friends, the glittery clip in her hair shimmered like jewels. Her gown was just as glittery, reminding him of pale pink champagne. Tiny sleeves fell just off her shoulders, displaying the graceful curves of her upper arms and shoulders and making him want to kiss every inch of exposed skin.

The dress's neckline dipped to a deep vee, stopping just short of baring the tops of her breasts, while the rest of the gown hugged her torso and hips, flaring at the bottom in pink waves. Dayne hadn't known his mouth hung open until Eric's hand beneath his chin nudged it shut.

"You look amazing," Tess said.

"Thank you." Kat gave Tess a quick hug. "How's Rosie doing? Are she and Tiger still getting along well?"

"You should see them together." Tess whipped out her phone and pulled up pics Dayne had already seen of Eric's Dutch Shepherd K-9, Tiger, and the pretty Australian sheepdog-shepherd Tess had adopted from the Haven.

Kat shifted to look at the phone, and *holy hell*. He'd thought the front of her dress was eye-catching. *I'm doomed.*

The back of the dress draped—no, make that *swooped*—teasingly low to just above her waist, leaving most of her back exposed. All that smooth, creamy skin called to him like an ice cream cone to a kid on a 95-degree day. He wanted to lick every last inch. Someone gulped, and damned if it wasn't *him*.

Jaime unclipped his cell and began snapping shots of Dayne. "I gotta send these to Nick and Matt."

Kade and Eric joined in, and the air filled with the snapping clicks of cell phone cameras.

Dayne gritted his teeth so hard they squeaked. "Knock. It. Off."

Kat stepped closer, massaging her chin as she examined the tux. "Something is a bit off. I wonder…" She pulled open the right side of the jacket, exposing his Glock. "Must you really wear this dastardly weapon of death? It ruins the cut."

He shot her an unwavering stare. "I really must."

She released the jacket. "Touchy this evening, aren't we?"

Tess giggled. "That, he is."

"Buddy, you look so hot right now, *I'd* do you." Jaime held up his phone and snapped another shot.

"Knock it off, Romeo." Markus gave Jaime's bicep a none-too-easy punch, and Dayne shot his friend a look of gratitude.

Eric smirked. "He is pretty, though, isn't he?"

"Fuck all of you," Dayne snapped.

"Dayne, really," Kat admonished, but from the hint of a smile spreading on her face, she wasn't offended in the slightest. "Hmm." She tapped her finger on her chin and began circling him, eventually stopping behind him. When she tugged at the hem of his jacket, her fingers grazed the top of his ass. A lightning bolt of sensation shot down the backs of his legs, then up the front to— Dammit all to hell, they had an audience.

Her hands released his jacket and he exhaled a breath of relief. That was, until she came to stand directly in front of him. Things were about to get worse. Even her flowery perfume was making him hornier than a rhinoceros in a rose garden.

He tried focusing on anything besides the way she smelled. Or the way her dress dipped torturously low toward her softly mounded breasts.

Tiny pink gemstones sparkled at her ears and from a thin gold chain around her neck. The tips of her toes—painted light pink—peaked out from delicate gold sandals. *Yeah, focus on her toes.*

Again, not working. Even the woman's toes were sexy.

Kat rested her hands on his shoulders then smoothed them down the front of his jacket. "This looks good." He swallowed, hard, as his slacks tightened painfully over his dick. Luckily, she blocked everyone else's view.

When her hands parted the sides of his jacket and her eyes dipped to his waist, a bead of sweat trickled between his shoulder blades. As she skimmed the tips of her fingers along the front of his cummerbund, flames licked at his balls.

"Kat, no!" He grabbed her wrists, holding them away. "The tux is fine." He could barely choke out the words as he struggled for control. Of his libido *and* his emotions. Where she was concerned, both were inextricably entwined.

Her eyes were questioning at first then she looked down— at his giant, throbbing boner.

Her cheeks flushed, and her eyes flared with awareness of what she'd unwittingly initiated.

"Yeah. We're done here." Releasing her wrists, he spun and stalked away to cool his jets in the bathroom.

When the door shut behind him, he went straight to the sink and cranked on the tap. He cupped his hands and splashed cold water in his face.

Time to face undeniable, scary-as-shit facts.

He wanted her like nobody's business, and it wasn't just about sex. It was about—*more*. She was getting to him. Hell, she'd already gotten to him. But getting involved with her could have dire consequences and not just because being around her messed with his head.

His feelings for her went way beyond a one-night stand or even a brief fling. What worried him was the long run. Could they really fit into each other's worlds?

His guts twisted at the thought of never seeing her again when this was over. If he didn't stay clear of the trigger that would set them off, they could both wind up burned and bleeding, with their hearts cut into tiny pieces.

Chapter Twenty-One

"Ready?" Kat asked as the limousine braked in front of her twenty-two-story building on Madison Avenue—a subsidiary Vandenburg Enterprises location with a banquet-ballroom on the top floor.

Dayne sat across from her, staring through the tinted windows at the throng of reporters gathered on either side of the red carpet leading to the main entrance. A slight frown downturned his lips—lips she sorely wanted to kiss her again, but she didn't dare test those boundaries. Nearly five days had passed since then, and he hadn't touched her. It was as if someone had flipped a switch. Funny, how she'd been determined not to get more personal with him. Now it was all she thought about.

"Vultures," he grumbled.

Subtle, fresh cologne filled the limo. While she'd been examining his tuxedo at the castle, she'd breathed in the same scent. He was so strikingly handsome in the tux, so broad-shouldered and sexy her breath hitched. The same as when she'd seen the erection straining behind his slacks.

Emotionally, he didn't want her. Apparently his body never got the message. Just thinking about it made her skin hot and her gown feel like it was smothering her.

He reached for the handle, not opening the door. "Give me a few seconds to look around."

She nodded and slipped on her pink silk wrap.

He stepped out, and cameras flashed. Most of the reporters still didn't know who Dayne was, but they saw what she saw—an extremely authoritative-looking man whose raw good looks would turn heads. So they took his photo anyway.

Seconds later, he held out his hand. His fingers closed around hers as he assisted her onto the runner. More cameras flashed, one after the other. She pasted on her smiling, public face, preparing for the inevitable and repetitive questions.

"Miss Vandenburg, is this your date for the evening?"

"Who is he?"

"What's your name, sir? Are you an FBI agent?"

"Miss Vandenburg, is it true someone tried to kill you?"

Yes, she wanted to scream. Then a microphone appeared in front of her face, so close to her nose she flinched. Dayne knocked it away, then his arm came around her shoulders and he ushered her quickly to the front door.

As soon as they were inside, he cut loose with a string of fascinating words she'd never heard before, finishing with, "I still don't know how you put up with those animals."

She patted his arm then placed her hand in the crook of his elbow. "You get used to it."

"Maybe *you* do." He guided her to the elevators where a building security officer held one open for them. "That's something I could never get used to."

Emptiness filled her soul because that was something any man would *have* to get used to. If they wanted to be a lasting part of her life.

The elevator whisked them to the top floor. The doors

parted, and they were greeted by orchestra music, laughter, and the clinking of fine crystal. An enormous chandelier, hand-picked by her mother, hung over the floor where nearly fifty couples danced.

As soon as she handed her wrap to the coat-check person, Dayne leaned closer. "How long do we have to stay?"

"Unfortunately, too long. This is *my* charity gala, so it would be rude and inappropriate for me to leave early." Although it would have been nice to stay home with Dayne's friends, especially Tess. She and Eric's fiancée were about the same age, and when Tess came to the Haven a month ago to pick out a dog, Kat had liked the other woman and wanted to get to know her better.

Worried he'd bolt, she tightened her hand around Dayne's arm. He might not be anything more than her bodyguard, but she was proud he was her "date" for the evening. Even if it wasn't a real date.

A waiter appeared, holding out a silver tray loaded with slim, delicately cut champagne flutes. "Thank you." She accepted a flute, and when Dayne didn't take one, she handed him her glass and took another from the tray. "Drink it," she said when the waiter moved off. "You're too stiff." She held back a snort. He certainly had been earlier. *Stiff, that is.*

"I'm on duty."

"You're *always* on duty. Try breaking the rules this once. It might make you feel better to have a little drink."

"I don't drink champagne."

Aside from that one beer at his parents' house, she'd never seen him drink alcohol. "Do you drink anything other than beer?" She guided them to the far side of the ballroom where Senator Graham chatted with several other wealthy New York businessmen. All wore tuxedos, but none held a candle to her *date*.

"Occasionally, scotch."

She held up her champagne flute, signaling to a nearby waiter who sprinted over. "Yes, Miss Vandenburg."

"Please find Mr. Andrews some of that Chivas Regal Royal Salute. The fifty-year-old bottle."

"*Fifty?*" Dayne's brows shot to his hairline.

She rolled her lips inward, trying not to giggle at the shock on his face. "Technically, it's pushing seventy years old now. The Chivas brothers bottled it in 1953 as a tribute to Queen Elizabeth II on the day of her coronation. There were only two hundred and fifty-five bottles vinted."

"Would you like ice, sir?" the waiter asked.

Dayne made a scoffing sound. "Neat," he said, and when the waiter disappeared in search of the Royal Salute, added, "No self-respecting scotch drinker would dare water down liquid gold with ice." He deftly deposited his champagne flute on another passing waiter's tray.

"There are people I'd like to introduce you to." She took his arm and serpentined through the couples milling about, stopping occasionally when one of the hired photographers took their picture.

"That's another thing," Dayne said. "Do you ever get tired of having your picture taken?"

"Hazards of the job." On the other side of the ballroom, Colin stood with Penny, Elaina, Nat, and that wretched Crystal Lockwood. She gave a slight twist of her lips. One look at that woman was enough to make the air go sour.

"See someone you don't like?"

"Does it show that much?" When had he come to read her thoughts so well?

"It does." He squeezed her hand, making her realize how much she missed his touch. "Don't worry. I don't think anyone else can see it."

"That's a relief." Since birth, she'd been carefully schooled in the art of masking her dislike for someone, especially at charity events. Even the truly detestable wrote sizeable checks.

They joined a group of three older men in their sixties. "Senator Graham." She kissed the senator on the cheek. "It's always an honor to have you at one of our events."

He smiled down at her, reminding Kat of why she truly liked him. For a high-powered state representative, his warmth was genuine. "Katrina, it's an honor to be invited. You look lovely as always."

"Thank you, John. I'd like to introduce you to Dayne Andrews."

"Senator," Dayne said as the two men shook hands.

Next, Kat introduced the other men. "This is Charles Worthington, CEO of Worthington Consolidated. And Max Rocher, owner of Rocher Industries." Dayne shook their hands.

"What do you do, son?" Senator Graham asked.

Beside her, Dayne tensed. "I'm an FBI agent."

The senator's face lit up. "What fascinating work that must be. I'll bet it keeps you on your toes."

"That it does." The tension ebbed from Dayne's body, leaving her wondering if he'd expected to be ridiculed because of his occupation.

"What kinds of cases do you work on?" Charles Worthington asked.

"It depends. I'm a K-9 agent, so I get assigned to a lot of search-and-rescue operations. Occasionally, I work on homicides, bank robberies, and terrorism investigations."

"K-9?" Max Rocher's brows knitted. "So your partner is a dog?"

Dayne grinned. "She is, and she's the best partner I ever had."

They all laughed, and Kat smiled up at him with a smug look intended to convey: *See, you fit in better than you expected.*

"Did I just hear your partner is a dog?" Senator Graham's wife, Betty, slipped her arm around her husband's waist.

Kat's heart squeezed at the affectionate gesture. Forty years of marriage and they still loved each other.

The waiter who'd taken her order for the Chivas Royal Salute arrived with a cut crystal tumbler containing an inch of gold liquid. "Sir, your scotch."

Dayne took the glass then held it up to the light, turning it around in his hand before taking a sip, then smiling like she'd never seen him smile before. "So this is what I've been missing all my life."

"Is that the fifty-year-old Salute?" Senator Graham pointed to Dayne's glass.

"It is." Kat nodded.

"Well, son. You must be someone very special to our Katrina. She doesn't whip out a ten-thousand-dollar bottle for just anyone."

That was true. Even her father rarely passed it around when he was alive. With Dayne, she hadn't thought twice about it.

Dayne choked. Clearly, he'd had no idea what that bottle cost.

Charlie gave him a few pats on the back. "Don't waste any of it. Enjoy every last drop."

Dayne chuckled. "I'll do that."

For the next ten minutes, Kat listened while the older men threw question after question at Dayne about his cases, funding for federal law enforcement, the FBI budget… Each time, he answered intelligently and articulately. Even Betty Graham seemed fascinated, and a few other couples had joined their circle to listen in.

Kat took in the strong lines of Dayne's profile, admiring the easy, natural way he had with these old bastions of industry and politics.

From the corner of her eye, she caught sight of another couple she wanted to introduce Dayne to. "If you'll excuse us, I'd like to introduce Dayne to the mayor and his wife."

"It was a pleasure to meet you." He shook hands with the senator, Charlie, and Max, as if he'd known them for years.

She started to guide Dayne toward the mayor when Betty Graham touched her on the arm, pulling her down to whisper, "He's quite handsome, and a hunk, too." Betty winked before walking off.

Heat crept into her face. *Yes, I know.*

The grin on Dayne's face was more of a smirk.

"Heard that, did you?"

"Yep. Handsome, huh? And, a hunk, too."

"Maybe a little," she admitted, averting her face so he wouldn't see how affected she was by Betty's comment. "You're a natural at this."

"I wouldn't say that," he muttered.

Unexpectedly, she was thoroughly enjoying the evening. Despite the tension still lingering between them.

The mayor of New York City was a few inches shorter than Dayne but had the presence of royalty. In a way, he was. The duly elected ruler of The Big Apple.

"Mayor D'Amici, Mrs. D'Amici, I'd like to introduce Dayne Andrews."

"Special Agent Andrews." The mayor clasped Dayne's hand, shaking it exuberantly. "Good to see you, again."

This time it was *her* brows that shot to her hairline. She had no idea Dayne knew the mayor.

"What a pleasure." Fran D'Amici extended her exquisitely French manicured fingers for Dayne to clasp. A tiny spurt of jealousy hit Kat. For her, a perfect manicure wouldn't last two days. Not with all the dog care she did.

"Are you here without your beautiful partner?" the

mayor asked.

"Sadly," Dayne said, "dogs are generally frowned on at charity balls."

"Nonsense." Fran waved a dismissive hand. "We love dogs as much as Kat does. You should have brought her."

"From what I recall, your partner is smarter than many of the people here tonight." The mayor chortled loudly.

"When did you all meet before?" Kat looked from Fran and the mayor to Dayne.

"Last year," he said, "I assisted on a protection detail at City Hall. Our paths crossed a few times."

"Tony absolutely loves dogs." Fran patted her husband's arm.

"Yes, I know." Kat smiled warmly at the mayor. "The Canine Haven is grateful for your generous contributions."

"Excuse me, Mr. Mayor, Mrs. D'Amici." Colin's voice came from directly behind them, and Kat cringed inwardly. After their last awkward conversation, she'd hoped to avoid him most of the night. "I see you've met Katrina's bodyguard. The FBI agent," he added with a subtle sneer in his tone.

Kat gripped the champagne flute tighter, annoyed by Colin's condescending manner.

"Yes," Fran said, briefly resting her hand on Dayne's upper arm. "We've actually met before, and he's still as charming and handsome as ever."

Kat sent the mayor's wife a grateful smile at her show of support. Even Fran had picked up on Colin's snotty attitude.

"Yes, well." Colin cleared his throat, clearly not expecting to have his attempt at undermining Dayne so bluntly rebuffed. "I need to steal Katrina away for a moment."

Kat bit back a frosty reply. She didn't want to leave Dayne's side. Not because he couldn't handle himself. He could and most definitely was. But she was enjoying his company. As much as Colin deserved to be shot down, it would be rude of her to say no.

Colin clasped her hand, tugging her toward the dance floor. Along the way, he took the champagne flute from her and thrust it at a waitress, sloshing some of the contents on the young woman's uniform. "Take this."

The orchestra played the *Prelude to the Sound of Music*, one of her favorite songs. Colin swung her into his arms, and when they were far enough away from where Dayne eyed them over the mayor's head, she ground her teeth then lit into him. "That was uncalled for. Dayne *and* the waitress."

He swung her around again. "Bringing that agent here as your escort was uncalled for. This afternoon I called to confirm I was picking you up today. Someone named Kade answered and told me you'd already gone. With that FBI agent."

"You and I never had plans to go together." She flexed her fingers, forcing him to ease up on his tight hold.

"I logically assumed we would." His eyes blazed. "We *always* go to these things together."

"You shouldn't have made that assumption. Despite our conversation the other day, we are *not* a couple and never have been."

His eyes softened. "I want to change that. Then you won't need him hanging around. You'll have *me*. He doesn't fit in here, and he doesn't belong here with you. *I* do."

"You're wrong." Rage raced through her body, and the heat creeping to her face had nothing to do with Colin's closeness or any sort of passion. "He fits in just fine. In fact, he's got better manners than you at the moment."

"You don't mean that." He tugged her closer so their chests touched.

When she looked into his face it was like staring into the eyes of a stranger. Why had she tolerated his obnoxious behavior for so many years? Because he was one of the few people who didn't want her for her money.

She'd rather have no one than put up with him anymore. Viewing her life from Dayne's perspective had changed *hers*.

Over Colin's shoulder, she glimpsed Dayne standing in the middle of several pretty women vying for his attention. Even as he said something that made them all laugh, he tracked her and Colin around the dance floor.

"Katrina? *Katrina?*" Colin hissed. "If you'd stop drooling over your bodyguard for a minute, you'd see the man you're supposed to be with is right here in front of you."

"No, Colin. He's not." With dozens of couples staring at them, she jerked her hand from his and walked away. Her hands trembled. She may have just permanently alienated a man who'd been her friend for most of her life. *Did I do the right thing?* If she didn't, it was too late now.

As she neared the group of women milling around Dayne like a harem, including Elaina, Penny, and Nat, one voice rose above the others. A voice she detested.

Crystal Lockwood.

The daughter of one of the most powerful Wall Street investment bankers was, to put it mildly, an untrustworthy, backstabbing b-i-t-c-h. *There. I said it.* Well, thought it, anyway. The woman had always been horrid, and she wondered who Crystal was venting her bitchiness on this time. It was a shame that she and her father were on every socialite invitee list in the city.

Kat paused behind Penny and the other women, trying unsuccessfully to see over their heads at whom Crystal was shouting.

"That is *the* ickiest celery-green dress I've ever seen," Penny said. "It reminds me of vomit."

Kat had to agree. And with every move and shake of her arms, Crystal's unrestrained breasts jiggled and threatened to make a guest appearance from the frighteningly low-cut dress.

Elaina snickered. "She must be wearing a quarter inch of pancake on her face, and those false eyelashes are long enough to trip over."

Nat shook her head. "Someone really needs to tell her that shade of blond exists nowhere in nature. It makes her look like a banshee."

That seemed a little harsh, even to Kat. *But it's so true!* The way she viewed her world really had changed in the last two weeks.

She touched Penny's shoulder. "What's going on?" The orchestra continued playing, but more people had abandoned their conversations and were gathering around.

"Katrina!" Crystal squealed as she rushed forward and curled her fingers around Kat's forearm. "There must be a mistake with the invitation list. Apparently, you'll let *anyone* in these days."

Behind Crystal, Dayne's jaw went harder than diamonds. His eyes flared with barely controlled fury and a muscle ticked in his cheek. The grip on his scotch glass was so tight, the tips of his fingers whitened, and she half expected the glass to shatter. He'd thrust his other hand into his pants pocket. From the visible bulge, it was clenched into a fist. There was only word to describe his overall demeanor. *Dangerous.*

Everyone crowding around them alternately shifted their attention from Crystal to Dayne. To their credit, the orchestra didn't miss a beat.

"This man"—Crystal jutted her chin in Dayne's direction—"is nothing but a thief. Not even an expensive tuxedo can hide the dirty little street urchin you really are and always will be."

"What's going on here?" The mayor had come to stand beside Dayne, as had Senator Graham, Charlie Worthington, and Max Rocher.

A veritable show of support, although Kat still didn't understand what was happening.

"I'll tell you what's going on. Our little Katrina is slumming it this evening." Crystal's words dripped with venom. "Still trying to be something you're not, I see." The last barb was aimed directly at Dayne, who stood frozen like a statue.

Green eyes as dark and furious as she'd ever seen them glared at Crystal. His lips pressed together tightly. The only part of his body moving at all was his jaw as it repeatedly clenched and unclenched.

"Dayne?" She extricated her arm from Crystal's claws and went to him. "What on earth is she talking about?"

The room went absolutely silent. Even the orchestra stopped playing, which was just as well since everyone on the dance floor had stopped dancing to witness the unfolding drama.

"Why ask *me*? I'm only a dirty little street urchin." Undisguised challenge lit his eyes, and the anger radiating off his body was hotter than a furnace.

"Crystal?" She turned to the other woman. "Let's go and discuss whatever this is about in private."

Ignoring the suggestion, Crystal crossed her arms, plumping up her barely concealed breasts. "This man stole a valuable family heirloom from me. You should toss him out on his ass. Better yet, call the police." Two security officers materialized from the shadows. Large, hulking brutes, although Dayne could probably flatten them with one hand tied behind his back.

Slowly, she turned to face Dayne. This had to be a mistake.

His voice was low and controlled. "It's your party."

He's testing me, but why?

Clearly, something had transpired between Dayne and

Crystal. Knowing Dayne, she couldn't imagine him having anything to do with someone like her.

Lily's words came back to her in a flash: *You, brother dear would probably still be in jail*. The story he didn't want told.

Kat fisted her hands. Something deep inside her brain snapped as loudly as a dry twig. *Crystal is lying*. The truth of it flared as brightly as the chandelier over their heads.

This *was* her party, and she wasn't about to let the likes of Crystal Lockwood ruin it, and she certainly wasn't about to let that creature dishonor a man she'd come to respect and admire as much as her own father. She stalked toward Crystal, her breasts heaving as she reined in the urge to do what she really wanted. Slap the woman's face. Kat had never liked her. No one did. Only her father's wealth and notoriety had protected her all these years. In reality, Crystal was the lowlife, and it was high time someone told her so.

Protocol be damned.

"This *man*"—she pointed to Dayne—"has more honor in a single hair on his head than you have in your entire body." Her voice shook but she was on a roll. Not even the shocked look on everyone's faces deterred her in the slightest. Not even Colin's. "Everyone knows you're nothing but a sniveling, lying, spoiled brat who'll do anything to get attention."

Crystal's jaw dropped.

A few snickers floated around the room, followed by Penny's voice. "You tell her," then Elaina's. "It's about time someone told that bitch off."

From the corner of her eye, Kat noticed a few cell phones held high to capture the moment. Her mother would be appalled, but it was too late to stop this train from speeding down the track.

"Well, I never!" Crystal parked her hands on her hips, and in doing so, one of her distended nipples popped out from the edge of her dress.

Kat smiled sweetly. "Well now you have." Most of the guests who'd been standing near Crystal had wisely stepped away.

"Kat," Dayne warned. "You don't have to do this."

"No, I *really* do. Pardon me," she said to a nearby guest, "may I borrow this?" She reached for their champagne flute and tossed the contents in Crystal's face.

The other woman's head dipped, taking in the pale-gold liquid dripping down her cleavage, darkening the edges of her dress. "How dare you!" she sputtered then lunged for Kat, screaming, "Why you—"

Dayne's arm shot out. He flattened his palm dead center in Crystal's chest, shoving her back. Only the guests standing directly behind her prevented Crystal from falling off her four-inch stilettos.

Cell phone flashes popped in her peripheral vision. *Sorry, Mother.* This was bound to make the front page of several high-profile newspapers.

Colin shoved through the crowd. "Katrina, have you lost your mind?"

"Actually, I'm only just regaining it." And it felt darned good.

Dayne had insinuated himself between her and Crystal, who'd begun readjusting her breasts and practically begging for support from those around her. To no avail, Kat was gratified to see.

His eyes danced with amusement and his lips quirked. He canted his head to Crystal. "What do you want me to do with her?"

"Nothing." She grinned. "This time, *I've got this.*" Her grin spread as he flashed her a brilliant white smile. She raised her arm and snapped her fingers. The two security officers rushed in.

"Please escort this…*woman* from the premises. Put her

in whatever conveyance she arrived in—cab, Uber, bicycle, broomstick—and be sure to put it on my tab."

"Yes, ma'am," one of the guards answered, then both men grabbed Crystal's upper arms and dragged her backward to the elevators.

More cell phones flashed. Half the room applauded and cheered. Kat ignored them all, preferring instead to bask in the glow of Dayne's warm gaze and brilliant smile.

Chapter Twenty-Two

Holy hellfire.

When Katrina Vandenburg stepped outside her comfort zone, she *really* stepped outside. More like, leaped a thousand miles beyond the perimeter.

He wanted to applaud and cheer. To beat his chest with his fists and roar. He was too stunned to do a thing but watch as the look of exhilaration diminished in her eyes. She was realizing what she'd done. *For me.*

The hell of it was, he'd never been more turned on in his life. It was better than any aphrodisiac. Kissing her in front of everyone was tempting, but there was only so much decorum a girl could ditch in one night.

"Buy you a drink?" Without waiting for a response, he signaled to a waiter. She definitely needed a drink. A good stiff one.

She nodded. "Thanks, sailor."

"Scotch for the lady," he said to the waiter. "Make it that fifty-year-old QE2 coronation Chivas."

"Right away, sir." The waiter disappeared.

"Oh boy." She took a deep breath as the hired photographers aimed their cameras at them.

"Yeah. Oh boy." He couldn't stop grinning.

His friends always had his back. They'd do anything for him. No one had ever done something like *this* for him. This would make the headlines of every paper in the city. She had to know that, and she'd done it anyway. One of the richest women in the country—if not the world—had stuck up for him. Without any explanation. Pride didn't begin to describe it. Pride for her and for the incredible woman she was. Her faith in him nearly sent him to his knees.

The gossip around them grew louder, and he had to lean in to be heard. "Thank you for defending my honor," he said against her ear.

"Someone had to."

He held back a laugh. "I've never had a woman do that before." That was the truth.

The waiter arrived with her glass of Chivas. She downed half of it, then handed him the glass. He downed the rest, setting the glass on another passing waiter's tray.

"Better?" he asked. A very pretty blush tinged her pale cheeks.

"Much." She took a fortifying breath. "I would very much like to dance with you, but first, protocol dictates I say something."

"Protocol, hmm." He massaged his chin with his thumb and forefinger, struggling hard not to, again, grin like a total idiot.

"Excuse me for a moment." She winked then turned to address the crowd. "Ladies and gentlemen, please forgive the interruption. My behavior was inexcusable."

"No, dear. Hers was," Betty Graham interrupted. "You only did what every last one of us has wanted to do for years. So here's to you." Betty raised her glass, as did everyone else with a champagne flute, wineglass, or tumbler.

More people applauded. More cameras flashed.

Dayne held out his hand to whisk her away to the dance floor before her adrenaline wore off. The moment her slim fingers contacted with his palm, electricity shot to every cell in his body, sending all kinds of inappropriate thoughts to his brain.

Amethyst eyes sparkled. Eyes he could stare into all night. Which was the stupidest thing he could possibly do. If dancing was the only way he could hold her in his arms again, he'd take that and live for the moment.

The orchestra had begun playing again. He didn't know what kind of music it was and didn't care. Dancing had never been his forte. Tonight, he'd wing it.

"Kat!" Colin blocked their path. "You need to apologize to Crystal."

"Not a chance in hell." Still holding Dayne's hand, she pushed past Colin.

Over his shoulder, Dayne watched the man's eyes narrow to slits. He couldn't help what he did next and shot the asshole a sly grin that said it all. *She's mine.* For tonight, anyway.

When they reached the center of the dance floor, she placed her hand on his shoulder. He tucked her against him and rested his other hand at the small of her back—her very sexy, very bare back. He trailed his fingers lower, to the slight curve of her buttocks. Her body trembled, and her lips parted.

Man, I'm in trouble here.

He swung her into a slow, easy waltz. *Thank you, Mrs. Evans.* The teacher who'd taught all the teenage boys in his class how to dance right before senior prom.

"To coin a cliché," Kat said, "you dance divinely."

"Liar." He nuzzled his chin against the silky curls artfully arranged atop her head and breathed in her scent. "I dance adequately, and you know it."

She laughed, a sound that went straight to his groin. One little laugh and the instinct to kiss her turned into a full-blown, flat-out craving. When she pressed her head to his chest, he thought he'd die and go straight to Heaven, bypassing the stairway to Hell where, as a teenager, he always assumed he'd wind up.

Being near her always left him supercharged. Leonardo DiCaprio had nothin' on him. Tonight, he was king of the world.

They danced in silence and in perfect rhythm, as if they'd always been meant to do this. Three songs went by before the need to have the answer to his burning question got the better of him. "Why?" he said huskily in her ear.

She lifted her head from his chest. "Why, what?"

"Why did you do that? You must have broken every rule of decorum and protocol in the book."

"It needed to be done," she said simply, but there had to be more to it.

With two fingers, he tipped up her chin. "And?"

"And"—she locked eyes with his—"I meant every word I said. You *are* more honorable and courageous than anyone else in this room."

His heart beat faster. He'd thought he was in deep trouble before, but now... *I'm in deep-as-a-diamond-mine kind of trouble.*

Now he understood what the *more* was. When he'd signed on for this bodyguard gig, he never expected to fall for her. Katrina Vandenburg. Who'd have figured? She was turning out to be the most wonderful woman he could possibly imagine.

"Don't you want to ask *me* something?" He still couldn't believe she hadn't pumped him for information. Then again, hadn't she shown him many times over that she was anything *but* what he'd pegged her for?

Her glossy pink lips twitched. "No."

He snorted. "Liar."

She gave his shoulder a gentle squeeze. "Of course I want to know. But it doesn't matter to me. Whatever happened between you and Crystal Lockwood is *your* business. I figured if, and when, you wanted to tell me, you would. If not, I don't need to know."

He stared into her eyes, searching for insincerity, knowing there wasn't an insincere bone in her body. She was telling the absolute truth. Kat trusted him. Completely and unconditionally. That only made him want to tell her everything.

He maneuvered them to the edge of the dance floor where there were fewer couples. What he was about to say was for her ears, and hers only.

"When I was eighteen, Crystal's Lamborghini broke down outside my parents' hardware store. She'd gotten lost and wound up in Newark, of all places. I fixed her car and after that, she started coming around the store. Not because she cared. Because she wanted me on her arm and in her bed."

He waited for Kat to ask the next obvious question. When she didn't, he answered it for her.

"I never had anything to do with her, but I couldn't stop her from hanging around the shop. She was a walking, talking ad for poison control. Toxic didn't begin to describe her, and I did everything possible to avoid her."

Kat frowned. "Knowing Crystal, she didn't like that."

"Nope." His gut tightened. "The next thing I knew, Newark detectives showed up to arrest me. Crystal had filed a police report saying I stole her diamond tennis bracelet, an heirloom her grandmother had given her on her eighteenth birthday. She came from a wealthy family. I came from the streets."

Kat's frown deepened. "So the police took her word against yours."

"They did. At first, anyway. I was about to be sentenced in criminal court. Lucky for me, the lead detective on the case was a crafty old sonofabitch and figured out Crystal's game. Turned out she'd sold the bracelet to feed her cocaine habit. When her parents asked what happened to the bracelet, she needed a scapegoat. Me."

"I take it you didn't go to jail."

"No. The detective threatened to arrest Crystal for filing a false police report if she didn't admit to her lies. Eventually, she came clean. I figure she was humiliated by the police then incurred the wrath of her family for losing granny's diamonds. The worst part was that my parents almost lost their store."

"Why?"

"Lawyers. We went through three because they all thought I was a lost cause, and no lawyer wants a reputation for losing cases. They only stuck around long enough to suck my parents' bank account dry. My folks had difficulty stocking their shelves and their reputation was dragged through the mud by what happened."

"That's awful." Anger flashed in Kat's eyes. "Your parents almost lost their livelihood and you almost went to jail for a crime you didn't commit."

The tug on Dayne's heart was totally unfamiliar to him. "Don't be angry for us. The store survived, and during all the legal proceedings I got hooked on law enforcement. That's what led me down the rosy path to Quantico."

"Are you saying I should forgive Crystal for what she did to you and your family?" Her look turned skeptical. "I think that ship has sailed."

"I agree." He nodded solemnly. "How do *you* feel about everything that happened tonight?"

"Honestly?" She let out a tiny huff. "Exhilarated. And

guilty. My mother would have been shocked at my behavior." She giggled, an altogether feminine sound. "Perhaps it was time someone put Crystal in her place, but she really was only crying for attention."

"Maybe." Then again, her cry to the police had nearly stolen his freedom. Sympathy from him would be a long time coming, if ever. "You're kind for saying that." One of the kindest people he knew. He winked. "Your mother would be pleased."

"I hope so." The sadness in her eyes told him how much she missed having her parents in her life.

The stalwart determination not to let anything more happen between them was in dire jeopardy of being blown to hell. Because dancing with her only worsened the growing ache in his heart and his head. Because holding Kat in his arms this way...

Would never be enough.

• • •

Kat stood near the ballroom doors, saying goodbye to her guests. From his tactical position twenty feet away, she noted Dayne alternating his focus between his conversation with Charlie Worthington and Max Rocher, and her.

She shook a few hands, said a few words, occasionally glancing at Dayne and trying not to relive every moment of dancing in his arms.

The warmth of his hard body against hers. His fingers skimming her bare back, scorching her skin and reminding her of things she shouldn't think about. She'd wanted to press her lips to his strong neck then lick and suck on his skin, tasting him like a yummy dessert.

Betty Graham landed a quick kiss on her cheek, knocking her out of her stupor. "Thank you for a most entertaining evening."

"It will be difficult to top this one." Senator Graham dropped a kindly peck on her other cheek.

"I'll do my best. Hopefully, with a little more decorum next time."

"Nonsense." Betty waved her hand in her typically dismissive gesture. "You were perfect as always."

Just thinking about tomorrow's society page headlines made her nauseous.

Charity Ball or Cat Fight?
Billionairess Gone Wild!

She pressed a hand to her forehead. Her mother would have a fit, but it was far too late to take anything back now.

After a few more guests departed, she yawned and made her way through the thinning crowd to Dayne. Seeing her approach, he said something to the other men and headed toward her.

"Are you ready to blow this joint?" she asked.

"Yeah." He grinned.

They collected her wrap then headed to the elevators. Several other couples joined them. Dayne stood on the opposite side of the elevator, watching her intensely, as if he wanted to eat her up.

I wish.

The doors opened, and they made their way to the exit. Dayne stepped outside and signaled to her driver. The white limo pulled up to the stairs. Seemingly satisfied there were no threats, he motioned for her to join him.

Dayne waited for her to settle in the back seat. Before getting in, he looked one last time in either direction then sat across from her. Soft amber sidelights glowed from the door panels, casting the hard planes and angles of Dayne's face in shadow.

"We should be back at the castle in about forty minutes,"

the driver—Sean—said through the open window separating him from the passenger compartment.

"Thank you, Sean," she answered.

"Cold?" Dayne asked in a low, sexy voice.

The limo pulled from the curb into traffic.

"A little." She tugged the shawl tighter around her shoulders.

He pushed a button on the console and a blast of hot air shot from the vents. "Better?" His eyes dipped to her mouth.

What was he doing? Besides driving her crazy with need for something she couldn't have. *Him.* "Some."

When her shawl slipped, exposing her bare shoulders, Dayne's eyes tracked the movement. He pressed another button, and a low hum accompanied the rising privacy window.

"Come here."

"Why?" Her pulse picked up. Being any closer to him than the three feet separating their bench seats was a dangerous thing.

A corner of his incredibly sensual mouth lifted. "Because I asked you nicely."

Confusion swamped her. In the last five days, they'd both made a point of keeping their distance. This time, she had to be sure. If she gave herself to him, there was no going back. Now, her heart was involved.

"Do you really want me?" She licked her lips, unable to ignore the heat in his eyes or the promise of passion in his outstretched hand.

Both corners of his mouth lifted as he gave her a sexy grin that made her heart race. "Baby, I've *always* wanted you."

She raised her arm, and as the distance between their hands got smaller and smaller, her pulse tripped into the danger zone. He tugged her from the bench and onto his lap. "Dayne, I—" His lips cut off her cry of surprise.

His mouth was hot, wet, the kiss scorching and dizzying until she could barely breathe. The throbbing between her legs became unbearable, and she dug her fingers into his back through his tuxedo jacket. *More.* She wanted to feel his incredible body.

Kat slipped her fingers beneath his cummerbund then pulled the shirt from his waistband, seeking his flesh and all but sighing when her fingers found it. Taut, hot skin over rippling muscle.

He groaned into her mouth, sweeping his tongue deeper as she slid her hands to the front of his slacks, grazing the handle of his gun—a stark reminder of the danger that had brought them together. The danger still out there.

"Christ, I do want you." He trailed his lips down her jaw to her neck, pressing hot kisses over her collarbone to the tops of her breasts.

"Oh, Dayne. Yes." If she hadn't already been firmly seated in his lap, she would have melted onto the floor.

When he shifted their bodies, clear evidence of his arousal pressed firmly against her bottom. She would have emptied all her bank accounts right then and there to be naked and straddling him as he impaled her slick folds. Before she'd even completed that last thought, moisture dampened her panties.

His fingers began a long, sensual path up her legs, hiking the long folds of the dress to her waist. When his fingers connected with the satin straps of her garter belt, an appreciative sound rumbled deep in his throat. "Sexy. So fucking sexy."

It *was* sexy. Everything *about* the man was sexy. The way he kissed. The way he smelled. How he was touching her now.

Dayne was right. The attraction between them had always been there. Their first aborted attempt at sex had been about grief and stark need. This time it was about them and their sizzling chemistry and passion ready to combust.

His big, warm fingers flicked teasingly at the garter then continued a fiery trail to her bare upper thigh.

The closer he got to the juncture of her thighs, the more anticipation thrummed in her veins. Through her silk panties, he stroked her until the garment was soaked, and she writhed against his hand.

Finally, he hooked her panties aside and plunged two fingers deep inside her. She arched against him, pushing him deeper as she rode his hand.

"Oh yes," she whispered. *God, yes.* Beyond those simple words, she had no more thought, only feeling. Incredible, wondrous feelings as he pumped her pussy, swirling his thumb over and around her clit.

With his free hand, he tugged the bodice of her dress down and fastened his mouth and teeth on her nipple. She bit back a cry as a piercing stab of pleasure shot to her breast.

He suckled and nipped, flicking the tight nub back and forth with the tip of his tongue. Her breath hitched, and her chest heaved. She moaned as the orgasm pulsing low in her womb pushed her closer and closer to the edge.

"Come for me, Kat," he said around her nipple. "Let it go, sweetheart."

It was the *sweetheart* that did it.

Bright lights shimmered behind her eyelids. Dayne smothered her cry with his lips on hers, swallowing her moans.

She came hard around his fingers, clenching and spasming as wave after wave rocked her body, leaving her trembling in his arms. As she floated back down to earth, the boldness of what had just happened hit her. *I just had an orgasm. In a limousine.* No one ever told her how hot it could be, or how deliciously, dangerously sexy it was.

Kat nearly whimpered when he withdrew his fingers from her wet, sensitive pussy and tugged her dress back into place.

"That was beautiful. *So* beautiful." He slipped the same two fingers he'd just fucked her with into his mouth, sucking them then licking his lips. His lids lowered, and the look he gave her was so carnal, so erotic she had to look away.

"Don't be embarrassed." He stroked her cheek. "Not everyone can let themselves go and just *feel*. After everything that's happened to you in the last two weeks, you needed that."

She *had* needed it, but the things he'd made her feel, physically *and* emotionally were so...personal. They shared a connection that went deeper than sex. At least, she hoped they did.

He pulled her head to his chest, cradling her to him. Being around this man was a roller-coaster ride of emotion, sensation, and lustful cravings.

His heart beat strong and steady beneath her cheek. She gave in to the rock and sway of the limo, closing her eyes, completely drained from the night's double adrenaline rush.

"Kat," he murmured. "Wake up." *Wake up?* Until that moment, she hadn't realized she'd fallen asleep. "We're home."

Home. She liked it when he referred to the castle as home, as if it were *their* home. The thought was there, twinkling like a star in the dark heavens.

"What time is it?"

"Midnight." He lifted her easily, settling her on the seat beside him before tucking his shirt back into his slacks and straightening his cummerbund.

Now that their erotic moment had passed, would her coach turn into a pumpkin? Would Dayne turn into a goose, a lizard, or a field mouse? As far as the menagerie went, he was still there, still as devastatingly handsome as ever and looking at her just as hotly as before.

He dropped a quick kiss on her lips. "Let's go to bed."

Renewed awareness throbbed between her legs and she smiled. "I think that's a wonderful idea."

They walked hand in hand to the door, passing Kade's SUV.

"I asked them to stick around and keep an eye on the place while we were out." Dayne nodded to the guard, whom she didn't recognize and who looked decidedly younger than the previous guards.

The second Dayne opened the door they were beset by two wildly happy, tail-thumping, furry beasts. Remy and Angus.

"'Bout time you two kids got home." Kade didn't look up from where he knelt on the floor, tossing some tools into a plastic toolbox. "We tweaked the system a little more. Ain't no one getting in here without—" He broke off, staring wide-eyed at Dayne.

Angus bit into his chew toy and tossed it at Kat's feet. Remy leaned against Dayne's thigh, gazing up at him adoringly.

Markus joined them, arching a dark brow. "We just had the dogs outside. You should be, uh, uninterrupted for the rest of the night."

"Duuude," Jaime said, drawing out the word in a suggestive tone. "Pink looks good on you."

Pink?

"And that's our cue to leave." Kade snapped the toolbox lid shut then stood. "C'mon boys. Let's get a beer. I'm buying."

They said their goodbyes to Dayne's friends then set the alarm. Trying not to laugh, she strode to him then used her thumb to wipe off the glossy pink lipstick smeared around his mouth. "We forgot about my lipstick."

"Yeah. We did." He pulled her into his arms, kissing her until she clung to him. All it took was this man's lips on hers and she turned into a rag doll. Mindless and boneless.

He swung her into his arms and carried her up the stairs. The dogs followed, and he gently nudged them aside before kicking the door shut and setting her on her feet.

He shrugged out of his jacket and yanked off the cummerbund, dropping them onto her armchair. When he moved to his bow tie, she stopped him. "Let me." With unsteady hands, she tugged on the bow tie and slipped it from his neck, letting it fall to the floor.

His hands skimmed up her bare back, unhooking the straps and slowly dragging them down her arms. As he pushed the fabric past her waist, her heart pounded, and she licked her lips. She wanted his hands on her skin, his erection inside her.

When the dress dropped to the floor, she rested her hands on his chest and kicked it aside.

"We really should hang that up," he whispered against her ear, sending chills down her neck to her breasts and nipples.

"Later," she whispered back, surprised at how husky and sexy her voice sounded. She linked her arms around his neck and stood on her tiptoes to take his mouth in a searing kiss.

With their mouths fused together, their tongues dancing wildly, he lifted her and carried her to the bed. Very gently, he laid her on her back then slipped off her strappy sandals. As he stroked his hands up her calves then her thighs and garter belts, her skin erupted in goose bumps.

"Dayne," she breathed, her breasts rising and falling faster. "You're taking too long. Get inside me." Before all that pent-up, protocol-be-damned sexual need and lust pooling in her core blew like an overloaded fuse.

"I give the orders. Remember?" His eyes darkened. "Spread your legs." She did as he commanded, expecting him to yank off his shirt and slacks and give her what she was dying for. When she reached for him, he pressed her arms down on the pillow above her head. "Don't move."

He released her arms then skimmed his hands over the tops of her breasts, down her belly to her thighs. She groaned and thrust her hips off the bed. With every tender stroke of his fingers, he was killing her.

Deftly, he unsnapped the garter belts and proceeded to slowly, torturously, roll her silk hose down each leg.

"Damn you," she whimpered, writhing on the mattress. Her body burned for him, and all he wanted to do was play with her undergarments.

He chuckled. "Sorry, babe. Not every man gets a chance to do this and those things are too sexy to ignore." Then he kissed his way up the inside of one thigh, leaving a sizzling trail directly to her pink lacy panties. "So pretty." He hooked his fingers around the waistband and dragged them down her legs.

Cool air washed over her naked body, but the way he looked at her—hungry, feral, and utterly male—flamed her with enough heat to fuel her private jet.

As he began unbuttoning his shirt, she wet her lips. Special Agent Dayne Andrews undressing was the most erotic, masculine dance she'd ever witnessed. Taut skin stretched over firm, rippling muscle as he shucked his shirt and stepped out of his slacks and tight briefs.

His erection jutted out—long, thick, and heavy. Her body trembled as he leaned over her, caging her body with his arms. Unable to wait a second longer, she curved her fingers around him, stroking up and down, reveling in the steely strength of him as she guided him to her entrance.

"Condom," he growled.

"Oh shit." At least one of them still had their wits about them. She leaned over and yanked open the bedside table drawer. She grabbed the box inside and tore it open. Several condoms fell on the bed, but her fingers shook so badly she couldn't tear open the wrapper.

"I've got this." Dayne took the condom from her and ripped it open. In seconds, he was fully covered.

He repositioned himself between her thighs, nudging gently at her entrance. *Too slow.* She understood he probably worried he'd hurt her, but her body was on fire.

She grabbed his muscled buttocks and pulled him inside her as she thrust her hips against him. "*Oh*," she cried as he stretched her tight walls.

"You good?" he breathed.

"Yes." Better than good, actually. Tiny pricks of energy buzzed all around her.

"Jesus, Kat." He groaned and closed his eyes for a moment. "You feel amazing. You feel like…" He kissed her deeply, then deeper still until it seemed like they were connected on a soul-deep level.

"Like what?" she whispered when they came up for air.

"Like I just found heaven." He began thrusting harder, penetrating deeper.

It does feel like heaven. Being in his arms, being one with his body and mind. *I wish this moment could last forever.* Because she'd never been more cherished, safe, or completely turned on.

He slipped his hands beneath her buttocks, changing the angle, driving deeper. With each slap of their hips, something wonderful built in her core, growing until her inner muscles tightened and she clung to his back.

Her heart pounded faster. Dayne's features tightened, his expression one of intense concentration. As much as she wanted to watch all that masculine beauty straining above her, she couldn't. Waves of sensation ripped through her body and she cried out again and again, trembling in the aftershocks of the most beautiful orgasm.

Dayne's presence in her life might only be temporary,

but she hoped not. The one thing she knew for certain was that they'd just shared something wonderful. Something she would never, ever forget.

• • •

Dayne's heart raced and his breath came in great heaves. Holding off his release to watch Kat shatter in his arms was worth every torturous moment.

Still gasping, he lowered his head to her breasts because he no longer had the strength to hold it up. Her heartbeat fluttered against his forehead.

When his vital signs returned to somewhat normal, he lifted his head. Her eyes were closed, her lips parted slightly. *Beautiful.* There was no other word for her or what just passed between them.

He ran his tongue over her lower lip, savoring her sweetness. Then his stomach grumbled.

Soft lips smiled against his. "Hungry?"

"Uh-huh." *For her.* He kissed her again.

She giggled. "My lipstick wasn't enough to satisfy your appetite?"

"No nutritional value. These on the other hand." He cupped one of her breasts and sucked on her nipple. When she sighed, his cock twitched with more life than he thought he had left in him. Usually he'd need at least forty minutes to recover. Around her, his body broke every record in the book.

His stomach growled again, louder and more insistent this time.

"I'd better get you some food to go with that scotch." Her fingers skated over his ass, sending shivers up his back. "I can whip up a salad to go with the casserole Francine left us last night. She also made zabaglione."

"Zabaglione? Is that an Italian sports car?" It wasn't, but he'd definitely never had it before.

"No, silly." She smacked his bicep. "But it *is* an Italian specialty. Whipped egg custard flavored with Marsala."

"Sounds amazing." He dipped his head to suckle on her other nipple. "And sweet," he said around the tight little bud.

"It is." She sighed, a deeply sexy sound he loved. "It definitely is."

Watching her this way, naked and with nothing between them but the sweat on their bodies, was something he could do for the rest of his life. That and making love to her every night. Fast…slow…it didn't matter. He'd give her whatever she wanted or needed. Whatever pleasure his body could provide.

Her stomach grumbled. "That wasn't very ladylike of me."

"There's nothing about you that isn't ladylike." *Or all woman.*

"Thank you." She giggled again. "But I should probably go heat up that casserole."

He groaned. Guess round two would have to wait. Reluctantly, he withdrew from her and rolled onto his back.

Kat rose, and he was treated to a tantalizing view of pear-shaped buttocks as she reached for the long purple robe hanging on the spindle of a really old mirror. His mouth watered. Whether it was from the promise of one of Fran's casseroles or the sight of all that shiny material caressing her lush body, he didn't know.

Definitely the latter.

She sent him a seductive smile over her shoulder as she left. Remy and Angus padded to the side of the mattress. His K-9 rested her muzzle near his arm, while Angus stood on his hind legs, trying to mimic Remy but only managing to get the tips of his paws on the bed. After giving Remy a quick head rub, she and Angus lay down, snuggling together like furry peas in a pod.

He stared at the ceiling's domed light fixture. Strands of clear crystals cast alternating shadows and gold splotches of light on the walls, reminding him of a toy his mother had given him one year for Christmas before she died. A kaleidoscope. It was old, chipped, and beat up, but he'd loved it. The colorful, symmetrical designs inside the tube were always different, changing with each turn.

He wasn't the same man who'd walked into the Vandenburg castle two weeks ago. That man wouldn't be thinking the crazy-ass thought tumbling over and over in his head. Could they really make this thing between them work when this was over?

After depositing the condom in a trash basket under the bathroom sink, he examined the expensive-looking toiletries on the counter. Crystal canisters with gold and silver lids. A gold-handled hairbrush. How could this ever work? He didn't have a clue.

I'm fucked. Because he'd fallen for her. Hard.

Returning to the bedroom, he shoved his legs into his slacks and headed for the door. The box of condoms on the nightstand caught his eye. He grinned and grabbed one, stuffing it into his pocket before heading downstairs.

Kat stood at the counter, humming as she sliced a cucumber. Her back was to him, her robe clinging lovingly to the same curves he'd touched everywhere and wanted to again, but he couldn't move. Watching her prepare a meal for him made his heart squeeze in a way that was fan-fucking-tastic and terrifying. Because he was getting *waaay* ahead of himself. First, he had to catch a killer. Then they could see what happened.

He padded to where she stood then skimmed his hands up and down her arms. "Mmm," he murmured against her hair.

Grrr. Angus trotted into the kitchen, shaking his head back and forth. The toy clamped between his jaws rattled and hissed as air escaped from one end that had practically been chewed clean off.

Dayne pulled Kat's hair aside and kissed the curve of her neck right below her ear.

"Mmm is right." She set the knife on the counter then turned in his arms.

He leaned down to kiss her when Angus's slobbery toy landed on his bare foot. He nudged the sticky thing off his toes.

"Angus, that's disgusting." Kat parked her fists on her hips and the edges of her robe parted slightly. "Tomorrow we're going to the Haven to find you a new toy." She slid her hands up Dayne's chest then down his pecs and nipples. "I'm sorry about that."

"That's okay." And yeah, it was. In fact, *everything* was okay. With her fingers teasing his nipples and her robe about to part down the middle, revealing her warm, luscious breasts…

Angus yipped, nudging the toy back onto Dayne's foot. He reached for the toy and picked it up by one end. *Yuck* didn't cover it. He was about to toss it to the other side of the kitchen when something black poked through the torn end.

He froze. In the span of time it took for his heart to beat once more, missing pieces of a very convoluted puzzle slammed home.

Why the killer had murdered Becca.

She definitely had something on him.

Why the killer had gone to the Haven that night.

The press had been all over Becca's crime scene, more so when they figured out a billionairess had discovered the body. Every news story reported that the victim's puppy was being cared for by Kat at the Canine Haven. He and Detective Paulson had assumed that since Kat had been at Becca's crime scene *and* at the Haven where the killer murdered Amy, that Kat was the common denominator. But she wasn't the *only* common denominator.

Angus had been there, too. The killer had been looking for the puppy.

"Dayne, you're scaring me." Kat gripped his arm. "What's wrong?"

He shook the toy over his hand. A slim piece of black plastic about an inch and a half square fell into his palm.

A memory card.

Chapter Twenty-Three

"We're in!" The CCU tech clapped his hands together over the keyboard. The poor man had been called in on a Sunday but seemed just as eager as the rest of them to crack the encryption.

Kat leaned closer to view the list of photos on the memory card. Her shoulder brushed Dayne's and she inhaled the same shampoo he'd used on her hair that morning.

After finding the memory card in Angus's toy, they'd tried accessing it on Dayne's laptop but since it was encrypted, they'd been forced to wait until a forensic expert could work his magic. They'd also been worried that all the tiny teeth marks in the covering had damaged the contents. Regardless, the discovery had left them brimming with so much excitement, sleep hadn't been possible. So they made love well into the early morning hours.

Her cheeks still burned from Dayne's stubbled jaw as he'd kissed her again and again. Every time she moved, her bra rasped against her nipples, tender from his wicked tongue and lips. She even had to keep shifting on the hard chair to ease the delicious throb between her legs from the many times he'd entered her.

With the discovery of the memory card, they were that much closer to finding Becca and Amy's killer. Soon this could all be over.

She tightened her fingers around her coffee mug. What if Dayne left when the case was solved? What if he didn't feel the same way she did?

I'm falling in love. They hadn't even been on a date yet, but her heart didn't care.

There was so much to talk about. So they came from different backgrounds. That didn't mean they couldn't work hard and make compromises.

"Good job," Dayne said, looking just as handsome in jeans and an untucked button-down white shirt as he had in his tuxedo. "Open them."

Detective Paulson set his mug on the table and pulled up a chair. "There." He pointed to the screen. "Can you magnify that tag?"

The tech moved the cursor over the car's license plate and clicked several times. NJ C24-BM. The shot had missed the third letter on the right side.

Dayne scribbled the plate number on a pad. "Looks like a gray Nissan. Could be the same one that followed us last Sunday on our way to Englewood."

"I saw a gray car parked on the street outside Becca's office the day I found her." She rested her hand on Dayne's shoulder. Paulson caught the movement then turned back to the computer. "You told me to close my eyes and I recalled a New Jersey license plate."

"You also said the car had a dented rear fender." He pointed to the image where a dent graced the left side of the bumper. "Open the rest of the files."

One by one the tech clicked open the files. All distance

shots of the same vehicle.

"That's the corporate building Kat and I drove to in Englewood," Dayne said. "The last address in Becca's GPS app."

Paulson leaned back in his chair. "The detectives and agents who went to that location interviewed managers from every office in the building. The ones that would talk to us didn't know Rebecca Garman. Naturally, the law firms said they'd get back to us."

"Naturally." Dayne and Paulson exchanged knowing looks. Like Dayne had said, law firms wouldn't confirm or deny anything until they'd covered their asses.

The next files showed a man exiting the car wearing a dark suit. His back was to the camera, and a series of successive shots showed him walking to a stairwell beneath the building.

"Stop!" Dayne leaned in. The last file was of the same man with his head turned in profile. He pulled out a folded sheet of paper from his pants pocket—the sketch of the man who'd attacked Kat. "It *could* be him. Kat?"

She studied the image. "I can't tell. It's only a profile."

"That's the last one." The tech looked from Paulson to Dayne.

"Print them," Dayne said. "We have five out of six characters on that tag. Can you run a DMV query and see how many vehicles with the same sequence are gray sedans, especially Nissans?" He tore the top sheet off the pad and handed it to Paulson.

"I'll see what I can do." He took the sheet to his desk and started tapping away at the keyboard. "Got it," he said a few minutes later. "Printing now."

Dayne grabbed the sheets from the printer. His brows drew together as he scanned the pages, then he grabbed a pen and made notations. "There are fifteen gray sedans on the list, including six Nissans. I can get a team of agents to help you track down the owners, and another agent to run all the names for criminal histories."

"I'll take that assist." Paulson grabbed his jacket.

"Keep me posted."

• • •

By noon, Kat sat at her desk, staring at two distinct piles. The first contained newspapers and mail that had been accumulating for the last two weeks and the other, a stack of resumes Emily had solicited to replace Amy.

Sadness filled her heart as she picked up a framed photo on the desk. Walter had taken it a year ago at the Haven. Kevin, Fiona, and Amy had surprised her with a birthday cake. The last birthday her friend would ever share with her. *I still can't believe you're gone.*

A birthday party, especially one that had been arranged by Colin, didn't interest her in the slightest. Not for the first time, she hoped he'd cancel. After last night, he probably hated her.

The doorbell rang, and she heard Dayne's and another man's voice. Not Colin's. Good thing, because she had no interest in seeing him. At least, not for a while.

She glanced at the front-page article of the *New York Post*: "Socialite Cat Fight." The other big city papers had similar headlines.

Dayne leaned against the doorjamb, frowning at the stack of newspapers. "Your weekly roses just arrived. Pink."

"Did Manny deliver them?" She hoped not.

"No." Dayne's voice held a discernible edge.

A tiny bit of guilt twisted in her belly. "I hope he doesn't lose his job."

"He did, but not because of that." The crease in his forehead deepened. "The shop owner said Manny stopped showing up for work the same day we saw him in the city."

"I wonder why. He's been working there for years."

Dayne shrugged. "I made sandwiches. Want me to bring you one?"

His thoughtfulness brightened her mood and she smiled. "Thank you, but I'm not very hungry right now. Maybe just some fruit, if you don't mind."

"Fruit coming up." A few minutes later, he returned carrying the bowls of zabaglione and strawberries they hadn't gotten to last night. A distinct gouge in the middle of the custard resembled a finger swipe. "No sense letting this go to waste. You were right. It *is* good." He dipped his finger in the zabaglione then held it in front of her mouth.

Hmm, this could be fun. She closed her lips around his finger and sucked off the custard. His eyes darkened as she licked his finger clean. "Aren't you hungry, too?"

"Yeah." His eyes glittered in that sexy way she'd come to love. "I am."

She dragged her index finger through the custard then held it out for him. Sporting a wicked grin, he closed his lips around her finger, his eyes glued to hers while he slid his tongue up, down, and around, licking and sucking as he swallowed. "Mmm," he mumbled then picked her up by her waist, plunking her ass first on the desk.

"What are you doing?" She giggled then her laughter died as he pulled apart the knotted ends of her silk wraparound dress and pushed the garment off her shoulders. A quick flick of his fingers later, and her bra slid down her arms.

"Oh yeah." His lids lowered, his eyes flaring with heat. With that one look she was jelly in his hands, willing to go wherever he wanted to take her. Which, clearly, was right on her desk.

He eased her down, parting her thighs to stand between them then cupping her breasts and rolling her nipples between his thumbs and forefingers. Her body was a musical instrument, and he played her like he was a master violinist.

Closing her eyes, she moaned and arched into his hands. His throaty rumble was as arousing as his touch.

Something cold hit her breasts and she opened her eyes to see generous dollops of zabaglione on her nipples. Just before he dipped his head, the side of his mouth lifted into a devilishly handsome grin.

His tongue flicked at her nipple, swiping away some of the custard. He swallowed. "So sweet." Then his mouth fastened on the tight bud, laving, until it glistened and jutted pertly, an erotic pleasure point connected directly to another part of her that throbbed and pulsed with need.

Sex had never been like this before. If he left her, it never would be again.

"We shouldn't let these go to waste, either." He grabbed a whole strawberry from the bowl then dunked it in the zabaglione and dragged the custard-laden berry between her breasts, down past her belly button, to the lacy edge of her purple panties. He bit into the berry, chewing as he held the rest of it out for her.

She took the remaining piece into her mouth. Sweet juices hit her tongue and she swallowed, licking her lips as Dayne began dragging his tongue down the custard on her body. When he'd licked her clean, he pulled her panties down her legs, taking her shoes with them.

Kneeling, he pulled her to the edge of the desk and draped her thighs over his shoulders. The second his lips met her wet, throbbing sex, she arched off the desk and nearly bucked to the ceiling.

With his fingers, he parted her folds then impaled her with his tongue. Her belly quivered and she clawed her fingers through his thick hair. Pleasure surged outward then ripped through her body, leaving her limp, sated, and smiling.

The sound of a zipper broke through her haze of lust. Crinkling paper, then he was there. Hard and full, and entering her slickness. His face was beautiful in all its strained harshness as he thrust into her.

She locked her legs around his ass, gripping his biceps to hold her in place. Papers rustled, falling to the floor.

"Baby," Dayne whispered harshly, "I want to watch you come again. Can you do that for me?"

Oh god. "Yes," she moaned, locking her legs tighter as he stroked harder, faster. "Yes." She couldn't have stopped it if she tried. Another wave built then crashed over her in a tidal wave of pleasure. "*Yes!*"

He stiffened, thrusting hard and throwing his head back before crying out her name. His chest expanded with heavy breaths. He cradled her head in his hands, staring intently as if he were searching for something.

"What is it?" She reached out to cup his face. A face she'd come to love in such a short time. *I do love him.* Nothing in her world was more certain.

"Not a thing," he said between gasps. "I—"

The gate bell chimed.

He eased out of her then deposited the condom in the wastebasket and zipped his jeans. His phone shrilled, and he glanced at the screen. "Colin's here."

"Oh no." She let him help her to her feet then gathered up her clothes. "I should talk to him." While she dressed, Dayne's expression soured by the second. "I owe him an explanation about last night." From the thunder clouds in Dayne's eyes, he didn't agree. "Look, I know you can't understand. That's just the way things work in my world."

"*Your* world?" He caught her hand as she turned to leave. "In *my* world, you don't owe him a thing."

"Please." The angry, adamant look in his eyes tore at her heart. She hadn't meant to draw a metaphorical line between the differences in their lives, but it was there nonetheless and neither of them could deny it existed. Crossing that line and meshing their lives would take time. "Let me take care of this in my own way."

She left him standing in her office, a grim expression on his face. No, not grim. Disappointed. He was disappointed with her, and she felt horrible about that.

In the foyer, she pushed the button to open the gates. A minute later, the rumble of Colin's Jag came from outside. Remy and Angus watched expectantly. She opened the door then signaled to the young security guard that everything was okay.

"Kat, we need to talk." Colin rounded the car, stalking up the steps. His expression was also one of disappointment.

I'm getting it from all sides today. Although she probably deserved it. "Let's talk in here." She led the way to the sofa and sat.

Colin settled next to her. "What in the world is going on with you? Your behavior last night was unbelievable. I didn't even recognize you."

She sighed. "I admit I didn't recognize myself." Telling Crystal Lockwood off still felt darned good.

"It's that FBI agent." His tone turned bitter. "The minute he came into your life you haven't been yourself." That much was true, and she liked the changes. "Are you sleeping with him?"

"Colin!" His prying question lit her fuse. "That's none of your business."

"Then you *are*." She opened her mouth to again object to his invasive question, but he held up his hand. "I don't want to know, but for God's sake, you need to think this through. He's not one of us, and he never will be."

"Did it ever occur to you that's what I like about him?" *More* than liked. *Loved*.

Colin made an exasperated sound. "I get it. Chad hurt you, and you were on the rebound when Andrews walked into your life. When you were attacked, he must have seemed like something out of a movie, coming to your rescue. Do you have any idea how much it hurts that I wasn't the person you turned to? You're shutting me out of your life."

"I never meant to shut you out." Losing him would hurt, but if he couldn't accept their platonic relationship, she'd have to.

His brow wrinkled. "How do you know he's not after your money? We all know Chad was."

"He's *definitely* not after my money." She uttered a laugh. "In fact, sometimes he even seems to resent it." Which was both good *and* bad.

He stood to pace in front of the fireplace. "Do you really see yourself with this guy? He's a federal agent. He's used to calling the shots and ordering everyone around. A guy like that could never be happy following you to charity events, standing to the side while the press interviews you. He'll always be in your shadow and he'll come to resent it. He'll come to resent *you*."

"I think he's confident enough not to let that bother him." She frowned. Wasn't he? *I think so. I hope so.*

Colin ran a hand through his perfectly coiffed hair, something she'd never seen him do. "He'll never be able to provide for you because he doesn't have to. You have enough money to buy out his net worth a million times over. Every man wants to provide for his woman. Do you think he can be with you, knowing that he doesn't have to?"

She'd never considered those things. "I don't know," she admitted, fear coiling in her gut that she'd been so insensitive.

"You have to admit there's truth in what I'm saying."

"Some. Perhaps." An ache grew steadily behind her eyes. One that matched the growing ache in her heart.

"He'll leave you as soon as the newness wears off. As soon as he realizes being the pet of a very rich, very famous woman isn't all it's cracked up to be."

She leaned back and hugged a pillow to her chest. Dayne was a proud man. He had every right to be. But was Colin right? Was it fair to do that to Dayne? Worse, was she setting herself up to be with a man who would leave her when he realized how difficult their relationship would be?

Her heart told her what they had was more meaningful than a fling or a byproduct of the intense circumstances that had brought them together.

Colin sat beside her, his voice softening. "You're infatuated, but it will pass." Again, he took her hands in his, and this time, she was too numb to resist. "I promise it will."

Her chest tightened. "I don't want it to pass." She was falling more in love with Dayne every day. "Colin." She jerked her hands away. "It's time for you to go."

"Okay. For now. But one day you'll see that you don't have to be in love with someone to make a good life with them. For people like us, the best matches are made for other reasons. *Practical* ones." He stood. "Remember, I'm here for you. I've *always* been here."

After he'd gone, she remained on the sofa. Colin would never be the one for her. That hadn't changed. But he was right. There were other things to consider. Like whether her love was enough to keep Dayne and make him happy.

Her lids lowered, and she could barely keep them open. It was one p.m., and already she was exhausted enough to sleep until tomorrow. She dragged herself to a window and watched one of the guards patrolling the tree line. When she turned around, Dayne stood there, watching her silently.

Needing to go to him—to feel the comfort of his arms around her—she took a step closer then stopped. Her scalp prickled with unease. Rather than being pleased at her stalwart defense of him and their relationship, his expression was unreadable.

"What's wrong?" She reached for him, but he shoved his hands through his hair, momentarily shutting his eyes. When he looked at her again, her throat constricted painfully.

He didn't say a word. Didn't have to. Dark brows drew together and the pain in his eyes was so sharp she felt it dead center in her chest.

Kat didn't understand how or why, but she knew.

I'm losing him.

Then slowly, her heart cracked into tiny little pieces.

Chapter Twenty-Four

Dayne hadn't meant to eavesdrop.

Who was he kidding? Of course he had. Although he wished to hell he hadn't. Every one of his senses was numb—no, make that mashed to a pulp—as if he'd been run over by a truck.

Colin was a prick, but he was also a shrewd attorney. The bastard had made his case and won. Kat hadn't caved. Dayne had.

"Didn't you hear what I said to Colin?" she cried.

The stark anguish on her face about killed him. "I did." Every word had been a knife slice to his guts. She'd stuck up for him, and he couldn't have been prouder. But he'd also heard the doubt in her voice. Doubt she had every right to feel.

She touched his arm, and his blood sizzled with need and so many emotions he couldn't name. But he had to let her go.

"I don't understand what's happening here." Her brow furrowed. "Are you angry with me?"

"No. I'm not." It was all he could do not to take her in his arms, but that would only put off the inevitable.

She cupped his face and he turned into it, loving the softness of her fingers on his cheek and knowing he would never feel her touch again after today. "Colin was wrong. So we have a lot to work through. We can do it. I *know* we can."

Gently, he tugged her hand away, wishing she were right. Knowing now that it wasn't possible. "I know you think so, but it's too much to ask. We *are* too different. We could never make it work." He'd been crazy and selfish to think otherwise. It was just that he wanted her so badly. Wanted to *be* part of her life.

She planted her fists on her hips. "How can you believe anything Colin said? You heard how he tried to manipulate me. Don't let him manipulate *you*."

Dayne shook his head, feeling more miserable than he'd ever felt in his life. "He made valid points. I *don't* know how I feel about never being able to buy you anything because you already have everything money can buy."

"No, I don't. I don't have you! *You're* all I want." Her eyes clouded with so much despair, he nearly fell to his knees. "Don't do this."

"I have to." The pain and hurt on her face were killing him faster than any bullet could. "We'd only wind up hurting each other. I don't fit in here. It's better to end it now." Before he lost more of his heart to her.

"You fit in just fine last night," she insisted.

He had, but it didn't change a thing. "You shouldn't have to defend my honor or explain anything on my behalf, and I don't want you to. The price is too high."

"What does *that* mean?" she cried.

"It means there will always be someone out there accusing me of being a thief or a gold digger. Of only wanting your money and of being nothing more than your 'pet.'"

"I don't care about that." A single tear trickled down her

cheek.

There was only one thing he *could* give her. Her freedom.

"It's not about living in your shadow," he continued, barely able to get the words past the enormous lump in his throat. "It's about us being able to just be *us*, and that's something that can never happen. You're the most generous, kind, and compassionate person I've ever met. *I* was being selfish. All I've done is turn your orderly world upside down. Today's headlines are proof of that."

With an angry swipe, she flicked that lone tear away and gritted her teeth. "I don't care about the headlines. I never did."

"You should. The kind of publicity you got last night could damage your reputation and every business dealing you have. I don't want to be responsible for that. I can't go through that again." The last time he had, his family had nearly lost everything. He couldn't allow that to happen to Kat.

Her mouth fell open and she took a step back. "That's what this is about. Not me. *You*. You have so many insecurities and fears about your past. About what Crystal did to you and your family and that woman who wouldn't marry you because you weren't going to be a rich doctor. That's why you're so easily swayed by Colin. You're afraid it will happen again and you're afraid to give us a chance."

Remy and Angus padded into the foyer, their heads hung low.

Some of what Kat said was true. Hell, all of it. Christ, he hadn't meant for things to come to this but they had, and now he had to reap what he'd sown. What they'd *both* sown.

"I'm sorry, Kat. One day you'll see this is for the best." So why did it feel like his entire world was imploding?

Her eyes went wide with a mixture of shock and outrage. "That's bullshit. How can you end this so easily? Don't you feel *anything* for me?"

More than you'll ever know. His throat clogged with so much emotion and regret he had to look away. Anywhere but at the heartache written all over her face. And as for this being easy on him, walking away from her would be the hardest thing he'd ever do in his life.

Her lips quivered until she pressed them together. "If that's the way you feel then get out!" She pointed to the door.

A surge of protectiveness so fierce and ingrained soared to the surface. "Not happening." Not with a killer out there. Their future wasn't together, but he damn well intended to make sure she had one.

"This is *my* house and I don't want you here." Tears spilled freely down her cheeks, each one like acid burning through his heart.

"You may not want me here, but you need me. In case you've forgotten, someone may be trying to kill you."

"I haven't forgotten. I'll hire more security to take your place. I'll hire an army if I have to. Just get out. *Please*, Dayne," she implored on a choked sob. "Go. I can't take this anymore. It hurts too much."

Jesus. He didn't think there was anything she could have said that would convince him to leave her. That did. He couldn't hurt her anymore. But he wouldn't leave her alone, either. "I'll make arrangements for Kade or another FBI agent to take my place tonight."

Somehow, and against every instinct and fiber of his being, he forced his legs to move. Numbly, he went to his room and packed his and Remy's things. His only recourse was to do everything in his power to catch this guy before he got to her.

When he returned to the foyer, Kat was nowhere in sight. Before opening the front door, he stared at the spot on the floor where she'd been standing.

Sure enough, she'd eviscerated him. Left his guts in a bloody heap on her pricy Italian marble floor. He didn't know how his heart was beating, not when it was shattering.

It was his own damn fault. He'd gone and fallen in love with the last woman he should want. And could never have.

...

Kat lost track of how long she cried. Hours probably. The pillowcase was damp beneath her cheek, as was the wad of tissues clutched in her hand. The early evening sky outside her window had turned gray and dreary.

True to his word, Dayne had arranged for another agent to stay at the castle in his place. Special Agent Beth Shanahan. The woman seemed pleasant and capable enough, but it wasn't the same. She wasn't Dayne.

"Oh, Angus," she said to the puppy. After Dayne had left with Remy, Angus had cried nonstop for twenty minutes. Only after she'd tucked him to her side did he settle down. "He should have given us a chance. How could he do this?"

Angus didn't answer, just watched her from soulful puppy eyes.

Her belly shook with renewed sobs. The ache in her heart was so deep and raw. She hadn't known she could hurt this badly. Was this what love did to a person? If so, the pain was too great to bear.

She gripped the sheet tighter. It felt like she was dying inside. Maybe she *would* be better off settling for a good match, instead of holding out for true love. That way she could never be hurt this badly again.

She hadn't expected to fall in love, hadn't been prepared for it. But he was gone, and she had to accept it. People she loved—her parents—had left her before, and she'd survived. Somehow. She'd busy herself with work, maybe go into the city more often. Perhaps get back into the nightlife scene.

Her stomach roiled at the thought. That kind of life hadn't been for her before Dayne, and it wasn't now. She'd only be fooling herself. Trying to become something she wasn't so she could forget him.

"I *can't* forget him, Angus." The puppy snuggled closer and licked her nose. It didn't matter that she'd only known him a fraction of the time she'd known all her other friends, because she *knew* him, and they were connected in a way she hadn't known existed. She was completely in love with him and without reservation. Nothing would ever change that.

Isolation and gut-wrenching grief washed over her in painful waves, and her body quaked with renewed sobs.

All her money and the power that came with it… She'd told Dayne the absolute truth. None of it mattered. The one thing she wanted in the entire world—she couldn't have.

Him.

Chapter Twenty-Five

"It's deer blood. I swear it." Daniel Fitzgerald pointed to the knife Dayne found in a camouflage backpack in the trunk of Fitzgerald's gray Nissan sedan. The blade was caked with dried blood.

He held the end of the knife handle with a rag. According to the ME's report, it was the right size and type. Smooth edged and about five inches long.

Fitzgerald pulled his cell phone from his pocket and began pecking away. "I have pictures of the deer I killed back in December. See?" He handed Paulson the phone.

Dayne eyed Fitzgerald cautiously. With Kat's life still on the line he wasn't taking any chances.

Before driving away from the castle hours earlier, he and Remy had parked by the gate, waiting for his replacement. After that, he couldn't just sit there on his ass doing nothing, so he'd hooked up with Paulson to assist with interviewing owners of the last two gray sedans on the list.

Fitzgerald didn't look anything like the subject in Becca's photo or Kat's sketch. This guy was about five-four, blond hair, clean shaven, and with gray eyes. The suspect Kat described was five-ten, with a mustache and beard, and brown hair and eyes.

"Can you account for where you were on Tuesday, March twenty-seventh between four p.m. and midnight?" he asked.

Fitzgerald thought for a moment, then his eyes rounded. "Yes! I was in Baltimore for work. I haven't submitted my voucher yet, so I still have all my receipts."

Dayne tipped his head to the condo. "Get them."

They followed Fitzgerald inside. Minutes later, he supplied a short stack of receipts with time and date stamps that further solidified his alibi. Fitzgerald hadn't been anywhere near Becca's office or the Haven on the days in question.

Dayne dragged a hand down his face. He wanted this guy, and he wanted him bad. But Fitzgerald wasn't their man. He gave Paulson a quick shake of his head.

Back outside, he pulled out the list of sedans he'd left on the dashboard. Check marks accompanied every vehicle on the list but one. All the other registered owners had been interviewed and discarded as suspects. They were either too old, too young, didn't fit the description, had alibis, or any combination thereof. One vehicle remained, although it was registered to a woman.

Paulson stood by his unmarked unit. "Who's next?"

"Carolyn Mauser. Nine eighty-five Oak Court, Edison, New Jersey." The address was about twenty minutes away. They'd already run all the registrants for the vehicles on the list and knew Carolyn Mauser had no criminal history. Being a woman, she couldn't have been the one to attack Kat, but they couldn't be certain Becca's killer and Kat's attacker were one and the same. It also didn't mean someone else hadn't used Carolyn Mauser's vehicle.

"Meet you there." Paulson got into his car.

Dayne was certain the memory card photos were the key

to the investigation. The only other thing he could do was sit outside the building in Englewood tomorrow morning and see if the same gray sedan showed up.

He sat behind the wheel and started the engine when Paulson ran over.

"Wait!" the detective shouted. Dayne lowered his window. "We've got something." Paulson enlarged whatever he'd pulled up on his cell. "Verizon came through with their subpoena production."

"On a Sunday?" He couldn't keep the surprise from his voice.

"No." Paulson shook his head. "The original email was dated Friday, but the departmental email server kicked it back as being suspicious. Eventually, it got through."

"And?"

"The subscriber for the last call on Rebecca Garman's phone." Paulson paused. "It's Carolyn Mauser."

They stared at each other, processing the ramifications.

Carolyn Mauser owned a gray Nissan, similar to the one Kat saw parked outside Becca's, and with five of the six license plate digits on Becca's photo. Carolyn Mauser was also the last person to talk with Becca right before she was murdered.

Or someone else using the same phone.

"Did that name pop up in any of Rebecca's case files?" Paulson shook his head. "But remember, one of the case files is missing. Stand by." Dayne tugged his own cell from his belt. "I want to check something."

First, he ran Carolyn Mauser through DMV. He didn't recognize her from her DL photo. Next, he ran her address through TLO—a widely used commercial database—and found three other people associated with the same address. From their DOBs, two were teenagers, a girl and a boy. The third was an adult. Christian Mauser.

He went back into DMV and ran Christian Mauser. When he pulled up the man's DL photo, his blood ran cold. He held his phone out to Paulson.

"Oh fuck."

Yeah. Oh fuck.

Christian Mauser was five-ten, brown hair, mustache and beard, and with brown eyes. The face staring back at them looked a helluva lot like the man in Kat's sketch and could very well be the subject in Becca's photo. The critical word in that sentence being *could*.

Kat had described her attacker's eyes as being cloudy, but Dayne couldn't enlarge Mauser's image enough to verify that.

"One last thing before we head down there." He took his phone back from the detective then ran Mauser for a criminal history. "Negative. The guy's squeaky clean." Yet something had the hackles on the back of his neck waving back and forth in warning. "Let's get down there. Fast."

...

Kat yawned. Her abdominal muscles ached from crying hours on end. She pulled the gauzy taupe curtain aside. It was only eight p.m., but the sky over the river was as black as ink. Like her mood.

Dayne was out there somewhere because she'd sent him away. No matter how many times she relived their last conversation, the end game was always the same. She loved him with all her heart, but being near him would have been unbearable.

Angus sat up from where he'd been curled happily at the foot of her bed. She and Agent Shanahan had taken him out earlier and met Hakeem, the new guard on duty. He was so young. Surprisingly young to be armed with a gun.

Needing to be more comfortable, she changed out of her dress and into jeans and a light blue sweatshirt. No sooner had she settled back onto the bed to find something—*anything*—on TV to keep her mind off Dayne, when her cell phone rang. It was Agent Shanahan.

She swiped to answer the call. "Beth, is everything all right?"

"No, Miss Vandenburg." Beth's voice held a note of urgency. "Hakeem just told me there's a fire outside the castle. On the northwest corner. I'm going outside to check it out. Stay here."

Kat bolted from the bed, upsetting Angus who pranced worriedly to the edge of the mattress. With the phone still pressed to her ear, she ran to the other window and yanked back the curtain. "Oh my god!" Flames shot from one of the hedges. Smoke billowed and blew past the window.

She flung open her closet and shoved her bare feet into a pair of Ferragamo flats. With her heart racing, she picked Angus up and hastily made her way down the stairs. The pup wriggled and struggled in her arms. At nearly twenty pounds, she had to set him on the floor.

The keypad on the wall by the door blinked green. Beth must have deactivated the system, and since the fire was completely outside the castle, the smoke alarm hadn't gone off. Yet. She hoped it didn't come to that.

Kat peered out one of the windows to see flames licking higher. She was about to call 911 when her cell phone rang again. It was Hakeem, the outside guard.

"Miss Vandenburg," came Hakeem's worried voice. "I know the castle is made of stone, but you'd better play it safe and come outside. I've already called the fire department."

"Thank you." Through the window she glimpsed flames spreading to Walter's beloved hydrangeas. Even with the wet spring season, the shrubs were catching fire quickly. Through the thickening smoke, she searched for Beth but didn't see her. "Where's Agent Shanahan?"

"She's with my partner," Hakeem answered. "They're hooking up the garden hose. Please, hurry. The fire's getting worse."

"C'mon, Angus." Her heart raced as she flung open the door. They'd be fine. The fire department was only two miles away.

The puppy bounded down the front stairs, barking his head off. "Angus!" She chased after him, worrying the little guy would get run over by a fire truck if she didn't corral him quickly. "Beth? Hakeem?" As she rounded the corner of the castle where Angus had disappeared, a wave of heat and smoke hit her in the face. A chemical smell raked at her nose and throat, making her cough. *Gasoline.*

"Angus!" she screamed, staggering back. *Where is he?*

Barking drew her attention to the grass near the edge of the adjacent tree line. Angus's tail whipped back and forth as he sniffed something on the grass. Was that—?

The security guard lay face down, unmoving. And was that blood on the back of his head?

She touched her fingers to the young man's head and they came back sticky with blood. "Hakeem!" she cried. "Hakeem!" She slid her fingers to his neck, searching frantically for a pulse. While she waited for the telltale thumping of life, something else caught her attention. Beth and the other guard lay ten feet away, also face down in the brush.

Fear snaked up her spine. That hadn't been Hakeem on the phone. No one had called the fire department, and no one ever would. Beth and the guards were dead, the fire intentionally set. *To get me outside.*

Leaves crunched behind her. Too late, she realized her mistake.

She'd played right into the killer's hands.

Chapter Twenty-Six

Carolyn Mauser's gray Nissan sat in the driveway. A lamppost in the adjacent yard illuminated the tag number—NJ C24-BMV—and the sizeable dent in the left side of the rear bumper.

They still didn't know for sure if this was their guy, but every fiber of Dayne's being said it was. They needed more than just a similarity to a photo and a sketch. Like hard evidence that would stand up in court.

He parked on the street in front of the house. Nine eighty-five Oak Court. Paulson pulled up behind him.

Remy snorted, pacing behind back and forth in the kennel. *"Bleib."* His dog shoved her head through the window, uttering an unhappy whine. He gave her a quick scratch behind the ears then joined Paulson on the sidewalk.

"How do you want to play this?"

"By ear." He tugged a flashlight from his belt, stopping to shine it through the garage window. Aside from two bicycles, several storage bins, and some garden tools, the garage was empty. The other vehicle registered to Carolyn Mauser, a blue Chevy Equinox, wasn't there.

He jerked his head up. *A blue Chevy Equinox*. Like the one he'd seen two weeks ago on the street corner near Amy Thorpe's house. He'd thought it had been sitting at the stop sign too long. Coincidence? Damn, but he should have gone with his gut right then and there. If his mistake got Kat killed, he didn't know if he'd survive it.

He pulled his creds from his back pocket and continued up the walk. "Let's just get our feet inside the door, first." He pressed the doorbell. A gong sounded and a moment later, the curtain covering one of the door's glass side panels shifted.

A woman's face appeared, and she eyed them warily. Not that Dayne could blame her. It was eight o'clock on a Sunday night. He and Paulson held up their badges. Slowly, the door opened.

"Can I help you?" Carolyn Mauser looked like her DMV photo and description, about five-three, blond hair, and blue eyes. She wore a blue skirt and tan sweater. A gold cross hung from a chain around her neck.

"Yes, ma'am," Dayne said, taking in the large wood crucifix on the wall behind her. "I'm Special Agent Andrews with the FBI, and this is Detective Paulson with the Orangetown Police Department. Is your husband at home?"

She shook her head. "No. Christian is working tonight." *On a Sunday?* He and Paulson exchanged looks. "He's an accountant," Mrs. Mauser added quickly. "It's tax season, and he's been working almost every night for the last two weeks. Can I ask what this is about?"

"Is your husband's office located at the Sylvus Corporate Center in Englewood?"

"Why, yes." Carolyn's blond brows furrowed.

Check. One more piece of the puzzle snapped into place. Now they could connect Christian Mauser to one of Becca's last known locations, but it still didn't connect the guy to her or Amy's murder.

"Is this about the car accident?" Carolyn asked.

"Yes, it is," Dayne lied, nodding emphatically and hoping Carolyn didn't pick up on the fact that most law enforcement officers wouldn't be investigating a simple motor vehicle accident on a Sunday night. He had to keep the conversation going. Anything to get inside the house. "May we come in? We'd like to get some more details."

"Of course." She opened the door wider and stepped aside. Two teens, a boy and a girl, sat at the kitchen table, staring at their laptops. They looked up questioningly as Dayne and Paulson came in. "Mary, Seth...please go upstairs while I speak to the officers." Wordlessly, the teens closed their laptops and went upstairs. "We can sit in here."

They followed her into the living room. Along the way, Dayne noted several framed family photos on the wall, including a wedding portrait of a younger Carolyn Mauser and a heavyset, clean-shaven man with brown hair and blue eyes. *Not* brown eyes.

Christian Mauser's DMV description said the man had brown eyes. Kat said her attacker's eyes were brown but murky, the way someone's eyes might look if they wore colored contacts.

"I'm actually happy you're here." Carolyn sat on the sofa, indicating two armchairs. Dayne sat in one, Paulson the other. "The insurance company has been giving us so much trouble over our claim, and the accident wasn't even our fault."

"How so?" Paulson took out a notepad.

"We were sitting at a traffic light and were hit from behind. The other driver's insurance company actually thinks we had something to do with the accident." Carolyn fingered the cross around her neck.

"Why is that?" Dayne asked.

"I suffered a slight case of whiplash and went to the

doctor. Our next-door neighbor is an injury lawyer and suggested we make a claim of pain and suffering against the other driver's company. My husband didn't want to make a fuss, but I pursued it anyway. As soon as I began making inquiries, the other insurance company started asking all kinds of questions. They didn't believe my injury was real. They think we're part of some insurance scam and working with the people who hit us in order to make a false claim."

Check, check. Becca had been working for an insurance company investigating scams such as the one Carolyn had just described. Another connection between Becca and Christian Mauser. It still wasn't enough.

"Did your husband receive any injuries from the accident?" Dayne asked, still trying to keep the conversation going until something else pinged, because he knew he was on the right track here.

"No." She waved a dismissive hand. "Aside from being extremely annoyed, that is. Ironically, he recently broke his nose, but not from the accident."

He stiffened. Kat said she'd hit her attacker in the nose with a palm strike. Maybe even broken his nose.

"How did he break it?" He flicked Paulson a quick look, taking in the detective's equally rigid posture.

"Someone opened a door on him at work."

"When was this?" Paulson asked.

"Almost two weeks ago."

Triple check. Dayne gave a mental fist pump. The timing was right. They had their man. He was sure of it.

Carolyn's eyes narrowed. "What does this have to do with the accident?"

"Probably nothing," Dayne reassured her in a calm voice. Inside he was anything *but* calm. "The insurance company may try to make it seem like too many injuries in one family and in such a short time period is suspicious in nature."

She nodded. "Ah, I see."

"In the interest of time," Paulson added, "perhaps we could speak directly with your husband. Would you mind calling him?"

"As I said, he's at work." Carolyn frowned, and Dayne worried how far they could take their subterfuge before she caught on and kicked them out. "He doesn't like me disturbing him at the office."

"It's important," Dayne added. "Anything you can do to help us facilitate things would be greatly appreciated."

Again, she fingered her cross. "Well, all right." She rose and went into the kitchen.

He and Paulson followed her to listen in. She removed a remote phone from a receiver on the kitchen wall, pushed a button then held the phone to her ear. While they waited, Dayne studied the wedding photo on the wall outside the kitchen.

"What are you thinking?" Paulson whispered.

"If this is Christian Mauser—and I think it is—he lied to the DMV. He could have lost weight, but he can't change his real eye color."

"He's not at his desk phone," Carolyn called out. "I'll try his cell."

"Thank you, Mrs. Mauser," Dayne replied, then lowered his voice. "It's still not enough."

"I agree." Paulson nodded then tucked his pad and pen into his jacket pocket. "We need more."

"He *what*?" Carolyn's voice rose. "That isn't possible. I saw him leave for work every day." Dayne and Paulson joined her in the kitchen, taking in her stricken expression. "Thank you, Adam." She returned the phone to its cradle. For a moment, she didn't say anything but remained staring at the wall. Finally, she turned. "I couldn't reach him, not at the office or on his cell phone, so I called Adam. He and Christian share an office. Adam said Christian has been calling in sick every day for the last week. He hasn't been to work, day *or* night."

"Did he come home last night?" Dayne asked.

"Yes." She nodded, the worry in her eyes deepening.

"Have you seen him tonight?" When she shook her head, warning bells shrilled in his mind. As much as he wanted to cut to the chase, they needed to tread carefully, or they'd lose her cooperation and miss out on getting the evidence they needed. "When was the last time you saw him?"

"This morning. At breakfast."

Gently, he urged her into the hallway outside the kitchen. "Is this your husband?" He pointed to the wedding photo. "He looks very different from his driver license photo."

She touched the frame. "He's lost over a hundred pounds since we were married."

"DMV records indicate he has brown eyes." Dayne pointed. "In this photo, his eyes are blue."

"He wears brown contact lenses. He has an acute sensitivity to light." Her lips twisted, and her expression turned to one of confusion. "I didn't know he told the DMV he had brown eyes. He probably did that because he always wears his contacts."

"I'm sure that's true." And to hide his identity. "Where are you from, Mrs. Mauser?"

"Minnesota." The skin over the bridge of her nose wrinkled. "Why?"

"Where is your husband from?"

"Minnesota. That's where we met."

"Did he ever go by any other name?"

"No! What is going on here?" She looked from him to Paulson, her eyes narrowing. "What are you not telling me?"

He and Paulson exchanged looks, one that said they were running out of excuses. And running out of time. Christian Mauser was on the loose and no one knew where he was.

Time for the Hail Mary.

"Mrs. Mauser, what I'm about to say may come as a shock. Trust me, we wouldn't say it if we didn't think it were true."

"Oh god." She slid the gold cross back and forth along the chain. "Please, just tell me. Is he dead?"

"No." He shook his head. "But we need your help and we need it fast. We believe that your husband may not be who he says he is."

Her jaw dropped. "What do you mean?"

"Do you have something of his we could borrow? A hairbrush, a toothbrush, something he touches every day?" Something with DNA or fingerprints.

"I don't understand this." Her grip on the gold cross tightened, her knuckles whitening. "I need to call Christian again. I need to talk with my husband."

Dayne exhaled a tight breath but let her go. They waited while she dialed. A minute later, she returned, her face paling more by the second.

"He's still not answering. I don't know what to do."

"Mrs. Mauser…Carolyn. Please." He used her first name to establish a more personal link she might respond to more readily. "We're looking for someone. Someone dangerous, and we're running out of time. We need your help, and we need it now. If the person we're looking for isn't your husband, then his fingerprints and DNA will definitively rule him out as a suspect." It was him. Dayne knew it.

Carolyn's eyes flicked back and forth. "He's a God-fearing man. He's active in the church. We both are. He wouldn't hurt anyone. I know it. I know it in my heart." The chain around her neck tightened then broke. The gold cross fell to the floor with a *ping*.

"Please, Carolyn. With your help, we can rule him out within twenty-four hours. By the time he gets home, this could all be over."

Yeah, with my hands around the fucker's throat.

Her eyes took on a faraway look as she processed the implications of what he'd just said. He wanted to press harder but worried they were about to lose her.

"O-okay," she whispered.

He cast a quick look to the crucifix on the wall. *Thank you, Jesus.*

Her gait was unsteady as she led them upstairs then through the master bedroom into the bathroom. She opened a drawer and pointed. "That's his, and so is the toothbrush in the cup."

Dayne grabbed two tissues from the box on the vanity, one for the hairbrush and one for the toothbrush. He handed one tissue to Paulson, who went for the toothbrush, while Dayne took the hairbrush.

"Thank you, Carolyn." He nodded to Paulson. "We'll get you a property receipt."

Minutes later, they placed the items in separate evidence bags Dayne dug from the back of his SUV. Paulson filled out a property receipt, going back inside the house to give it to Carolyn Mauser. While Dayne waited for the detective to return, he tried calling Beth Shanahan and the security guards on duty outside the castle and the Canine Haven. Nobody answered. What were the chances of none of them answering at the same time?

He tightened his hand around his cell and punched up Kat's number. It went to voicemail.

"Mike." He grabbed the evidence bags. "Get these to the nearest lab and run them for prints. Call me if you get a hit. I'm heading to the castle. No one's answering there."

"You got it."

"And send patrol cars to the castle and the Canine Haven. Tell them I'll meet them there."

He pounded to the Interceptor and fired up the engine. *Please don't let me be too late.* Two seconds later, he was peeling rubber up the New Jersey Turnpike.

Chapter Twenty-Seven

Before she turned around, she knew. *It's him.*
The killer.
An uncontrollable shudder swept through her body, and her heart began thudding painfully in her chest. Cold, stark fear prevented her from getting a single one of her body parts to move. Sucking in a deep breath, she started to turn when he grabbed her hair and yanked. Hard.

Excruciating pain radiated through her skull as he dragged her backward, twisting her hair tighter. She screamed, flailing her arms and clawing at his hands, but it was no use. His grip was too tight.

Panic exploded in her mind, and she drew in quick, shallow breaths, trying her best not to tighten his hold and add to the throbbing pain in her scalp.

Don't give up. Fight!

With a rough shove, he pushed her to the ground on her belly and rammed his knee between her shoulder blades. She breathed in a mixture of damp grass, smoke, and gasoline.

Again, he grabbed her hair, pulling it tighter and forcing

her to angle her head backward. Something sharp dug into the tender flesh of her neck.

A knife.

She uttered a choking cry. *The knife he murdered Becca with?*

"Where is the memory card?" His voice was low and raspy. "Where is it?"

She gasped for air but that only dug the edge of the blade deeper into her skin. She couldn't see it but felt it—blood trickling from the open wound. "The F—"

No. If she told him the FBI and the police had the memory card, he'd kill her. She had to give him a reason to keep her alive. "It's in my bank box."

"Goddammit!" he roared then rammed his knee more forcefully into her back.

A jagged rock bit into her ribs, sending a stab of agony through her torso. "I can get it for you," she grit out. "First thing tomorrow morning."

"Lying bitch," he growled at her ear. "I don't believe you. I already know it's not at the dog shelter. Is it in the house?"

"N-no." Once he realized she couldn't produce the memory card, he'd figure out the police had it. Then he'd have no reason to keep her alive. *I saw his face, and he knows it.* Either way, he was going to kill her.

All she had to do was stay alive long enough to get free. Long enough for the police to arrive. It sounded so simple. It wasn't. He had a knife and was *much* stronger than she was.

She had to stall for time. Better yet, get the hell out of there.

Angus's shrill barks rent the air. The puppy darted in, trying to bite the killer's arm. The blade at her throat disappeared as he took a swipe at Angus.

"Fucking dog."

"Nooooo." She flung her fist into his forearm, making

enough contact to offset his aim. Angus darted away, his barks becoming more insistent. Rage bubbled up from somewhere deep inside her. *If he hurts that puppy, I'll—* What? What could she do?

A siren wailed in the distance. She still couldn't see the killer's face but sensed his body going taut.

"Get up." He grabbed her upper arm and jerked her to her feet. She gasped as tendons and ligaments screamed in protest. "Move!" A hand at her back shoved her so hard she nearly stumbled.

She started to turn but he shoved her again, forcing her across the grass. Angus had stopped barking, and she flicked her gaze back and forth, searching for him. Finally she glimpsed his golden coat as he bounded beside them. Relief poured over her.

"Where are we going?" Wherever it was, it couldn't be good.

He grabbed her again by the hair, jerking her against his chest. His breath was hot in her ear. "Inside, to get the card. Then, somewhere I can set your soul free." The growled words reeked with menace and fury.

Set my soul free?

Coming from a homicidal madman wielding a sharp knife, that couldn't be good.

Sirens grew louder as he forced her toward the castle steps. When she didn't come up with the memory card, he'd gut her on the spot. She'd never have the chance to convince Dayne he was wrong. They *could* make it work. For that to happen, she had to live.

Over the blood pounding in her ears, his mumbled words slithered over her like a venomous snake. "*He* will set me free. *He* will show me the path to righteousness, guiding my sword to set all sinners free of shame." With that last word, he twisted her hair tighter.

She bit back a cry. *Sonofabitch!* He was out of his mind. And angry.

I'm angry, too. Pissed as hell, actually.

This evil man, this—*fucking asshole*—had no right to take her life. She'd never get married or have children. Never love or *be* loved. Only vaguely did it register that she was really getting the hang of this cursing thing.

Fuck. That.

She took a deep breath and spun. Sections of hair parted from her scalp. She screamed then reared back her fist and slammed it into his face.

It was a glancing blow. Momentum sent her flying against his chest, but he'd released her hair.

He coughed, then coughed again, dragging in a wheezing breath.

Right then she didn't care if she broke his windpipe because she was free.

"Angus!" She tore across the driveway, hitting the tree line at a dead run. Branches whipped at her face, slicing into her skin. Her heart hammered, and her pulse roared in her ears. The woods were nearly pitch black and she stumbled, righting herself before face-planting into a rock. She glanced to her right, gratified to see Angus keeping pace.

Crunching leaves and branches came from behind her. *He's coming.*

She ran faster, pushed herself harder until her thighs and calves screamed in protest.

A sliver of light from a break in the clouds lit something ahead. Water. She veered around the puddle then tripped, forcing her to step into the water. Mud sucked at her foot and she went down on her knees. Mucky water splashed in her face, obscuring her vision.

Oh shit. Shit. She couldn't see.

She drew in ragged breaths, swiping at the muck in her

eyes while reaching out blindly to steady herself. Her hand made contact with the very thing she'd tripped over. At first, she couldn't identify the object. A second later, she froze. Her throat constricted, and she nearly screamed. The thing she'd tripped over was—

A body. The clouds gave way just long enough for her to glimpse an embroidered nametag.

"Oh no." She covered her mouth with her hand, swallowing hard to keep from vomiting the remnants of food in her stomach.

It was Manny—the flower delivery guy.

Angus whimpered. "Shhh," she crooned. If he barked, he'd give away their location.

The puppy quieted, prancing nervously a few feet away.

She pushed with her hands, but the mud sucked her in deeper. More crunching. Closer this time. A burst of adrenaline refueled her determination. Stifling a cry of rage, she tugged first one foot free of the mud, then the other. One of her shoes came off as she pulled from the muck.

"Angus, let's go," she whispered, and they took off again.

She had no idea how far they'd run from the castle. Fifty yards. Eighty. A hundred...

Her chest heaved, her muscles ached, and the foot without a shoe was cut up from sharp branches and rocks and stung like a *mother.*

Another break in the clouds glinted off a building up ahead. The old document bunker. She hadn't been inside the place for years. The thing was like a fortress, with concrete block walls and heavy, locking metal doors. If she could get there before he caught up to them, she'd be safe until help arrived.

Kat raced to the building and tugged on the handle. It didn't budge. It should have been unlocked. They hadn't stored anything there since the fire twenty years ago. Now all her family's valuable documents were either stored in a bank vault or on hard drives.

Twigs snapped. She jerked her head around. "Open. Dear God, please open!"

She gritted her teeth, pulling harder on the handle. Her arm and shoulder muscles screamed from the strain. It still didn't budge. The snapping of limbs behind her grew louder.

Kat planted her shoeless foot on the concrete wall beside the door. With another mighty heave, the door squeaked then opened. She fell backward on her ass, and a bolt of pain lanced up her spine.

A dark figure crashed through the trees.

Her pulse rate ramped higher. She pushed to her feet, opening the door just enough for her and Angus to slip inside. With a shaking hand, she fumbled for the light switch, praying the power hadn't been cut off. Long, tubular bulbs flickered to life. She pulled the door shut and twisted the lock on the knob.

The handle jiggled and she jumped back, holding her breath. The handle jiggled again then went silent. Relief had her sagging to the point where she almost collapsed on the floor.

Her chest continued sawing as she sucked in damp, musty air. She turned to take in their surroundings. A charred desk in one corner. Burned remains of the old oak filing cabinets. A lone fire extinguisher, and—

A river of sweat trickled between her shoulder blades. *The other door.* She'd forgotten there were *two* doors to the repository. Was it locked?

She ran to it, reaching out to test the knob.

The door burst open, slamming into her forehead. She staggered back. The room spun as she fell to her knees.

A door slammed shut. When her vision cleared, she looked up...

...into the face of pure evil.

Chapter Twenty-Eight

Dayne's red-and-blue strobes ricocheted off the trees bracketing Tweed Boulevard. He turned off the main road, and before he made it halfway down the drive to the Haven, other strobes flashed in the distance.

His heart rate didn't slow a beat as he hit the final turn. He still couldn't reach Kat, Beth, or any of the guards on their cells, and he'd called every one of them three times during the thirty minutes he'd hauled ass up the Turnpike. The two local PD cruisers parked in front of the Haven should have eased his anxiety. They didn't. Nor did the ambulance quickly closing the gap behind him. The PD must have called for it.

His heart leaped into his throat. He shoved the gearshift into park, jumped out, and ran to the nearest cop. "Who is it? Who's the ambulance for?" He held his breath. *Please don't be—*

"A security guard." The cop jerked his thumb to the back of the Haven. "Someone knifed him in the gut. Don't know if he'll make it."

He let out the breath he'd been holding. Mauser was here.

Somewhere on the grounds. Knowing the guard had been taken out was bad enough. At least Kevin, Fiona, and the volunteers were long gone for the day.

"Call for more backup and stay alert," Dayne warned. "There's a homicide suspect on the loose and he's here. Name's Christian Mauser." He gave the cop a quick description. "Tell your partner, then meet me at the castle. I'll leave the gate open." Two seconds later he was back in his SUV and speeding toward the gate. He punched in the code then hit the button to lock the gate in the open position.

Dayne slammed his foot on the gas pedal. Remy snorted from the back seat. "Sorry, girl."

He skidded to a stop in front of the castle, pausing only to grab a flashlight from the console and pop open Remy's door. The pungent smell of gasoline and smoke hit him in the face, growing stronger as he rounded the northwest corner. He clicked on the flashlight, taking in the smoldering shrubs first and then the three bodies lying on the edge of the grass.

The guards. And Beth. *Shit.*

Strobe lights reflected off the trees, indicating the other cop had joined him.

Dayne drew his gun, maintaining a firm grip on the flashlight as he aimed the beam over the yard and the brush line. He ran to Beth and the guards, feeling each of their necks for a pulse. Luckily, they were still alive.

"Call for more ambulances," he shouted to the cop rushing over. "I'm going inside." He ran to the front steps. Remy loped next to him. Cautiously, he pushed the door open. It was another five minutes before he cleared the place. No sign of Kat anywhere. Or Angus.

Before leaving her bedroom, he grabbed her lavender sweater for Remy to get a scent.

Christ, if anything happens to her... The thought gutted him.

He ran back outside just as two more cruisers skidded to a stop in front of the steps. Dayne's cell vibrated and he yanked it from his belt. *Paulson.* "What've you got?"

"Two clear prints from the hairbrush, and we got a hit. A big one. Christian Mauser's real name is Robert Fulbright."

"I know that name." He tried to remember why but couldn't.

"You should," Paulson continued. "We *all* should. Eighteen years ago, Robert Fulbright killed his entire family in Oregon. His wife, mother, three children. The guy disappeared without a trace."

Dayne gripped the phone tighter. Jesus, he *did* remember that case. The killings happened before he became an FBI agent, but Becca told him all about it because she'd worked the case before transferring to New Jersey.

The rest of the puzzle locked into place.

Becca had photographed Christian Mauser in connection with her insurance fraud investigation. She'd either recognized him, or he'd caught her photographing him. So he killed her then stole the file from her office.

"Dayne, you there?" Paulson shouted. A siren screamed through the phone. But the detective was all the way down in Edison.

"Yeah." He gripped the sweater in his hand even tighter. "Send more patrol cars. Tell them to start searching the roads in and around the Vandenburg estate. Tweed Boulevard, Bradley Hill Road, and Park Road."

"Already on their way."

Dayne ended the call then held Kat's sweater out for Remy to sniff. When his dog had inhaled her scent, he tucked the sweater through his belt. *"Such!"*

Remy tore down the steps, nose to the ground, circling until she found a track and followed it to where the cops stood by Beth and the guards' prone bodies. His K-9 zigzagged then circled twice more before heading across the driveway to the tree line. She turned to wait for him, expecting him to clip on her search lead.

"*Voraus!*" He waved his hand in the air for Remy to keep going then he hit the ground running.

He aimed his flashlight dead ahead, doing his best to keep up. Occasionally, Remy stopped, circled, then took off again. Dayne's pulse raced faster than he thought possible. Sweat soaked his polo. He prayed they wouldn't be too late.

He recalled the day he and Remy had found a track that led all the way through the woods to the Blauvelt State Park parking lot. He'd been sure then that Mauser had left his vehicle there. If Mauser got Kat into his Equinox before they caught up, he could take her anywhere. And kill her.

Fuck. He hadn't put out a BOLO for the Equinox. Another mistake.

He pounded through the trees, not caring how much noise he made. If—*no, when*—Remy found Kat, she'd alert and start barking.

As if reading his thoughts, Remy's barks sliced through the air, getting louder as Dayne neared where his K-9 stood in a moonlit clearing up ahead. Judging by the rigidity of his dog's posture, she'd found something. The slumped form on the ground at Remy's feet was definitely a body. Time—and his heart—seemed to slow.

Please don't be Kat.

The beam of his flashlight lit on the corpse. He sucked in a tight breath, letting his head tip forward in the most relief he'd ever experienced in his godforsaken life. It wasn't Kat.

The man's nametag glowed in the overhead light. Manny. Beside the body lay a bouquet of mangled pink roses. He'd bet his ass this was the same bunch of flowers Manny had with him outside the Vandenburg building in the city. Meaning, the man had been dead for days.

Meaning Christian Mauser aka Robert Fulbright had been watching them for who knew how long.

A chilling fear gripped his soul. If Remy tracked Kat's scent only to find another corpse, he didn't know what he'd do.

He'd made a mistake. A big fucking mistake.

Chapter Twenty-Nine

Kat's belly lurched as the killer secured the lock on the knob then slid a knife from a leather sheath on his belt.

"It's too late. You've ruined *everything*." The blade was long and sharp and shiny as he raised it above his shoulder, ranting louder, "Because of you, *bitch*, I have to start all over again. Do you have any idea what that means?" Spittle flew from his mouth. His eyes radiated madness.

You're not the only one who's mad. She gritted her teeth. *It can't end this way. I won't let it.* Although how she'd get out of this, she didn't know.

He tightened his grip on the ebony handle, raising the knife higher. "God will cleanse your soul. *He* will put you on the righteous path, saving you from your sins. *He* will set your soul free. I am *His* servant."

On top of everything else, he really was out of his fucking mind. *Sorry, Mother.* Swearing—even to herself—just seemed like the right thing to do at the moment. Besides, if she was about to die, it wouldn't really matter anyway.

Frantically, she searched the room again, but nothing had

changed. No deadly weapons had miraculously materialized since the first time she'd checked. With every step closer he took, she crab-walked backward. Angus lunged for his leg, latching on the way he'd done to Remy. Only this wasn't playtime.

The killer's eyes narrowed as he glared down at the puppy. More spittle flew from his lips then he kicked Angus, sending him tumbling over and over. The puppy hit the wall with a *thump* and lay still.

"No!" she cried and crawled to Angus's side. Her heart dropped as she touched his limp, unconscious body. *Oh god no. Poor Angus.*

"You bastard!" she screamed, balling her hands into fists. Fury, the likes of which she'd never known, erupted inside her. For the first time in her life, she wanted to hurt someone. *Physically* hurt them.

Kat lunged for the fire extinguisher. The tank was probably empty, but it was all she had. She aimed the nozzle at his face then squeezed the trigger. Thick white spray splattered his face, completely obscuring his eyes, mouth, and nose.

The knife fell to the floor, clattering on the concrete. He sputtered, dragging in wheezing breaths and wiping the foamy chemical from his eyes.

She lunged for the knife but he grabbed her wrist, giving a vicious twist as he picked up the knife in his other hand. Pain shot up her arm to her shoulder, and she screamed.

A dog barked. *Remy.*

The doorknob jiggled then went silent. Heavy pounding rattled the door.

"No one can save you but me," the killer snarled, although there was a sense of peace and acceptance in his eyes. He raised his arm again—the one holding the knife. Her heart hammered, and she gasped for air. "Our Father, God, who art in heaven…"

The doorknob rattled again, quieter this time. She

tightened her muscles, preparing to ram her knee into his groin when he shoved her roughly backward, slamming her head against the concrete wall.

Pain wracked her skull. Her vision clouded, but not so much that she couldn't see him advancing on her.

"All hallowed be thy name. Thy kingdom come; Thy will be done."

She gulped and stared into a set of soulless eyes. *I'm not ready to die.*

Dayne, please. Hurry.

Then she screamed.

• • •

Dayne dropped the credit card he'd used to open the locked door and yanked his Glock from the holster. Kat's scream echoed inside, and his heart nearly stopped beating.

He turned the knob, ramming his shoulder against the thick metal door. It wouldn't open. He re-holstered, using all his weight on the door. Finally, it creaked open and crashed inward against the concrete wall.

Mauser snarled, releasing Kat then lunging at Dayne. Remy leaped, latching onto Mauser's forearm. The knife fell to the floor.

Dayne rammed his fist into the guy's face. Bones cracked—Mauser's.

The man went down and when he tried to rise, Dayne pummeled his face again and again, holding him up by the shirt so he couldn't fall back to the floor.

"Dayne! *Dayne!*"

He jerked his head to the sound of Kat's voice. Was she hurt? Still gripping Mauser's bloody shirt, he searched her face and body for injuries, seeing none. Then he looked at Mauser, whose bloody, mashed-in face was nearly unrecognizable. He released the guy's shirt. The back of Mauser's head hit the floor with a solid *whack*.

Outside, footsteps pounded. Uniformed police, guns drawn, crowded into the bunker.

"FBI." Dayne adjusted his position to reveal the badge on his belt so the responding officers wouldn't mistakenly think *he* was the perp and unload their guns on him.

"You good here?" one of the cops asked, warily ey眼 Mauser's bloody, still form.

"Yeah," he answered. "We're good." All things considered. His hands shook, his body still so amped up on pure rage he could barely think straight.

Another cop called on the radio for an ambulance while others began securing the scene.

Kat crawled to the other side of the room and gathered Angus in her arms. At first, the pup didn't move. Remy padded to Kat and nudged Angus with her snout, licking the puppy's face.

"Please wake up, Angus. Wake up!" Tears streamed down her face.

She's alive.

Dayne took his first easy breath in hours, although it was an unsteady one, to be sure. He wanted to haul her into his arms but stopped himself. Touching her again would be too painful and would only rekindle something that needed to burn out.

You gotta let her go, man.

The puppy's head moved, and he began wriggling in Kat's arms. Her laugh came out on a sob. That's when he noticed it. The trickle of blood oozing slowly from a cut on her neck. *That motherfucker hurt her.*

He clamped his jaw. It was all he could do not to prop Mauser up and beat the shit out of him all over again.

Kneeling, he touched his fingers to Kat's neck to inspect

the wound. Touching her again warred with his resolve, but he had to stay strong. For both of them. With no small effort, he forced his emotions back into that deep, dark hole he'd stashed them in. "Are you alright?" He knew *he* wasn't because he was choking on his own heart.

When she lifted her head, he feasted on her beautiful eyes. "I'm fine. Thanks to you."

He cleared his throat then tugged a packet of tissues from his thigh pocket, gently pressing one of them against her neck. Luckily, the cut wasn't as deep as he'd initially worried it was. "Hold this here and keep a light pressure on it."

When she did, their fingers brushed and the instinct—no, *need*—to hold her, kiss her, and tell her he'd never leave her again became unbearable.

"Sir?" Two EMTs crowded in. "Can you give us some room to work? We need to check her out." Without waiting, one of them knelt and began inspecting Kat's wound, effectively pushing him away.

They were right. Her medical condition trumped his need to stick close. Still…

"Dayne!" Paulson rushed into the bunker, his eyes bugging as he looked at Mauser. "Holy shit. Guess I missed all the action. How 'bout filling me in? My chief wants an update."

With a hand that still shook, Dayne touched Kat's cheek. "You're safe now."

She looked up at him, her eyes brimming with gratitude and the same sadness eating him alive.

"Make sure she's okay," he said to one of the cops then stood and pointed to Mauser. "I don't care how bloody he is. Cuff him." He waited until Mauser was securely restrained with handcuffs.

It about killed him not to look at Kat one last time. Somehow, he managed. His heart slowed to a dull thud, and he walked out the door.

Chapter Thirty

Two weeks. Two long, lonely weeks and no word from Dayne. Not that she really expected him to contact her. There was nothing more to be said.

Taking a deep breath, Kat touched up her lipstick in the private powder room. A thin red line remained on her neck from where Mauser had cut her. Looking at it day after day brought a tightness to her chest. Like her broken heart, it might never heal completely.

Music from the ballroom thumped through the walls. *Happy birthday to me.* Birthday, yes. Happy, no.

Despite her protests, Colin had insisted she attend the party he'd been planning for months. So much had gone into the black-tie event that she didn't have the heart to cancel. The only way she'd agreed to attend was if her friends—her *real* friends—came, too. Emily, Francine, Walter, Kevin, and Fiona had given her the support she'd needed.

She plucked a tissue from the box on the counter and dabbed at her lips. The person staring back at her from the mirror was a stranger. She might look the same, regaled in a glittery gold evening gown and yellow diamonds, but her soul would never be the same. Dayne had done that. He'd shown her what it was to love someone so deeply, and with such absolute fervency, that no one else could ever take their place.

Before he'd come into her life, her world had become a prison. He'd changed that, made her want to experience life again outside the walls she'd been hiding behind.

Had she really driven him away? Not intentionally. Perhaps she *had* said or done things to make him believe he would never fit into her over-the-top life. It didn't matter. *He* was the one who thought he didn't belong with her. As long as he believed that, they could never be happy together. Above all else, she wanted that for him. Happiness. She loved him that much. *Enough to let him go.* But with each passing day, her heart broke a little more. Maybe he really had spared them both more pain.

If only things could have been different. If only...

The tightness in her chest worsened. There was no sense weeping over *if only*s.

At least Christian Mauser, whose real name she'd learned from Detective Paulson was Robert Fulbright, would never hurt another living soul. At a minimum, the man would be behind bars in New Jersey for the rest of his life. First-degree murder charges in Oregon could get him the death penalty.

With his jaw wired shut from the injuries he'd received at the end of Dayne's fist, he'd asked for a priest then confessed everything. Eighteen years ago, he murdered his entire family, waiting for each of them to return home one day from work, college, high school, then coldly slit their throats. In his confession, he claimed they were failing God, had lost their way, and he'd killed them to save their souls.

Apparently, Fulbright had planned those murders in excruciating detail and had set up a new life for himself in

Minnesota. A few false identity documents and voilà, he was Christian Mauser. Eventually, he married and moved to New Jersey, where he began his new life—until Rebecca Garman figured out who he really was.

Mauser had seen Rebecca taking his picture. He'd confronted her and killed her before realizing she'd hidden the camera's memory card in Angus's chew toy. Media coverage of her holding Angus outside Becca's office the day she found the body was a roadmap to where Angus was—at the Canine Haven. Mauser had gone there in search of the chew toy. She and Amy were just in the wrong place at the wrong time. When Kat glimpsed Mauser's face that night, she became a target he had to eliminate.

If Dayne and Remy hadn't found her in time… She shuddered at what would have been her fate. Even Angus might not have lived.

Angus had suffered a slight concussion from being thrown against the wall, but he'd recovered nicely and was now a permanent part of her household. Rebecca Garman's husband had given Angus to her, saying the pup had been his wife's, and having him around would remind him too much of his loss.

The only good news over the last two weeks was that Beth and the security guards would recover. She'd sent them flowers and visited them in the hospital several times.

After capping her lipstick, she dropped the tube back into the gold box on the vanity, plastered on a pathetically wan smile, and headed back to the party.

The first thing that hit her was the gaiety. Music, laughter, and dancing. She *so* didn't feel it. The next thing she noticed was the gift table. In the last ten minutes, the stack of wrapped boxes had grown by at least two feet. Expensive, extravagant gifts she didn't want or need.

A champagne flute appeared in her hand. The urge for

something stronger welled up inside her. "Wait," she called to the waitress. "Can you dig me up some of that Chivas Royal Salute? Neat," she added. *Wouldn't want to water down liquid gold.*

"Of course, Miss Vandenburg." The young woman took the flute and disappeared into the crowd.

"Happy birthday, Kat." Walter kissed her on the cheek, as did Emily, Francine, Kevin, and Fiona, who joined them just as the waitress reappeared with her glass of Chivas.

"Thank you." She clinked glasses with her friends and took a sip of the fifty-year-old scotch. The whisky slid down her throat to her belly, leaving a soothing warmth in its wake. Just what she needed. A little numbness.

Walter continually flicked his eyes to the ballroom doors where several men in tuxedos milled about.

"I must say"—she glanced from Walter to Kevin—"you both look exceedingly dashing in black tie."

"Thanks." Kevin grinned and waggled his eyes at Fiona. "Told ya."

Fiona made a choking noise in her throat. "That tux has gone straight to his head. He'll probably wear it tomorrow morning while he's cleaning out cages."

"Ladies," Kat said, "might I add that you look equally stunning?"

"You didn't have to buy us these dresses." Emily fingered the beaded strap of her blue silk evening gown.

"Nonsense. It was my pleasure." Again, she caught Walter eying the doors. "Looking for someone?"

"No." Walter chuckled. "Just comparing cummerbunds."

They all laughed, and for the first time that night, Kat thought she might actually survive the party.

Loud clinking came from the front of the ballroom. Colin stood on the dais, tapping a knife on the side of his glass.

The worst part of the party was about to commence.

Standing in front of two hundred guests and pasting on more smiles she didn't feel in the slightest.

"Katrina," Colin called out. "Would you please come up here?"

The ballroom quieted. Heads turned her way.

"You can do this, Kat," Emily whispered.

"Right. I can do this." *Suck it up.* She walked to the stage, setting her glass on a nearby table, when what she really wanted was to chug the contents in one very un-ladylike slurpy gulp.

At the top step, Colin took her hand then set his glass down on the Baby Grand piano. *Oh, faux pas.* One did *not* do that to a Baby Grand. He clasped her shoulders as he leaned in to kiss her on the lips. As always, she presented her cheek. A hint of annoyance lit his eyes as he reached for his drink.

"Katrina." He raised his glass, as did everyone in the room. "Happy birthday."

"Happy birthday!" came two hundred voices, followed by applause.

Thank god they hadn't sung the happy birthday song. Yet. That would probably come right before the cutting of that tasteless, five-tiered cake taking up an entire table in a corner of the ballroom. It couldn't hold a candle to one of Francine's or Lily's cakes. Even Dayne's cookie sandwiches would be preferable.

"I'd like to give you *my* gift first." He set the flute back on the shiny black piano then pulled a small velvet box from his jacket pocket.

No. Oh hell *no.*

"Colin, don't," she whispered loud enough for him to hear. "I know I made myself clear. I can't do this with you. *Ever.*" She reached out to stop him before he opened the box, but he ignored her and went down on one knee, flipping open the lid. She groaned, experiencing a dropping sensation in the pit of her stomach. Gasps came from the crowd. This was worse than she could possibly have imagined.

Over the past two weeks the rift between her and Colin had grown, but embarrassing him in front of two hundred people wasn't her style. Then again, he'd done this to himself.

"Katrina, will you marry me?"

She opened her mouth to politely, yet firmly, reject his offer when a deep voice boomed from the ballroom doors.

"No. She won't."

Dayne!

Her heart fluttered, and her insides began tingling so much her entire body seemed to vibrate with hopeful energy. She could barely breathe. *He's really here.*

He shoved one hand in his tuxedo pants pocket. In his other hand was a gift-wrapped package. Remy and Angus sat on either side, each wearing white bows around their collars.

"At least," he continued, "not until I give her *my* gift."

Everyone watched as he strode past the tables. Whispers accompanied his progress as he wended his way through the crowd that parted in his path.

"Is that a dog?" someone said. "I didn't think you could bring a dog in here."

"Katrina!" Colin reached for her, his face livid.

She evaded him and met Dayne at the bottom of the stairs.

"You're not on the guest list," Colin hissed from the dais.

"*I* invited him." Walter beamed a thousand-watt smile at Kat, one that thoroughly explained his surreptitious glances at the ballroom doors.

She wanted to kiss the old man then yell at him for keeping her in the dark.

"What are you doing here?" Her heart raced as she gave him her first genuine smile of the evening. *God, he was handsome.* "What are you *all* doing here?" She reached down to pet Remy and Angus.

"We came to give you your birthday present." One side of his mouth quirked as he handed her the gift. She took it but couldn't tear her gaze from his and the love shining in his eyes. At least, she hoped that's what it was. "Open it."

She turned the gift over and slipped her fingers beneath the tape. As the beautiful gold foil paper parted, she gasped, letting the wrapping fall to the floor. The cover of the book was pristine. *Dogs of Character*, by Cecil Aldin.

Gently, she opened the book and her jaw dropped. A first edition, 1927 and signed by the author. "Ohhh," she breathed. The very book her father had searched for and never found. Her heart blossomed with so much love she thought it would burst from her chest. "You remembered."

"Yeah." He shrugged. "Turn to the next page."

She did and saw he'd inserted a handwritten note. She read the words three times. Just to be certain she wasn't dreaming.

I love you with every breath I take. Forgive me? Dayne.

Her throat constricted with worry. The words were incredibly beautiful, but she couldn't take it if he left her again. "I don't understand. What's changed in the last two weeks?"

"First, I flew to Oregon to help out the authorities there. After that, I talked with my friends and family. I needed time to sort things out in my head."

"Did you?" She held her breath.

He nodded. "You and I *are* different. This won't be easy. There'll be a helluva lot of compromises to be made by both of us, but I want to find a way to bridge our worlds. I love you too much not to. Are you still willing to see where this takes us?" The warmth and sincerity in his eyes filled her with so much promise, hope, and elation she could barely keep from flinging her arms around his neck.

She nodded back, slowly at first, then more vigorously as tears slid from the corners of her eyes. "Yes." If that's what it took, she'd make compromises every day for the rest of her life.

"I'll do anything for you." He framed her face with his hands. "I love you."

She smiled and her body trembled with joy. "I love you, too."

He kissed her. Right there in front of a gasping crowd.

"You've *got* to be kidding," Colin hissed.

Clapping came from nearby. Dayne ended the kiss in time for her to see her friends clapping enthusiastically. Kevin whistled loudly and then the entire crowd joined in.

"Whatdya say we get out of here?" he whispered against her ear.

"Sounds like a plan," she whispered back.

He swung her into his arms and carried her through the cheering crowd. Remy and Angus trotted after them, with her friends in tow.

Moments later, they were all standing in front of a cream-colored stretch limo she didn't recognize. The driver opened the passenger door, and Dayne herded the dogs inside.

"Whose limo is this?" she asked him.

"Mine." The sexy wink he gave her sent a tingle straight to her core. "For tonight, anyway. Hey, Walter." He grinned at the older man. "You guys mind taking the other limo home?"

"Not at all." Walter grinned back, giving Dayne what looked like a distinct nod of approval.

Kat swore a telepathic message passed between the two men. Considering Walter hadn't been Dayne's biggest fan after their initial meeting, Dayne certainly seemed to have won him over.

"Happy birthday, Kat." Emily kissed her on the cheek, followed by Francine, Fiona, and Kevin.

Without her wrap, she should have been freezing in the March night air, but all she felt was a soothing warmth and happiness from being surrounded by friends that loved her, and Dayne. It was a happy birthday after all.

She slipped her hand into his then settled with him into the limo. The dogs sat happily panting on the opposite seat. The second the door closed, Dayne kissed her, his lips firm yet gentle, his tongue thrusting inside her mouth, tangling with hers as he pulled her onto his lap.

She kissed him back, clinging to him, wanting him to feel every ounce of love she had to give. Beneath her dress, her nipples tightened painfully. The bulge of Dayne's erection beneath her buttocks hardened and lengthened.

"Dayne," she whispered.

"Mmm," he mumbled between dropping hot, wet kisses on the curve of her neck and the tops of her breasts.

"You're turning me into a limo sex maniac."

He grinned against her mouth. "If you've gotta be something, I'm okay with that." He pushed a button, lowering the driver's window. "How long until we get home?"

"Traffic's light tonight." The limo pulled away from the curb onto Park Avenue. "Should be about forty-five minutes, tops."

"Take your time." His grin broadened as he pushed the button again. The window rose and clicked shut. He readjusted her on his lap so she straddled him.

"I want you." She licked into his ear and was rewarded with a sexy groan. "Now." With unsteady hands, she reached between them, intending to tear off his cummerbund and tug down his zipper, but he stopped her.

She pulled back. "What's wrong?"

His smile broadened then he tipped his head, indicating to something over her shoulder.

The chauffeur window? She twisted her neck to see what

was so funny. "Didn't you—" *Oh.* "Ohhh." Two sets of eyes watched them curiously. *Canine* eyes. She snorted and held a hand over her mouth.

Dayne shifted her in his lap so she was snuggled comfortably with her head against his shoulder, then he tipped up her chin. "Honey, as much as I want to let you have your way with me in a stretch limo, we can't. Not in front of the children. Do you think you can put a lid on all that lust for at least forty-five minutes?"

She giggled, snuggling deeper against him and sighing. "I suppose so." She smiled against his chest, weightless and filled with so much happiness, she could float away.

Will it always be like this?

It *would* be. As long as she was with Dayne.

Their mouths came together, and their breaths became as one. This was where she was always meant to be. In the arms of this beautiful, humble, courageous man.

Epilogue

Yankee Stadium - American League Championship Series, Game Seven

The crack of a bat split the air. The crowd—including Dayne and his friends—roared with over fifty thousand other fans jumping to their feet as the Yanks tied the final game of the series with Boston 3-3. The next batter struck out, ending the top half of the seventh inning.

"More beer?" Dayne asked. Everyone nodded or gave him a thumbs-up. They'd all come in two limos, courtesy of Kat, who'd arranged everything.

"Yo, Dayne." Jaime joined him at the bar, clinking his empty bottle against Dayne's. "A luxury VIP suite, huh? Not a bad birthday gift at all."

He pulled another six-pack from the kitchen's refrigerator and set it on the bar. *Nope.* It wasn't. The best part was that his family and all his friends were there to celebrate with him.

His mother and father sat in the exterior cushioned seats, along with Lily and her kids. His friend Matt, his wife Trista, and their little boy, Joe, had driven up yesterday and spent the night in one of the castle's guest rooms. Nick, Andi, and their little girl had arrived that morning and would be sticking around for a few days. Eric and Tess, along with Tess's brother, Jesse, had driven in that afternoon and were also staying in the castle. There were as many bedrooms in the place as in a small motel.

Kade, Markus, and Jaime were the only bachelors left in the bunch. Not that Dayne and Kat had gotten married yet. Another thing he hoped to rectify, and soon. Before the seventh inning stretch ended. For that, he needed another beer.

Across the suite, Kat and his friends' wives were deep in conversation that elicited a round of giggling. Nick and Andi's baby, Rose, lay in Kat's arms, fast asleep. Over the baby's head, she caught his eye and winked.

"Man, you are totally whipped." Nick slapped him on the back.

"Yep." He nodded. He totally was, and that was okay with him. *More* than okay. It was fan-fucking-tastic.

Eric and Matt joined them.

"Happy birthday, pal." Eric gave him a bear hug.

Matt clapped him on the shoulder. "Another year gone by."

Yeah, and he couldn't wait to see what the next year would bring.

His mother, father, Lily, and the kids joined them inside the suite. The kids went for the tray of cookies and brownies, while his mother and Lily mingled with the other women. His father rested his hand on Dayne's shoulder.

Dayne couldn't take his eyes off Kat and the baby. There was no doubting she'd make a great mother.

Marriage was definitely in their future, but they were still working through the bumps and hurdles life continually presented them with. Like accepting the extravagant luxury VIP suite overlooking home plate. One of the many compromises they'd each made since Dayne and Remy had officially moved into the castle five months ago.

In exchange for him accepting the suite as a birthday gift, she'd gone camping with him in the Poconos. They'd grilled burgers and dogs then made love under the stars. The guys were more than right. Not only was he totally whipped, but he was 100 percent head over heels in love and couldn't be happier. He fingered the small box in his pocket.

Kade leaned in. "Does she know?"

Dayne shook his head, unable to speak. His throat had gone as dry as a desert.

"The seventh inning stretch is wasting away, here," Eric prodded.

"Yeah, bucko." Jaime nudged Dayne's shoulder. "She's not only rich, smokin' hot, but she loves baseball. If *you* don't ask her, *I* will."

"The man's right." Markus's amused expression took him by surprise. "What are you waiting for?"

What *was* he waiting for? He'd bought the ring a month ago, hanging on to it like a big chickenshit, waiting for the other shoe to drop. For someone to shake him awake and give him the bad news that he'd been dreaming. That the most wonderful woman in the world didn't love him. But she did, and she was standing ten feet away.

His father gave him the encouraging nod he needed to make his feet move.

"Kat," he said, joining her by the other women. "Can I borrow you for a minute?"

"Sure." She handed the baby back to Andi then he led her to the center of the suite and knelt, tugging the black velvet box from his pocket and flicking open the lid. Damned if his palms weren't sweaty.

He took a deep breath and swallowed, but that didn't do a thing to slow his racing heartbeat. "Katrina Vandenburg. You are my heart and my soul. With every breath I take, I love you more than the last. Will you marry me?"

She covered her mouth with her hands. Her body shook with sobs. Happy sobs, he hoped. He held his breath, waiting for the answer that would forever change his life. She nodded and lowered her hands. "Yes. It's about time. Yes!"

He didn't know which was smiling more, his face, or his heart. He plucked the ring from the box and slid it onto her finger. Then he stood and kissed her, pulling her against his chest so he could feel her heart beating against his.

A series of *aws* came from around the room. Dayne caught his friends fist-bumping his dad.

"There's something else I need to say." He had to say it now, so there'd be no lingering doubts in her mind. "I'll sign a prenup."

"Oh, Dayne." She blinked rapidly. "You don't have to do that."

"I know I don't." He kissed her palm. "I *want* to. I want to prove to you that I love you for *you* and nothing else."

"No, you don't understand." Tears spilled from her eyes and he tried brushing them away with his thumbs, but they kept coming too fast for him to keep up. "That's the one thing in this world I don't doubt. That you love me for me, and I love you for you. Don't you see? I don't care where you came from, and I don't care where you go. As long as we go there together. That's all that matters."

Hot tears welled behind his lids because he'd just learned the most important lesson of his life.

Home isn't where you come from. It's where you make it.

In the warmth, comfort, and joy of her loving arms, he was finally home.

Acknowledgments

My thanks to Kayla Gray and MK Mancos for your unwavering willingness to critique my books year after year. A very special thanks to my brother Matt. Your uncanny ability to troubleshoot a plot is invaluable. To my editor, Candace Havens. You have the patience of a saint! Last but by no means least, to everyone at Entangled who works so hard behind the scenes to publish my books and get them out there in the world.

About the Author

Tee O'Fallon is the author of the Federal K-9 Series and the NYPD Blue & Gold Series. Tee has been a federal agent for twenty-three years and is now a police investigator, giving her hands-on experience in the field of law enforcement that she combines with her love of romantic suspense. When not writing, Tee enjoys cooking, gardening, chocolate, lychee martinis, and spending time with her Belgian sheepdogs, Loki and Koko. Tee loves hearing from readers and can be contacted via her website https://teeofallon.com where you can also sign up for Tee's newsletters.

Don't miss the Federal K-9 series…

LOCK 'N' LOAD

ARMED 'N' READY

DARK 'N' DEADLY

Also by Tee O'Fallon…

BURNOUT

BLOOD MONEY

DISAVOWED

Discover more Amara titles…

Honor Avenged
a *HORNET* novel by Tonya Burrows

Leah Giancarelli would have crumbled if not for her late husband's best friend, Marcus. She has her issues with his team, though—after all, Danny would still be alive if he'd never accompanied them on their last mission—but Marcus has always been by her side…until after one impulsive kiss, he becomes so much more. But Danny's death was only the beginning. Whoever hired the hitman is looking for something, and they think Leah knows where it is…

Flatline
a novel by Linda Bond

People are dying in Dr. Joshua Salvador's ER. His medical assistant hangs on to life by a thread. The symptoms seem horrifyingly familiar, and he suspects the deaths are targeted at him. But before he can figure things out, top TV investigator Rachel Wright is standing in the middle of his ER, convinced an outbreak, an epidemic, or even a botched flu vaccine could be the cause, and she's going to tell the world.

Dangerous Desires
a novel by Dawn Altieri

Three years after her fiancé is killed, Emma Sloane is ready to move on. But her plans are derailed when she's attacked…and women who look just like her start turning up dead. Homicide Detective Jake Quinn is shocked when the victim of his new high-profile case is a witness from the one unsolved murder that still haunts him. Neither expects the immediate attraction they feel. But can he find the killer before it's too late?

Printed in Great Britain
by Amazon